Path to the Gods

Part of Hyades Wars, Book 1 in the Orcs series

I0685251

Michael Ryan

Hyades Wars Publishing
Hyadeswars.com

ISBN-13:
978-1-7329292-0-3

ISBN-10:
1-7329292-0-3

Body of Work

Path to the Gods
book 1 in the Orcs series

Darkster, Even the Gods Tremble
book 3 in the Orcs series

The Troublemakers
book 1 in the Humans series
book 2 in the Orc series

The Troublemakers, Halfling
book 2 in the Humans series
book 4 in the Orc series

Schula and Downs, Love Triangle
book 1 in Life's Mysteries

Tales of Hyades Wars
book 1 in Short Stories

Acknowledgments

This book is dedicated to my wife, children, and other family members, without whom the inspiration and consequent publication would not be possible. My love for the genre of science fiction/fantasy as read in books, seen as film, and played as tabletop and video gaming is the basis for this book, and the Hyades Star Cluster universe I have created.

Special thanks to Jericho Benavente, also known as Serathus for Artwork created, based on my designs. Font for cover page was created on cooltext.com.

This book has been edited by Sandra Ely from Polished Pearl Author Services.

Content

Prologue

He had gotten the news and hurried home. He'd opened the door so quickly and violently that the wood was ripped from the hinges; he didn't even notice. As he raced passed his seven children, stepping on two and accidentally kicking a third in the head, he entered the main part of the house. It was dark, save for a low-watt bulb that hung precariously from a fixture in the ceiling. It barely lit the tiny room's dirt floor and ragged furniture; it did, however, hide the filth and cracks that plagued the walls, floor, and ceiling- not that orcs cared what condition their houses were in, he certainly didn't. Besides, this was going to be a great day.

He followed the whimpers that he heard and the scents that he picked up with his nose. They led him into a room toward the back of the house. It was here in this shanty, lean-to addition that he found his wife. She was obviously uncomfortable as she lied on a thick wooden table, draped in old, worn linens. She snapped at him, "Nice you show up!"

The large orc responded, "I stay away long as I can, but udder orcs complain you stink. He here, yet?"

Her painful eyes met his. "Da baby?"

"No, Stupid, da doc."

Muga took his insults in stride, even in her current condition. He was big, and stinky, and stupid, and well...simply vile. Yet, there were a hundred other females waiting to have him and she was lucky; he was a real find. "No doc. Docs not come after you kill da last one."

There were so few doctors delivering babies anymore. More often than not, a suspecting father killed or seriously harmed a doctor that didn't deliver a live baby; sometimes, it happened just because the baby didn't look like the father; sometimes, because the doctor had inappropriately touched the mother during child birth, which was virtually impossible not to do, considering the area of the body babies came from. Most orcs were driven to tinker with anything they could get their hands on, so would-be doctors simply decided to accidentally blow themselves up as dedicated mechanics instead. At least they died doing what they loved to do.

The large orc put his huge hand on Muga's forehead, "I help now. No doc ok."

Muga half-smiled and returned her attention to the pain. She began to push, and her breathing was labored. She dug her left hand into her husband's chest and squeezed as her agony intensified. Her nails dug deep into his green, muscular skin. He wiped her forehead and ran a cool, damp rag across her face, barely noticing his own discomfort.

"Muga, dis one betta looka like me."

Muga spit through her gritting teeth, "Sure hopa not. Dis family oogly 'nuff." She growled and arched her back as the pain reached new levels. She bore down harder.

Blood was all over the table, the floor, and the large orc's chest. Muga's water broke and sprayed on everything in the back room. As she growled, so did he. He began to bob up and down in a ritualistic manner, matching her thrusts. His teeth were bared, and he was exhaling in deep guttural snarls. She looked up helplessly as anguish overtook her. Her eyes were wild. She screamed and called out to her god.

The large orc positioned himself below her. His blood was boiling. His temples were throbbing. His muscles were tight and constricted. He struggled to see everything through the layers of mucus and blood with his one good eye. He looked up at Muga and commanded her, "Push one mo' time. Da baby comin'."

Muga was convulsing. She pulled her hand from her male's chest and bore down one final time. She stiffened everything in her body and focused all of her efforts on removing this vile contaminant from her body. What she removed so far was plenty of fluid from hers and her husband's bodies. And then...

It was here.

The large orc couldn't contain himself. "Him oogly, lil bastid!"

Muga was weak. She struggled to talk, but found the strength when she saw her new prize. "Yeah, him looka lika you mudder."

He laughed a big belly laugh. "You do good, Muga. Him lil, scrawny, too. Maybe we feed him to da chicklens."

Muga felt the warmth of her baby as the large orc gave him to her. She smelled him. Actually, she smelled him, herself, and her stinky ass husband. She held the baby by his head and flipped him clumsily and counted his fingers and toes. She looked over to her very proud husband with an apparent war wound deep in his chest and questioned, "What we call him?"

There was simply no response except a shrug of shoulders. The large orc wasn't in the business of naming little, green turds. What did he know about such things? He honestly tried, but his mind kept coming back to "Poop". *"Oh well,"* he thought.

Muga realized that her useless husband hadn't named any of their previous eleven children. She rolled her eyes. "What 'bout Bomb lika you?"

The large, bloody, stinky orc pushed out his chest in pride and tried to show indifference, "Dat a nutty." He turned his head and looked away, but he couldn't keep his eyes off of the female he loved. He wanted her to name their new baby after him; however, he wouldn't show his weakness.

"Ok, not Biggabomb lika you. Him keep Bomb, but maka a Nutty, too. Nuttybomb."

The large orc was pleased. He thought for a moment about his own name. Biggabomb was fitting. He was large for sure and he was strong like a bomb; the name was one to be respected. It meant big and strong. So, how would a name that means crazy and strong go over? It was a no-brainer. "Dat name is a good." He pushed out his bottom lip and nodded in agreement, over-accentuating his mannerisms to affirm his satisfaction.

Muga was exhausted; she desperately needed rest. She handed Nuttybomb to his father. "Go put a him to kids." She closed her eyes and began to drift to sleep.

Biggabomb carried the baby by its arm and dragged it into the next room. Very few races were built like orcs. Even newborn babies were hardy enough to be tossed around without harm.

Several of his other children cried out, "Eewwwe! Him still gotta slime."

"Shutta up! Keepa you brudder safe or you die!"

The children stopped all noise and became perfectly still. The three closest to their father held their hands over their ears to somehow cut down on the pain from his deafening bellows. Sure, the large orc had yelled at them before. Hell, he even stepped on them and kicked them on the way in today, but they knew to never, ever underestimate an orc's intentions when the word die, or a variant thereof, was even so little as muttered, especially in regard to his newest prize. The oldest boy dragged Nuttybomb carefully away from his father by his umbilical cord and began to play quietly.

The large orc headed out the door with a smile. "Dis gonna be a great day!"

One
The Pecking Order

Nuttybomb's name didn't earn him much respect so far. He was still smaller than quite a few orcs his own age. Even his two younger brothers were around his size. This meant that the bigger children, and not necessarily older, were more than happy to beat him up regularly. It wasn't always like that for Nutty, though. Some events happened that propelled him to where he was, physically and socially; and like clockwork, everyday seemed to be much the same. Still, name and all, he decided to earn his own respect. This day started like most other days.

Right after the sun came up, he and five of his siblings made their way up the dusty road from their house to an intersection. He typically struggled to carry a bag or a box with his items in it. He lagged behind the others, sometimes dropping his things and having to pick them up.

The walk took around an hour and he gauged his progress by landmarks along the way. There were a number of flat, dilapidated shacks that were used as houses that he passed. He could tell that most were made of wood framing with tin nailed or strung along the outside walls and roofs to give some protection from the elements; others were made of straw; some had electrical wires that led from community power poles to them; most had vehicles in front or on the side that were junks of rusted metal. It was hard to keep them in good shape because parts were stolen off them with regularity. Several houses had old iron or shoddy

11

wooden fences that were used to enclose the house or vehicles from harm. Bottles, paper, and trash littered everything.

He passed an ox farm where a number of trees lined the property. He guessed they were to provide cover to the animals from the relentless sun. As his eyes surveyed the land, he could pick out a pump house in the distance. There were several tractors toward the back of the property as well as some equipment. The house appeared slightly better than those he had just passed. The wind changed direction slightly and his nose picked up the aroma of dung; it was a familiar smell that reminded him of his mother's cooking. Every time he thought about that, he smiled. Boy, how his dad picked on Momma's cooking.

As the wind changed directions, it brought with it dust and sand from the farm and red dirt road; the rainy season hadn't begun yet and things were pretty dry. The planet that Nuttybomb lived on was more arid than many worlds and very hot; its proximity to its mother star was close, but it was also in a circular orbit. Had it been in an elliptical orbit, the atmosphere probably would have burned off while the planet was at its closest point and orcs wouldn't have been able to live there.

Nuttybomb wondered why he thought of such silly things while other orcs thought about building radios, cars, and household appliance stuff. Then, he wondered why he even wondered. His wondering mind was the cause of much ridicule from his absentminded friends and the reason for his fights as well. He wiped some dust from his runny eyes and put those crazy thoughts out of his head.

He came across the next landmark. This was also his first stop. It was at the corner of the first Crossroads he would pass. There were iron poles in the ground on each corner where signs used to be. Now they were bent, rusted stubs, varying in height where they were sheered from different vehicle accidents. Traffic was light and loud; a few old trucks and motorcycles made their way through the intersection, their drivers making sure to rev their engines. This was done to show status or to intimidate others. Most orcs strived to have the fastest and loudest vehicles. Again, Nutty wondered why things were the way that they were. He shook his head and forced himself to concentrate on the task at hand.

As his siblings went ahead, he entered a rickety, wooden machine shop. His nostrils were filled with the smells of smoke and machine oil. His eyes were burned by the sparks thrown from a welder. The orc that was welding a motorcycle frame together killed the flame to his torch when he noticed Nuttybomb enter. He appeared aggravated and squinted his eyes as he questioned the young orc's reason to bother him. "Boy?"

Nuttybomb stepped forward and dipped into a bag. He was careful not to move too quickly. He thought that somehow, if he was careful, he wouldn't be beaten to death or eaten- not that he really had any reason to even think this way, but the orc in front of him smelled of danger. He was nearly as massive as Nutty's dad and sported a large gutting knife that was pierced through his jaw from one side of his face to the other. He'd kept it as a souvenir. It was rumored that he had killed the owner of the knife in a war and kept the knife in its wound as a trophy of sorts. The skin had scarred over the holes and the knife looked like part of the orc's face now. Over the years, he continued to decorate the knife by adding jewels, feathers, and anything that he thought looked good. It was a gesture of *"don't screwa wit' me"*. Obviously, the wearer of this trophy was tough and mean. Nutty carefully pulled out a compass that he had traded for and handed it to the older establishment owner. "Here ya go, Guthrak."

Guthrak put down his torch, rubbed his chin with one hand and took the compass with the other. He studied it for a bit and his appearance changed from menacing to businesslike. "Whatcha want fo' it? Ain't gonna pay big."

"Dint figure so." Nuttybomb paused as he thought of a good price; then, he blurted out, "A heat coil."

"Heat coil? You nut!" Guthrak began to negotiate with the child, but knew that a coil wasn't worth much and the compass was the perfect front fender ornament for the bike he was working on. He softened his tone, "Ok, but don't tink I do dis always, Boy." With that, he got the coil for Nuttybomb and sent him on his way.

Nuttybomb was thrilled. With the coil he just obtained, he was going to finish his school project and show the other kids that he was not some boob that they could just beat up at will. He could build things that none of them could. He didn't have to beat anyone up to feel good, not that it would make him feel bad either. It was just that he didn't understand why they took such pleasure in it. He wondered if life would be different if orcs thought more about what they did. If they acted differently, how would that change things? Hmm. He felt like beating himself up. What a boob!

He caught up with the others and they all stopped at the last important landmark. It was a market that had some makeshift tables made of wood that laid atop some stones; there were awnings that hung from the front of the building to the edge of the road. It was quiet this time of morning and not too busy. Nutty and the others shelled out some coins for a bit of bread and water. They sat for a minute or two, and then, continued on.

The youngest complained about still being hungry. While the two oldest took turns pounding on the youngster in an attempt to shut him up, Nutty remembered something and formulated a plan. They were coming up on the old lady's house. It used to be a farm or something and still had fruit trees. The old lady that lived there was as blind as a bat. She would collect fruit and sit on her porch. She was scarier than Nutty's own dad. But Nutty was smart and told the others how to shut up their little brother.

Within a couple minutes they were passing the old lady's property. Four of the kids crossed the street and Nutty stayed on the same side as the old lady. The old lady's eyes widened when she spotted the children. She leaned forward on her chair and growled. The porch that she sat on cricked as her weight shifted forward. She clutched a basket of fruit and held it close to her chest, attempting to protect it. Her eyes followed all the children. Even if she just saw spots, she knew where they all were.

Nutty nervously addressed her, "Are you Old Lady TacaTaca?"

Her curdling voice cut the air with, "What lil bastid?"

Nutty was taken aback. He hesitated, but repeated his question, much louder and slower.

The old woman leaped from her chair. "Fuck me Old Lady TacaTaca? You lil bastid!" She ran toward Nutty at a pace he couldn't fathom, especially for an old hag like her. She obviously misunderstood him. He took off quickly to put some distance between him and his attacker. When she realized she couldn't catch him, she threw all her fruit in his direction, one at a time, until the basket was empty. Nutty's siblings picked up the fruit as it rolled toward them. Then, they ran for their lives.

As Nutty reached his destination, his siblings were jeering him, "You dint even show you butt. She gonna kill you. Her gonna puts *you* in da baskit."

Nutty smiled. "Still gots da fruit for Kajo."

Kajo smiled wider than Nuttybomb. His face was bright red in fruit juice. He licked his lips and rubbed his stomach. "Dat wuz goods fruit."

Nutty thought a bit about Kajo for a moment. He was the youngest surviving son. He was Nutty's size, but dopey and like today, he typically had food or juice all over his face. He limped because of a malformation to his right leg. Nobody knew why or even questioned it; these things just happened among the orc population. Half of all children on the planet wouldn't even reach adulthood. Nutty thought that maybe it was something in the water or maybe it was because of the heat; maybe, even as tough as orcs were, they were prone to diseases that their bodies couldn't fight against. It's one thing to fight another orc or a wild dawg, but how did one fight an enemy one couldn't see?

Nutty's mind drifted to sum up each sibling as his eyes went from one to the next.

Pretty was one of two sisters. She was older than Nutty, second oldest of the children. Physically, she was a bit shorter than Nutty and a bit heavier. She smiled a lot, showing the few teeth that she had. She was cute as far as sisters went, but she was nice and usually quiet. Nutty thought that this was smart. Young girls didn't want to draw attention from boys due to the fact that boys were mean by nature and could easily hurt them. Nutty was glad he seldom had to come to her aid.

He glanced at Booma. Booma was much bigger than Nutty. He was the oldest boy. He often teased Nutty by saying things like how he played with Nutty's umbilical cord and let the dawg chew on it. He would wait for their dad to leave so he could sneak into the alcohol. Then, he would give the empty bottle to Nutty when Dad came home. Nutty thought he was a big poop that way. But, he saved Nutty's hide in dozens of fights. Being alive was the payoff for the teasing he had to endure. It all evened out in the end.

He thought briefly about Guta, who was very ill and at home. She was the third oldest for now. She got the fever and was fighting for her life. She was mostly crippled now and smelled terribly. Nutty would bring her fresh water to drink and wash her face for her. She couldn't do these things herself, certainly not able to go to builder school like him. He wondered if she would survive as she was one of two sets of twins and the last remaining alive. The other three had already passed. Maybe twins were weaker than individually born orcs.

Nutty wasn't sure, but he was glad not to be a twin…Just in case.

Then there was Gardawg. He was a pain in the butt! He was a year younger than Nutty, maybe eleven months; anyway, he was just mean. He skinned animals and shoved the poor bloody things in his sisters' mouths. He lit the house on fire…twice. He cut off one of Nutty's toes while Nutty slept, and of course, it found its way into Guta's mouth. Of all the children, Nutty especially disliked this one. They all had their moments, but this one never had a good one. He was just wired wrong. Nutty had thought far too long about Gardawg and moved on.

His eyes gazed upon Runzda. She was around two years younger than he was. He guessed that would make her eight years old. He checked the math, not knowing why, but he needed to know such silly things. He calculated Booma to be fourteen, Pretty to be twelve, Guta to be eleven, himself to be ten, Gardawg nine, and Runzda was younger. He thought Kajo was six. Yeah, six. So, one child died between Runzda and Kajo. He shook his head yes without realizing it as he determined that she was, indeed, eight years old.

Then he noticed that Runzda was looking back at him. She asked, "Why you look at me and shaka head?"

He replied, "Just tinking."

Booma rolled his big, red eyes and exclaimed, "Here he go again wit' da tinking." With that, he found the opportunity to close his left hand into a fist and bop his little brother over the head.

Everyone laughed, that is everyone except Nuttybomb. He had little sparkling lights dancing in blackness before his eyes.

Gardawg, like an overexcited forest monkey, yipped and shrieked uncontrollably. He grabbed Nutty's arm and bit down on it with his mangled teeth; he flailed his arms and legs, connecting several times with Nutty's face and trunk.

Pretty stopped laughing. She yelled, "Gardawg, stop!" She could see that this was going beyond the teasing and harmless poking that occurred daily. About once per month, the wild, mean, senseless child had to be stopped from hurting, or worse, maiming another. Gardawg wouldn't stop. He had latched on to Nutty's face with his own mouth.

Other children that were waiting for their ride to arrive circled the two Bomb children. They yelled and cheered, only fueling the fire in Gardawg's eyes. He took part of an ear, a finger, whatever he could.

Booma sighed in disgust. He pushed past some of the children and hit Gardawg with his full might, landing a fist to the cheekbone. Gardawg's body went limp. He released his bite as his body fell to the dusty, red clay.

Nuttybomb was stunned; he was still trying to grasp what happened; he was dizzy and bloody; he hurt everywhere. He heard the cheers end and looked around frantically, not knowing if an attack would start again. He didn't even know who attacked him.

Booma stood Nutty up with one hand and ridiculed, "You asgusting! Learn a fight! You dumba Nutty!"

Nutty aimlessly followed the others into the back of a large truck that had just pulled up. It was the same truck that picked the children up every day to transport them to builder school. It was a basic truck with wood beams as railing that enclosed the flat bed. It was here that the children sat and made fun of Nutty. Nutty wasn't thinking clearly; he barely noticed the other children. He hung his head in pain, almost in a state of sleep and hugged his box. He drifted off.

**

"Da wires go lika dis," the old orc screamed.

Nutty awoke in a chair with his head on a table. He shook his head to clear the cobwebs; it took a few seconds for him to gauge his surroundings and figure out where he was. He vaguely remembered stumbling into school with his box and heat coil before putting his head down on his table and collapsing. He heard children's voices over the hurried sound of what he thought were hammers. Schoolmates were at tables like his, performing various tasks. As his vision came into focus, his brain recognized the voice as his teacher. The sound of the voice had to bounce around in his foggy mind until it clung to something, he thought, hence the delay.

"Oh, you waka up now? Do wires, Lazy!"

Nutty looked up to see his teacher hovering over him and nodded his head as he tried to make sense of where everything was, how to make things work, and figure out where he was. Wait! His body hurt. He was tired of thinking; thinking, thinking, thinking. Who cared about wires?

Nutty spotted his box that he carried earlier. He wearily leaned down and picked it up from the floor.

His teacher mistook Nutty picking up the box as an attempt to find the proper tools. The teacher, satisfied with himself, walked away.

Nutty saw that his lunch was missing. Not only that, the heater coil he had traded for earlier that day was gone too. In its place was a pile of orc dung. One of the little bastards went in his box after stealing his stuff. He was furious. He raised the box and yelled, "Who bastid makes a fuckin' dump in box and taka my stuff?" Spit hung from his lip like a mad man.

The teacher tilted his head slightly and waited. The room fell silent. Nutty's chest was heaving as his heart and lungs were in overdrive. He waited for someone to confess so he would kill anyone that admitted to such an atrocity. Just who the hell did they think they were to keep abusing him? His fiery eyes looked from one victim to the next, trying to sense just a hint of ownership. Five seconds; ten seconds; fifteen. Someone muttered, "Pee Peebomb". Then the room erupted in laughter. None laughed as hard as the teacher. They all simply went back to wiring their motors.

Nutty dropped the box in defeat. His eyes, now sad, caught a curious look from another's. They were the prettiest eyes he had ever known, warm and understanding, and appeared to reach out to him, wanting to take away his pain. He recognized them immediately; they belonged to the beautiful face of Uhra.

Uhra was this pretty little girl that Nutty used to play with. They had been good friends until recently. They would walk home together after school to Nutty's house. Uhra's aunt would come by and pick her up from there. Usually, they would just throw rocks. Sometimes, they would try to kick a bottle all the way home; mostly, they would talk.

Nutty's mind wandered to a fateful day that changed that.

***

The two were walking. Nutty would cleverly tell a joke and Uhra would giggle. This was kind of new. Nutty thought Uhra was acting differently; she talked less now, and she smiled a lot. She always bumped into him and didn't compete with him to see who could kick the bottle more. He thought that maybe she was growing up faster than him. He still wanted to knock her over and race to see who won. That's what orcs did, but even if he started to, she simply would have nothing of it; her interests laid elsewhere.

She had started calling him Younut. This was typically followed by a giggle. He didn't like the fact that she might be teasing him; he had enough of that from the other idiots. Orcs seemed to do that in excess. However, he figured it was innocent enough.

They came to the Crossroads. Some older kids had stopped there on motorcycles and obviously saw Nuttybomb and Uhra approaching the intersection. The older kids left their bikes across the street and waited for their prey.

What Nutty and Uhra found were three delinquents. They wore dark clothes with lots of leather and metal spikes. They were garnished in additional metals such as chains and bolts. "Hey, Boys, dis wunz pretty," the biggest kid exclaimed.

The other two laughed and one followed, "Which one?"

The three of them busted a gut. They exaggerated their posture and volume to enhance their invulnerability. Maybe they thought it was just funnier to be louder and more obnoxious than most.

Had Nutty not been part of the joke, he probably would have laughed too. He was surprised to find other kids as clever as him. He found himself wanting to impress Uhra. "Wow, you lika boys?"

The three looked around at each other and stopped laughing; the insult began to take hold. Uhra smiled.

The boy that insinuated that Nutty was pretty needed a response. It had to be witty, maybe harsh, and certainly quick; it had to reestablish him as a male, and a dominant one at that. He walked closer to his prey to buy time as he thought of what to say. He pushed his chest out and his shoulders back. He curled his mouth in a snarl as he neared Nutty. He spat, "No, pretty lika jail bitch."

Nutty smelled the stench of the biker's mouth. It reeked of alcohol and rotten meat. He saw tattoos on his face and nose rings. There were scars all over his face. He was a kid- well, sort of. He was older than Nutty, but only by a couple of years. Nutty was forced to assess the situation. These weren't school kids; they were hardened criminals.

Nutty was reminded of something his dad had said about pecking order. Was this the leader? He wasn't the biggest of the three. He seemed to be the brightest, though. Dad had said, "Sometimes you hit the biggest one. You knock him out and the others are afraid; or you take out the leader. The followers sometimes don't know what to do." If in doubt, Dad would just kill them all. Nutty was not his dad.

Then, he realized that he must have been just standing there looking at the biker.

The biker's attention was now on Uhra. The biker pulled out a long knife and pointed it at her. The knife made a searing, scratching sound as it slid from its holster. His eyes remained focused on Nutty. "I'ma gonna play wit' her anda you gonna watch. Den I kill you."

The other two bikers moved forward instinctively. Nutty thought that this was not going well; there was no more humor. Nothing funny could be said to break the ice and cause these killers to withdraw. He desperately sought to say something. He didn't notice the crowd that started to gather. His face was hot; his common sense was gone; he was afraid; he was unsure, but mostly, he was protective of Uhra.

Nutty growled, "Screwa you!" He threw a hard punch that landed to the jaw of the knife biker. As the knife biker stumbled back, the next closest biker took his place. Nutty swung wildly and hit that one too. He, himself was hit in the face by the third biker and fell backwards. Uhra screamed in horror as the knife biker regained his balance and swung the knife toward Nutty's face. The blade caught Nutty in the cheekbone and took his left earlobe off as it swung around. Nutty didn't realize how lucky he was at that moment. By falling backward from the punch he had taken, he received more fist than knife from this assault. He landed on his back and hit hard though.

He felt kicks to his ribs; he was a little dazed. Then, he saw Guthrak throwing bodies around. Yes,

Guthrak! Guthrak had an easy time disarming the battered bikers. Quickly, they felt fear from a real killer, a war veteran. He threatened to kill them if he ever saw their "oogly" faces again. That was all they needed to hear. Just like that, Nutty was okay.

Guthrak extended his huge hand to help Nutty to his feet. "You really am nut. Dose kids killas."

Uhra was already holding her fingers over Nutty's ear that was partially missing to help stop the bleeding. She whispered into it, "Younut," and giggled.

Nutty was a little worse for wear, but overall, he was okay. He and Uhra followed Guthrak over to the machine shop. Guthrak told the two to stay there while he got some water and would be back in fifteen minutes; he left the door open and disappeared.

Uhra still pinched the hole in Nutty's ear. She looked closely at it and wiped some blood from his cheek. Her face was against his now and could feel her breath on his neck. She kissed his face and whispered how proud she was of him. She was his best friend.

Nutty was a little dizzy. He assumed it was from blood loss; he was shaking a bit. Uhra was licking his cheek and moaning softly. He wanted to push her away. Friends didn't do that; it was weird, but it felt good. No, he didn't want to push her away. He didn't want her to stop...but stop she did.

A loud crash came from behind her. They both jumped in horror at the sight of her father entering the room. The large doors were wide open and there were dozens of orcs looking in. They had seen the fight and were talking about it. Her father was working on a power pole just a hundred yards away when he heard

25

what was going on. He investigated the fight as well; what he found was far worse.

Nutty looked quickly at Uhra to see how he should respond. He found that her eyes were fixated on him, but not his eyes. He looked down in shock to see that his appendage had slipped out of his pants and was upright. He jumped, and his eyes met hers. She bit her lip and smiled nervously. It seemed that *his* power pole was being worked on as well. He didn't understand it, but the situation didn't look good. He had a better chance of talking his way out of the biker fight.

Uhra gulped and backed up. Fear now took hold of her as her hands came up to somehow defend herself involuntarily. She began to shake and whimper. She closed her eyes as tight as she could while her father drew nearer. His thunderous footsteps were slow and deliberate. He growled with each one.

While she was terrified, Nutty was worse. His eyes remained open the whole time. His hands fumbled in a desperate attempt to get everything back into its clothing. He was surely going to die now.

Uhra's father came into Nutty's space. He leaned over so he was face to face with Nutty. His head turned a bit and drew a deep breath. He brought his enormous fists into the air. The veins in his temples pulsed; the veins in his arms, back, and chest bulged over massive muscles, tensed to the breaking point. With his teeth bared, he opened his mouth and screamed a deep, vicious growl.

It was the loudest thing that Nutty had ever heard. He waited, frozen, for the blow that would end his life. He waited, and he prayed. He waited and was wet; he was very wet. So was Uhra; her father too. What had happened? What was still happening? Nuttybomb lost control of his bladder and was still unloading on everything within ten feet.

As Uhra's father was distracted, Nutty finally got into his clothes and rushed past him. Uhra was still standing with her hands in the air crying as Nutty made it to the door. The crowd was hysterical. Nutty somehow made it out of there alive and left the laughter behind him.

He couldn't help to think about what was going to happen to Uhra. He was probably going to lose her as a friend now. No... he was definitely going to lose her as a friend. If her father didn't kill her, she certainly couldn't see him anymore. Maybe she wouldn't want to anyway. How many friends are happy with somebody peeing on them? Or leaving them for dead? Or embarrassing them like that?

Well, he was alive. He tried to reason that it could have been worse. He thought about what would happen when he saw her again. He would see her again. He sighed. He hoped he would see her again. Maybe he hoped he would never see her again. He didn't want to face her; he couldn't.

His mind considered how events might have been different, what he could have done differently. The whole father thing took maybe a few seconds. How quickly things can change. He also thought about what his dad had said about pecking orders. One thing was clear: from that day on, he would be at the bottom of every pecking order.

Nutty's mind came back to school. His eyes were still on Uhra's. Was he imagining that her eyes were warm and understanding? They understood what it meant to be humiliated. He peed on her for orcs' sake! Was that it? Did she have feelings for him? Good feelings? Not just hate? He missed her. He wanted to talk to her. She looked away in visible disappointment.

The teacher rang out, "Ok. Today lasta day fo' some. Booma, Killza, Gurg, anda Motu go a fight skool now. No mo' here."

Nutty didn't care; get rid of the oldest kids. That way there was less of a chance that Nutty would take a beating. Then it hit him; if Booma wasn't around, Nutty had no protection. The day of the bikers was a day that Booma hadn't been there. He had gone to fight school that day for registration. As bad as Booma was, he was still better than most.

Nutty was on his own now.

Two
War A Comin'

Biggabomb clasped his hands and put them behind his head. He leaned back in a chair that was much too small for his enormous frame. His feet were without shoes and he placed these sizable pedals on a crate that he used as a table. His toes were as big as apples and each one had broken, crusty nails that threatened to curl under and into his skin. "Dunno," he stated carelessly.

Nuttybomb entered the house. Booma and the other kids went to the lake bed to see boat races. Nutty wasn't interested in that today; he was tired and beat up. He was hoping to just go home and relax. Instead, he found his father and another large orc talking. The other orc's back was facing the door that Nutty just entered. The orc hadn't noticed Nutty enter.

"I do know," the orc with his back to the door exclaimed. "War comin' or no, him's pee was stickin' out!"

Biggabomb saw Nutty. He said, "Oh, he here now. Just aska him."

To Nutty's surprise, the conversation was about him. He was in shock when he realized who the orc was that had his back to him. The orc had turned his head at this point. It was Uhra's father!

Nutty almost collapsed. He froze and waited for what came next. Maybe he was still going to die.

Uhra's father turned completely and stood up from the mangled crate he had been sitting on. He was a figure to behold, the same size as Biggabomb and just as fearsome looking. He fought to calm himself and glanced at Biggabomb. He slowly forced his posture into a non-threatening form. With his words chosen carefully and his tone as respectful as he could control, he asked behind angry eyes, "Why you pee stickin' out wit' Uhra?"

Nutty's eyes widened and his jaw dropped; his heart stopped; then, it raced. Was his father going to let him die now? Had he committed a crime punishable by death? Maybe he would just lose a limb. Damn, that was gonna hurt. He looked over toward his dad for help, but his father simply nodded. Nutty spoke, but no sound came out.

Uhra's father looked angry. "Boy?"

Nutty swallowed and responded in humiliation, "Dunno." Then, he slouched and hung his head.

"Dunno? You know!"

Nutty didn't know how to explain; it just happened. He didn't even know what happened. He was so ashamed; his body had failed him. Uhra's father hated him; was probably going to maim or kill him. He lost his best friend; his brother was going into training for the army, and now, Nutty would have to fight the whole world alone. His sister was dying. His emotions were running so hot that he couldn't even think. Still, he tried. He had to, or he might be killed. "It wuz out by itself. It stand up. Why it do dat?" Tears welled up in his eyes.

Muga was serving boar cakes when she heard what was being said. She broke in with, "Eh, Biggabomb's pee do dat, too."

Biggabomb yelled, "Shutta up and mova you, fat ass!" He looked at Uhra's father. "Boy lika his old man." A big belly laugh followed.

Uhra's father sat down and fought back laughter, but to no avail. He realized what had happened. He didn't like it, but it made sense. At Nutty and Uhra's age, these things came up, so to speak. Uhra's father introduced himself to Nutty in a far less threatening way than the first time, "Me Gunza. You dad be me captain. He me Chief."

Nutty's mind was reeling. He figured out that he wasn't going to die now. He didn't urinate on himself. He blurted out, "Ok?"

Biggabomb directed a question toward Gunza. "Is ok den?"

"Is ok if him not do to Uhra."

The two turned to see Nutty. He was shaking his head in a fearful "no" manner with his eyes wider than an orc elk in a battle truck's headlights; definitely "no" to whatever he wasn't supposed to do.

Gunza confirmed, "Is ok den. You tell him and I go?"

Biggabomb stood and clenched Gunza's forearm. "Yes, friend. Tonight I tell all tings."

***

Biggabomb explained that in the last few wars he was the Warchief's bodyguard. He was second only to the Warchief in charge of the whole army. Gunza was part of his bodyguard and the two fought side by side for years. Uhra's aunt had just died. With Gunza going away to fight a war, that would leave Uhra alone. So, Gunza had asked for Uhra to stay with Muga.

31

The whole "pee" incident, although possibly damaging to Nuttybomb and Uhra's relationship, paled in comparison to what might happen to Uhra if she was left alone. She would be prey to every orc scum on the planet, and an easy target at that. Nutty knew that he must not screw up.

Then, Nutty thought of something. Why was he never told about his father's high-ranking position? He was never told that his father fought in any wars...never told about Gunza being a friend. He heard of other orcs boasting of their accomplishments. Why was that not the case in his house? What did his father have to hide?

When asked, Biggabomb explained that most orcs were dumb. They were more brutal than thoughtful. They were also very territorial, jealous, short-tempered, warlike, crude, and basically walked around with chips on their shoulders; and those were just a few of their wonderful attributes. Biggabomb didn't feel the need to boast; what good would come from it? He never told the children of how he killed a dozen or so idiots that had something to prove to themselves. They would seek Biggabomb out and try to advance through the ranks by eliminating him. When there was no war, Biggabomb liked to keep quiet and stave off trouble. Surely, his kids didn't need to know. They might tell school kids and that might cause a flare up. But, things were different now; war was comin'.

When all the children came home, Biggabomb explained some more in detail. They all sat on the dirt floor along the walls. Muga put some blankets on the crate near Biggabomb so she could sit and hear her male tell his children about his exploits, and he did tell some.

Mostly, he explained that the Warchief was usually the biggest orc in a clan, or the most powerful. The Warchief usually rose to power by dominating others through brute strength. It wasn't unheard of for one to take over a village, then a city, then several more until he folded a whole army into his ranks. Sometimes, one came to power by assassinating the Warchief above himself, thereby stepping into the role by default. Some even ruled whole planets. Rarely, but occasionally, some Warchiefs ruled more than one planet. They were very powerful indeed, with massive armies and fleets of ships at their disposal. He further explained that another name for Warchief was Warlord.

Brutes were the next largest orcs. Biggabomb and Gunza were Brutes. Actually, they were very large Brutes. Their clan seemed to have very big Brutes. Brutes as large as them probably ruled other worlds. In fact, when the "Grate Attakk!" came to invade the Eastern Continent, the warriors were quite small. The invading Warchief couldn't match up with Biggabomb and his bodyguards. Biggabomb did point out his kill of the invading Warchief with unparalleled pride. Then, he dug his finger into his belly button and pulled out some fur and what may have been old food.

He went on to wrap up that boys and tolkienz rounded out the pecking orders. Then within these pecking orders were ranks.

All the children except for Gardawg were glued to every word. While the rest of the family waited in anticipation of what Dad would say next, Gardawg was busy putting a spider in his dying sister's mouth. Upon seeing this, Muga yelled at him. He simply ignored her.

Nutty flew across the room and walloped Gardawg in the face with his fist. He hated the bastid that had no remorse for anything he did or anyone he hurt. He threw punch after punch, sending Gardawg to the ground, blood splattering around the room. Nutty had so much pent up angst in him; he was taking it all out on his younger brother; his brother that deserved it. How dare Gardawg do that to his ailing sister! That was it. He was never going to do it again.

Biggabomb had seen enough. He pulled Nutty from his bloody brother. Nutty was screaming, "I screwa kill him!" Gardawg's right eye was hanging out of its socket. His jaw hung unhinged from his skull. Biggabomb was shocked. He would have stopped the scuffle earlier if he had known that Nutty would do so much damage so quickly. But Nutty was usually passive and didn't seem capable of what he had just done.

In fact, nobody had ever seen Nutty like that before; Gardawg never wanted to see it again.

The story telling was over for the night. Biggabomb picked up Gardawg and took him away to find a doc. He held the boy's eye on his forehead as it dangled so it wouldn't get lost. As the two passed Nutty, Gardawg saw him with his good eye and clung to his father. He was terrified of his older brother.

The other children were shaken by what they witnessed. Muga put blankets and fruit sacks on the floor so they could sleep. Nobody could take their eyes off of Nutty. He was pacing and grumbling to himself;

he was spitting and growling as he walked back and forth. He stopped at the front door, waiting for his little brother to come home. When he saw that he wasn't anywhere to be seen, he went back to pacing.

After setting up the children's sleeping blankets, Muga attended to Guta. She washed her face and hands with an old cloth, dipped in water that was boiled earlier in the evening. She kept an eye on Nutty, hoping that he would calm down, all the while doing the only thing she could for her little girl.

Guta's coloring wasn't good. Before she was ill it had been bright green like the peas Nutty loved to eat. Now she was a pasty yellowish-green. She was thin, so much in fact, that her veins were visible as dark greenish brown lines under her sickly-toned skin. Her hair was all but gone.

Muga understood why Nutty did what he did. She didn't completely approve of his actions, but she found herself trying to aid all her children. When she finished with Guta, she went to Nutty.

Nutty was unaware of her standing in front of him; he was still out of control; anger surged through him.

Muga reached her hand to him and calmly spoke his name, "Nutty."

On his first pass, he brushed past her.

Again, "Nutty?" This time, she said it a bit louder and accentuated the consonants. He swatted her hand away as he paced.

The next time, she grabbed his arm and screamed his name in his face, "Nuttybomb!"

His eyes met hers. They lacked the usual love and respect she so often associated with her amazing son.

Her open hand flew in a broad arc and caught his cheek. "Stoppa or Momma gonna killa you!"

Without thinking, Nutty's reflexes began to cause his body to attack her. His body wanted to finish the kill it was deprived of earlier. Something inside him didn't allow it though; his eyes came back. He saw his loving mother standing before him. He unclenched his whole being and trembled; he slumped to the floor and cried.

Muga coaxed him to his blanket where she washed him up, much the same way she had just done with Guta. She rubbed his head.

Nutty wondered if his mother felt differently about him now. He might have killed one of her surviving children. He may have caused more harm than good. His mother might have to attend to two ailing children now. What had he done?

It wasn't long until he found slumber on the other side of his eyes. He dreamed bad dreams about his pee being out for all to see.

***

Muga was distraught; her eyes were watery. She tried to hide her emotion as she woke the children for school. Like every other day, the kids were awakened and sent on their way. That's what orcs did.

But Nutty wanted to know why she was so upset. Was she upset with him? Had Dad returned with bad news about Gardawg? His eyes surveyed the room for answers. Guta's bed was empty. He wondered where Guta was. He got up and went to Guta's bed. He just stood there. "Momma?"

Muga went into the back room. Minutes later she returned, an unbearable strain on her face. She saw the other children standing with Nutty. She simply said, "Guta gone," and fell to her knees, wailing.

Guta was removed during the night so the children wouldn't see her carried out. She was eleven years old. Biggabomb quietly buried her behind the house, then he left. Nobody knew where he went. He was probably as upset as Muga. Surely, he would drink a barrel of shlogger to get him through the next few days. That's usually what he did after losing a child. He never shed a tear around the children.

The children were at a loss. Some patted Muga's head, others rubbed her arms. Nutty leaned down and hugged her. In an attempt to console her, he let her know, "See you when skool done, Momma." The children looked at each other, not knowing if they should leave her.

Nutty said, "Ok. Bye."

They left her to sob on the dirt floor and went to school.

School, school, school. Let's all build a radio. No, let's make something that just makes loud noises; it was all nonsense. He could make the stuff without thinking. Nuttybomb found it strange that he thought of some things at the strangest times. While the other kids worked on their projects, he again wondered. Why did his right foot swell up two days ago? The left foot was just as big now. He thought his feet were much larger than several days before. Was this normal? He unwrapped the rags on his feet to see if there was any change in size. He put them up on the table for a better look. Nope, still as big as water rats. He would never get his old shoes on again. He was caught wiggling his toes as he studied them carefully.

Uhra was standing next to his chair. He looked up to see her staring at his feet too. She looked puzzled and asked, "Are dems brokes?"

"Of all things," he thought, "my feet." With everything going on, with all the stuff that had happened between them, with all that he wanted to say, he was made to talk about his feet. He couldn't help but smile. This just seemed to be the way things worked. He had planned for days about what to say and how to say it. Their friendship had changed. Or had it? Hmm. She asked about his feet. That seemed like the old Uhra he knew. He shrugged and responded, "Yeah, dems both me tinks."

It was clear that each had things to say. Neither knew how. Nutty tried but was cut off by his teacher.

"Bigga news. War a comin'. I tell you 'bout tings. Bad tings."

Nutty found that the children were hanging on their teacher's words, just like Nutty and his siblings had the night before when Dad told them stuff. Nutty listened, too. Dad didn't finish because Nutty beat the poop out of Gardawg. Maybe this was his chance to hear about everything.

The teacher told them an invasion force was headed to their planet and that the situation was potentially grim with, "Bad orcs a comin'. We has no a Warchief. Him die. Maybe skool a close. Maybe forever. Two more hour you go home. I go to fight da bad orcs. We gettin' da Warchief now. Maybe a Nutty's dad."

All heads turned; everyone looked at Nuttybomb. The room was perfectly silent. Uhra nervously smiled.

Nutty's feet were still in the air. He saw half of the students between them because his feet sat upon the table at eye level. "Perfect. Just perfect," he thought sarcastically. Okay, maybe he was always beat up because he was odd. He prided himself as being intelligent, but obviously he couldn't be all that smart. He still hadn't taken his feet down when Uhra had approached him. No, he was too stupid to do that. Maybe he could somehow get his pee out of his pants and make it screwin' dance or something, just to top things off. He realized his toes were still wiggling.

Then, something occurred to him. He copied his dad from the day before. He clasped his hands together and nonchalantly placed them behind his head in a carefree manner. This gave the appearance that he was lounging without a care in the world. He simply waved one hand away at the pesky bunch of kids and muttered, "Maybe. Maybe if him wants to."

In reality, he was shocked. His dad? A Warchief? He saw his own disbelief reflected in the faces of the other children, but he knew not to show it.

Kor, a sharp-tongued, stupid jerk, was the first to mock, "Yeah, right. Him dad a nutty, too!" His words prompted the others to laugh, but that was short-lived.

"Kor", Nutty began as he lowered his feet to the ground. With his feet under him, he rose and warned, "Don't maka me a kill you." There was fire in his eyes; he began to pant. His breathing altered. He clenched his fists and leaned in Kor's direction. He appeared to be waiting- no, daring- Kor to escalate the confrontation.

Kor shrunk into his chair and looked down. He didn't challenge Nuttybomb. The pecking order came to Nutty's mind; one down at school and fifty to go.

***

Nutty returned home later that day with his siblings to find orcs coming and going to and from his house all day. Gunza and Guthrak were there most of the day, except for quick trips to meet others to get updates about the coming war, or whatever else they did. Later that night, Nutty found out they were there to help protect Biggabomb from possible assassination. Nutty thought that surely other Warchief wannabes would challenge the hierarchy and lay claim to the throne.

While Nutty was apprehensive about war, he had to admit that the talks between the adults were mostly positive. The females seemed to speak more about the darker side of things while the males spoke of victorious battles. More males than females visited.

Nutty saw that his dad was busy...Busy and drunk. Biggabomb was forced to face war in his current state. He was asked to lead? How could this be? He was talking about plans while grieving, without a clear head. Right or wrong, Nutty currently viewed him as an average orc, big and all, with some smarts, a gambling problem, and a bit of a drunk; not quite a leader of leaders.

Still, Gunza and Guthrak thought highly of him. They were big and tough. They commanded respect and they bowed to him. What did they know that Nutty didn't? It then occurred to him. There was plenty he didn't know; his dad was in wars, had friends, and had killed other orcs. Nutty recounted the same questions he had just asked himself yesterday. The answers were the same. His father was completely different than what he knew.

Nutty saw that Gunza and Guthrak were preparing to leave. He thought it would be a good time to talk with his dad. It wasn't long before the two left and things settled down. Nutty approached his father and began talking about his father's history.

Biggabomb told Nutty about some fierce battles he had been in. He seemed to get some pleasure from the nostalgia. He began to talk about battle plans he helped to develop that won battles for his clan. It seemed to turn on a light bulb in his head. He told Nutty to wait for a minute while he retrieved some things.

Biggabomb came back shortly with some old books that were leather bound with string. He called Booma over to join Nutty and himself. He addressed Booma, "Boy, you know how read these?" Booma had just started fight school. He was the oldest son, and hopefully, next in line to his father's glory.

Booma flipped through some pages and settled his eyes and thoughts on one. "Not a really. It all X's and O's."

Biggabomb shook his head with a bit of displeasure. He took the book back that he had handed to Booma and passed it to Nutty. "How 'bout you, Boy?"

Nutty opened the book and began to observe. The bindings appeared loose and the leather was worn. He suspected this was from age and wear. The pages were from mildus tree bark that was stripped into thin sheets and dried. The book had a feel of importance to it. Nutty brushed the thought aside and studied the first page. He saw the movement of troops and how a trap was set with certain formations. He was quiet for about a minute.

Biggabomb waited, "Boy?"

Nutty saw a flaw in the plan. It was a sound plan, but he wanted to see what his father thought. "Why not take bridge first and cut off company to north? Den you no need reserve."

Biggabomb took the book back to see what his son was talking about. His eyes widened. He looked at Nutty and back to the page. The kid was right! "Dat worka good, too. How 'bout da next wun?"

Nutty again surveyed, analyzed and found nothing. "Nope, it looka good."

"Looka all and say to me."

Nutty went through the book and over the next couple of hours made some strong tactical points. His father was shocked and amazed; mostly, he was very proud. His son, without formal training, was a sound tactician. He had the ability to see an enemy's move and counter it or to draw an enemy into a trap. What also struck him was Nutty's attention to detail. Nutty made points about rewriting the whole thing with minor changes and clarifying some notes. By cleaning up the language, there would be no ambiguity to leave room for mistakes.

Biggabomb instructed Nutty to write his own notes on blank pages. Bigga would look at them in the morning. Nutty did so with difficulty as his hand had swollen and was very stiff. He worked late into the night as everyone else slept on their makeshift beds. He thought up his own plans to add to his father's. He was careful to draw everything in detail and included potential counter moves and contingencies against those possible enemy moves. It was utter genius, but to him, it was child's play.

Nutty thought about things his father told him, such as the enemy already landing on the far side of the world. He talked about the planet's defenses being fragmented due to different Clans being led by different Warchiefs. Biggabomb needed to mobilize quickly. He anticipated leading his army in a week or less. Nutty thought of the possibility of never seeing him again. What army would protect Nutty's home village while the main army was away? Wasn't Booma leaving for good, too?

Nutty's endless questions and diligent work brought him to the inevitable sleep that his body required. He drifted off with the book on his lap. The pen slipped to the floor.

"Getta up," Muga pleaded with her children. "Skool now."

Nutty's body jumped in a startled way. Without much sleep his nerves were on edge. He was half wedged between the crate he used as a chair and the wall. He figured that he must have slipped from the crate during the night, but didn't really care. His body ached. He guessed that he slept in a bad position for a while, enough so that his joints hurt. He caught a glance from his father as he started to get up from the floor.

"Is good Nutty. I lika. You smarta boy." Biggabomb flipped through the pages of the book with a look of deep pride. His head nodded "yes" several times. Then, he stopped, and his brow rose. He twisted his head a bit as he contemplated what was obviously wrong on one of the pages. He started, "Nutty, no. Dis wun not good. Looka." He leaned down and showed Nutty the area that concerned him. He went on, "Dis make left flank weak. But," he paused for a moment and then continued, "could swing out here, no?"

Nutty listened carefully and watched as his father ran a thick finger across the page to indicate the movement of troops that he spoke of. He saw his error and that his father was brilliant to remedy it and make it even better. "Wow, Dad! Dat even betta. You not just great warrior, you smart planner, too." Nutty wanted his last experiences with his father to be positive. Even if the props came from a kid, he hoped his dad realized how proud Nutty was of him. He was a great dad; he provided everything the family needed. He didn't just provide for them, he protected them; he protected the whole world. Nutty might never see him after this next week. He didn't see the harm in boosting his father's ego to make him happy.

Biggabomb was digging something out of his ear while Nutty was speaking. He heard the weight of those words and simply smiled. He might have been proud beyond belief, but it didn't show. Even as Nutty waited a bit for a response to his kind words, his father's mood seemed to change.

"Nutty, I be gone and nobody home to fight in town. I need you protect Momma and family and maybe town, too. You smarta den alla dem. But don't maka fight wit' town. You lead wit'out fight. You smarta, but still just boy."

Nutty felt the weight of the words now being thrown at him. He didn't know how to fight, or protect, or lead; and yes, he was just a boy. He raised his hands with his palms face up and shrugged with a dumbfounded look on his face. He begged for some common sense. "How?"

His father was now his Warchief. He spoke in terms that captains and squad leaders used. He touched on logistics and mobilization, not to mention bravery, commitment, and recruitment. There was no question that he felt as strongly as he did about Nutty's ability to do what was necessary to organize a defense in town. He understood the opposition to a child giving orders. He explained how to overcome that and to move forward. The Warchief abolished the boy's requirements for school and designated him to be "Big Town Army Controla".

Then, his father said something out of context. "You hands as big as you feet now. You gettin big." That big belly laugh followed.

Nutty saw that it was true. Both of his hands had grown, fairly quickly too. Even still, he wasn't an adult. There was a lot of responsibility placed on him. This couldn't possibly be real. He thought for a second that his father was teasing him; his father transitioned a little too easily between life and death to the size of his hands and feet. He had to know, "Dad, you sure 'bout me lead town army? For real?"

"It already done. I maka Guthrak know. Him shop be you base to work." His father puffed out his bottom lip and crossed his arms. He made his usual head nodding gesture to show his affirmation of not only making the right decision, but also to reassert he was the Warchief, and it was made regardless of outcome or possible conjecture.

The other children had already left for school. It was quiet, save for the random banging of big iron pots and cooking utensils in the back room. Smoke was building in the house. It was already muggy and musty. The smell of rotten food, dirty feet, and Biggabomb hung heavy in the air. Muga was cooking something, probably for that night's dinner. Biggabomb caught the odor once he cleaned the green mucus from his left nostril; it hung across his hand and ran up his arm. He made his daily cooking comment, "You cooka smell lika you feet."

Muga was quick in return, "Yup. I soaka my achin' feets and denna cooka you dinna in it."

"Putta you ass in it. I eat dat, too. Fat giv a flava. Ha ha." The old man was proud of himself. His cooking insults were something he lived for. Actually, Muga lived for them, too. Nutty thought she would miss them while Biggabomb was gone.

Biggabomb needed to leave for a bit to finish up some things. He mentioned inspecting the troops and out the door he went.

Nutty soon followed. He headed to Guthrak's machine shop. The walk seemed to take much longer today than others. His feet were enormous, and his legs hurt. He was clumsy, even by his awkward standards, but he did make it there. He went inside to see Guthrak.

Guthrak was taking things down from overhead. First, some metal tubing; then, some chains. The light that shone through the doorway enhanced the sight of dust that permeated the room. He saw Nutty standing at the door. "You comin' in, boy?"

Nutty entered. He didn't know if he should ask to use the machine shop or if his dad had already asked, or even worse, told Guthrak to give it up. What was already worked out? He hesitantly probed, "Guthrak?" He waited briefly, then followed, "Wut you gonna do wit' dis place when you go?"

"Didn't you dad talka you?" Guthrak asked.

"Yeah?"

Guthrak was a little confused. He didn't want to dance around with the child. It wasted time and was just annoying. He had too much to do and wasn't in the mood to go back and forth. "It gonna be army center for town." There. It was stated, plain and simple. Nothing to argue about.

Nutty agreed, "I know. I mean, where I put stuff?"

Now Guthrak was really confused and even more annoyed. "What you talkin' 'bout? You crazy sumptin'? I know you Chief kid, but you head inna ass? Why you put stuff in dis place?" He put his hands on his hips and raised one eyebrow. This better be good.

"Me be Big Town Army Controla."

Guthrak lowered his hands. He blinked several times as he looked at the boy, then the ground, and back to the boy. He looked utterly lost. He turned away as he ran his right hand over the top of his head. He mumbled, "Chief kid" under his breath and walked slowly into the back room and didn't come out the rest of the morning.

Nutty gave up after waiting for what seemed like an eternity. He walked outside and stood at the corner. He thought about logistics. This was the Crossroads to town from over the river or down to the mines. This location controlled everything. He made mental notes and began formulating a plan to protect the town.

He decided he would go to the school tomorrow to recruit his schoolmates. His father had explained that he could pull kids from school and even close it down, if necessary. As he thought of where the different orcs would fit into his plans, he began to go door to door. He would recruit everyone. He started on the road that led west, went to every house and business on the same side of the dirt road all the way west, and hit everyone on the opposite side returning.

During the day, he kept his conversations brief. He said that there were orders from the Warchief himself for all to participate in the war effort. This was an exaggeration of the truth. By Biggabomb appointing Nutty to control such matters, it was really the same thing, just indirectly. Nutty let all those he spoke with know about a meeting at the school in two days.

So, Nutty would use the school. He would work out using it in two days to bring all of the town members together. It would be there and then that he would fully explain what was expected of them. He would walk the north road tomorrow. He decided to ride the truck to school in the morning, recruit kids and work out closing school for the following day, and then, he would talk to orcs in their houses and businesses while walking home. He patted himself on the back.

There was one thing he wasn't pleased with during the day. While walking west, one of the bikers that he had a run in with some time before passed him on his motorcycle while riding east. The biker slowed and turned around to come back and tell Nutty something. He said, "Me taut dat wuz you. War a comin'. You gots no army. Me clan killa you! Bye jail bitch!" Then, he sped off toward Nutty's town. About an hour later, he passed again, this time going west. He pointed at Nutty and laughed as he headed toward the town of Wivvaflow.

Later that evening, Nutty finished up organizing things and lay down for the night. His father had helped him with some details and left for a city to the north for a couple of days. His mother attended to Gardawg. The little bastid would be okay.

Three
Big Town Army Controla

Uhra was always on Nutty's mind lately. Even with the frenzy of organizing the town's defenses, Nutty couldn't get her out of his head. He wondered if he could protect her. He wondered if she would provoke his body like she had several months earlier. She would be staying with him and his family. Would that affect their friendship?

Once again, Nutty felt he thought differently than others. Most orcs he knew were not "tinkers" (thinkers). They figured stuff out, but were predominantly "bruisers". Some didn't necessarily have feelings for females, they mated and had families, but not like his own. They weren't even supposed to feel fear.

His father had told him some strange things about orcs, especially on other worlds; things that were alien to his own clan- his entire world, for that matter. He wondered what it would have been like if he wasn't birthed by his mother and raised by his parents. Apparently, orcs on other worlds hatched from cocoons like chicklens from eggs. It was believed that some just grew like plants that needed dark, dank areas to take root. Regardless, it was commonplace that females weren't important to the males, other than for the need of procreation and food gathering. None of them went to builder schools. Things were simply different.

It occurred to Nutty that there were barriers to the language his clan spoke. There was ambiguity with limited language structure that left some things said up to interpretation. This was clear in his father's war plan notes. Nutty decided, then and there, that if he had the opportunity, he would make changes to the language he used; he would make it more rigid. Maybe he could teach this newer language in a kind of school. If builder schools could teach masses to learn how to build electronic equipment, then surely, he could use them to teach a better language.

Language barriers or not, he needed to focus on his job. He would just do the best he could. Besides, maybe the fact that the invading orcs were different than those he knew would help his clan. His clan obviously had an inherent instinct to protect its loved ones. The females weren't just pieces of meat; well, mostly, he thought as he smiled to himself. The females could organize, do a bulk of the production, and be docs while the males fought. He wondered if it could work to implement such an idea; innovative, but possibly not well accepted. Still, it was his clan's best chance of surviving if they were attacked. He would approach this conversation carefully.

Nutty stood off to the left and behind an old, rugged orc that held a megaphone. He was distinguished, yet, ragged in appearance. He had long, gray hair that flowed from the top of his head. It was held tight in a pony tail clasp at the scalp, so his hair hung behind his head, giving view to patches of gray tuft that clung to his jowls. When he spoke, a spattering of drool and spit flew from his lips and hung like a cave bat from his scarred chin. He seemed calm, but not necessarily reassuring; his voice was a bit thin and high-pitched for a male orc. Nutty wondered if the unusual tone was from an injury of some sort. The partial hole in his leathery neck and marks from past stitches in the skin pretty much confirmed his suspicions.

The device he held was mostly black with apparent wear around the edges that revealed its metal composition. There were spots that had been welded, soldered, and taped in repair to keep it functioning. The thing whistled at times as it was pointed in different directions. The crowd would hiss in dismay as the crude contraption screamed over loud speakers and sent inaudible rings throughout their ears. There were hundreds, maybe a thousand, clan members standing before him and many more outside that heard what was being said through a number of speakers that picked up the old orc's words by long wires that ran from the megaphone to the speakers.

The spacious room was lit fairly well. It had a particularly high ceiling that further echoed the annoying sounds that came from the megaphone. Chairs, crates, and whatever else orcs could sit on were used. Food, drink, and whatever else the crowd brought with them littered the aisles. The crowd was loud and rambunctious. That was until a certain part of what the old, rugged orc said hit them. "Anda now...Nuttybomb...Hims a Big Town Army Controla."

The crowd wasn't nearly as raucous as they had been a second before. Their ears attuned to what they had just heard, and their brains were now trying to make sense of it. Sometimes, it took a while for orcs to absorb what they saw or heard and process it. Some understood right away. Many looked around in bewilderment. All those in the room watched as Nutty took a few steps up to the megaphone. Who was this Nuttybomb? Surely, he wasn't the little kid that played with their own kids? Definitely not the "pee" kid. There was a collective groan of disappointment as Nutty stepped up.

Nutty decided to throw away the speech that he had prepared. There were obvious concerns about him being in charge which needed to be addressed. He took the megaphone with both hands and adjusted it down to an acceptable height, so he wasn't craning his neck and head upward to speak. His hands and feet had grown. He had widened in his shoulders and chest, but still seemed small for his age. He understood that he had obstacles to overcome. How would the crowd react to him? Would they accept him at all? When he spoke, he was polite and careful. "Tanka all fo' comin' to skool. Dis a great town wit' great orcs!"

Some orcs cheered, unwittingly to the hostile stares of many others.

Nutty continued, "Tank you. War a comin' fro' udder world."

Most in attendance booed with gusto.

Nutty went on, "Our armies go to Eastern Continent to fight wit dem."

A loud voice shouted sarcastically in a deep bellow, "And you gonna save us?" A young adult orc, maybe in his twenties, stood up to ask that question. He was lean, but looked strong. He didn't appear as crude as many of the others in the room.

Nutty began to explain, "We all save us."

"How? You gonna lead us? You a just a pee boy!"

To that, the crowd both busted out in laughter while jeering, and screamed in disbelief. Questions were flying aimlessly. Orcs were standing from their seats with fists waving in the air. Many felt the same way that the young orc did.

Nutty's voice boomed, low and strong. "Dat's 'nuff! Sit down!" he added with a snarl and widened eyes.

Some sat right away, others weren't sure how to react. This was a child giving orders, but they were orders. There were hundreds of males that thought they could kill the boy easily. They just weren't sure what would happen to them if they attempted to do so. Also, there was a high risk that some wouldn't be able to control themselves; orcs didn't always reason very well.

Guthrak came toward Nutty from the back of the room. He stood in front of Nutty, turned, and faced the audience. Within a few seconds, Gunza also came forward and turned to face the audience. Guthrak looked over his shoulder and spoke to Nutty, "Go 'head, Boy. You be ok."

Nutty pushed things a bit, but kept as calm as he could. It didn't matter if he was the son of the Warchief. He could still be killed here and now. It helped that Guthrak and Gunza were backing him up, but could they really think they could stop a riotous mob? Nutty began, "Listen. We work together, den we be a ok. We gotta support from fight skool to protect airport. Anda maybe war no come here if our armies win on Eastern Continent. Some a you already good fightas from udder wars, but not go to Eastern Continent. I needa you to help fight here if has to."

The orc in his twenties, obviously not satisfied with Nutty's words, or possibly that he wanted to be the local leader, scrutinized Nutty again. "How olda you, Boy? You's justa kid. Anda pee boy, too." He looked around and raised his hands repeatedly to gain support from all the orcs around him. Many rose to their feet, pumping their fists in agreement.

Nutty didn't want a riot, but he felt the hair standing up on the back of his neck. He was beginning to lose a little control himself; he was angry with the young orc. He didn't like the hostile crowd. He was trying to be rational, and again chose his words carefully, "It not smart to oppose me. I aska you to sit down till I finish."

The young, brash orc had little regard for Nutty, his position, or any authority. He waved his hands in downward motions to quiet the crowd. When he sufficiently controlled the crowd, he defiantly bellowed, "No! It not smart fo Peeboy to oppose me." He had left his seat and entered the main isle just moments before he spoke. Now, he was approximately fifteen feet in front of Nutty.

A female's voice cried out, "Sitta down anda shutta up; you stupid."

The young, brash orc turned, and when realizing the words were directed toward him, retorted, "Shutta up you oogly, old bitch! I killa you!"

He had no idea who he was speaking to; he probably didn't care. If he knew what Nutty knew, he might have cared a little more.

Nutty saw the young, brash, ignorant orc threaten his mother. There was no rationality or choosing words to appease the crowd. No posturing, no recruiting, no

55

nothing. Nutty leaped over Guthrak and Gunza in an instant. He was enraged. He was on the young, brash, ignorant, injured orc, covering fifteen feet in a millisecond.

The orc tried to avoid Nutty, but to no avail. Nutty was a crazed animal, teeth bared, eyes wild. His fist came across the orc's face like a sledgehammer. Then, the other flew. Bone-crushing blow after bone-crushing blow felled the larger foe.

The crowd moved back and away from the fray. Some were actually frightened, something not normally seen in orcs. Some of the beaten orc's friends did not move away, however. They may have felt fear, but they came to the aid of their fallen friend. Eleven in total started to encircle Nutty. Guthrak and Gunza took up their places behind Nutty.

The beaten orc's face was unrecognizable. His nose was simply gone. Maybe it fell off or was pushed back into his brain. His head hung to the side, torn muscles in his neck straining to keep the weight of his head upon a fractured neck. Still, he barked orders for the others to take out the current leadership and his lackeys. Nutty had heard of orcs in battle that had lost limbs and continued to fight, using them as weapons. Orcs were truly amazing physical specimens.

Nutty was utterly mad. His head spun as his burning red eyes glared from one opponent to the next. He waited, no, anticipated the actions of the enemies that would come. And when they were slow to act, he urged them to engage him. He dared them to lay injured like their fallen friend. He simply growled, "What you wait for? I killa you all!"

Gunza was impressed. He had been in battle countless times with Biggabomb. The two had fought other clans; hell, they faced many enemies. The worst were those damn Spidanoids; fast and strong, giant bug-like aliens with huge talons. They ripped apart their foes with a brutality that was unmatched, even by orc standards. Gunza, Bigga, and Guthrak came out of that scrap okay. These orcs standing in front of him, Nutty, and Guthrak were just punks. They weren't to be underestimated, but certainly seemed in no way as threatening as other enemies.

Anyway, Gunza would die for Bigga's kid if he had to. Biggabomb saved his hide more than a few times. If he had to return the favor, regardless of cost, he would gladly do so. Besides, he felt a sense of pride in knowing Bigga's kid. This kid was a warrior like his dad. He would probably protect the kid whether he was Bigga's or not. Then, for an instant, he thought maybe this kid would protect himself. He sure looked vicious. But there were eleven orcs ready to fight against him. One wrong move or miscalculation and the kid could be hurt. Whether by design, or just out of carelessness, Gunza made a remark about Nutty, "Ok, I tink him's startin' a get mad." Gunza smirked.

Something happened that diffused things; some of the orcs recognized Gunza as being a top officer. He wasn't just an officer, he was a killer. He was a huge, monstrous, fighting machine without fear or regard for his own life. Nutty's appearance was that of a rabid dog that was cornered. He was frothing at the mouth, sweating, and mumbling threats under his breath; he was wild. Yet these two paled in comparison to

Guthrak. This guy had a knife shoved through his face that he kept as a piercing.

Maybe it was a reality check for the eleven. They surely would have died that day. They pulled their fallen friend up and left with their tails between their legs, so that never happened. The crowd cheered as they disappeared.

It took some time for Nutty to calm down. He began to understand what had just happened as the levity of the situation took hold. He saw his mother; she wasn't harmed. Her eyes conveyed her understanding that he had become something more than the boy he was. She smiled and sat down in her seat.

As he looked around, assessing the situation, he saw Uhra. She approached him with a big smile. She stopped in front of him and leaned forward, her arms reaching around him for an unexpected hug. His heartbeat slowed as her warm embrace soothed him. She loosened her grip and giggled, "Younut." There was the sound of some light-hearted snickering throughout the room, and Nutty himself, couldn't help but chuckle a bit.

His muscles weren't as tense as they were just moments before. But he wasn't completely relaxed either. He carefully pushed Uhra away and nervously smiled at Gunza. Gunza crossed his arms after pointing toward the megaphone. He simply snarled, "Letta us finish dis talk wit' dem all, Nutty."

Nutty nodded in agreement. He turned away from the crowd and took a few steps back to the raised platform where the megaphone sat in pieces. He didn't remember throwing it, but he might have without thinking about it when he sprang at the orc that threatened Muga. He waved it a few times and played with the button on the underside. This just caused the top to fall off and drop to the floor. He laughed.

He turned his attention to the crowd and spoke with an assertion at an audible level that few could have duplicated. This time, he was direct with his words. He clenched his right fist and pumped his arm in time with those words he felt needed to be accentuated with a physical show of force.

If Gunza was proud of the boy before, he was awestruck by what he was now experiencing. If he wasn't following Biggabomb into battle, he would swear his allegiance to Nuttybomb.

The kid sat everyone down and asserted himself. He swore to protect them. He built them up and praised their blood lines. He spoke of honor and valor, fighting da good fight. All would participate. Schools would be better. He boasted that the males were the strongest in the world. Production would go up by bringing females into the workforce. He was sure to let them know how beautiful their females were, the best on the planet, in fact. They were even more attractive as strong contributors. This, combined with sharing of technologies and products, would advance their standing as the prominent clan in the region: militarily, socially, and economically. He knew to explain to those that didn't care about social values and the economy of Big Town that they simply didn't understand the importance of what he was saying. By the end of the speech, they all understood what they had to do to be a successful state as a military power. He told all those present that day to spread the word to all.

Gunza thought about the possibility of Nutty being his son through marriage with Uhra. It seemed he had misjudged Nutty in the beginning. However, the real test for Nutty would be while Gunza and the other boys were off to fight. Would Nutty protect his daughter? Would he violate her? He was still a kid, albeit a bigger kid now with hormones and a pee. Gunza was one once; he shuddered at the idea.

***

The crowd had left, and most were enthusiastic. Gunza had taken Uhra home to finish some things up before his journey to the Eastern Continent. Biggabomb was coming back from his trip to see Muga and the kids before he left, too. Guthrak had left some instructions about his shop with Nutty and then he was off as well.

Nuttybomb couldn't have planned it any better. It seemed like he had gained enough support to move forward without a hitch. Several hours after the speech, there were still three or four hundred orcs hanging around, just chatting about the new plan.

Nutty had chosen a team of advisers to head up certain departments. Over those several hours, while talking with them, he overheard some things being said by remnants of the crowd that gave him great pride, as well as a bit of a laugh. He heard things like, "We do have da bestest females in da world," and "Him's right, we da strongest. We win all da wars!" Over the next few months, these same types of comments would ring throughout the Town.

Over his council and the vague dialogue of those still loitering, a raspy, "Nuttybomb," caught Nutty's attention. A hunched, well-aged orc had addressed him firmly.

"Ole Man Boppa," Nutty countered as he bowed to the ancient veteran.

"No, son. It me who bow to you, now. My boy die in Eastern Continent. You dad be new Warchief. Anda you be Big Town Army Controla."

Nutty was stunned. Ole Man Boppa was a Warchief from fifty years before. His son, Warchief Dagga, was the Warchief who had died, leaving Biggabomb, his senior officer next in line. Biggabomb didn't fight to become Warchief. He simply acquired leadership by no contest. Nutty didn't know what to say. He blurted out, "You son, Boss Dagga da great Warchief, him die wit' honor."

Ole Man Boppa rolled something around in his mouth. He thought about how this kid carried himself, the way he talked. He had seen him obliterate the orc that threatened Muga. The kid came from good stock. Biggabomb was Dagga's best guard, the strongest, toughest, smartest he had ever known. This kid seemed to be a chip off the old block. He half spit a wad of brown leaves and mucus out of the left side of his swollen cheek. "You needs anyting, son, you come a to me. I help."

"We win war fo' you son, Sir."

Ole Man Boppa liked this kid standing in front of him. He smiled, attempting to hide the pain of his recent loss, renewed by Nutty's words. "I have no doubt of dat, son."

Nutty had thought of something at that moment. It was something he hadn't thought of before in any detail and he thought that asking the Ole Man would help both of them. "Would you help set up defend to da mines? It mean lot to me anda town."

"Hm hm hm", he chuckled. "Me an ole man, I can show you how tho."

"Yes, Sir. It helpa lot."

***

Biggabomb was exhausted. He was successful in his travels by uniting several other clans, mostly through diplomacy. He was bombarded with Nutty's accomplishments from earlier that day by Muga as soon as he got in the door. These weren't the ramblings from a mother's point of view. Others that came and left had vowed their support and attested to what she told him.

Bigga heard how strong Nutty was, how well he spoke, all about his great ideas, and some silly nonsense about females. He wasn't gone all that long. How did his kid reach so many and become so popular so quickly? And, what of school and language changes?

Nonetheless, Bigga wasn't going to be home for very long. He ate while he interacted with the kids. He knew Muga was having a hard time with him leaving, but he had to. So, he would spend the little bit of precious time he had with his family and hope Nutty would be home soon, so he could say goodbye.

Gunza showed up with Uhra. They were to stay the night until Bigga and Gunza went off to war. Uhra would stay with Muga until, if ever, Gunza came back alive.

Gunza sat down to talk a bit with his friend and boss, careful not to interrupt any conversations or important moments he might be sharing with his family. He noticed Gardawg and said, "Hey, da boy lookin' betta."

Bigga swatted at the troubled child, "Hims still a pain in da ass tho." Gardawg dropped to the floor and laughed. Bigga's halfhearted attempt to hit the boy was seen as a joke. Gardawg hugged his father's leg and then crawled off to get into trouble somewhere else.

Gunza had all girls. He never swatted at them. The fever took his wife and two of his little ones. Only he and Uhra survived. He laughed, too, when he saw Bigga and Gardawg's antics.

Bigga continued to talk, "So, what I hear bout Nutty?" He handed a bottle of alcohol to Gunza, who swigged a gulp before answering.

"I nevva seen nuttin' lika it befo'. Maybe lika time when Ole Man Boppa rally us when we wuz pups."

Bigga laughed his belly laugh. "I 'memba dat. Wow! We fighta good afta dat. Really? Dat good?"

"Bigga, you boy sumptin' else. Hims… umm… special."

Bigga was noticeably proud. He owed his friend and best guard a resounding, "Tanks my ole friend."

The two war veterans drank through the night between Bigga consoling Muga and the kids stirring. They talked about great battles, fallen friends, and females. They laughed. They boasted. They passed gas and toasted. They gave their own solemn wishes should one of them fall in battle. They were partners, as close or closer than males and females that were bound through marriage. They understood hardship, carnage, and loss. But they strove for victory and anything needed to attain it. They were like brothers connected through a tragedy that could never be spoken of. They would fight to protect each other, putting themselves last. They were the best of friends. They were orcs!

As the sun rose, Nutty came through the door. His last few moments with his father should have been better spent, certainly longer, but with an enemy on the move, Biggabomb was off to fight. There were pleasantries and back slaps just before he left. There were some kind words and hugs. There were some tears. But there was war... and then, there was silence.

Nutty was in charge now.

Four
Over the River and Through the Woods

Some news came in the form of a "Runna". Runners were the orcs that brought information back and forth between different army headquarters. They delivered mail, helped to resupply, or whatever they could as part of their back and forth responsibilities. Runna Bigeye lumbered into the doorway at Guthrak's shop and gazed upon Nuttybomb.

Bigeye noticed Nutty was busy, so he waited for Nutty to acknowledge his presence before he spoke. Such was the way in most of this world of orcs. Speaking out of turn might result in catastrophic results; all too many ignorant orcs lost limbs or lives, and Bigeye didn't want to be another statistic. Bigeye was a replacement of such an unfortunate predecessor that walked into an angry general's wrath. That orc didn't do anything; he simply happened upon a general that didn't have his morning drink yet. No way was Bigeye going to make the same mistake.

Nutty finished going over some plans with Booma, who was coordinating defense with the fight school. Nutty lifted his eyes to meet Bigeye's. Bigeye lowered his head to his alpha male in discernible obedience and nodded ever so slightly.

Nutty began, "Ah, come in." Nutty waved his large, right hand to welcome the runner. "What da word wit' da war?"

Bigeye came wearily closer, but soon realized Nutty wasn't in a threatening mood. His posture straightened a bit as he fumbled to find the correct greeting and title for Nutty. His mind grappled with several variations and committed to words as, "Chief Nuttybomb, da Homeworlders are puttin' a good fight to da Invadas. Warchief Biggabomb winna two battles at Big Ridge. But udder Homeworlders lose at Gunna Pass and Red Town. Warchief Biggabomb say he to tella you dat he can't win in south too, anda you be ready for Invadas in three weeks."

Nutty looked over at Booma. Booma boasted, "We be ready, Nutty."

Nutty puffed out his bottom lip as he shook his head in general "yes" motions. It occurred to him that his father made similar gestures when he agreed with information he was processing. He also wondered if his father's mind wandered and considered things others didn't. Obviously, his father was much smarter than Nutty ever gave him credit for. He must have contemplated about a variety of different things in order to problem solve. Surely, this is partially why he was so successful and revered.

Nutty redirected his thoughts from missing his father and words unsaid back to Booma. "Booma, it come to a me dat da town to da west will probably attack us. Dems use mostly bikes to fasta attack. Canna we refit our bikes wit jet engines fro' da airport? I mean, any engines left?"

Booma smiled. "Ya. I can get some. You got bikes?"

Nutty thought for a moment. He began, "Well, we gonna raid Wivvaflow anda take ders." After Booma laughed, Nutty continued, "We go in two weeks. Until den, we close borders and place mines. You start trainin' all males at fight skool. I have a plan."

Booma held his belly and laughed. "Nutty, you a always got da plan."

Nutty explained to the quiet, obedient Runner what was needed. The Runner agreed to contact all the orcs that Nutty instructed him to. Then, Nutty dismissed the Runner and thanked him; this was a first in orc history; never had there been any regard for a lowly Runner. Nutty even got his name and addressed him as "Bigeye" when he thanked him.

Some Warchiefs gained power through diplomacy while others took it by brute force. Nutty had no aspirations of being Warchief; his father was quite capable of being one. Nutty was planning to take Wivvaflow by removing its main strength though. Without its bikes, Wivvaflow was severely handicapped. Nutty planned to secure his western front by debilitating the adversary with force and then, using diplomacy by having the upper hand. Maybe he could bully Wivvaflow into submission and absorb its forces into his own. Either way, Wivvaflow was his first military threat and he would plan everything to the T. He began working out diversions and traps and thought out contingencies and possible counter attacks. He developed exit strategies and calculated potential losses. He had to do this right: his town, his family, his mother, and his best friend- Uhra, were relying on his ability to lead and protect them. He had three weeks. He couldn't fail. He mustn't.

***

It was dusk on this warm summer night. Intermittent rain had begun over the last week or so, and with it, enormous stinger bugs that sucked the blood from their victims. Buzzing wings drowned out all, but the loudest sounds. This would help in troop movement being undetected. The lack of rain on this night was ideal for troop movement as dry roads were easier to traverse, although the humidity of the rainy season had arrived in earnest.

Gardawg and Kor were paired by Nutty to begin the first part of his plan. Nutty saw Kor as sheepish and careful, but Gardawg as a loose cannon. He thought the two would keep each other in check. As predicted, they did just that.

They waded through murky water in the dark to avoid being seen; Kor made sure of this. Several times he had to keep Gardawg from racing forward in an attempt to keep noise to a minimum. They crossed the river from Big Town to Wivvaflow's bank on the other side, whereupon Kor signaled with his left hand toward a Big Town company commander that had positioned his troops below the bridge that connected the two towns. Then, Gardawg and Kor made their way through a few miles of woods until they came upon a tall, wire fence. They were running behind schedule because of Kor's constant stopping and checking things out before they continued. Inevitably, Gardawg would move ahead and keep them on pace while Kor always reminded him to be quiet. They crouched low behind a wooden crate and some tall grass and began to examine their surroundings.

Beyond the fence was an impressive building. It was easily as large as any in Big Town and was enclosed within a similar fence to the one that Gardawg and Kor ducked behind. Machine parts were scattered throughout the yard and there were bike parts everywhere. The building's outer walls appeared to be dressed in vertical strips of corrugated aluminum that hung on slight angles, exposing steel beams and light from inside.

Inside was obviously busy; shadows could be seen moving between the metal slats and the sounds of drills and hammers clattered relentlessly. Orc whistling, and occasional drunken singing, evolved into laughter. Two orcs stumbled out a door on the side as they clumsily carried some engines and placed them along the outer walls of the building. Just as quickly as they emerged from the building, they stumbled back in.

Gardawg and Kor began making their way south along the fence that led to a field that was darted with trees and overgrown, wild grass. Gardawg impatiently trotted awkwardly, less aware than his cautious counterpart. He giggled like a little school girl as he vibrated the ground with the foul air that emitted from his rear end. He held his nose and waved the area behind his butt so that Kor could fully appreciate the magnitude of stink he had created. Following as closely as he could, Kor nearly died. Even his conservative demeanor and keen sense of his surroundings were lost on such a worthy gift. Funny how many an orc's courtship had begun in such a way. The mere fact that Gardawg was sharing such a precious rarity was a sign of true, albeit new, friendship. Kor fought between laughing and vomiting.

Another had caught the smell and deciphered trespassers above the sounds of stinger bugs. A carnidawg lunged from behind wild grass and tore through Gardawg's left arm. It pulled him to the ground, nearly severing the forearm from the elbow. Gardawg's eyes opened in fear at the sight of the monstrous beast that was devouring him. He raised his other arm in a futile attempt to block the next attack which was aimed at his throat. His right hand was ripped to pieces in an instant as the carnidawg's ravenous appetite for flesh drove him to finish his kill.

Kor stepped forward and landed a blow to the back of the carnidawg's head. He swung repeatedly, not knowing what to do, other than try to stop his new friend from dying. He knew if he fired his weapon, he would be heard, and the mission wouldn't be accomplished. All he could do was to keep punching. At first, the punches went unnoticed as the carnidawg snapped through Gardawg's bone in his upper right arm. Gardawg fought back a scream; pain and sheer terror had now gripped him. The carnidawg turned on Kor and clamped down on his left arm as a punch was thrown. The carnidawg was quicker than either of the orcs and was the alpha predator on this world. It was powerful and quick, didn't feel fear, and only wanted to kill.

The carnidawg turned its head with blazing speed and grabbed Kor's mid-section, taking his entire torso into his ravenous mouth. The sound of bones crunching and fluid replacing the air in one of Kor's lungs was blood curdling. Kor pushed back helplessly with both of his arms against the monster's head, trying somehow to free himself from death's grip. His eyes shut as his body involuntarily went limp, slipping into unconsciousness. The carnidawg still thrashed Kor's body wildly; more bones cracked; more blood flowed.

Gardawg stumbled to his feet. He saw his new friend being consumed. He threw his own ravaged body toward the beast and opened his own mouth, nearly unhitching his jaw. He found the throat of the carnidawg with his own teeth and drove home, deep into the rough skin of his foe. He instantly severed an artery. The taste of blood fed his own frenzy as he wrapped his torn arms around the neck of the beast and hung on desperately. His legs instinctively wrapped around the beast's chest.

The carnidawg released Kor and fought to reach Gardawg. It could barely get its front paws, furnished with massive, razor sharp claws, to get Gardawg clear of its throat. It shook its head and lashed its paws upward, catching Gardawg's legs each time. Gardawg's lower half was being shredded, but he held on.

Kor wearily opened his eyes. It took several seconds for him to realize what was happening. He couldn't believe that he and Gardawg were going to die this way and end up in the belly of a carnidawg. He realized that he was too helpless to do very much as he was weak and dizzy. He recognized how severely his chest was crushed. Gardawg looked worse than he did.

***

Lightening crashed, and the winds howled. Thunder clapped furiously, drowning out almost all other noise. Rain, which was coming from the north, began to fall in earnest. The river began to rise; the dirt roads were becoming muddy, making travel difficult.

Nutty and his groups of Big Town troops were spread behind a long embankment just on the northeastern edge of Wivvaflow. They were waiting for the sign they needed to begin the next phase of the mission. Nutty wondered if the sound of thunder and the constant flash of lightening may have muted and blinded him and his orcs from the explosion that should have happened by now. It was hard enough just to hear the orc next to him. He looked directly at Thunda, a big, crude orc he had handpicked to work alongside him. As he struggled to hear Thunda over all of the weather's fury, he pleaded, "What? Talk louda!"

Thunda clenched his battleax hard enough so that his big knuckles turned white. He leaned closer to Nutty. He inhaled deeply and shouted, "Sumptin a wrong! It take a too long fo esplosion! You tinka we should move?"

Nutty was constantly assessing the situation. He thought that he should give his dumb brother and cowardly schoolmate a bit more time. So, he answered his impatient underling with a hardy, "We wait a few mo' minutes! It be a soon!"

Thunda rolled his eyes and sat back. He began shaking his head "no".

Just then, a tall, fairly slender orc named Quicklip griped, "You stupid a ass! Get offa me foots!"

Nutty found himself watching the two bantering back and forth over the next minute or so. He would normally break them up to be quiet so as not to compromise the mission, but nobody in town would possibly hear these two going at it beneath the chaotic thunderstorm. He used this time to evaluate personalities, dispositions, and traits. He figured that by knowing these things, he would better know where to place troops within his ranks.

Thunda fired back at Quicklip, "I no see you a scrawny ass! Now shutta up!"

Quicklip wasn't pleased with Thunda's reply, so he fired off a volley of his own with, "You Mudder see a my ass all last night!"

Thunda wasn't as quick with his words as Quicklip, and certainly not as creative. He usually reasoned things out with his brawn; if he was going to win this fight, he would do it physically. He thought a threat was in order though. "I should squasha you skinny ass! No! I cut you a ass up you back wit' me a ax and make a crack all da way up to you neck. Den you be bigga ass a den you already are!" Thunda was pleased with himself; proud of how quick witted he was with that last reply. He busted out a hardy laugh and rubbed his loving ax in satisfaction.

Quicklip smirked. "Not bad, Thunda! You Mudder like big asses! And a she rub my ax lika dat last night!"

Thunda went from play to kill in an instant; he swung his heavy battleax in a flash. Quicklip stepped back just as quickly and caught the ax with two crossed short swords. He balanced himself in such a way that he could match Thunda's strength by using leverage.

Quicklip boasted, "You too stupid anda slow!"

Thunda leaned to the side to throw off Quicklip's balance. Then he freed his right fist and found Quicklip's jaw with it.

Quicklip was just as fast with his reflexes as he was with his mouth however, and Thunda landed a glancing blow. Quicklip, unfazed by the sloppy fist, taunted, "You stupid, slow, anda weak too!" Quicklip threw his right sword through Thunda's left foot, spiking him to the ground. Without a thought, he rattled off two jabs from his now free hand into Thunda's face.

Thunda caught Quicklip's hand under his own armpit on a third attempt. He dropped to his back and separated Quicklip's shoulder from its socket. Thunda yelled out, "Ha!"

Quicklip dodged beneath Thunda's ax and drove his remaining sword down to the throat of his opponent.

Nutty intervened with his own knife, blocking what may have been Thunda's demise. He surely didn't want any of his orcs to die before the mission was done. He had seen enough and stated so. "No mo' fightin'!"

As he said that, Thunda had rolled just far enough to avoid Quicklip's sword anyway. As he did so, he also kicked with his free foot and swiped Quicklip's legs out from under him. Looking up, he caught Nutty's angry stare. "Yes, Chief!"

Quicklip concurred, "Ok, Chief!"

The two gathered themselves and picked themselves off the ground. Quicklip grabbed the sword that was installed in Thunda's foot and pulled. "I'll take a dat now!"

Thunda grimaced and followed with, "Let a me help you!" With that, he took hold of Quicklip's dangling arm with one hand and his shoulder with the other. He pushed the two together, reuniting the ball and socket as painfully as he had separated them.

Quicklip snarled, "Tanka you! You Mudder put it in dat hard last night!" He then giggled as he turned around and picked up his other sword.

Thunda growled, "Dis gonna be a you last night if you a keep it up!"

"Wanna drink?" came from Nubbs. Nubbs was a short, stocky orc. He wasn't quite as tall as Thunda, but nearly as muscular. It seemed like every square inch of his body was tattooed. He wore many scars, both those physically that could be seen outwardly, and those that developed through years of neglect and punishment from growing up in broken homes and mostly living in the streets. He wore rings through his ears, nose, lip, and eyebrows. He, like the others, was also handpicked by Nutty. Nutty liked the way that he thought things through before acting. Also, he was a good fighter. Nutty saw him win many more fights than he lost over the last two weeks in fight school. Nutty picked most of these orcs because they had been in fight school for a few years. They were all good fighters as far as he could tell. Hopefully, they would listen well and not fight each other.

As they drank, Nutty prepared them again to move as soon as Kor and Gardawg exploded the far bridge that divided Wivvaflow in two. Not only would it be the distraction that Nutty needed to divert attention from his troops, it would cut half of the town from its army on the other side of the now raging river.

Nutty and his orcs waited.

***

The carnidawg was unwilling to succumb to the little green pest that was clinging to its throat and chest. It thrashed and thrashed, but Gardawg hung on. It threw itself forward and down, its massive weight falling upon its prey.

Gardawg's arm snapped. Its muscle and skin which was already ripped to shreds simply couldn't hold the arm together. Gardawg screamed and had to release as the bones in one of his legs splintered and he lost his arm.

Kor knew that he had one last chance to save them both. He found his anger which is inherent in orcs and lumbered a few feet to defend his new friend. He growled and spit over his pain as his determination brought him next to the unaware carnidawg. He screamed in mad ferocity as he thrust his hand into the carnidawg's eye and beyond. He grabbed as much soft tissue as he could, clawing, scratching, and pushing as deep as he could with all his might. The last thing he saw before he collapsed was the carnidawg going into convulsions and Gardawg's eyes rolling back.

***

It's funny how the mind works, especially for orcs. Evolution-wise, orcs were generally considered a step up from dogs or maybe wild boar. They shared similar thoughts of eating; that's about it. Sure, orcs went a step further and thought about killing something, being loud, or having sex. Whereas a dog associated its own yelp as being related to pain, an orc reasoned that yelping was the result of pain. The difference of having thumbs and slightly larger brains allowed orcs to develop languages and rudimentary writing skills. It also allowed them to make tools and shelter. Their brutish attributes and hardy genetics caused their rise as the dominant species throughout many parts of the star cluster. For orcs, moments of clarity seldom occurred. It was often at the end when it was too late that somehow things connected the wires •in their brains correctly.

In this case, clarity was illusive. Gardawg was struggling to bring things into focus. What he saw first was his father. Biggabomb was furious; he stood over Nuttybomb waiting for an answer.

Nuttybomb and Gardawg were wet. Nuttybomb was trying to explain to Biggabomb that he found Gardawg in the river. Gardawg had fallen in so Nutty jumped in to save him. Unfortunately, Nutty was only three and his language skills were far from developed. He tried to explain that Gardawg made a boat with a motor, but it didn't work because the river was too strong, and the boat tipped over.

Gardawg watched as Biggabomb screamed at Nutty, "Him only a two-year-old! How da hell a him make a boat?"

Gardawg's mind was reeling; he was wet and cold; he felt pain throughout his body. He talked some; mostly he didn't make much sense. He felt strange and light; like he was in a dream. He knew what was going to happen next. Actually, it seemed like a memory, but something was different. He muttered that he had built the boat like Nutty had explained. He saw his father and brother slowly look up through the roof of their home; they were looking up at the rain. Gardawg was confused. Where was the roof? He looked up at the intense lightening. He blinked several times, pain gripping him and causing him to shake. He closed his eyes; things were fuzzy again.

Biggabomb turned the steering wheel and lowered the gears to reduce speed in the rickety truck that he drove. He and his passengers leaned to the left to balance themselves as the wheels slipped slightly and dug into the loose dirt. Things clanged and squeaked. The belts in the engine whined as they passed from pulley to pulley. The smell of the engine was ever present. Oil burned from the top and fuel sputtered in and out of the mixture tank before meeting compressed air. Like the wheels, the gears slipped as well, grinding momentarily before finding their grooves. An occasional backfire caused laughter for those in the truck.

Those outside the vehicle flinched every time the truck belched its thunderous clap. Some initially perceived the sounds to be gunshots. It wasn't inconceivable for an orc to haphazardly fire a weapon inadvertently as a knee-jerk reaction. But that hadn't happened so far and Biggabomb was pretty sure that nobody would shoot in town on a well-lit day like this.

Biggabomb pointed out a large building to his two kids. Gardawg sat directly to his left with Kago. "Dis is Wivvaflow bike factory."

Gardawg was excited and happy. Normally it was hard for him to sit still, but occasionally he was distracted enough to be somewhat normal. He was so glad that his father was taking him and his little brother out this day. Gardawg was six today. He got to spend precious time with his father and get something, too. He asked his father, "Do dems only make a bikes der?"

Biggabomb was happy to talk with his kids. Well, in truth, he didn't mind as long as they weren't total asses. He responded, "Well, mostly dems maka bike der. But dems maka engines and udder parts, too. You a smart fo' askin'."

Gardawg perked up and smiled as he spoke. "Am I a smart kid?"

Biggabomb didn't see any harm in telling the truth. Orcs really didn't care about such things as intelligence; they relished noise and bright colors; they liked to drink and fight. Being smart was not getting killed. He began to drive slower as he explained things to Gardawg. "You used to be a smartest kid in da town. You even save mama after da earthshake. She did be pinned unda stuff and a fire be comin' fo' her. You a tied rope ova da roof and pulled da stuff offa her. Denna you tie it so it not fall. You goed back and a pulled her out. You saved her life!"

Gardawg was shocked. "I did?"

"Yup. You wuz only three. Den da fever a get you. You die like a twice. Den you a lived. You not dat smart afta dat."

Gardawg was intrigued by what Biggabomb was telling him. He didn't realize the gift of intelligence that he had lost to disease. "Am I still lil smart?"

Biggabomb laughed. "Nope! Now, you justa Daddy's lil smart ass!" He pet the top of Gardawg's head as Gardawg nuzzled under his father's arm. Gardawg's happiness brought him to laughter, too. Biggabomb pointed out another landmark. "Hey boys, dat is da fuel tanks dat energy da whole town."

Kago dropped his mouth wide open like the innocent child he was and asked bewildered, "Da whole town?"

Biggabomb laughed uncontrollably. He couldn't fathom why that would be so important to a four-year-old. While the two children laughed in response to their father's abrupt outburst, he gathered himself and said, "Yes, Kago…da whole town. And a up here on da right is da bridge over da wivva."

Gardawg thought again about the river. He recalled pulling his little sister, Runzda from the river. He could see and feel it like it was yesterday. He thought for a moment that he was cold, wet, and in pain from that event now.

He saw his mother. He helped her cook.

He saw Booma playing with Guta. He saw Nutty again; Nutty was telling him to complete the mission.

Finally, he saw Guta. She wasn't sick; she looked well. She instructed him to close his eyes and so he did. Then, she said, "In you life, you were deprived of greatness by events not of you making. You saved Mama and Runzda. You will be rewarded soon, I promise. Now, I save you." After pausing for a moment, she made him repeat what she said. She chanted, "It is not my time. Not my time. Not my time." Then, she spoke softly, "I will see you soon, Gardawg. Keep saying, *it is not my time.*" Gardawg followed Guta's chants. He chanted along with her, over and over. She told him to open his eyes when she clapped. He chanted the words. He was starting to feel fuzzy again. Then, Guta clapped. There was clarity.

Gardawg awoke to a flash of lightening and thunderous clamor. His body twitched; he was in agony. He laid there for a moment as he looked around. He moaned, and his body shuddered for the rain was blinding and cold. Through it he saw two limp bodies; one was the carnidawg and the other was Kor. He began to crawl over to Kor.

Along the way, he managed to pick up one of the bags that he and Kor brought on the mission. It wasn't easy, but he used the stump of his right arm and slid it through the shoulder strap. He groaned as he lifted it upward, over his raw, torn-off elbow joint. He dragged his body and the bag filled with explosives to his friend. Moving ten feet and getting the bag took no less than five minutes. He wondered how he and Kor could possibly finish the mission now.

Kor didn't look good; his body was misshapen. He was a very pale green, much like Guta over the last few months before her death. When he breathed, blood gurgled in his mouth and chest. Gardawg tried to wake him, but Kor continued to breathe quickly and erratically, all the while his eyes remained shut.

Gardawg was surprisingly clear-headed, even with his injuries and pain. He thought about the strength potions that were in one of the bags he brought. They were actually some kind of poison from snakes that was mixed with the sap of trees. They caused some sort of adrenaline boost. Gardawg thought for a minute and reasoned using one might kill Kor. They didn't always work on orcs that were severely wounded. On the contrary, they often killed them. He knew that he had to act though. He, himself was probably going to die soon. He had no hands, or much in the way of legs and was bleeding out. He had to try to revive Kor at any cost. So, he dipped into the bag with his broken, bloody face and retrieved a syringe needle with a florescent yellow liquid inside. Knowing that he couldn't complete the mission in his own state, he held the needle in his mouth and plunged the tip through Kor's chest, piercing his heart. Gardawg injected his friend with the concoction and waited.

Kor began to move in less than a minute. He began to choke and turned on his side to spit blood from his mouth. He caught a glance of Gardawg and weakly whispered, "You looka like a shit!"

Gardawg barely heard him between the claps of thunder. He felt himself slipping away; he was slumped over and beginning to convulse. He barely managed to get out, "Stabba me wit' needle in da bag."

Kor had a hard time hearing and understanding Gardawg. He watched his friend fall over and his eyes roll back again. Then, what Gardawg said dawned on him. This time he fought through his pain and found a needle that he promptly injected into Gardawg's heart. He also knew the possible consequences of doing so, but he, too, reasoned that there was no other choice.

As the rain lightened a bit over the next thirty or so seconds, Gardawg began to regain consciousness. During that time, Kor had noticed that the bike factory had closed. It was quiet and dark. He was amazed that nobody heard the fight with the carnidawg just fifty yards away. He gave his attention to Gardawg.

Gardawg was awake, but obviously not himself. He wasn't wild and carefree. He was beaten and battered; he was death walking. He told Kor what they needed to do. "Listen. You a put bag a esplosive on me and a drive me to fuel tank. Den you go a to bridge and blow it up." Gardawg was using his eyes and head movements to convey what his lack of fingers could point to.

Kor understood. He at least had extremities to drive. He tied the bag of explosives to Gardawg's chest and dragged him as quietly as he could to a fuel truck that was a half block away. Kor was gasping for air; his heart throbbing in his temples.

Kor dragged Gardawg into the truck. After he hotwired it, he drove another block and carried Gardawg to the fuel tank. He laid Gardawg beneath it and placed the fuse in his friend's mouth under the cover of darkness.

Gardawg spoke quietly as he again began to drift, "You a good friend. I wait till you blow bridge. I see you on a udder side a life." The fuse that was in his mouth had slipped out as he spoke.

Kor embraced Gardawg's shoulder and nodded. He weakly muttered, "You a good friend, too. C-ya der." Kor reinserted the fuse in Gardawg's mouth.

Kor left Gardawg, knowing that they would probably never see each other again. He pulled himself along the perimeter of the truck as he choked up blood. He leaned his weight against the tanker to keep his weakened legs from sending him to the ground. He dragged himself up by his arms along the running board and opened the cab door. As he climbed in, he was spotted by locals.

Mayhem ensued. Orcs began to enter the street from every direction. They were starting to encircle the truck. They were screaming, "Invada!" Shots were fired.

Kor heard a hiss. His front driver side tire was blown out. He was thrown back in his seat as he felt like he was punched in the face. It wasn't a fist though. It was a bullet that impacted his cheek and thrust him backward. He threw the truck into gear and rolled toward his destination in slow motion.

Orcs were now climbing onto the truck. Kor found his weapon and fired to his left, knocking one orc from his driver side door. Why he didn't use it on the carnidawg didn't even occur to him. Another orc made his way through the passenger window and grabbed the steering wheel. He was too fat to get his bulky body all the way in; this kept him from reaching Kor's gun. Meanwhile, another jumped on the running board to replace the orc that was just shot. The truck limped slowly down the street.

Things weren't going well. If the bridge wasn't taken out, the mission would probably fail. The truck had lost another tire now. Kor thought about how crappy this damn truck was with tires. He had to drive another half block without tires and orcs shooting at him; plus, he could barely see and think.

The orc outside his door grabbed his left arm from the steering wheel and began punching Kor in the face. Kor aimlessly fired to his left and caught the orc in the chest with a bullet that ripped through it. Kor's left hand was freed and it somehow found its way back to the steering wheel.

The fat orc that was stuck in the window to the right found Kor's right thigh and bit down hard. Kor screamed and his foot slipped off the fuel pedal. The truck was limping ever so slowly and drifting right as Kor's strength couldn't match that of the orc that was holding the steering wheel. Kor turned his gun on the fat orc and pulled the trigger, but nothing happened; the gun had no more bullets.

Kor leaned down to his right and grabbed the face of the fat orc with his teeth. The fat orc let go of Kor's leg and the steering wheel. Kor located the pedal again by feel and again the truck lumbered forward. Kor absorbed blow after blow to his head. The fat orc, now with free hands, pummeled Kor's head. Kor was starting to pass out.

As before, another orc climbed aboard and replaced the orcs that were shot. In the frenzy, this orc was shot by one of his own Wivvaflow orcs. He pulled Kor away from further pummeling as he tried to hang on. More bullets flew.

Kor had an idea. He spotted the release valve on the dashboard. He sluggishly flipped the switch and opened the fuel valves on each side of the truck. Fuel began to drain from the tanks on each side of the truck. Orcs were running around the truck, splashing fuel all over themselves and each other as they ran through it. Their feverish attempts to capture the Invada left them thinking of only that.

The truck approached the bridge. Another orc attempted to climb into the truck right over the orc that was shot. The weight of both orcs pulled Kor from inside. The fat orc had finally gotten through the window and pushed Kor out. Kor's foot was stuck under one of the pedals. The truck rolled to a stop at the edge of the bridge.

Kor had failed. As he hung upside down, he was beaten unmercifully. One of his eyes was ripped from his head. It hung from its socket and swayed back and forth against his forehead. Half of his tongue was cut out. Zealous Wivvaflow orcs fired their weapons into the air. And then…

It ignited. A stray bullet had lit the flow of fuel behind the truck. Fifty orcs burst into flames. Flame followed the trail of fuel for half a block until it met the truck. Then, the truck erupted. Metal fragments and rubber were distributed throughout eastern Wivvaflow as the explosion sent projectiles into orcs everywhere.

Kor, partially obstructed from the blast by the fat orc on one side and two orcs on the other was thrown into the river. His limp body was carried away by the raging torrents. The bridge, which took the brunt of the shock, partially collapsed. It would completely fail some ten minutes later as the superheated fuel compromised its structural supports.

Kor hadn't failed after all.

***

Nutty and his troops were over a mile away. They heard the blast and saw the sky light up in the distance. The flame wasn't characteristic of charges that Gardawg and Kor would have used to detonate the bridge. Nutty was trying to rationalize what was happening. He thought that even if it wasn't the charges and the bridge wasn't destroyed, it was enough of a diversion for him to move ahead with the mission. However, that was a huge gamble. If the bridge still existed, then the Wivvaflow army could very well stop Nutty from succeeding, and maybe worse. A scarcely protected Big Town would be an easy target for invasion.

If the first explosion gave uncertainty, the second was bewildering. A massive explosion rocked Wivvaflow just seconds after the first. The shock wave threw Nuttybomb and his troops to the ground. They were stripped of weapons, helmets, and various gear. Night turned to day and a mushroom cloud rose approximately a half-mile away. The sound of the blast was deafening. Nutty had no idea what had happened.

What he did know was that the explosion surely crippled most of northern and eastern Wivvaflow. Even with the possibility of a Wivvaflow army to deal with, he and his troops may never get another chance. He ordered his troops to gather their stuff and to move out.

As Nutty cleared the embankment, he and a dozen orcs swung around in the direction of the bike factory. His other orcs headed downtown to grab whatever bikes they could. The plan was to work their way south in two groups, hopefully avoiding detection until they were able to obtain one bike per rider, steal as much equipment as possible, and meet at a rally point before heading back to Big Town. At least, that was the plan.

Nutty's group began to move south toward the bike factory. It traveled through alleyways that weren't well-lit, hugging close to the edges of buildings and behind vehicles. This was still difficult because the explosions (and subsequent fires that resulted) were casting shadows against the cover they so desperately sought. Even though the explosions were distracting to locals, it brought many of them outdoors that would have normally been inside. Thankfully, they seemed to be drawn to the fires like moths to a flame. They stood around, staring in an apparently collective daze. Some were seen heading toward the fires, maybe to help those in need, or perhaps to get a better look. Either way, Nutty and his group covered several blocks undetected.

Nutty signaled those behind him to circle around a vehicle near an abandoned building. Across the street he saw an ale bar with a few bikes outside. He left a few of his orcs to wait for his return before they attempted to hot wire them. Again, Nutty began to move his squad.

Nutty's squad was doing well. They were organized and followed him closely. They were quiet as they moved, too. He was surprised to see how easily Thunda moved. Even with his short, seemingly heavy gait, he was rather stealthy. Quicklip hid well, despite his height. The others, with different physical builds and ways they moved, also worked well to conceal their presence. They had a couple more blocks before reaching the bike factory. So far, so good.

The group scurried along a wooden fence line that brought them to a well-lit corner. This corner was one of the Crossroads that connected the main north-south road with an east-west road that led toward Nutty's other group of orcs. He pondered over how he would cross this area without being seen. The lighting, combined with the probability of traffic on a main road, made for a potential recipe for disaster.

Nutty decided to openly walk across the street, visible for all locals to see. He instructed his orcs to wait a minute or two and follow in pairs. He hoped that they wouldn't be recognized as foreigners. On the contrary, they might appear to be walking toward the fires like other locals. They were ordered to conceal their weapons, keep talking to a minimum, and follow his lead. If he was seen, they were told to abandon the mission and head to the rally point.

Nutty's hair rose on the back of his neck. The sense of danger enveloped him as he walked out into the light and made his way across the street. He used his large hands to cup around his face like he was straining to see down the street. There was a dozen or so Wivvaflow orcs close enough to identify him, but they were disinterested as they watched intently down the same street that he pretended to watch. After twenty steps, Nutty made a hard left into a dark alley. He poked his head around the corner where he couldn't be seen to watch his orcs follow what he had done. He was secure now and couldn't be seen by locals on the street. He waited for his orcs.

Thunda and Quicklip began their deception. Quicklip, closest to the Wivvaflow orcs, took advantage of his height. He pulled a hood down over his head and moaned as he pointed in the direction of the fires. Thunda, to his left, was blocked from view of onlookers. Quicklip's hood and out-stretched hand covered his face. His moan did catch the attention of another, though. The Wivvaflow orc asked Quicklip if he knew what was going on down the street. Quicklip responded, "No. Looka bad though." This was satisfactory to the puzzled orc as he never made eye contact with Quicklip and was easily drawn away to the bright lights that flickered blocks away.

Nubbs and another strode right down the middle of the street. Nubbs actually walked over to a pair of locals and offered them a drink. The locals accepted and drank, never even thinking twice, about who was kind enough to share alcohol.

Nutty, Quicklip, and Thunda went from cringing to laughing. Thunda said, "Not even you do dat, Quicklip."

Quicklip retorted, "No cuz you would a drink it all befo' we get der."

Thunda chuckled and simply agreed, "Yup."

Nutty quieted Quicklip and Thunda as Nubbs approached. Once they were safe, they all watched anxiously as the last groups came in twos, keeping to the opposite side of the street and never being as brazen as Nubbs. They all made it safely. Under normal conditions, they all would have been seen for what they really were, but they had surprise, deception, and a bit of arrogance on their side. Luck and opposition stupidity helped a bit as well.

Nutty wasn't able to see the damage that his troops to the west could. Because those to the west could travel farther by way of back roads and quiet industrial areas, they were closer to the location of Gardawg's explosion. They would later report that buildings within three blocks of ground zero were obliterated. Fires burned throughout the area, skipping over some dwellings as cinders were carried hundreds of feet into air. The heat grew more intense as they moved further downtown. Bodies lied burning in the streets; the disgusting smell of singed carnage wafted in the stifling air. Vehicles seemed to randomly ignite, adding more fuel and burning embers to the already volatile mix of expanding destruction.

In the meantime, Nutty hoped his western forces were doing well. He would get a briefing if he and they made it to the rally point. From there, they would continue homeward; that is, if all went well.

Nutty focused on the mission at hand. He continued unnoticed all the way to the bike factory where he and eight orcs broke in. Once inside, he made a call with a two-way radio. Within minutes, two Big Town trucks pulled up and twenty or so more troops loaded machines and parts as quickly as they could.

Once the trucks were loaded, all that were free to mount bikes did so. They each hotwired the bike they sat atop. Some picked which ride they desired, the red ones were claimed first. Others worked quickly just to accomplish the mission and attain a piece of raw power of their own. To those, working on a bike to make it louder, faster, and meaner was more satisfying than getting one that was already complete. Yes, to the tinkerer, these types of bikes were a real find!

Thunda, a bit slower than some of the others was last to get a bike. He looked mildly uncomfortable as he lowered his large frame over a less than well-endowed piece of two-wheeled glory. He immediately complained, "I no like a dis bike. It a too small!"

Quicklip snapped, "Like a you brain, dummy!"

Thunda snarled and retorted, "Bike not too small for me to pick a up and beat a you wit'."

Some of the other orcs in the group laughed.

Quicklip loved the banter. He had to continue. "Dat not da only ting you beat! And a dat small, too!"

Nutty intervened, "Dat's 'nuff. Let's go!"

With the trucks loaded, the building was ordered to be burned. Nutty, the bikes, and the trucks rolled out and headed north of town.

Minutes later, they came upon the few orcs left behind earlier that were waiting to hot wire the bikes outside the bar. They stayed in cover, and when the opportunity arose, they jumped from where they hid.

A few Wivvaflow orcs came outside from the bar to see what was happening. When they saw Invadas trying to hot wire their bikes, they began to run without thought across the street. Nutty and his twenty-one bikers sped by, zigzagging to avoid ending their rides prematurely by colliding with locals. As the orcs from the bar ran across the street to stop the Invadas from stealing their bikes, they were cut down by two heavily loaded Big Town trucks. Their bodies rolled as they were swept along under the trucks, bones breaking and blood spilling. Nutty's orcs that were in hiding laughed hysterically. They were able to hot wire the bikes without difficulty and soon followed Nutty and the others to the edge of town.

The second group to the west had just as much success. They stole another thirty or so bikes. They also reported extreme damage near the center of town with fires all over and met little resistance before meeting up with Nutty, unscathed. The mission was nearly complete. They just needed to head east over the bridge to get home.

Nutty's two-way radio rang out, "Boss, der a problem."

Nutty pushed the button on the radio and replied, "I here. What is wrong?"

The radio operator on the other end shouted, "Our bridge is out! Our bridge is out!"

The raging river had taken out the bridge to Big Town. This presented a real problem for Nutty and his orcs. How would he get them home on vehicles without a way east over the bridge? He concluded that the only way was going back to the edge of Wivvaflow and heading north. This was not what he wanted. Surely, Wivvaflow knew what was happening by now. He was sickened to think that he had to take his orcs back into harm's way. Maybe he could race there and get far enough before a Wivvaflow force could catch him. He had to try.

Nutty and his orcs headed west. He figured if there was one saving grace, it was that Wivvaflow forces couldn't use the bridge to attack his hometown. Then again, what difference did it make if he and his troops didn't survive to defend it later? He didn't count on this as a contingency. He swore to be more diligent in his planning. He needed to get home.

Five
Things Heat Up

Muga, Pretty, and Uhra were cooking lots of food. They hurried to finish before the troops came home. Muga and Uhra accidentally bumped into each other in the builder school kitchen as they worked.

Muga joked with Uhra, "Honey, you ass a betta nevva get dis big or we both not fit."

Uhra laughed. She liked Muga and respected that she was Nuttybomb's mother. She also knew she needed to stay on Muga's good side if she was ever to have a relationship with Nutty, so she replied, "My ass a bigga dan a trukk!" She also knew that she wasn't particularly big, but figured she would be better accepted if she poked fun at herself. She hoped it worked.

Muga smiled. She wasn't exactly born yesterday. While she pulled the mudbread from the oven, she sought an honest answer from Uhra, "So, you lika a Nutty?"

Uhra was careful to respond without sharing too much information. "Guess so." She half smiled and turned away so Muga might not read her. She found a rag and wiped the counter to appear busy.

"Guess so? They ain't much a guessin'. You do or don't."

Uhra was feeling cornered. She thought if she was a mother, she would want to know, too. But what difference did it make? Again, she masked her true feelings with, "I like all you kids, Muga."

Muga was amused. "Gurl, nobody like all a my kids! I don't even like all a my kids!"

Uhra and Pretty both chuckled. Pretty looked at Uhra and boldly stated, "You lika him."

Uhra simply responded, "Yeah. We beed friends fo' long a time now."

Muga blurted out under her breath, "Yeah, I beed friends wit' Biggabomb for lika million years anda I can't a stomachs the stinky bastid!"

The two younger girls chuckled again. Muga on the other hand missed her Biggabomb. She worried that he might come home disabled; maybe he would never come home at all. She pushed the thought from her mind and focused on Uhra.

Muga said, "Anyway, Nutty is a big boy now. He gots all a us in a his hands." Again, she tried to evoke emotion or some sort of response from Uhra that would tell all.

Pretty stopped working and stared at Uhra, matching Muga's gaze.

Uhra looked from Muga to Pretty and realized that they were fishing for her to give some sort of incriminating information. She hoped to put things to rest once and for all with, "Oh, yeah. I guess he is in charge a evvyting now. We just have a do what he says."

There, it was done. She took control from Muga and put it on Nutty. It didn't matter how she felt about him. It didn't matter that she couldn't wait to see him again; his eyes, his dopey smile, and his awkward posture. She smiled internally when she thought about how big he was getting; he was broad and muscular. She was really attracted to him. Plus, he was the most important orc in town. She was so proud of him. She blurted out, "I'm so proud a him!" Her excitement was obvious, her timing couldn't be worse. She thought that she just went from putting things to rest, to opening a can of worms. She put her foot in her mouth instead of fixing things.

Muga just smiled in her motherly way. She had a bit of a smirk, like the cat that swallowed the canary. She only made a sound that dragged out for what seemed like a lifetime in a low assured way, "Mm-hmm."

Pretty laughed.

Uhra's cheeks began to fluster. She wasn't sure why she cared that either of these two needed to know how much she cared for Nutty. It really didn't matter, especially if Nutty could do whatever he wanted. Muga was his mother, but what difference did it make? "Yeah," she thought, "what difference it make?"

Uhra stared off as she began to think. She began to become oblivious to any concerns about Muga and Pretty. She didn't notice that the two were still waiting, or at least, hoping for a response that might give them a clue as to her intentions. To this point, Uhra had been coy. She was just vague enough without lying to leave doubt as to what she was thinking one way or the other. Truthfully, these feelings were new to her. Did she love Nutty like a wife loves a husband? She certainly didn't want anything to happen to him. Her thoughts and feelings went deeper and deeper. She thought…

How often had nerves or anxiety kept those from accomplishing goals where they would otherwise excel easily? How many geniuses never put themselves on the line for fear of ridicule? How many diseases that may have been cured, weren't? How many talents have gone unnoticed, trips not taken, businesses not opened, or homes not purchased? How many relationships that were meant to be lifelong, never even came to fruition because of ego or pride?

Then, she asked herself these questions: How many statistics to validate the point really mattered, other than specifying odds of probability to reduce such fears, anxieties, or uncertainties? Did they really matter? Who wanted to be part of a statistic that stated failure anyway?

Uhra smiled and made eye contact with Muga. She decided to try something; a different approach was needed. If it worked, she was off the hook, but if it didn't, well, she would cross that bridge when it came.

She began, "Muga, you a know dat Nutty be a my bestest friend evvas. Right?"

Muga turned her head a bit like a carnidawg trying to make sense of what it was hearing. "Yeah?"

"Well, I beed tinkin'. At first, I no figure why you ask if I lika Nutty. We beed friends. But you keep a askin'. Why a you keep askin' bout Nutty? Do he lika me or sumptin'?"

Then Uhra shut up and waited. This might have put Muga back on her heels. Did Muga buy that Uhra thought that they were just friends? Uhra didn't feel that way of course, but Muga didn't know that for sure. Plus, Uhra insinuated it without actually saying so. It's not like she lied. Also, Uhra hoped to find out if Nutty ever told Muga that he liked her.

Muga thought for a minute. She tapped her long, cream colored fingernails on the counter in an irritating rhythm. Then, when she was satisfied with what to say, she responded, "Nope. I don't tink Nutty evva say he like you to a me."

Uhra was visibly disappointed. "Oh?"

Did Nutty not like her; not like her in an attraction kind of way? Was he never going to really notice her, because he was too important now? Did he just like her like a friend? Friends didn't always last; mostly, they would drift apart over time. Orcs weren't a race that committed easily. Or, she thought, maybe Nutty just didn't tell Muga. Right? Anything was possible.

"Nope. But, I asked you if you lika a him? No udder reason."

Uhra wasn't committing to Muga either. She kept her words short and vague. "Oh, ok. Just a makin' sure."

Just then, the three were startled by screams that came from outside.

***

Things in Big Town were clicking. Nuttybomb had thought out everything he possibly could to ensure that Big Town had the best opportunity to defend itself, and just possibly, bring a fight to the Invadas. He did doubt his ability to make one correct decision after another when it came to war though. He was simply untested.

For instance, he thought the risk of making raids on Wivvaflow was clearly necessary. Rumors about Wivvaflow attacking Big Town were confirmed as fact. But attacking a stronger opponent was more than dangerous; the results could be disastrous. One reason for this thought, and the most important, was that he had no doubt that his own small number of older kids was no match for Wivvaflow's vicious adult males in a head-to-head fight. In fact, Wivvaflow frequently attacked its smaller neighbors, taking what it wanted and enslaving its opponents' males; it was opportunistic that way.

Normally, it outnumbered Big Town two to one in troops and equipment. But it never attacked Big Town as it didn't have an air force to match Big Town's. Additionally, some of the greatest chiefs had come from Big Town. The inherent boasting and embellishing traits of orcs further added to Big Town's mystique. Big Town's chiefs became unbeatable that way. They were bigger than life, almost gods. On the other side of the river, Big Town orcs perceived Fokra, the Wivvaflow leader as a force to be reckoned with. His cruelty was legendary, and his victories were nothing short of remarkable. His army was invincible.

But things were different now. Wivvaflow saw Big Town as weak and an enormous potential prize for the taking. Big Town was led by a kid running other kids. There were no chiefs; there were no fighter planes; there was no army. There was only the town's name which other cities respected because of its association with great chiefs.

So, Nutty planned things out the best he could. His recent speech in the school was the basic plan that was being followed. He adjusted individual tasks based on abilities and performances. He, himself, was being trained by Booma and one of the fight school instructors. He labored day in and day out as he helped other orcs build and place weaponry, manufacture vehicles, and mine precious metal ores. He knew that there was no better way to evaluate production and find ways to expedite tasks efficiently without knowing every facet of the jobs being performed.

So, every orc had a variety of tasks to help in the cause. The population was still nervous about the coming war however. Even still, the orcs hustled as they prepared, drinking ale and hard stock to sustain them over these long, hot, steamy days. The occasional loss of a finger or two was insignificant in the whole scheme of things. They all pushed on, morale high as faith in their leader's might and cunning gave them strength as well.

Booma was only a grunt and not a very good one at that. He was loyal to Nutty and knew what was at stake though. He pushed his cadets harder than ever. He learned from instructors at night and taught what he learned during the day. He was tired and sore, but he endured.

Females did work in the kitchens, the mines, and makeshift medical areas. While Muga, Pretty, and Uhra made food, the younger ones such as Runzda and Kago made uniforms. They sewed day in and day out. They made leather pouches, boots, and holsters. They made blue jackets and trousers. Blue was chosen because the most available dyes came from a local flower known as the Bulbus. Also, Nutty thought that a uniform look would help unify the troops. He needed every advantage he could think of to prevail under these less than perfect circumstances.

The airport, which had no aircraft, was basically shut down. Minor protection was placed there to keep the runway open for cargo and Runnas. There simply wasn't enough of a need to keep orcs there when they were required to be in other places for other jobs. Actually, very few new fighter planes were being produced because all of the capable adult males that could be mustered were fighting on the Eastern Continent.

***

The door flung open. Three older kids rushed into the room in a panic. They were ranting over each other, canceling out the others' words. To Muga, it sounded like her kids at home fighting over boar cakes. The thought of that would normally warm her innards. She longed for normalcy again and the thought of little ones running around as her sloppy ass husband lounged in his chair and drank was missed. But this was different; something was obviously wrong.

She pointed to the tallest boy in the center of the group and asked, "You, what a happen?"

The boy was winded. He must have run the seven miles with the other two from where he came. He was dirty from head to toe. He wore ripped clothing and he was full of soot. He spoke in spurts as he tried to calm himself and catch his breath. "Der beed a accident in da mines. A esplosion wit' cave-ins."

Muga gasped. She looked with shock at the two girls she had been cooking with the last few hours. Pretty's eyes were wide open. She didn't know what to say. Uhra had her right hand over her mouth in stunned disbelief. They all knew how terrible a mining accident could be. They all knew there were probably casualties. The question was, "How many?"

Muga turned back to the boy that just spoke and questioned, "Do dems need a help ova der?"

The boy nodded his head, "Yes".

101

The other two boys nodded in agreement. The shortest boy to the right kept his mouth open. He had some drool hanging from his lip that dangled and swayed back and forth as his head motioned. It cleaned his lower lip of soot as it rubbed and stuck occasionally.

The third boy was a little bloody. There wasn't anything in particular that stood out about him. He just stood there, mimicking the first boy's nods to affirm his responses.

Muga went on to ask, "How bad is it, boy? Any orcs get hurt or die?"

The boy nodded his head. He responded, "Umm, seven deads and a twelve hurt so far."

Muga couldn't believe that she never heard an explosion or felt shaking. It was hard to do with all the rattling and banging that the town's orcs were doing while building and blowing things up, she thought. Regardless, she went with the three boys and her two cooking girls to see what they could do to help.

While the girls raced to put the massive quantities of food away in bowls and even the pots that they were cooked in, the boys moved boxes, swept, and moved tables. In short time, they were finished.

They all rushed outside into the muggy night air. The smells of smoke and ash filled their nostrils. The night sky was orange to the west, a sign of multiple fires burning in the distance. For a moment, each of them tried to link the fires in Wivvaflow to the mine collapse, but even their orc brains couldn't make an inaccurate correlation between the two.

Muga was sickened; possibly by the thought of not knowing how many orcs were lost in the mining explosion; or more likely, because her inane sense of loss for her baby was taking hold. She just didn't feel right.

To the south, the sky was dark. Stars weren't visible, probably due to being blocked from dust and soot thrown into the sky by the mine collapse. The rain, which was heavier earlier in the evening, had now dissipated. Cloud cover wasn't noticeable, yet the sky was littered with stars in some areas, and devoid in others. The patchwork of heavenly art dabbed in various colors was eerily haunting. Even orcs gave pause when gazing upon such rare scenery, especially when it wasn't something they were used to seeing as part of their daily routines. Maybe they didn't recognize beauty, but they recognized change. The sky was undeniably angry tonight.

Scattered lights throughout the community sparsely illuminated the road they needed to take south to the mine. The truck that they climbed into had no lights of its own. Muga struggled to see as she drove the other five toward the mining disaster.

Pretty, who was usually quiet, stated, "I hopes da mine isn't real bad."

Muga agreed. "Me too, Pretty." A sense of dread clawed at her.

Uhra added, "Yeah. And a I hopes dat Nutty and his boys is ok, too."

***

Nutty and his troops made their way west, back toward town. There was no chance of being quiet this time. Their engines were loud, their exhaust pipes belched fire. The vulnerable factory district, which was accessed easily because of the explosions, was now bustling with activity. Fires were being extinguished. Locals were putting together posses to hunt down and destroy the Big Town kids that caused so much destruction. Word was beginning to spread.

Nutty wondered if they could go off road to avoid the busy section of town. He knew he could take his boys north and back across the river at Gravestone, a neighboring town. But would these bikes get through the hilly, wooded terrain? That was questionable indeed. He decided to go into town and get out of the area as quickly as possible. Speeding through would probably give him and his boys the best chance for survival. Hanging around and getting bogged down in the woods would just allow Wivvaflow more time to organize parties to hunt them down. So, off to Wivvaflow they went.

They passed a small number of rickety shacks. Most were like those in Big Town, made of wood, tin, or block. They weren't well-lit, if at all, and included familiar fences and stripped vehicles. Had it not been for the knowledge of the undertaking at hand, Nutty envisioned how easily he could have mistaken this stretch of road for his own hometown. But he knew all too well where he was and what might happen in this hostile environment.

After several minutes, the band of inexperienced kids arrived at Wivvaflow's eastern fringes. The heat of fires were becoming more noticeable the closer they got. Nutty began to sweat. He was feeling the unrelenting burn of distant, superheated flames on his cheeks and exposed arms. His eyes were becoming irritated, too; his body coped by forcing tear drops to wash away the dry heat; salty water from his ducts ran down his face. His other riders were experiencing the same mild discomfort. Nutty wondered how unbearably hot it must have been a mile or two South, at ground zero.

Nutty also wondered which was hotter, the Wivvaflow fires or the orcs' tempers.

He was about to find out.

***

Muga and the other five orcs arrived at the mine's entrance. It was very dark here due to the choking volume of dust, soot, and smoke that filled the air. Quite quickly, all that approached found their mouths, noses, and lungs filled with the concrete mixture of floating debris. They all covered their mouths and noses with any materials they could find. The sleeve of the shirt was the most common. Others were assorted rags or even socks.

They made their way to a group of miners that were at work trying to rescue orcs that were trapped or injured. Other females were already on the scene to administer first aid. A triage unit was being assembled just outside, to the west of the mine's main entrance. Just outside of the tents that were being pitched, injured orcs lay on cots and some dead were lying on the ground, covered with blankets.

The younger orcs that bore witness to this seemed to be more shaken than the adult females and the elderly males that weren't fit for battle. They were less accustomed to seeing death firsthand. The older orcs knew how common death really was. They had even built up a tolerance of sorts to the inevitable. Hell, many experienced half their families dying before adulthood. Many had rocked their own children to sleep for the last time, their little bodies finally succumbing to the fever. Even still, the thought of others perishing senselessly affected them as well.

What struck Muga the most was the fact that orcs were grumbling about being led by kids...stupid kids that had no idea what they were doing. Why were females and kids working the mines? Why were they attacking a neighboring town that they had been peaceful with for a hundred years or more? How could this be allowed to happen?

While mothers sobbed and old orcs screamed, the outcry for justice was exclaimed. When the tally of seven dead and twelve seriously injured was noted, the head of Nuttybomb was sequestered.

Six
The Getaway

Even over the sounds of engines roaring, the clamor of irate townspeople was palpable and the picture that came into view was foreboding.

Wivvaflow orcs had come to the edge of town, seeking the heads of the Invadas. More than a dozen well-trained adult males, armed with military-issued weapons, were organized alongside the road. Along with their citizen counterparts, they brandished torches and close combat weapons. Sixty or more angry orcs stood between Nutty and his kids from trying to get away. Among them was Captain Morbid.

Morbid was known for his unbridled desire to inflict as much pain against his opponents as possible. Rumors of his torturous techniques weren't unfounded either and the embellishment of such atrocities wasn't that far over the top. He was said to have enjoyed each kill more than the last as he perfected the art of causing suffering. In this case, even orcs that boasted about what they saw, didn't give the wrong impression. There was no misnomer when it came to this sadistic agony inducing psychopath.

Nutty's group approached furiously fast. He sent his two trucks ahead first, each with multiple guns and crew to fire into the crowd. They sped down the middle of the street, taking out several Wivvaflow orcs that were too slow or stupid to get out of the way. One of the crewmen in the lead truck received a bullet himself, a superficial wound to his shoulder. He shouted obscenities and pumped his fist as his truck bounced over a couple victims. Otherwise, the two trucks made it virtually unscathed as they made clear of the area.

Just behind and to each side of the trucks, Nutty and his kids opened fire from their guns as they approached the crowd. Their bikes lacked the armored cover the trucks ahead of them benefited from though. Some of them took return bullets that knocked them from their mounts. Several bikes, now without riders, careened into the crowd. The crowd began to thin as some sought cover. Others disbursed, wanting no part in the butchery that was beginning to occur. A few froze, becoming statistics as stray bikes severed their heads from their bodies.

Later, it was stated that some of these heads were still screaming at the Invadas as they approached. Several bodies, without realizing their monumental losses, continued to swing their weapons unwittingly for several seconds. Inexorably, they fell to the ground, never inflicting any damage.

Events were unfolding quicker than Nutty could wrap his head around. He was enveloped by enemies. His troops were coming to a halt as bikes cluttered the street. They could no longer fire their weapons safely from the distance they hoped they could. No, now they would be forced to engage the enemy in close quarters.

Others followed Nutty's lead as he flew from his moving bike into the crowd. He was afraid, not a trait that he thought other leaders shared. He would never let his troops know how he felt though. He thought briefly about Uhra and Muga. Beyond that, there was no time for indecisiveness. He acted without much thought of himself and hoped that those behind him would follow his actions.

His body dismounted awkwardly, traveling much faster than he had anticipated. His bike lurched to the right and eliminated a few orcs ahead of his own orcs trailing in that direction. He somehow found one of his knives while in flight and did his best to assail any target that he met. The knife found its way into the face of one orc while the force of his body severed the spine of another. Partially dazed and somewhat confused, he jumped to his feet as soon as he could.

He turned around to gauge his troops. Bikes were still coming in hot, riders flew into the enemy. Wivvaflow forces were dropping like flies. The noise of battle was thunderous; bullets were still flying. Screams were audible this close. Nutty's face was spattered with blood from his comrades and his enemies. The mayhem that was evolving was mind boggling and Nutty was directly in the fray.

Nutty made his way back to his troops. He slashed and punched, dropping another orc as he proceeded. One after another enemy stepped in front of him, swinging knives, swords, hammers, clubs, and virtually everything that might harm him. He continued fighting for his life, his troops, and his loved ones. He felled each enemy within reach, never thinking twice about the outcome, just ensuring survival.

Within a minute or less, he made it to a group of his orcs. They were struggling against the remainder of well-trained enemy troops. But numbers were on their side. They fell back slightly, defending against the might of adult males. In most cases they only won by rushing the enemy in numbers. Nutty saw this and thought about ants attacking a wasp. The wasp might kill a few ants, but in the end, it would be overwhelmed.

Somehow, Nutty was able to help in several of these outcomes. Invariably, he would step forward, pushing his own orcs out of the way until he landed a blow that would drop his foe. The combined effort of his strength, speed, and agility, as well as the numbers of his troops, reduced the remaining enemies to a pittance.

As Nutty stepped forward to engage his newest enemy, he saw that his troops weren't faring well against this one.

This enemy was cunning. He lulled Nutty's troops onto his knives, one by one. He would lean making them think that he was going to attack from one side, only to strike his weapon from the other hand. He was fast and equally strong and made short work of these kids without much effort.

This area of battle was littered with Nutty's bloody orcs, lying on the ground, writhing in pain. Those still standing stepped back, behind their leader. His pushing orcs to the side was taken by his own as "get back". They watched and waited for his next move. Nutty quickly surveyed the area around him as he stepped cautiously toward this menacing foe. He saw Quicklip, Thunda, and Nubbs engaging the last few Wivvaflow orcs. They were doing well, so his attention immediately went back to the formidable enemy before him.

The enemy spoke slowly, raising the tone of his words at the end of each sentence, but never in volume. His easy flow of words and nonchalant posture gave him an air of confidence. Nutty's orcs, licking their wounds, affirmed why.

"I am a Captain Morbid. You must be a Nuttybomb." The orc smiled as he licked his lips.

Nutty was puzzled. How did this guy know who he was? He had only overseen Big Town for how long? Maybe a few weeks? Nutty looked bewildered.

Morbid saw the youth's reaction and began to toy with him, "Don't be confused, boy. Tings are as they are meant to be. You and you a friends will die here. It's ok, really. I'ma da one to defend Wivvaflow now. Dis is da way it be now."

Nutty didn't know what to make of this newest turn of events. He sought in the back of his mind what to say, but nothing came.

"You are Nuttybomb?" Morbid asked.

"I am." That much he was sure of.

"Good," said the maniacal orc before him. He slid forward between bike parts and orc limbs. His swagger was overtly offensive and demoralizing. His decorated armor and long flowing cape showed his stature. He addressed his adversary in the same unrushed, polite way he began, "Well, den. Let's get on wit' it."

Morbid looked from side to side. Nutty's attention was drawn a bit to the hundred or so Wivvaflow orcs that were gathering around the battle. They didn't appear to be an immediate threat, but they were still a potentially lethal obstacle to get past. That is, if Nutty survived the confrontation with Morbid.

In an instant, Morbid swung down on his preoccupied opponent. Nutty jumped in horror; he was caught unaware!

Nutty blocked the first attack. The knife in his left hand caught the overhand attack cleanly. Soon, his right hand would do the same. He ducked and turned. His foe was too fast, too strong. The attacks came furiously. Nutty couldn't mount an attack; he was completely defensive. It was the best he could do to just avoid being ripped apart. Within a minute or two, he had lost the knife in his left hand. His right hand came around, attempting to block a volley of attacks from all directions, but that too was futile as he lost that defensive capability as well.

He was astounded by the speed and ferocity of this larger foe. He never would have guessed that he would see such a combination of power that came from such bulk in blazing rapidity.

Nutty stepped forward, a risky proposition at best. He ducked under a combination of slashes and kicked hard to the knee of this immensely skilled and mighty warrior.

The warrior laughed. "Boy, you have to do better dan dat!"

Nutty slumped to the ground in defeat; he couldn't defeat this guy; he was simply outmatched.

The warrior said to Nutty, "Surely, you won't just a sit here and die."

Nutty was hunched, his laurels resting on the back of his legs for support. He was quiet.

"Ok, den." The warrior drove his right knife toward Nutty's throat.

But Nutty was cunning and he was fast. He had legitimately lured the warrior into his own trap. He grabbed the wrist of his foe with both hands and jumped up as hard and as quick as he could. His knee struck a hard blow against the warrior's elbow, releasing the grip of his weapon. Nutty caught it in midair and sliced across his enemies injured arm.

***

The warrior stepped back. "Good, Nutty! That was a very good move." Biggabomb was sure to compliment his kids when they did well. That is, unless he was drunk or tired. In this case, he saw potential in Nutty. Nutty wasn't his oldest son, nor was he the best fighter. In fact, he routinely got his ass kicked at school.

Nutty responded, "Do you have to fight so hard? I'ma sick a bein' hurted!"

Biggabomb made sure that Nutty fully understood what was going on. "You need to learn to fight, Nutty. Der will be da enemies dat are stronger or faster. Dis prepares you for dose enemies."

"But, I'ma tireds."

"Too bads! We do it again!"

This routine went on for several years. Then, for some reason, it stopped. Maybe Biggabomb was disinterested in teaching Nutty. Maybe Nutty wasn't worth the effort. It wasn't like fighting with knives would help Nutty every day in builder school anyway. Bringing knives to school wasn't permitted. Plus, Nutty wouldn't stab Gardawg or Booma. They were the ones that beat up Nutty with frequent regularity.

Nutty forgot about the training he received. For one thing, he wasn't violent by nature. He liked to think about things. He could be lost in thought, daydreaming for hours at a time. And he loved to hang out with his best friend, Uhra. These things, along with not knowing the importance of Biggabomb to the

113

survival of his race, obscured the sparring behind more important things to him.

Nutty was glad when the long days of training finally ended. At the time, it seemed senseless. It wouldn't be until years later that he would draw upon the strength of his training in a variety of ways. It would be then that he would also think about his father. Today was the first.

***

For the love of the gods, Nutty thought. He could fight; he just never wanted to. But now, he was entangled in a death grip with one of the most famous and infamous warriors on the continent. They were grappling for just the slightest advantage, so they might end each other's lives. So far, neither orc had a clear advantage, although Morbid had scored more secondary blows.

Nutty was a bit bloody. He had been cut across his face, both arms and his chest. Each wound wasn't that bad, but collectively, the blood loss was adding up. Nutty stepped back as another swing from Morbid resulted in a cut to his wrist.

Morbid stepped back as well. He was very gratified in the job he was doing. He was cutting Nutty to pieces, one slice at a time. Outwardly, he only sported the mark of a slight bruise and cut above one eye. Nutty's attacks resulted in some punches and kicks, not the sort of blood splattering blows that Morbid had landed.

Morbid suggested to his less experienced foe, "Maybe you should just a slice youself, boy. Dis way, you won't be so tired and a you can die however you a want to. Ha ha!"

114

Nutty wasn't laughing. He was becoming tired. But what could he do? Every time he saw an attack coming, he tried to parry it, only to get caught bloody from a different angle. At least his nerves were a bit calmer. He wasn't shaking like several minutes earlier.

He knew he needed to be on the offensive. Things couldn't continue to go this way, that was for certain. He took this moment to rethink the fight to this point. He thought about each of his wounds and how he received them. They came from different angles, not those assumed, based on Morbid's motions.

A light went on in Nutty's head. He chuckled, partially at Morbid's words, but mostly because he could see what was happening. He figured it all out!

"Morbid, dat a really funny. Howevva, I will be takin' my troops home a tonight. Oh...tanks fo' da bikes, too. Anda...I will pleasure in seein' you die."

Morbid's outward appearance changed. "No, boy. Da bikes a stay here. Nobody goin' home tonight! And da only one a dyin' is you!"

"Well, 'bout dat...I don't a wanna die, so too bad! Anda I'ma take you cape too cuz I likes it." Nutty laughed hardily.

On cue, Nubbs let out a huge rumbling noise from his hind quarters. Nutty's troops burst into laughter. They didn't know how Nutty was going to beat Morbid, but just his confidence made them loose. They were enjoying the show. What was better than a good fight and some witty banter? It was perfect.

"You take a dis too lightly, boy!" Morbid's tone wasn't so even keeled as earlier. He was getting annoyed. "Busides, you showed nuttin' so far. Anda you just a pee boy, I hear!"

Nutty wasn't going to let name calling upset him. That was in the past. He would remain clear-headed from this point forward until Morbid's demise. He would throw some insults back in turn, trying to incite anger in his enemy and take him out of his game.

Nutty smiled as he said, "Oh? I'ma pee on you dead body after I kill a you."

Morbid was done talking. He lunged forward, duplicating his movements of deception. But Nutty saw them coming. After ducking a few slashes, he timed one and countered. This time his knife cut across Morbid's left hand. Two of Morbid's fingers dangled. He stepped back in disbelief.

Nutty taunted, "You won't need dose fingers where I sendin' you." Then, he stepped back and smiled, further irritating Morbid.

Morbid growled in pain, "Lucky shot, boy!" With that he came at Nutty again, this time a bit quicker and more determined. Nutty found it harder to dodge the hasty moves of Morbid. But Morbid was a little sloppier, and once again Nutty countered well.

Morbid jumped back as his face and nose took the brunt of Nutty's well-timed return. Blood squirted from his nose, rushing down the deep cut in his cheek.

Nutty exclaimed, "Ouch. Looka like dat one hurt."

Nutty's boys laughed. Nubbs made some strange face with one eye higher than the other and he stuck his tongue out. His elastic skin and adept facial control was used to mimic Morbid.

Morbid was angry. His words weren't easily contrived and willed to a perfect monotone. Indeed, he was well beyond flustered. He was not going to die at the hands of this child. That was absolutely impossible. He stated what he thought was obvious, "Dat wuz you last one, boy." He continued much louder as he barked, "Now, I finish you!"

Morbid lashed out as hard as he could. To almost any other orc on almost any other night, he might have easily cut through with little effort. But Nutty's training, his strength from recent work, and his ability to effect situations through thought, made him the exception.

Again, Nutty struggled to time Morbid's strikes so that he could counter. But Morbid caught Nutty's hand with a blade and Nutty dropped one of his knives. Nutty contemplated what happened and knew to counter differently the next time. But, he was down a weapon to an enraged and very capable enemy.

"What wuz you sayin', boy?"

Nutty gripped his hand in a tightly held fist in an attempt to somehow curb the pain. He blatantly smiled and asked, "Which part? Oh, 'I'ma pee on you dead body after I kill a you'?"

Morbid was mad. He wanted this little bastard dead. He didn't want to play any longer. This time as he screamed and lunged at Nutty, he was shocked. Searing pain and impact was felt in his throat. He stepped back to find Nutty's knife buried beneath his jaw. He tried to step back, but stumbled up against a vehicle in the street. Blood gushed down his body and shot up onto his face.

Nutty had followed every one of Morbid's steps to the vehicle. He never relinquished his right to finish the kill by removing his weapon from Morbid's throat. Upon Morbid slamming back against the door, Nutty used both of his hands to push his blade through to the other side of Morbid's neck.

Nutty couldn't help but fire Morbid's words back at him in defiance. He asked sarcastically, "What wuz you sayin', boy?"

Morbid tried to speak, but as the cervical spine separated below his head, agony ripped his body before it went numb. Nutty pulled his knife from Morbid's dying body before it hit the ground.

Nutty's troops erupted in applause. Not one wasn't impressed with the fight they just saw. Several back slaps and handshakes ensued. Then, they cleared the road of debris and loaded their injured and dead into the trucks that came back.

The Wivvaflow orcs that were standing nearby vanished beyond sight. They had obviously seen more than they wanted to.

Their great captain was cut down by the Invadas' leader, their town was still burning, and their army was unable to muster any more defense. The road was clear all the way to Gravestone.

***

Nutty had lost some troops, maybe a dozen or so. He was sad about that fact. He wished he didn't, but he also knew that he did what he had to; the losses weren't in vain. Big Town would have a fighting chance against any future attacks from Wivvaflow. He hoped they would think twice after what they had experienced at his hands.

The thirty-minute ride north to Gravestone had given him and his injured troops some time to bandage wounds. Most seemed to be fine; their injuries weren't so severe that they wouldn't heal over time. In fact, most of their bleeding had stopped. The broken bones and internal bleeding would take longer to mend, however. Nutty thought about rotating his troops to offer some much-needed recoup time when he and his boys got home.

Within a short distance to Gravestone, Nutty disembarked from the lead truck and mounted his bike. He decided to approach the gates alone, so as not to seem imposing. He rode up slowly until he was warned to halt.

"Who is dat rider?" came from a voice behind castle walls.

"I am Nuttybomb from Big Town?"

"Who dat?" the voice quizzed.

"I am Nuttybomb, Big Town Army Controla."

"The voice from a tower adjacent to the gates continued, "What you want here?"

Nutty explained, "I just tryin' to get back home. Our bridge is washed out connected to a Wivvaflow."

Nutty waited for a response. He looked at the stone towers on each corner of the fort that he sat outside of. The gates between two of the towers at the road were impressive; constructed of iron latticework intertwined for strength; obviously to keep out Invadas. Nutty couldn't see much more of the fortress or the city from his current vantage point.

He became a little nervous after waiting a couple of minutes. He tried contacting the quiet voice from beyond, "Hello?"

This time a different voice was heard. "Nuttybomb, why you bring army to my city?"

Nutty needed to be careful in what he said. Any wrong word or interpretation could spell disaster. "We just a tryin' to get home. Our bridge connected to Wivvaflow is washed out."

"Why you come from Wivvaflow wit' der army?"

Nutty needed there to be no confusion. "Dis is part of my army. We fight against a Wivvaflow, but we can't get home now. I ask you to let us pass." Nutty hoped that Gravestone's past problems with Wivvaflow would seal the deal.

The voice questioned, "Did dems attacks you?"

Nutty wasn't sure how to respond to this. He didn't want to seem like the aggressor, but he was. He wasn't going to lie. His town's ties with Gravestone were better than those with Wivvaflow's. He laid it out as clearly as he could. Of course, he colored it up a bit. But first, he wanted to know who he was talking with. "Who dis I talkin' wit'?"

"Dis is King Basha."

"King Basha, our two great a towns have beed friends fo' a long a time. I sure dat you, as a great leader, can see my problem. I have troops dat attacked Wivvaflow when we heard they wuz gonna attack us. We just kids fightin' dems, too. Some are hurt. We just tryin' to go home. But dis is da only a way. Will you grant us passage?"

After hesitating to even respond, Basha explained his own plight, "We want a no mo' trouble wit' Wivvaflow. Dems might come fo' you and follow you here."

Nutty couldn't guarantee anything different. "Maybe, but we hurt dems bad. I tink it will be some time before dem can attacks." Nutty paused as he thought, then continued, "I gives you some bikes fo' you trouble."

Basha thought, then exclaimed, "I, King Basha of Gravestone, grant you, Nuttybomb and you army, passage. You only a go down south road. No troubles. You leave three bikes. Any troubles and we attacks you." His voice was low and booming.

Nutty didn't even need to think about it. He made the appearance that he *did* need to think about it, though, so he paused before replying, "Hmm. Dat sounds fair, King Basha. No troubles from us. We don't want a fight wit' Gravestone. We just wanna get home."

The rest was easy. Three bikes were exchanged for passage beyond Gravestone's gates. Nutty's troops stayed along the southern road all the way back to Big Town.

Nutty learned about the mining accident that happened earlier in the day. He also learned that there was unrest over young orcs that had died in the accident under his command. As he made his way into the builder school, an angry crowd was gathering.

One mission was complete. What were the costs so far? Where were two of his orcs? He rushed in to get whatever information he could in the event he had to defend the town, or possibly, address the crowd.

Seven
Things Get Bad

The battle had been raging for weeks on the Eastern Continent. The Invadas, now known as the Crimson Brigade, were pushing east. Biggabomb had thrown everything he had at them, but they just kept coming. Biggabomb looked over the reports so he could learn everything he could against this more advanced Invada. He learned quite a bit, although not much of it was helpful.

The Crimson Brigade was from several other worlds in the same star system. Their home world was called Tempest. Whereas Hotta, Biggabomb and Nuttybomb's home world, was the second planet from their star, Tempest was the fifth planet in the system. It was considerably colder than Hotta with much more water and vegetation. There were more types of life forms there than on Hotta and they weren't as harsh. For instance, there were no giant plants that would trap a boar and emit acid to break down the boar's body into digestive juices. In fact, there were no carnivorous plants at all. But on Hotta, more than one thousand such types of plants existed. Life was just harder on Hotta.

Tempest was where Jarnar the Great first won control of his local town, and then region. Within four years he dominated the planet. His lust for power and love for technology led to better aircraft and spaceships. This gave him hopes of conquering neighboring worlds as well, which he soon did.

He first invaded Da White Rock, one of four moons that rotate around Orcra, the fourth planet in the system. Although Orcra couldn't sustain orcs, Da White Rock that orbited it could. Its huge volcanic activity and tectonic plates gave the moon warmth. Its gases released from volcanic activity over the millennia had provided it with a stable, yet thin atmosphere.

Da White Rock orcs, that were indigenous, grew to be somewhat smaller than orcs on the planets. Some have speculated that this may have been due to the low levels of oxygen, or possibly, the type of limited diet. For whatever reason, they were outmatched by the bigger, stronger, and technologically advanced orcs from Tempest. They had become the backbone of the Crimson Blade and were usually first into battle.

After conquering Da White Rock, Jarnar set his sights on Marshil, the third planet in the star system. From the first day, Marshil gave Jarnar problems. The distance from Tempest to Marshil was immense. This caused issues with resupplying troops and a whole array of logistical nightmares. In the end, Marshil succumbed to the Crimson Brigade. But not in Jarnar's time. Jarnar died two years before Marshil fell. Jarnar's son, Orcilla, was the Warchief who led The Crimson Brigade to its final victory.

It had been four years since the warm, wet planet of Marshil was conquered. Orcilla had reorganized and was now pushing to take Hotta. Marshil had become the launching point because of its relatively close position to Hotta. But that distance changed as the planets rotated around their star. The time that the planets were closest was every seven months. This invasion on Hotta had marked one of those times.

Biggabomb read more and wrote down some notes. The enemy's technology wasn't that much superior to his own. Sure, they could travel between the planets, but their weapons were similar. Their guns were better, but not by much; orcs shot like crap anyway. They were always better with close combat weapons. So, a knife was a knife, was a knife. One advantage that the Crimson Brigade had was its aircraft. Its planes were sleek and fast. They outmatched his Stug Fightas. So, if Biggabomb could take out the Invadas' aircraft, maybe he had a fighting chance.

The way to beat them was to do it quickly. If the war dragged on for seven months, the Crimson Brigade would resupply. Hotta had finite troops, certainly nowhere near what Orcilla could throw at Biggabomb.

Then, Biggabomb thought about Orcilla. What did he learn about this chief of three worlds? Not much. As far as Biggabomb knew, Orcilla hadn't even landed on Hotta. Unlike Biggabomb, Orcilla hadn't led one charge; he hadn't even fought in one battle. His father, Jarnar, participated in his attacks on the other worlds. What was the reason?

Biggabomb scratched his head. He just didn't have any answers.

With his oversized feet up and his legs extended, Biggabomb laid back and pondered about his enemy. His eyes fluttered as years of war kept his ears alert to the noises outside. Soon, he began to dismiss all external distractions and began to relax into a comfortable state, ready to doze.

***

Lord Carnidawg readied his troops for the invading army that was amassing some forty miles away. His own troops in heavy gear looked fearsome. Even in their yellow military uniforms and painted armor, they appeared formidable. Large chest plates and shoulder pads emphasized their defensive prowess. Their enormous weapons however, showed off their offensive capabilities.

The Wasp Legion, as they were so aptly named, began the long trek toward their new enemy. They hoped to swing around, well south of Biggabomb's troops, in an attempt to encircle the Crimson Brigade. The problem was that Carnidawg's troops, in all of their bulk, were very slow. They could pack a punch and take a beating, but if they couldn't outmaneuver the enemy, they wouldn't be able to tighten a noose around their opponent's neck.

Carnidawg moved out his army, sitting atop an armored monstrosity. It had a number of guns, some on turrets and some that were single mounted on swiveling pods. The tank, like the other vehicles and troops, was mostly yellow. It had rust that ran down from rivets and hatches. It was marked by streaks of dust and dirt that barely hid the damage from battle. These were mostly nicks from bullets that showed the unpainted metal beneath. In various places, a wasp was painted. This insignia matched the flags that blew in the wind above most of the military vehicles.

Behind the tank were other, smaller tanks followed by trucks. The trucks were huge metal beasts that belched smoke from their powerful engines through exhausts behind the cabs. A dozen or so troops huddled within the covered beds of each truck:, drinking, singing, laughing, and farting, but not always in that order.

There were some bots further back. They were clumsy-looking, walking boilers. They had effective guns that they utilized. Usually, one was an extension of an arm, while the other arm might have held a huge cutting or smashing weapon. Some had multiple guns and arms. A driver sat inside these clanging, bouncing, dung heaps. It has been said that more orcs died inside the innards of these death traps from choking fumes than those they killed on the battlefields. By looking at them, one could easily imagine truth in that.

Some bikes and various vehicles rounded out the attack force. Not one was new or clean; some vehicles, so dirty and worn, looked like they were painted tan. None of this mattered to the orcs. They loved the ear-splitting noise of their vehicles' engines; the occasional backfire was somehow reassuring. The aroma of oils, fuels, emissions, and dirt was their delight. War was coming. They were elated!

By now, the troops were chanting in rhythmic unison, "Hun, hun, hun… hunger." They were hungry for battle. The incessant chanting was somewhat of a battle cry for these hardened warriors. The slow, deliberate chant matched the speed at which they advanced. They were methodically moving into position, hungry for a kill, hoping to will themselves to victory through the horrible song.

***

Biggabomb was finally sleeping. Several days of hard hand-to-hand combat left him drained. He had sustained his share of war wounds recently, and even his strapping brawn needed some downtime. But it wasn't to be.

His information officer woke him carefully. He sat up from his olive-green blankets that were laid in the corner of a shack he was using as his command post. He rubbed his eyes for a few seconds. Then, his massive arms stretched above his head as he yawned. His rippling muscles popped, and veins already visible, riddled the surface of his skin. The information officer backed up wearily as he saw the size of Biggabomb's mouth. It could easily be imagined that a chomper that size could eat an elk with one bite. This orc was taking no chances!

Biggabomb addressed the officer. "Yes, Skull?"

The information officer was quick to respond and efficient in his use of words. "We find dat Wasp Legion movin' in south to cut off Invadas."

"Very good. Letta us show dem Invadas what we can do."

Biggabomb pumped out his chest in pride and a bit of defiance. He meant what he said. He knew that his Homeworlders were great fighters. If they could all work together, instead of quarreling with each other, he was confident they could inflict enough damage on the Invadas to halt their invasion and send them back home. He sent Skull on his way and called for his own officers.

Gunza, Guthrak, Headhunta, and Nukklez entered the room that Biggabomb waited in. After they squabbled over who was to sit where, they finally did so. Although they could be annoying at times, they were heavily relied upon as Biggabomb's elite squad of personal guards. They were fearless and loyal. Also, after years of fighting together, they anticipated each other's moves. This was vital to their success in protecting each other. They were all keenly aware of this and would all admit that they wouldn't want to fight alongside anyone else if they had the choice.

Gunza and Guthrak were Biggabomb's most important guards and for good reason. They were nearly as massive, mean, cunning, and intelligent as he was. They were eager to die so that he or any of the others in the group might live. They were true warriors and his best friends.

Headhunta was perhaps the strangest one in the group. He didn't speak much, so it was difficult to gauge him in any way unless it was during battle. His aloof disposition hid his love of bloodshed and pain that he caused. He was somewhat sadistic in that way. He forced himself to kill out of respect for his opponents, rather than compassion for their suffering. Otherwise, he would just as soon leave one squirming on the end of his sword for hours, watching their struggle with pain and their transition to the afterworld. Before he was recruited and promoted by Biggabomb, he routinely cut off the fingers of his opponents and left them in their mouths, lips stitched shut.

Physically, he was a bit taller than Gunza and a bit lighter. However, he seemed shorter than that as he carried himself in a somewhat hunched manner. His piercing eyes and slouched posture as he moved would raise the hair on the necks of even his closest battle brothers. Nobody ever knew what he was thinking as he never smiled, nor partook in small talk.

He fought hard and he fought well; that was enough for Biggabomb and his squad.

Nukklez was very similar in size and form to both Gunza and Guthrak. He was a little thicker in the midsection and joked about how much he loved to eat and drink Shlogger. He frequently exclaimed, "A barrel of Shlogger a day will keep da enemy away." This was a crude reference to the bitter stink that his flatulence gave off after drinking such large quantities of a potent drink. Truth be told, nobody ever saw him drink a whole barrel in a day. Those around him accepted his mild boasting and embellishing, as well as his use of third person when referring to himself.

On this day, he started the group conversation that way with, "Nukklez will sit here." Then, after everyone sat down, he began with, "Why you call Nukklez, Chief?"

Biggabomb addressed Nukklez's question, "I a call you hear to go ova da plans to kill da damn Invadas."

Guthrak pumped his fist with a solid, "Yes!"

Simultaneously, Gunza howled, "'Bout damn time!"

Nukklez stated that he was equally pleased with, "Finawy! Now, Nukklez will showa dems bastids who dems a screwin' wit'!"

Words of, "Dat's right," and, "Yeah" were exclaimed by all- all but Headhunta, that is. He looked down at the table the entire time, saying nothing, but turning his head in the direction of each orc as they spoke. His head rotated slightly on the opposite axis like a dawg trying to figure something out. He never blinked and never moved anything other than his head as he took in the conversation. His sullen, dark, twisted, mannerisms were simply chilling.

Biggabomb quieted his orcs and continued, "Wasp Legion movin' a south and we hold line here. Dis gonna be a tough. We needs to hit Invadas hard to west so dems commit troops ova der. It our only a chance to get Wasps in da fight to win."

Nukklez slammed his mace on the table in sheer joy. His weapon of choice was his beloved mace. He was proficient with it, but really liked it because it was different than what most of the other orcs in his army used. He referred to fighting with it as "clubbin". It gave him the ability to boast a bit.

He happily exclaimed, "We do it, Chief. We send dem Invadas backs!"

Gunza thoughtfully waited for Nukklez to finish before he began. First, he engaged his chief as a friend, "Bomb, we don't have 'nuff to win if dis don't work." He leaned forward, and his facial expression changed as if to emphasize the importance of what he was about to say. He went on to state, "We has no heavy arma. Our fightas are down wit' almost no fuel, too. Maybe we can hold Invadas fo' a while, but..."

Biggabomb interjected, "I know. But if a we don't, den we lose fo' sure. Plus, Wasps has heavy arma if dems can a make it to us. We gots no heavy arma wit' out dems. I tinka we should try."

"Ok. I always be you a friend and guard. You right."

Guthrak looked disgusted. "You two a gonna kiss now?"

Nukklez immediately laughed. Headhunta didn't.

Gunza snapped, "Watch it!"

Biggabomb turned toward Guthrak and jeered, "My old friend, you gonna kiss a me ass!"

Guthrak snarled under his breath, "Don't I always?"

The four talkative orcs laughed hardily. They talked about options and ironed out plans over the next thirty minutes. Then, they left to carry out their plans. Headhunta quietly followed, lurking in their early morning shadows.

***

Biggabomb would have liked to open his attack on the Invadas with artillery. The powerful blasts, although somewhat random, were both deadly and demoralizing. A few fighta planes could be used, but not enough to do anything more than get the enemy to keep its head down for a short while. Needing support or not, Biggabomb's Bone Crushas began their assault.

A line of fire began on the east side as a diversion, meant to lure the enemy commander to pull resources from his western and southern sides. This would allow the Wasp Legion to swing around from the south. This was a huge leap of faith from Biggabomb though. He would be thinning his own lines and taking much heavier fire than the Wasps to give them the advantage they so desperately needed.

The Bone Crusha vehicles raced ahead and were immediately under a heavy stream of rockets. Some crew members locked themselves in their vehicles with the intent of never returning. They drove their coffins on wheels deep into the enemy before enemy fire took their eventual toll. Most survived long enough to penetrate into the heart of the enemy. By the time small groups of Biggabomb's troops engaged the enemy, it did indeed seem as if his army was engaging in a full out assault on the eastern side.

Biggabomb needed to ensure that the Invadas didn't blink and second guess their decision to reallocate troops to the east. He and his own squad fought alongside his small groups of infantry. This was a gamble to validate his apparent attack in the east. He had led every attack against the Invadas. Lack of his presence would allow his enemy to see through his plan. No, he was going to make sure there was no second guessing. He figured that he was the finishing touch on this daring plan. Just to make sure though, he sent his few fighters just ahead to soften enemy positions to further drag the Invadas into his trap.

There was a problem, though. As the main fighting force of the Bone Crushas waited to attack to the west, Biggabomb and his meager forces were taking the full brunt of what the Invadas could throw at them. Biggabomb hoped he could hold on just long enough for his main force to attack in the west and push south to meet up with the Wasp Legion as it slipped around from the south. By outflanking and attacking the weaker side, they would essentially surround the Invadas. If things went well for the Homeworlders, they could force the Invadas to abandon their plans to invade any further. The downside was that Biggabomb didn't have an exit plan for himself or his eastern troops. This was their best opportunity to succeed and that outweighed the importance of his, or any of the other hundred lives, he put at risk.

Biggabomb picked times between enemy fire to show himself. He timed the shots and moved forward, ducking and dodging as he did so. His guards did the same. Nukklez dove to the ground as a hail of enemy fire raked the dirt around him. Guthrak took a bullet in his upper right arm, but continued on without a thought about himself. He met up with Biggabomb and Gunza under a corner building which was partially collapsed.

The three orcs opened with a volley of fire with themselves as cover for Nukklez. Nukklez stumbled in to meet them, a bit bloody and bruised, but not seriously hurt.

Nukklez screamed, "Wow! Dis da most fire in da whole war I tink!"

Gunza scowled. "It only gonna get a worse fo' us."

Movement just ahead of the group startled them. They saw Headhunta advancing forward under some debris. None of them even saw him show up. They looked around at each other, puzzled.

Guthrak joked, "If only I dat sneaky goin into da female's bedroom windows."

They all got the joke, although none laughed. Nukklez raised the corner of his lip on one side. "Dat how you get dat knife in you jaw?"

Just then, a blast sent concrete and debris flying around the orcs as they tried to hunker down. Gunza was closest to the blast and took some shrapnel in his one leg and side. Like him, the debris from the explosion blanketed the others with thousands of small pieces of concrete that imbedded in their skin and eyes. They were covered in light gray dust and blood.

It didn't take but a second or two to realize that their protection from the building they were huddled in was compromised. They quickly scrambled to get into better cover as bullets flew around them. Each was hit at least once. Guthrak was riddled down his left side with a half dozen holes. Nukklez hit the ground hard, unable to support himself on his right leg long enough to see where he stepped. As bullets ripped through his tendons and muscles, he stumbled heavily into a crater.

Biggabomb crouched down and surveyed, "Evvyone ok?"

Nukklez yelled, "Yeah. But dat wun hurt Nukklez. Leg no work now!"

Gunza and Guthrak nodded.

Biggabomb commanded, "Let's go."

Biggabomb moved his orcs into a safe position, just opposite the enemy's front line. His troops had taken heavy fire the whole time and had lost about thirty orcs. He ordered the remaining seventy to open fire. As they did, he and his guards came out of hiding and sprang into the enemy line.

Biggabomb's ferocity was unmatched this day. His attack on the enemy was shocking and they were unprepared for his furious wrath. He cut one orc down after another. Guthrak and Gunza fought alongside him, felling twenty or more enemies each. Nukklez handled a few as he crawled into battle and fought from his knees. Unable to keep up the forward pace that the other three were, he shot several enemies as they approached.

Each member of the squad saw Headhunta fighting alongside them from time to time. Then, he would seem to vanish behind a wall or burning vehicle. His fighting style was fluid. His movements never seemed to be forced and he seemed to have an ability to hit and run.

Biggabomb and his squad were forced to drop to the ground again under gunfire. Enemy tanks were approaching from the west, and with them, a battalion of infantry. The Bone Crushas shot sporadically to buy some time, so Biggabomb could figure out what to do.

Biggabomb took this little bit of time to communicate with his other squads and to get updated information about the Wasp Legion. He found that they were advancing as planned. His deception had worked! But the squads that he led in the east were all but decimated. Enemy tanks and artillery were exacting terrible tolls on his orcs. He needed to buy a little more time to fully execute his plan.

He poked his head up just high enough for his eyes to see through a hole in a block wall that he was lying behind. He measured distances in his head and mapped out a way to move around the tanks. He ordered the rest of his orcs in battle with him to fall back while he took his elite squad south and east.

They fought their way another fifty yards, just as they did before. Biggabomb made easy work of his enemies. He was much larger, faster, and stronger than they were. His elite squad covered his flanks and rear as they, too, were more than the opposing orcs could deal with.

Then, Biggabomb and his elite squad came upon something disturbing. They came to a clearing. Smoke and dust filled the air so that they could only see twenty feet in front of them. There was no enemy fire. There was just the sound of moaning and liquid sloshing.

The Bone Crusha Elite Squad tried to make sense of what it saw. Dozens of enemy orcs were lying in clusters with their bellies cut open. They struggled to pick up their innards and put them back in their bodies, unaware that Biggabomb and his orcs were upon them. None of their wounds were from ranged weapons. They had all been cut by a sword.

From within the fog of war stepped a figure. The figure slid into view, slowly revealing its identity. Headhunta!

Guthrak marveled at what he was witnessing. At the same time, even with one of the strongest stomachs an orc can possess, he was a little sickened. He found himself commenting in disbelief more than he was asking, "You did all dis?"

Headhunta was silent. He watched the blood that ran down his sword as he stepped effortlessly over writhing bodies. He studied the consistent flow of fluid over the same trickle down his lethal blade. He acknowledged nothing and said even less. He simply took up his position to the right of Gunza.

None of them needed to put the enemy troops out of their misery for the incoming tank fire accomplished that. Bodies were turned into objects of flight. The sound was deafening!

Biggabomb and his elite squad were also hit. Biggabomb was lifted and thrown violently. He landed some distance from his squad. His vision was blurred, and his hearing was lost. He tried to gather himself to fight as quickly as he could, but he couldn't. His body was shaking; he was in pain.

He struggled to figure out what was wrong. He wasn't sure what happened or why he was on his back looking up. He saw Gunza running toward him. Yes, Gunza. This familiar face could hopefully shed some light on things.

Gunza was bloody and there wasn't much clothing on his bulky frame. Biggabomb saw him speaking, but his voice was muted. Gunza sounded like he was talking under water. That struck Biggabomb as peculiar. However, what stuck in Biggabomb's brain was the look of shock on Gunza's face. Gunza put both of his hands up to shield Biggabomb from view of what was below. Biggabomb started to drift into unconsciousness, but not before he forced his friend's hands out of the way.

Biggabomb barely comprehended what he saw. The shell that detonated and sent him flying was followed by other shells that were packed with gases. Upon their impact, toxins were spewed all around Biggabomb and his orcs. He was gasping for air that was critical to his survival. He coughed blood into his mouth and out his nose. He saw yellow and green smoke wafting through the air. He saw his friend bending down to attend to him. He saw that his left arm was gone.

***

The angry mob was entering the building, shoving its way past several troops that had returned with Nutty. It had never occurred to Nutty that his own orcs would be waiting to lynch him when he returned. He had very little protection against the dozens of unsettled Big Town orcs that were yelling at him. He kept trying to put them off as long as he could until he got more information. But there was very little reasoning that could be done with angry orcs.

Still, he tried to make them understand. "Shutta up now! I still tryin' to help udder hurt or maybe dyin' orcs. We at war! Wivvaflow was attackin's us."

Nutty looked around to see bodies in the gymnasium that were covered by bloody blankets. He surmised that these must have been the dead bodies from the mining accident that was reported to him. The yells from the crowd lightened to a hushed whisper as he bent down by one of the cots that supported one of the mining victims. He pulled back the blanket and began chanting under his breath. He finished with, "You name will be remembered. Da Gods be proud a you."

Before information gathering, Nutty went to each body and did the same thing. The crowd was quiet, yet edgy. Still, they were respectful and at least took solace in knowing that he was compassionate toward their losses.

Nutty had just finished with the last victim when orcs were shoved out of the way by a new commotion.

"Bring him in!" Muga was directing the younger male orcs to carry the even younger soldier into the back room that was set up to accept the wounded. This soldier looked horrible. He was ripped to pieces and was unrecognizable. He was limp and bloody.

Nutty pushed as many of the gathering out of the way that he could. This reignited some in the already touchy crowd, but he hardly noticed as he attended to the business of finding out which soldier this was and what shape he was in. Of course, he wanted whatever enemy intelligence he could possibly attain as well, but that wasn't very likely with the soldier in his current condition.

Uhra came through the front door and pushed through the crowd and bodies until she came face to face with Nutty. She was elated to see that he returned. She was getting the feeling that she should probably be concerned with what was going on though. There was an awful amount of tension in the room; it was palpable. There were other concerns to deal with first, though, and she began to help where she could.

"Nutty, we got no docs here. Dems all at da mine. What we do?"

Nutty faced the crowd and ordered, "Evvyone outside! We no need another dead orc. We talk later."

The disgruntled crowd understood. Even as stupid as orcs were in general, they got it. They didn't want another dead kid. Even still, there were enough adult orcs in the group that could cause serious problems. They were injured in battle on the Eastern Continent and back to heal before returning to war again. Nutty couldn't afford a fight with these hardened veterans and he knew it.

One orc in the crowd asserted, "We be waitin' fo' you."

Nutty nodded to his antagonizer and then turned to Uhra. "Any medicine here?"

"Some. Most a dat all at da mine, too. Der no adrenaline stuff fo' him to stay alive neither."

Nutty wasn't sure what to do. There were a number of troops already occupying the cots that lined the walls in the next room. Several per day were coming back severely injured from the Eastern Continent. Most of those were missing limbs, eyes, or worse. Some would eventually die, regardless of what primitive methods could be administered. Medicines were in short supply now because of their constant use.

Thinking things through briefly, Nutty had the injured soldier brought into the next room and he followed behind. He ordered for a doc to be brought back from the mine, hoping beyond hope that one would return before this young soldier died. When the soldier was placed in a cot, Nutty went to him and tried to identify who it was. There wasn't much to recognize however. Most of the body was burned. Pieces of the face, ears, eyes, and identifiable features were all but gone. This poor kid was hanging on, but how?

Then it hit Nutty. Was this Gardawg or Kor? They were the only two aside from the miners that were unaccounted for. Nutty breathed a sigh of relief when he regrettably determined that it wasn't Gardawg. At least it gave his little brother a chance to be alive. "Yes" he thought. This was Kor, poor bastard. Nutty couldn't think of anything worse than what Kor was experiencing.

Maybe Nutty couldn't help him, but maybe he could get some information about Gardawg. Nutty began to ask his subordinates questions. "Where was Kor found?"

They replied, "Him wash up onna our side da wivva."

"Did you searcha da area fo' anyone or anyting else?"

"Yessa, but a find no ting."

Nutty questioned further, "Him say anyting?"

"No."

Nutty was getting nowhere. He asked Uhra to keep Kor as comfortable as possible. He also sent two soldiers as guards to watch over them both. Then, he went out the back and headed to Guthrak's shop, so he could go over everything to date. This way, he avoided confrontation with the angry crowd. They would just have to wait for him. Ultimately, he gave orders for some of his top orcs to meet with him and update him on details. Nutty's other troops were reorganizing and did whatever they were trained to do. Muga went back to the mine to check on the progress of aid given to the injured miners and to see when a doc would help Kor. Pretty stayed with Uhra to lend a hand, not that she could do much.

The two girls tried to think of ways to help Kor, but realistically, they didn't have faces or limbs to give to the injured boy, they had very little medicine for pain, and no way to keep him alive.

While thinking, something occurred to Uhra. She mentioned what was on her mind. "Do you know anyting bout da adrenaline shot?"

Pretty shook her head and responded, "Not really. I know dat it mix wit' some udder stuff. We got dat, but no adren...adren..." She struggled with the word, but continued, "You know the stuff dat I mean."

Uhra did know the stuff. "Yep, and I knows where to find it."

"Where?"

"By da wivva in da trees dat are bended funny. I can go anda get some. Be right back," Uhra exclaimed.

Pretty agreed with Uhra. "Ok."

Uhra raced against time to get the needed adrenaline to keep Kor alive. Pretty wet a rag and wiped Kor's face. She was careful to bandage him and clean him up. The little bit of skin that Kor had left, was easily wiped off with a rag. Pretty wept as she did so little for this poor soldier. She guessed that he was probably younger than she was. She couldn't stand to be there. She waited for Uhra to return, but that didn't happen.

Eight
From Bad to Worse

The room sounded of painful moans. Medical equipment beeped and some whirred as air was physically pumped into lungs of the seriously injured. No amputations were currently being conducted. Today's arrival of casualties from the eastern front was yet to arrive. Otherwise, moans would be drowned out by the screams of the unlucky amputees as medicines were minimal. The smell of copper from blood, mixed with the cheesy aroma of infection cut through the senses like a hot saber slipping through hot rolls.

Kor was still clinging to life. Pretty had gone to the mine when Muga returned to relieve her. Muga had come back with a doc and some adrenaline. The doc slowly and carefully injected Kor. After several minutes, Kor began to scream; his body flailed uncontrollably as pain overwhelmed him. Muga and the doc quickly restrained Kor by tying down whatever parts of his body were left. The doc administered what little relief for pain through medication as he could, without surely ending Kor's existence. His orders were clear, as unfair as they sounded; to keep Kor alive as long as possible so Nutty could find out about Gardawg.

Muga's heart ached for this kid. She looked into his eye and reassured him that he wouldn't have pain for long. She tried to gather whatever information she could to end any more of his agony. Furthermore, she wanted to know what had happened to her Gardawg. She knelt beside him and began to ask open-ended questions. Kor fought to speak, but couldn't find a way to formulate words. His pain was still unbearable and his mouth, without a tongue, fumbled through unintelligible noises.

Muga soon understood his plight and started with simple yes and no questions. Kor could nod to these. When she wanted details, she tried to piece his vowel sounds together to figure out what he was trying to say. After fifteen minutes, she found out that Kor and Gardawg fought a carnidawg and barely survived. She now understood that the initial injections of adrenaline had kept them alive. By this time, Kor was so weak that he kept slipping into unconsciousness. It was possible that Muga and Nutty might never find out what happened to Gardawg. Muga was beginning to feel a little anger like the crowd outside. She was tired of war and the losses attributed to them!

***

Nutty was dealing with issues on different fronts. He had a Runna waiting for him as he went over the Wivvaflow situation with Booma, Thunda, Quicklip, and Nubbs. Ole Man Boppa was also due to show up shortly with the mining accident's details. He sent for Uhra just because he missed her, but she hadn't shown up yet either. He was struggling to keep everything running properly. In the back of his mind, he was still aware of a possible invasion on his people from the Invadas, retaliation from Wivvaflow, civil unrest, supply shortages, an overabundance of casualties, uncertainty about Gardawg, training issues, logistical problems, and a myriad of things regarding time and timing. He questioned his own position and ability as Big Town Army Controla.

In response to Nutty's concerns, Booma responded first. "Trainin' happenin' as we a can. Da teacher comin' home wit' a hurt arm, so he will do builda skool again. I still do a fight skool. Da kids doin' goods, too."

Nutty pressed on one of his concerns. "What about if we is invaded? Are kids ready fo' real war?"

"No. I means, dems canna fight, but no strong like Invadas. Dems still kids."

"Hmm. Well, letta still make betta defend at wivva and north borders. Trenchas, steep embankaments, you know? Tings to slow down Invadas if dems a come here to Big Town. Maybe we can shoots 'em from cover instead a fight up close."

"Yes. Dat a good idea."

Nutty continued, "How is da fighta plane production?"

Booma looked displeased as he spoke. "Not a too good. Da best workas are on Eastern Continent or hurts. And, we short on metal cause kids and females slowa dan males. Plus, now we gots mine accident dat stopped metals all. We tryin'. Three planes go to Eastern Continent dis last month."

Nutty sighed, "Keeps on it, Booma."

"O' Course."

"Ok," Nutty acknowledged. He continued, "I also needs suggestions 'bout which soldias betta at close fight, wit' explosions, or shootin's."

"K. Anyting else?"

Nutty relied on his brother and these kids to run the city and fight a war under extreme conditions. He needed them more than they knew. He respectfully thanked Booma and sent him on his way.

Then, he asked, "Guys, anyting we did wrong in Wivvaflow?"

The three subordinates looked around at each other. They were puzzled. Hadn't they performed well? Didn't they steal all those bikes and supplies? Didn't they blow up the bridge and a huge portion of the town with minimal casualties?

Thunda pounded out, "I did good!"

Quicklip followed in his usual way, "Yeah, good at bein's loud anda stupid!"

"Shutta up or you be called Nolips!"

Nubbs chuckled between swigs of his prized ale. Thunda laughed hardily at his obviously witty comeback. He slapped Nubbs on the back and wobbled his head in an antagonistic way while he stared at Quicklip. He realized a little too late that his overzealous actions caused some ale to fly from Nubbs' mug.

Nubbs' chuckle turned to a growl as he scoffed, "Anda you be called Nohands if a you spills my a drink again!" He put his short, stubby pointer finger at Thunda's nose.

Thunda was taken aback. Still, he found a way with all his brain power to come up with, "Anda you will be called a Nubbs fo' a reason! Der is no sense fo' you to die ova ale!"

Nubbs and Thunda stood up simultaneously. Nutty jumped to his feet in an instant and bellowed in sheer anger, "Shutta up and sit downs before I killa both of yous!"

Quicklip cackled a scratchy sound as he tried to avoid bursting out in laughter and urinating in his pants. He just couldn't help it. Usually, it was him and

146

Thunda going at it. It was refreshing and entertaining to see Thunda getting in trouble without him having anything to do with it.

Nutty regained his composure before addressing his big-mouthed, self-proclaimed prince of banter. "Would you radder be called a Quicklip or Noballs? I offer you da option."

Thunda and Nubbs fell back in their chairs. Thunda refrained from slapping Nubbs on the back this time. He instead put his hands on his belly as he laughed uncontrollably. Quicklip just couldn't keep his mouth shut, ever! Quicklip stared at Thunda in anger, but he too found humor in Nutty's challenge. They all realized that Nutty had a knack for diffusing things, keeping things light, and getting the most out of them. Too bad they were orcs. They couldn't always control their impulsive outbursts. Nutty obviously understood their flaws. In the end, Quicklip eventually smiled.

Nutty, still standing, went back to his original question. "Well, anyting yous could do a betta?"

Quicklip thought of something and decided to share. "Da plan was good. But maybe we coulda got down da street to da factory betta."

Nutty liked this. He wanted his orcs to think. He wanted them to work out plans on the fly. He figured they would be more effective. "Ok. How?"

"Maybe not to walk right down da street. Was der a different way?"

Nutty was reaching his limits of what he could work out in his head. He was tired and overworked. "Not dat I can tink of right a now. But dat is good. How 'bout no fightin' wit' each udder?"

Nubbs shook his head "no". That wasn't an option when it came to Thunda and Quicklip. In fact, they all knew it. Again, they were orcs. It was understood.

Nutty finished on the topic with, "Tink about stuffs we can do a betta."

With that, Nutty and his orcs went over some other things, and like Booma, they were politely dismissed.

***

Muga was struggling. She knew that there was limited time to get all the information she could from Kor. He was now awake, albeit barely, and trying to answer more questions; and like before, he mouthed out sounds and motioned to get Muga to understand him.

She found out that he had continued his mission after killing the carnidawg, and at that point, Gardawg was still alive. She wept when she learned of her baby's injuries. To her, he was still her beloved and gifted child, unaffected by the fever. She was able to keep him in her heart over these last few years by thinking about him as he should have been...as he was, not as the way he became after the fever. As a baby, he had saved lives. She so wanted to save his. She yearned for him; she still wished that it was to be, regardless of his physical condition.

Muga pressed on with questions. She discovered after a frustrating time that Kor and Gardawg were separated so they could continue their mission. Then, she was horrified to learn Gardawg was strapped with explosives. Kor had continued down the road as he fought off countless orcs. Eventually, he was thrown into the river as the truck he drove exploded. He didn't know what happened to Gardawg.

Muga kept fighting to get details about Gardawg, but in the end, Kor expired into the beyond. His eye rolled back, and his labored breathing ended. A final gurgle of air left his perforated lung and he was gone. He had done his job and completed his mission. He couldn't fight any more; his fight was over when he slew the carnidawg. Against all odds, after his fate was already decided, he still made it to the bridge. Muga wept as she left his side. She prayed to her God that he found Kor to his liking, and then she prayed that she found Gardawg to hers.

***

Locals were scrambling as their cities were being leveled. Orbital bombardments were raining down like hail on the only homes they knew. Sure, it wasn't much, but every orc had a place he or she used as a dwelling. Many were left to the elements without shelter. Most were easy targets as the incoming onslaught found them unprepared. Few noticed the order in which events were unfolding; it really didn't matter. The Homeworlder's defenses were overwhelmed by the massive explosions that rocked the area.

The outskirts were hit first. Landing areas were cleared, and troops began to arrive. They had little opposition as their weapons and preemptive attacks cleared the way for these seemingly invincible Invadas. They grabbed several towns and set up command centers. The same thing that happened on the Eastern Continent, just weeks before, was beginning to play out on the vulnerable Western continent.

Homeworlders, outmatched and outmaneuvered, were unwittingly corralled into the jaws of the invading juggernaut. The Invadas fought in such a way so as to manipulate the directions their opponents moved in order to escape. This was a common element in the Invada's attacks.

What was different and horrifying to even the orcs of most pure and brutish decent, was what happened after they were captured. The adult males were offered to join the Invada's ranks as soldiers, or more accurately, as fighting slaves. This was optioned while they were separated from their females and openly told of their females' fates, as well as that of their children. Their females were being sent to the Invada's worlds where they would be used to populate their armies with newborn children; in essence, they would be raped and kept in prisons. The children would be trained as eventual soldiers and worked as slaves until that time. In short, any captured orc was subject to possible torture as guinea pigs toward the advancement of science or any other possible way to help the Invadas. All adult males that refused slavery as fighters were tortured and tested upon.

***

Nutty was incensed at the indiscriminate torture of his fellow Homeworlders as he thought before handling what he needed to with the newest Runna. He wouldn't be one to kill the Runna in front of him, although the Runna didn't know that. Nutty listened as the Runna carefully listed the towns on Nutty's very own Western Continent that had fallen to the Invadas. He heard about the landings of reinforcements and quietly speculated about what the invading armies might do next.

Then, the Runna informed Nutty about the Wasp Legion's victory. This apparently slowed the Invada's march across the whole continent. However, the happy news was short-lived as information about the Invadas using gas bombs and the disappearance of Biggabomb and his elite guards came to light.

The Runna didn't even know about Biggabomb's injuries. Biggabomb and his guards penetrated so deep into enemy territory, that they were assumed to have been captured or killed. The Wasp Legion had met up with Bigga's western army, but couldn't completely do away with the Invada's massive troop count.

Nutty couldn't help but think about his father being captured or killed as a real possibility. Even the wounded soldiers that came back from battle talked about how good the Invadas fought. Bigga and his orcs were woefully outnumbered, too. Then, his mind drifted to Gunza, Biggabomb's elite guard and best friend. He was missing, too. Nutty never seriously considered that his and Uhra's fathers might be lost together.

The prospect of such a thing was frightening. He didn't know how he would tell Uhra. He decided to tell her nothing until he had proof of what happened to Gunza...and his own father, for that matter. How would he tell Muga, his mother? He hoped the day would never come.

Ole Man Boppa showed up and gave Nutty whatever details he wanted. Between the mining accident, the attack on Wivvaflow, and Big Town and Wivvaflow exchanging shots across the river, casualties were mounting. Nutty was getting a clearer picture and that picture was bleak.

Nutty would have to confirm some numbers and probably call a town meeting to inform the angry crowd about the successes they had, as compared to their losses. He would have to speak with his mother about Biggabomb and Uhra about Gunza, but again, decided to wait. He also came to the decision to go back to the school to check on Kor and let the crowd know that he would be holding a meeting. Once he gave the Runna instructions and Ole Man Boppa left, he did just that.

***

It was twenty minutes later when Nutty got to the school. Nutty found Muga off in a maintenance closet crying and guessed that she already found out about Biggabomb. He was wrong though. "What, Momma?"

Muga wiped her eyes. She cleared her throat and talked in a way Nutty might be consoled. She said, "Nutty, I tink I have news."

Nutty was sure not to give his own information away. He simply asked, "What news?"

"Der was two esplosions in Wivvaflow?"

Nutty was a little surprised. This didn't have anything to do with Biggabomb; his assumption was wrong. This obviously had to do with Gardawg. He paused before he answered. "Yes. Why?"

Muga broke down. "Oh, Nutty, da first esplosion was Kor on da trukk. Da nexta wun wuz Gardawg." She clumsily spoke as her own feelings were dragged to the surface with each word. "Hims had bombs straps to hims. He deads, Nutty."

Nutty hung his head in disbelief. This couldn't be. Everyone made it back from the mission except Gardawg, his own brother. He looked up into his mother's eyes, his own eyes softened as he empathized with her. "Kor?"

Muga said, "He said most. Sorta. Him die, too. Da rest make sense."

Nutty didn't understand why Gardawg would strap bombs to himself. He shouldn't have. What would be the point in that? His mission was clear. "Why he strap bombs?"

"Dem both fight a carnidawg. Dem was dyin' anyway, Nutty."

Nutty didn't know what to say. How could anything he might say help his distressed mother? All he could find was, "Sorry."

Muga looked at Nutty. She breathed hard now. Her hand was shaking as she handed something to him. "It worse, Nutty."

Streams of tears ran down her face as she saw him take what she was giving him.

Nutty opened the piece of paper and looked down at it. It didn't take long for terror to grip his soul. His terror was soon mixed with anger. He began to shake like his mother. He screamed out, "I screwa kills dem all!" He dropped the paper to the floor and raced to the exit.

"Nutty, don't go alone," Muga pleaded.

Nutty turned for a moment toward his stricken mother. His eyes showed a desperation that she had never seen from him until now. Her heart was heavy for his loss. Her heart was bleeding for his safe return. She knew him all too well. She understood.

Nutty exclaimed, "I be back Momma." He turned and busted through the enormous, steel doors to the outside. He roared at the irritated crowd as he pushed a dozen or so to the side and screamed obscenities. He was wild. He was mad. He was dangerous!

Pretty had just entered through the back door as she saw the commotion with Nuttybomb. She went over to Muga and picked up the piece of paper. She brought her hand to her mouth and she gasped. "Oh no!"

Nine
How Bad Can It Get?

Nutty had given instructions and they were final. Quicklip would oversee the troops and Booma would be in charge of the fight school and aircraft production. Ole Man Boppa still had the mine. The teacher would run the builder school. Muga would be in charge of health and food, overseeing the docs and kitchens. Nutty planned on being back soon; he had to be. With Biggabomb missing, Invadas landing on his continent, and him leaving for a while, it was imperative to have clear and concise plans. Unfortunately, his instructions were rushed. More accurately, they were almost nonexistent. He left in such a hurry, there was no central control in his absence.

Now, this didn't matter to Nutty. He couldn't think clearly; he was tormented by the piece of paper he read. The tattooed biker who referred to him as Jailbitch, had taken Uhra by the river. The biker was holding her as a prisoner of war on the Wivvaflow side. He had given crude directions to her location and demanded that Nutty come alone. Against the advice of his commanders and his family, Nutty set out by himself to find Uhra.

Big Town troops fired concentrated shots over the river where Nutty crossed. Nutty was able to traverse the water that had now receded from its rushing mayhem to a subtle calm. He quickly came ashore and disappeared into the woods that lay beyond.

He thought about Uhra. He thought about her eyes...her smile...her sexy curled lip when she referred to him as "Younut". He thought about their walks together and recounted the many times they laughed while telling jokes and kicking stuff all the way home from school. Why her? What did she have to do with anything? She was completely innocent in this war.

Well, it didn't take long for him to know why she was kidnapped; she was his best friend. What better way to hurt him than to hurt someone he loved? Still, the tactics stunk. The thought of taking a helpless girl was appalling. All things considered, though, how many innocent Wivvaflow orcs died when Kor and Gardawg blew things up? That was blood on Nutty's hands, collateral damage that he knew might be a result, but didn't actually want to occur. Maybe this was exactly what he deserved, even if Uhra didn't.

Nutty brushed the thoughts aside as he concentrated on the directions he was given. All he needed was to take a wrong turn or stumble into a force of Wivvaflow orcs to spell disaster. He needed to be careful and cautious; "Cautious," he mumbled to himself. He began working things out in his head and then confirming them aloud. He was quiet enough though; there was no way he would say something that could be heard as he made his way to Uhra. He tried to think about what Biggabomb would do. He went over strategies in his head, again talking things out.

He came upon a large mildus tree that fit the description in the directions he had gotten. He cut around it and followed a trail to the northwest. This brought him to the main road he had just traveled out of Wivvaflow when he made his escape. He felt a little anger. Surely, the biker knew that this road would be guarded and well-traveled. Even if the biker didn't have the satisfaction of killing or capturing Nutty, somebody else might.

Nutty hunkered down for a while as traffic went by in droves. He was feeling so impatient; his nerves were on end. He wanted to get to Uhra, hoping that time would cut down his adversary's chance of harming her. This was an unnecessary delay as far as he was concerned. He wanted to rush across the street, but held up against his impulsiveness.

Thoughts of possible outcomes were occurring to Nutty. He might die. Worse was the fact that Uhra might. The town would be helpless to attack in his absence. There would be orcs totally opposed to his selfish actions that he took over those of the community. He sure felt like he was doing the right thing, but was he?

He guessed everyone would know how much he loved Uhra. He wasn't entirely sure until this very moment how much he felt for her. Nor did he know how much he cared if anyone else judged him or not. He was in charge and this was his decision to save her, period. He could deal with angry crowds later; first thing was first.

Nutty found an opening in traffic and made sure he was safe to cross the road. Darkness was now beginning to overtake the day's light, and this helped in his not being detected as he crossed. He ducked down into a ditch on the other side and stayed low as he traveled parallel to it until he found a break in the fence line. He looked around to be sure that he was unnoticed and proceeded into the field of high grass beyond.

The pace of his heart outpaced the distance he covered. The extra blood that pumped adrenaline and testosterone helped as it ran through his arteries to his lungs, brain, and muscles. He was feeling fresh and strong. He was a physical specimen; he had grown large in these last few months; his powerful muscles pushed him up and over the next few hills with ease. His breathing was without any difficulty as he covered mile after mile in short fashion.

Voices caught Nutty's attention. He immediately dropped to the ground below the height of the high grass, determining that the voices were a short distance ahead and to the right. After being unable to hear what they were saying, and finding their tones to be nonthreatening, he slowly stood and peaked in their direction.

What he saw were some farmers that were hitching a plow to oxen. They were unaware of Nutty's presence and busy working; they hadn't seen him while they worked. Nutty dropped back down beneath the grass and remained unseen as he made his way through the field. After passing a bit to the south of a wooden shanty, he quietly crossed a trail that led away from the little building to the south. It was covered in debris that he was careful to walk over without making a sound.

A heavily wooded tree line with thick underbrush was the next obstacle. Being quiet here wasn't an option. He made sure there was no one around and used the strength in his arms and hands to push through the foliage to make an opening. The thorns on the heavily defended plants made their mark on his palms, fingers, and forearms. He growled, but continued unfazed.

Nutty knew that he was close to his destination. He deviated from the directions given to him so he could gain the upper hand with surprise and avoid other orcs from seeing him. His keen sense of direction kept him on a parallel path to the one supplied on the piece of paper.

"Finawy," Nutty mumbled to himself. He came to a wooded hill that overlooked a valley he needed to get down into. Unfortunately, he couldn't continue straight down to the small building at the end of the valley. Where he sat, the way down was a sheer cliff. In fact, three of the four sides were rock-faced cliffs. This left only one way in. He would have to go back down the way he came and go around through the opening in the valley. This left him no chance of surprise.

He gave pause to assess his situation. He thought this would be a great place to see everything in the valley below. Actually, his approach to this lookout spot could be observed easily if anyone wanted to see him coming. He looked around at the other high points that overlooked the valley as he ducked. This whole area was ideal for protecting the building below, as well as the ascent from any side. Nutty worried.

Just then, he was startled! A rustling sound coincided with a hard blow to the side of his head. A flash of light danced before his eyes as a crack of thunder crashed in his right ear and buckled his knees. He swung a quick backhanded punch with his right hand in an automatic, protective response. He was lucky enough to catch an orc in the chest. He knew in an instant this was the orc that delivered the blow to his head. The orc stumbled back and dropped a metal pipe he had used on Nutty.

To Nutty's left came another hard hit. This time it was Nutty's left temple that was impacted with a blunt object. Nutty, already swinging around to his right, stood up in his now, impressive, full stance. As he continued to spin, his right backhand caught the second orc's forearm and pipe that he was holding. The pipe sailed into the nearby brush. The orc that had been holding it wasn't unhinged, though. He threw a punch with his other hand, glancing off Nutty's face. As the orc missed with his full punch, Nutty took advantage of the orc's unbalanced attempt. He dodged just enough so that the orc's inertia carried him just sideways and to the front side of Nutty.

Nutty, in a completely defensive reaction, brought his right hand behind and over the orc's head. In an instant, he pushed down, closing a tight grip around the orc's neck with his powerful arm. With his left hand, he pulled back hard on the orc's left shoulder. His strength was unbelievable. A loud snap was heard as Nutty separated the orc's skull from its spine that supported it. The orc dropped as Nutty released him. Nutty didn't take time to see the orc's eyes watch him for the next several seconds. They could only gaze as their owner's body betrayed them. The orc couldn't pump air into the lungs they relied on to carry oxygen to their depending body. In the end, the previously gazing eyes fluttered briefly until they went out for the last time.

A large, hunting knife buried itself into Nutty's right shoulder. Nutty felt a lightning bolt cascade down his arm, to his hand, and up into his neck.

However, he didn't scream. Orcs had a strong threshold to pain and he was no different. Instead, his training, natural ability, and instinct brought his left hand over the handle of the knife, and the hand that held it. The hand under his, slipped away, leaving the knife in Nutty's tough skin and muscle. The orc's other hand had found a way to take Nutty's personal knife from its holster. Nutty now had one weapon, and it was the one that was stuck in his shoulder.

Nutty stumbled to his left. He hoped it would buy him some time as he put a small distance between him and the orc that had just stabbed and disarmed him. He quickly realized that it did. He righted himself and saw the other orc, maybe ten feet away, apparently doing the same thing; both were sizing each other up.

Nutty's first impression of the other orc was how ugly he was. His head was misshapen, maybe due to an injury from a fight, or perhaps just a birth defect. Again, this was another trait that ran consistently throughout the orcs as a race. They were strong as hell and eager to fight. What they lacked in intelligence, they made up for in brute force. But, that one little, unseen flaw was their weakness to certain defects and diseases. Nutty shook the idea from his head as he summed up his opponent.

The next thing Nutty noticed was the orc's inability to call for help. Why didn't he alert anyone? Surely, he was a lookout. Shouldn't he have notified someone in the building below? Was this a perfect example of what Nutty had just briefly thought about? Was this guy too stupid? Or did he want to fight and have Nutty as a prize all to himself? It didn't matter; Nutty knew he had to take advantage of this opportunity and keep the fight to a one-on-one. After disposing of this threat, he could make his way down below.

Nutty watched the movement of the orc. The pipe he had initially whacked Nutty with was replaced with a knife. His opponent flipped the knife that he held from hand to hand. He spun it occasionally in his right hand before flipping it again. The orc did this several times, giving indication that he was probably predominately right-handed. Placement of his left foot in front of the right confirmed this.

Nutty watched the drool that hung from Oogly's face. He turned his head slightly and smiled. Not only was he momentarily amused by such a gruesome individual, like that of flatulence that friends occasionally shared, but he would arouse the orc's anger. He counted on the orc coming at him.

Oogly snarled as he raised his right hand, armed with Nutty's knife and charged. Nutty pulled Oogly's knife from his own shoulder and met the incoming knife, blade to blade. Metal met metal again and again. Nutty stepped back to bring Oogly to him, this time with the chance to prepare with a knife already in hand. Nutty had underestimated his opponent's skill with a weapon; it wouldn't happen again. This time, he wouldn't be pulling a blade from his flesh. He would already have his feet planted and a weapon ready. He would need to face this guy evenly. He had just struggled a bit at a disadvantage.

As Nutty stepped back, Oogly paused. He didn't follow like Nutty had hoped. Instead, his eyes shifted down to meet those of his fallen comrade. The lines in his forehead grew and his brow dropped. His teeth bared, and his open hand clenched into a fist. He looked up at Nutty, his eyes showing determination. He slowly stepped over his fellow orc toward Nutty. Although he was obviously angered, he didn't show the reckless abandon that typically accompanied so many orcs, nor did he rush toward Nutty as was assumed.

Then, it hit Nutty. The tattoo that Oogly sported on his left bicep was a Wivvaflow sergeant insignia. This guy was a veteran soldier. He was disciplined and obviously well-trained. Anger might not make him careless, at least, not to the point that he would find himself upon Nutty's blade. Although Nutty had lured Captain Morbid into a mad frenzy, maybe this guy was able to control his anger. Or maybe, he was better trained. Or maybe, it really didn't matter why. The fact was that he didn't seem rattled. This was going to be a fight of skill. Nutty readied himself.

"Nice tat, Oogly" Nutty quietly acknowledged the paint on his opponent's arm.

Oogly's tension left his face. "Tanks. I got it afta promoted to sergeant fo' killin's three Gravestone soldias." Oogly smiled. He looked at the blood running down Nutty's arm and continued, "You a arm marked, too, now." He laughed.

Nutty didn't have a tattoo to show as a trophy for his accomplishments. He only had the memory of deeds that he had done. He said in a low tone, without giving much thought, "Hmm…I got no tattoo fo' killin's you captain or da udder ten Wivvaflow orcs. I gots no tattoos fo' anyting I done." Nutty wondered if these words would provoke Oogly.

"I hear you a good fighta, kid. But you nevva gonna get a chance fo' tattoos afta dis fight. Dems don't tattoo dead kids. By da way, Morbid was da hothead. Don't get me wrong. Him good fighta, but we trains together. Him was easy." Oogly's tone never changed. He didn't lunge at Nutty. He actually seemed to enjoy the banter with his enemy. He smiled and waited for Nutty's reply.

"It gonna take mo' den you to kill me Oogly. I gotta get da gurl dat you are holdin'. Sorry."

Oogly looked confused. Who the hell was this kid to think that he was even in the same league? It was rumored that the kid came from good stock, but Oogly was a sergeant in the best army on the continent. He was well-trained, possessed exceptional skill, and had killed dozens of orcs in the chaos of combat. At the very least, he felt that he deserved the respect he was due. Still, he stayed composed. "Kid, firsta all, my name is Killa, Sergeant Killa, not Oogly, but tanks fo noticing. Second, I not holdin' anyone. I just gonna do my job anda kill you. Dat's it."

Nutty didn't know what to say. He was beginning to doubt himself. It was occurring to him that if this sergeant was here to kill him, how many other Wivvaflow military orcs were involved? Nutty was instructed to come alone and unarmed. He did bring the knife, but no gun. He wasn't expecting to be disarmed so quickly by this guy. Was he in real trouble?

Killa spoke easily, "Kid, no mo' talkin. Der is plenty mo' orcs down der. You can't win. Busides, you can't get down der lessa you killa me first." This time, Killa's smile showed a mouthful of rotten teeth. He was right; all the banter meant nothing. Nutty was going to have to fight him, period.

Doubtful or not, Nutty engaged Killa. There was a slice here and there. There were glancing blows from one or the other, but nothing that disabled either orc. As in the fight with Captain Morbid, Nutty was marked worse early in the engagement. Blood ran from several deep cuts; he was losing.

Nutty was in the worst struggle of his life to this point. Killa was virtually unmarked. He was unbelievably adept with a blade and always seemed to have good balance as he never over swung. He didn't lunge carelessly, he defended well, he was smart, quick, and he fought well; too well, in fact. He was nearly equal in size to Nutty, but his musculature was better developed.

The realization of how quickly the orcs were fighting was beginning to register in Nutty's brain. This was a furiously violent, yet stunningly beautiful display of speed and agility. Nutty nearly matched everything Killa threw at him. But nearly wasn't enough. There was so little time to think. Things were happening too fast to formulate a plan. One lapse could mean instant death and Nutty knew it.

Nutty stumbled ever so slightly as he stepped backward over the dead orc he had killed. He partially blocked a drive from Killa that caught him in the face. That was too close! The fact that a twenty-inch blade cut into the side of his mouth and touched his tongue within was a little more than awakening. He was damn lucky, and he knew it. He didn't feel pain as spit drooled out of the hole and mixed with blood running down his face. He had to be more careful as he avoided Killa and stepped over things.

Then, this occurred to Nutty, he wasn't fighting completely defensive, but pretty close to it. He couldn't muster much of an attack against Killa. Each time he tried, Killa was the one who inflicted damage on him. He had to do something. He was never going to save Uhra like this. He was being carved up, little by little. He had to take the offensive, if even just once. He decided to choose his timing wisely, and quickly worked his feet to get into position.

A flurry of measured swings came from Killa. He was self-assured as he drove Nutty in a circle, his knife just one swing away from dropping this annoying kid. He didn't measure his own footwork as he confidently moved forward over the dead orc. Once both feet were across the body, Nutty took the offensive.

It was a calculated risk that worked. This time, Killa stumbled back and Nutty's blade found its way into his opponent's throat. Nutty continued to fight without giving time to wait for the outcome of his well-executed attack. A dozen or so more thrusts in several seconds left Killa dead on his feet. Nutty survived; somehow, he survived.

Within ten minutes, Nutty was patched up and ready to move again. He didn't care to guess how much blood he had lost. He wasn't all that dizzy from the loss of blood or the blows to his head. He had taken his own knife back from Killa, giving him two close combat weapons.

Before Nutty made his way down to the building, he surveyed his surroundings and noticed movement across the other side of the valley on the hill above. He ducked down behind a few large rocks to avoid being seen. It was fairly dark by now and this gave him great cover. However, it also made it hard for him to make out what was moving.

As his eyes adjusted, Nutty saw an orc wave to another orc on the third lookout point. Both orcs gave thumbs up to each other. Then, they turned toward Nutty and waved. Nutty wasn't sure what to do. He didn't want to give himself away, so he took another calculated risk by standing up and waving back. Like they had just done, he gave a thumb's up. This seemed to satisfy the others as they must have assumed that he was one of their sentry counterparts.

Nutty went to the sentry to his right, under the cover of darkness and foliage. Having the upper hand, he eliminated this potential problem without incident. He was quiet and unseen, approaching from behind the threatening guard. The unsuspecting orc never knew what hit him.

Nutty quickly made his way around the ridge to the last orc on the hill. Like the last obstacle, this orc was bashed in the back of the head and disarmed. A quick choke hold left the orc struggling for air. Without it, the orc was forced into unconsciousness. The process was just as quick and quiet as the one before. Now, Nutty could make his way down to the valley.

As the range between Nutty and the building shrank, he became keenly aware of several things. First, it was now beginning to rain. At first, the wind began to howl through the trees; then, it started to drizzle. Lightning flashed every so often and soon, became more frequent.

The second thing that he noticed was what he smelled. He was downwind from the little building that he was approaching. He picked up the strong scent of several males. It was hard to determine how many. Their scents were mixed with heating oil for the lamps that were burning inside. His hair stood up when he smelled the faint scent of Uhra. His body's natural reaction to her smell, mixed with the males, was uncontrollable. He snarled as his heart pumped faster. His testosterone was accelerated through his body as his lungs forced oxygen to his brain. His senses, heightened by chemical enhancement and loads of adrenaline, were thrown into overdrive.

As Nutty came to the building's front door, the sound of thunder echoed throughout the valley. The lightning show was amazing. The rain was so heavy that it couldn't be perceived as such, the deluge sent water from the sky in massive quantities. Nutty was oblivious to the scale of the thunderstorm. He didn't care. However, it did provide him with cover as he came to the front door.

Sounds from inside the building were now audible. There was laughter and crude sexual jokes coming from the males. "Kill da bitch," was said, followed by Uhra screaming.

Nutty burst through the front door of the cabin. The door flung open and partially swung back, now hanging crooked from the top hinge. Nutty slowly put his right hand around the knob and finished removing the door from his way by pulling it off the last hinge and throwing the whole door behind him.

He didn't wait to plan out his entrance; he reacted to what he heard and smelled. What he saw was even worse! Male orcs were everywhere. Nutty's brain subconsciously registered their number and locations in the room. His eyes came upon a sight that he wished he had never seen. But this sight registered, and how! Uhra was dangling from the rafters with her feet a yard from the floor. She was naked and completely vulnerable. Her arms were bound and hung from the rafters while her feet were tied to bolts in the floor. Her extremities were tied in such a way that they formed the letter X, exposing every inch of her. Her young womanhood was at eye level for her taunting predators to humiliate her. Two orcs were holding lit cigars. Uhra had small burns in the shapes of circles all over her belly.

"Jailbitch," the biker to the far-right corner of the room addressed Nutty. He said it instinctively, without even turning around. He smiled a devilish smile and began to turn around. He started to say, "Do you lika my new gurlfriend?" But his sentence was cut short at "gurl" when he caught a glimpse of Nutty.

Lightning silhouetted Nutty's hulking body in the doorway. His bared teeth and deadly eyes shined against the dark, menacing night. Flashes of lightning and the constant sound of thunder perfectly encapsulated the anger that was welling inside him. He was wet and already injured.

As he took a step inside the building, he wasn't an orc. He was a monster! At that very moment, he may have been more dangerous than the hellacious storm wreaking havoc outside.

The room fell silent. Several orcs closest to Nutty wearily backed away from him. They could smell danger. One pulled a knife from a holster; another slowly armed himself with a gun. All thirteen orcs grabbed some sort of weapon. They looked around at each other, trying to figure out who was going to make the first move. That was figured out for them when Nutty saw that Uhra's legs were visibly broken. Her left leg had a compound fracture. The bone was sticking out of the flesh through the side of her calf.

Uhra cried out, "Oh, Younut!"

Nutty's head turned upward toward the ceiling. He roared an ungodly sound and flexed his muscles as his arms reached upward. His scream of madness enlarged his neck. His chest and shoulders popped. Deep cut crevasses between his bulging muscles accented his physique. The veins in his arms were close to explosion just beneath his skin as his muscles tightened to near breaking point.

Nutty sprang forward. His imposing image shocked most of the orcs in the room and certainly the ones closest to him. In an instant, he grabbed one orc by the head and threw him into another just behind. One was immediately killed while the other crumpled to the floor and started to convulse.

The reaction of the orcs was slow. They weren't fully prepared for what they saw. They were stunned and then, awed by Nutty's feats of strength and agility. Within a few seconds, several more were dead or injured enough that they posed no threat. But Nutty's initial progress wouldn't go unchecked.

Several bullets found their way into Nutty's belly before his teeth found the face of his next victim. His blade cut into the heart of this orc that tried to stop him with a gun. His same blade was a little late to stop another orc from firing his gun as well. Nutty stumbled as his legs were hit. Fortunately for Nutty, he closed the gap in enough time to prevent any further harm. Two other orcs weren't so lucky. They were killed by their own kind as fear gripped their comrades, sending errant bullets into them at close range.

Nutty dropped to the ground as a long blade was shoved beneath his armpit and into his ribcage. He swung his knife around and caught the orc that just landed a potentially fatal blow. The orc fell backward and looked down at his wound. He was slashed across his chest. It hurt like hell, but not enough to stop him. He was back on Nutty quickly.

At the same time, a large orc with a mechanical claw instead of a hand smashed Nutty across the face. The blades from the claw cut deep across and down through Nutty's forehead, eye, and left cheekbone. Nutty threw himself to his back. He kicked out with both feet and shattered the orc's knees. The orc fell to the floor in pain. This gave Nutty barely enough time to roll out of the way of the other orc.

Nutty grabbed the other orc's foot and dragged him to the ground. The two fought for position, each trying to outmaneuver the other. Nutty was stronger, even with his injuries. His anger helped his body to not feel as much pain as compared to when he was completely calm. The struggle became a grappling contest that Nutty eventually won. He clamped his legs around the orc's throat and eventually choked him out.

The time that it took to do this caused two things to happen. First, the biker shot into Nutty's right arm once and into his chest once. Secondly, the orc with the claw crawled over between Nutty and the biker. This shielded Nutty from anymore gunfire, but the Claws were ripping his left leg apart. Nutty kicked wildly this time, just trying to get the orc away from him. He landed strong kicks to the orc's face and upper body.

By this time, two more orcs entered the building. They were more guards that heard the commotion. One jumped on Nutty and bit down on his nose while Nutty flailed at the orc with the claw. The other ran in front of the biker to protect him.

Nutty grabbed the orc that was biting him by the jaw with one hand. Nutty's other hand forced its way into the orcs mouth. Nutty fought feverishly to pry the orc's mouth away from his own nose. The pain in Nutty's face was supplanted by that of his hand as the orc bit down. Nutty was absolutely uncontrollable at this point. He got to his feet and lifted the attached orc high above the ground, prying with his hands as hard as he could.

Uhra screamed when she saw what happened next. As afraid of the Wivvaflow orcs as she was, she never, not in a million years, expected to see what her eyes were telling her. She witnessed Nutty, the orc whom she loved, brutally kill the way that he did. Nutty held the orc's bottom jaw with one hand and roared. He pulled so hard with the other hand that he ripped the orc's head in half from top to bottom. The orc dropped and shook.

Nutty was on top of the other guard that just entered the room in a heartbeat. The guard shot into Nutty again and again as Nutty beat him to death with his sidekick's skull.

The biker and one other orc made their way out the back door as quickly as they could. They weren't willing to trade their lives for Nutty's. They scurried away, praying that they wouldn't have to face that monstrosity again. The biker cursed all the way home. The other orc would later spread the word about what he had seen.

Nutty stumbled over to Uhra. He was limping heavily to one side. If not for the fact that he was an orc, he probably wouldn't have been able to walk at all. He picked up a knife and cut her legs free. Her own pain was dwarfed by her concern for his wellbeing. She bit her lip and began to examine him. As he attempted to free her hands, Uhra could see how badly hurt Nutty was. He was riddled with bullet holes and deep bleeding cuts. The deep gashes in his face caused her to cringe. She couldn't see his left eye and thought it might be gone.

As she was cut loose, she cried out, "Oh, Younut! I wuvs you! You comes fo' me." She saw the long knife that was still implanted in Nutty's side as his hands were above his head. She was sickened by this. He came to save her, and in so doing, may have cost him his own life. This wound was bad. It pumped blood in spurts that matched his heartbeat. She wasn't aware of his broken vertebrae, and organs that were pierced by bullets. Being an orc or not, he had taken a deadly beating. She wrapped her arms around him and deeply kissed his mouth.

She proceeded with licking his facial wounds and softly kissing his head and neck as he dressed her and carried her all the way back to the river. In retrospect, the fact that they made it was remarkable. Most of the trip was quiet as the night meant less traffic and better cover. But they were both dazed and confused during much of the trek.

Covering fire from the Big Town side of the river gave them their final protection. Nutty waded through the chest deep water with help from some of his troops. His troops were in awe of his appearance. They pulled Uhra from his arms and he reluctantly let her go. He knew there was a real possibility that he might never see her again.

Nutty gently rubbed his hand across her face and whispered, "I wuvs you, too."

Ten
One Must Know One's Self

By any standards, Nuttybomb was in bad shape. His wounds were severe, but for some unknown reason he survived, despite the docs marveling as to how. His punctured lung and sliced heart should have killed him. His fractured skull and massive swelling to his brain certainly could have if the other two didn't. Yet, here he was in the old builder school back room, clinging to life. He had been unconscious for two days and was finally waking up.

As he stirred and wearily opened an eye, he saw a doc tending to his chest wound. He fought to wake up and forced his other eye open the best that he could. As he fully regained consciousness, he became aware of the intense pain that raked every square inch of his being. He heard wailing, and then, in an instant, realized that he was making the terrible noises that pierced his ears. He clamped down on his top lip with his jaw to conceal his crying out. His arms and legs were strapped to the table and were no help in his plight to massage the excruciating fire that was him.

Several docs rushed to Nutty and began covering his face with wet rags that smelled of some sweet chemical. They appeared panicked as they raced to induce him back into slumber. Nutty looked around wildly as if he was being attacked. The last thing he saw before he slipped back into unconsciousness was his own beating heart, palpitating in his open chest.

***

Nutty was walking in a cave, or more precisely, a tunnel. It had unfinished walls like a cave, but it seemed to go on and on like a tunnel. Either way, it was vaguely familiar. He only needed to hear laughter and to look over at Booma's goofy face to remember what he was doing.

He and Booma had made their way into the tunnel just on the Wivvaflow side of the river. They were forbidden to cross the river like they did, but the danger of being caught by Momma or Dad made it even more intriguing. They hadn't been caught before and figured that this day would be like any other.

Along the way, they were forced to step over areas of dank, smelly water. There were numerous spots where it ran down from the ceiling's abundance of vents and pipes. Nutty figured that these were pipes that drained down to where he was walking. He was correct. The tunnel was indeed a cave that served as a natural sewage conduit that carried waste to the river. As it turned out, it was a good thing that he stayed away from the putrid water.

After walking for a half hour, they arrived at a spot they had come to a dozen times before. And like those times before, Booma climbed up a rough incline and poked his head out of a small hole to see if the coast was clear. Once he did, he watched things that Nutty couldn't see. As usual, Nutty's impatience was loud enough to prompt a "shush" from Booma with an accompanying bop on the head. After this happened several times, Booma inevitably gave way to his nuisance of a little brother. It was better to give the pest some time, rather than get caught.

Nutty poked his head through the vacant hole left by Booma. First, he saw tall block walls that were topped with rows of razor wire to his left. They were run down and dirty, probably just there to keep things out...or in. This wasn't at all what Nutty had come to see. In fact, he just wanted to make sure that a prison guard didn't see him. Once he realized that he wasn't seen, he focused on what Booma had been fixated with.

His eyes found the naked female orcs that lined the street just ahead of him. He watched as they accepted money from large males and then walked around the corner. This was usually accompanied by moaning sounds and thumping that occurred rhythmically. Nutty wasn't sure why and he really didn't care. All he cared about was seeing the females carelessly flaunt their green skin all over the place.

Nutty wasn't accustomed to seeing naked females flaunting their unclothed bodies around in his town. He was taught not to even glimpse his sisters as they were washing or changing their clothes. For whatever reason, Nutty and Booma needed to travel to see such things. These became recurrent adventures for the boys.

More often than not, his sightseeing was cut short by another quick glimpse by Booma and the desperate race home so the two wouldn't get in trouble. This was a secret that the two kept with each other for years. At this time, they didn't know how instrumental these exploits would turn out to be years later.

***

Nutty's eyes opened. He had been dreaming. While he was still hazy, he thought about the cave that he and Booma used to travel together into the heart of

Wivvaflow. How many others used that same route? How many other kids used to do the same thing? Did the Wivvaflow kids use the same way to travel to Big Town? *Probably not,* he thought. The path would only bring Wivvaflow kids to the edge of the river on their town's side. Nutty couldn't see much benefit to them using it.

Then, Nutty wondered if any prisoners ever escaped through the tunnel. He thought that it would be an excellent escape route. From Wivvaflow, it led right to the river. That would be perfect for an escaped convict to get away.

Nutty was starting to awake fully. His mind was still fighting with the dreamy state he was coming out of though. He was wondering what types of prisoners were within those tall, dilapidated Wivvaflow walls. He had heard that they were prisoners from other cities; soldiers that were captured. If that was true, then maybe he could free them. Adult male veterans to boost his ranks would be more than helpful, especially against the ones that captured them. He started to devise a plan until he grasped the situation.

He was still in the back room of the school. Docs were dressing the injured and performing some small procedures. He was no longer strapped to the table where the docs had been working on him. With his arms free, he waved to a doc. "Doc," he said weakly and softly.

The doc dropped everything and came over to Nutty. "You doin' goods. Big hurts on you, but you strong."

"Ok. How is Uhra?"

The doc was cautious not to say things out of order. He first stated, "She goods." He gathered his thoughts before he finished, "Almost a have a cut her leg off. But I use metal and screws. She goods now."

Nutty sighed a deep, exhaled breath of relief that drew blood into his mouth. He choked a bit and coughed some brown and red mucus from his healing lung.

The doctor was quick to implore with his boss to be careful. "You lung is hurt a bad! Don't a breathe to deeps. Lil breathe only. Ok?" Then, the doc took a slight step backward. He hoped that he didn't come off as telling Nutty what to do. He didn't want to die for his mistake.

But, Nutty in his humble way, thanked the doctor for his concerns and all the help he had given to Uhra as well. He asked the doctor if he could find a Runna or to call on Booma himself. The doctor obliged.

Booma wasn't far away. He was summoned from just around the corner where he had been working on some of Nutty's responsibilities. He, like the officers under Nutty, took it upon himself to do the best he could until Nutty got better. As soon as he heard that Nutty was awake and doing well, he raced to his little brother's side.

"Heya, Nutty." Booma smiled wide.

Nutty was glad to see his oldest brother. Hell, he was glad to see anyone at all. He wasn't sure how he had even made it back to Big Town the night he rescued Uhra. He was a little unclear about everything that transpired since that day. He got some details from Booma before asking, "How tings been 'round here?"

"Goods, Nutty. Glad your goods, too," Booma replied.

"Tanks, Booma," Nutty said. He continued, "Looka like I gonna be healin' fo' a longa time here."

"Yeah, I guess. Hey, I gots dose books 'bout Grim. Dems come from da north while you wuz bein' fixed."

Nutty was temporarily pleased. Reading would give him something to do while he recovered. He could formulate plans, talk with his officers and Runnas, and a bunch of stuff throughout the day, but he would still be stuck in this damn bed. Yes, reading would be welcomed.

After discussing some basic ideas with Booma about using the tunnel in Wivvaflow as access to and from the prison, Nutty was able to iron out most of the details necessary for a mission to succeed. He discussed it with Booma and asked him to run the plan by the other officers to see what their input might be or to see what they felt they would need to complete another ambitious mission. Booma agreed with Nutty's ideas and soon left his weary brother to fall asleep. Nutty tried to read for a while, but he began to drift into unconnected thoughts. He stretched, yawned, and finally...slept.

***

Nearly a week later, Nutty woke up. He was in less pain than the last time he opened his eyes. He felt a little stronger and was eager to get back to his duties. He made sure that Uhra and the rest of Big Town were doing okay by questioning his doctors. Actually, except for Uhra, his closest family and friends visited him now that he was stable. Uhra still couldn't be moved because of her injuries and he missed her. There was still no word on Biggabomb or his unit.

Nutty struggled to get comfortable as he lied in bed. His massive headache and gallons of medicines made him nauseous. Knowing that Uhra was alright helped him get past his discomfort though. He wanted to make good use of his time as he recovered, so he decided to read the books about Grim that had finally arrived.

He was intrigued by the books as he studied them. They were leather bound, laced in decorative gold, and worn by age. They were obviously crafted with great care and saved. But why? Who exactly was this Grim? There were stories that he was a great leader. Conversely, there were others that depicted him as an old, insane hermit. The bindings and covers on the books were ornate. Surely, this Grim must have been something special to write stuff that would last hundreds of years. It's not like orcs read much. If the writings weren't special, they wouldn't have lasted so long. They probably would have been burned or maybe the pages would have been used to wipe an ass or something like that.

Nutty began to thumb through one of the books. It took him some time to figure out what he was trying to read. The writings were in old tongue and mixed with symbols. He began putting some together and found patterns throughout the pages. By doing this, he determined what specific combinations meant. He was able to decipher more easily as he dug into the content, one page at a time. He had no idea that he was one of only a few orcs in the world who could do this. He still wasn't aware of the things that he was capable of.

He found certain areas of interest and read those first. He flipped from page to page, and then back, as he was mesmerized by the quality of thought behind the words.

One area of interest read:

Occasionally, maybe once in ten thousand years, forces come together that impact changes far beyond the scope of normalcy or relative expectancy. Furthermore, these changes typically impact masses on a greater scale than ever experienced previously. Whether by genetic mutation, chance, or any other causes, actions are set into motion that are unequivocally unique in their magnitude. More often than not, these forces are initiated by exceptional individuals in response to species threatening events, and further fueled by the convergence of additional individuals with distinct abilities or intelligence in an attempt to stave off disaster. The locations of these convergences become hotbeds for scientific, political, or social advancements, further feeding the cyclical frenzy of unique individuals that lend their skill sets to the mix and complete the final pieces necessary to enact these forces and continue the cycle of advancement.

Why this happens is a bit of a mystery. However, history dictates that there is usually a trigger that begins the process. This may be a war, or perhaps, a natural disaster. The result is the need to change in order to survive. In most cases, species adapt over periods of time in a race to mutate before extinction of their kind. Some races, however, have the ability to reason, or they may have technologies to deal with their problems. Regardless, if the problems are so great that a species can't fix them, or if they don't have the ability to physically mutate, then they are likely to perish.

If there is no trigger, and sometimes that is also the case, the rarity of random mutation is greater than the previously mentioned millennium. In this case, I believe that a change in genetic code is so rare, that it happens perhaps once in fifty-thousand years. Yet, this does happen and individuals that shape the world with abilities beyond any of their fellow species are far more gifted and precious than the entire species that evolves to survive. The chances of extremely gifted individuals coming together at the same time are astronomically low.

But I have seen an individual who will be of such quality that the world will never be the same. While I have the gift of controlling energy through spells, this one will control millions through multiple abilities.

The world and the star will bend at his will and the other worlds will join him. Like Da Rampage before, the race will go out into the abyss, and make life better for his kind. Those that resist will be swallowed by his glory; those that follow will bask in his greatness.

Nutty looked through the pages in an attempt to find Da Rampage. His eyes followed a maze of images that his mind was unfolding. While searching, he came across another area of interest. There were simple proverbs that he was able to figure out. Some were:

One must know one's self before knowing one's enemy,
Death is but life's disguise,
Wishing is for fools,
He, who walks on water, never gets his feet wet.

Nutty pondered the thoughts of the information he had just read. He understood most of it upon first glance, but still found it difficult to concentrate. He continued on, wanting more. As he skimmed and discarded whole sections of the current book, he decided to search for specific information. He wanted answers to his and his species' existence. He wanted to learn about empires and rulers. Mostly, he was extremely curious about the things Grim had to say. This was a drastic departure from radio building that was taught in builder school and Nutty loved it.

He went from book to book, trying to take in as much information that his orc brain would allow. He settled on a thin book with torn and tattered pages. It was just as ornately covered as the others, but more beaten over time. Its dark pages and antiquated appearance made it even more appealing to Nutty than the other books. There was just something fascinating about it.

It was here that he found out about past rulers and other worlds. What he had learned about other worlds' orcs being born out of cocoons was a topic covered briefly. In fact, the small amount that was covered, referred to it being the norm. The orcs of Nutty's world were the exception. But why? Why was he born of his mother, unlike orcs from other worlds? How was it even possible that the same species could reproduce so differently? Also, why were orcs different in size from planet to planet? Although discussed, it still didn't answer the question.

Nutty read on and soon discovered that it did address the fact that the original orcs on a distant world reached out into this part of the galaxy. They conquered many worlds under the great leader, Da Rampage. Legend claims that he seized control of his local area on a planet named Fangus. Before long, he conquered the whole world and moved on to other worlds. He was said to have great powers and be a giant among his followers. It had been said that the orcs on Hotta became his direct descendants. Other planets were colonized by his followers. This would explain two things. One is where the orcs of Hotta came from. The other is why the orcs of Hotta are generally larger than those of the Invadas. It made sense to Nutty.

Nutty couldn't continue to read anymore. He was exhausted and needed sleep. His body was distressed to the point that its recovery was dependent upon the unusual amounts of rest that it required to heal itself. He eventually dozed, but not before taking some notes and referring them to Booma. He requested Booma to find the Book of Render. A great king is said to have faced Grim for control of Hotta. Nutty needed to know what happened. He was addicted to the mere thought of learning about these fabled, yet obscure characters.

Nutty would have to read more at a later time. He carefully rubbed his repaired eyes, stretched his arms without overdoing, and pushed out his legs while curling his toes. He was able to breathe more deeply than just a week ago, so he did and mustered a fairly healthy yawn.

To his surprise, the most beautiful thing he had ever seen arrived. Uhra clumsily made her way to visit him. Against the doc's orders, she got up on her feet and threatened him until he allowed her to see Nutty. It was common knowledge now that she and Nutty were an item. The doc was caught between her safety and her ability to sic Nutty on him. He chose the first rather than the latter to satisfy her.

She was in long, resin casts from her toes to her thighs. Her wrists were wrapped in white linen, as was her stomach. Her broad smile and bright eyes brought an unmatched happiness to Nutty. He fought to keep his undamaged eye open and easily smiled in return. They were both lucky to be here.

Nutty had so many things that he wanted to say. He wanted to know that she wasn't sexually violated. Realistically, he hoped against hope that she wasn't. Unfortunately, he was so exhausted, he could only muster, "Hi, Baby."

Uhra bit her lip in her usual, now profoundly sexual way, and simply greeted Nutty with, "Younut."

She leaned against the wall and held his hand as he drifted off to sleep. She knew they would talk. He gave so much to save her. She knew how he felt. She was happy just to be near him and his prognosis was good. She was secure in knowing that their prognosis as a couple was even better.

***

Nutty was doing much better. He was stitched up virtually everywhere. Most stitches had been removed, but some wounds needed several surgeries to repair. Skin graphs and internal tissue work kept some stitching fresher than others. Bullets that shattered bones and ripped tissue were removed several weeks before. He still had drainage tubes that kept fluid away from his lungs and heart. These were now hooked to a portable machine that he wore in a backpack. This set up allowed him to move as freely as his beaten body would let him. His one eye was still closed, and he was going to be permanently scarred across his face. The most important thing was that his heart and lungs were strong. He had no further signs of internal bleeding and showed no signs of brain damage. His massive headaches were a thing of the past too. By all accounts, it was a miracle that he lived. The fact that he was leading this mission...well...that was something of a legend.

Seventy of Nutty's kids were accompanied by twenty veterans that were healing before returning to the Eastern Continent. The veterans weren't needed as soon as was earlier expected because Biggabomb and the Wasp Legion had stalled the advances of the Invadas there, leaving them more time before needing to return to battle. In fact, the landings of Invadas on the Western Continent where they now resided also slowed as a result.

Nutty thought things through before sending his troops to their tasks. They were at the end of the tunnel, just below the prison. It was still unprotected where they stood. So far, so good. However, this was very near to the Wivvaflow Army base. There were twelve hundred vicious, vengeful orcs up there just waiting for the opportunity to kill Big Town militia, so Nutty needed this to work like clockwork. He checked and then double-checked the times that he had previously calculated. He confirmed orders with his officers. Then, the word was given.

This time, Quicklip and Nubbs made their way in the early morning, along and then, beyond the external borders of the prison. They scurried along a ravine until they came to the outskirts of the Wivvaflow Army base. Several well-placed shoulder mounted missiles at key locations cut the enemy's ability to regroup and counterattack. The first two, fired simultaneously, took out the main gate and communications hub. The next two, fired fifteen seconds later, left one fuel tank erupting and a series of small munitions boxes scattering bullets into everything within a quarter of a mile. This started more fires and explosions.

The prison became overrun by Big Town troops in the next few seconds. They took out the eastern towers with rockets and entered the courtyard by blowing out parts of the eastern wall. Veterans moved in to fight hand to hand while the kids supported them with suppressing fire.

In ten minutes, inmates on the main level were freed. They were briefly told about the situation and their commitment was questioned. They were given weapons and their knowledge of the prison was used to gain access to other levels within its walls. Ten minutes later, the second and third levels were freed.

By this time, Wivvaflow orcs were banding together in small groups and trying to defend their land from the Big Town Army. Fortunately, they weren't much of a match for Nutty and his army. They were held off for the remaining seven minutes until the last prisoners were released from their cells. On the western side, where Quicklip and Nubbs had come from, Wivvaflow troops that weren't on the base were now approaching.

Even though all prison guards had been subdued and the Wivvaflow citizens were held at bay, the actual Army posed a very serious threat. Quicklip estimated two hundred plus Wivvaflow troops and he reported the number to Nutty. Seventy kids and twenty veterans wouldn't do well against these well-trained killers. But, the additional six hundred Gravestone and Da Bend convicts, now armed to the hilt, offered resistance that overwhelmed the approaching troops.

Nutty's forces, now close to seven hundred, made their way through the tunnel. They detonated the opening by the prison. Smoke bombs hid their escape as six hundred and ninety well-armed troops simply disappeared. Wivvaflow was once again left dazed and confused.

There was no quibbling between Quicklip and Thunda. Nubbs wasn't drunk. The prisoners worked together for one common cause. In all, there were no casualties on the Big Town side. Another one hundred and eight Wivvaflow deaths and sixty more wounded were counted. It was a totally one-sided victory.

When Nutty and his orcs made it to the river, they crossed without taking any more fire. The Wivvaflow army, which was regrouping when smoke hid Nutty's escape, searched above ground for the rest of the morning. It never occurred to anyone that an underground escape was underway. Orcs could be so stupid sometimes.

To outsiders, Nutty and his ragtag team of kids were busy and effective. It was a testament to Nutty's leadership and the resolve of his followers. They were doing things that established armies struggled with.

To this point, Nutty was responsible for seven war-related deaths and sixteen significantly-wounded casualties to Big Town troops. He was also accountable by default for the eleven accident-related deaths and nineteen injured at home.

To his credit were the dozens of bikes and crucial equipment that he took from Wivvaflow, six hundred prisoners of war, and nearly one thousand, five hundred dead Wivvaflow troops and citizens. Another eight hundred and thirty-seven were reported wounded.

Word was beginning to spread about these unprecedented numbers and this leader of orcs.

Eleven
The Legend Comes Out

As impressive as the one-sided battles were going, Big Town civilians were not happy about their women and children being hurt and killed because of the apparent lack of sense from their appointed leader, Nuttybomb. It still seemed that a war with Wivvaflow was ill-timed, considering the eminent threat of attack from the Invadas coming from other planets. Gun fire across the river from Wivvaflow found a Big Town orc every day now. Unfortunately, when a seven-year-old boy was killed, this day was the day that the citizens of Big Town couldn't tolerate one more senseless loss of their own.

Nutty awoke to find a smoke-filled room. Dark brown paper, which covered the windows, was engulfed in flame. Red chaos danced upward, throwing cinders and hot ash, igniting the rug and furniture. The fire shot up the walls and ran along the ceilings. In a matter of seconds, the room was extremely hot and not breathable.

The door opened with a loud crash that could be heard for several blocks from the outside. From Nutty's point of view, the sound was muffled by the thick particles and smoke, as well as the noise of crackling flames that were devouring his surroundings. Nubbs burst in. His face was a pleasant surprise to Nutty, who was to his feet and heading toward the door at this point.

Nutty had been sleeping in the back room of Guthrak's machine shop. The shop was close enough to the school, which was currently set up as a hospital. This made getting back and forth a short trip. Also, it was at the corner of the Crossroads, the major junction between Wivvaflow to the west and homes to the east. The mines were to the south and the road out of town to Gravestone was to the north. It was as convenient a place as any for Nutty to catch some shut-eye and dash out to any location quickly; it was centrally located.

Nubbs stumbled into the burning room and fell to the floor. Nutty made his way toward Nubbs through the fire which was hot enough to ignite the flammable blanket that hung across the room and separated the two. Nutty pulled the blanket down in a hurry. The heat was more than he thought he could stand. He couldn't breathe, his eyes burned, and his nose ran. He gasped for air as he bent down to grab Nubbs.

Nubbs was unconscious. This was peculiar to Nutty. He thought that surely, he would have succumbed to the smoke and heat before Nubbs. Nubbs just entered the room and fell down. Nutty was in the room for a longer amount of time.

Then, something occurred to Nutty. The dim light which shined through the open doorway, was just bright enough for Nutty to see blood on the back of Nubbs' head. Nubbs wasn't stricken by the effects of the fire; he had a wound before he came in. Nutty grabbed Nubbs by the arm and dragged him toward the door. The two were traversing through a raging fire now.

Nutty's arm was ablaze! More accurately, the sleeve and wrappings on his wounded arm were. Nutty slung Nubbs through the doorway to the outside. He immediately followed, well aware that there were bodies moving about as he left the shop. His senses were sharpened by the adrenaline and endorphins that kicked in as his body automatically prepared him for the peril that was cast upon him.

He ducked a barrage of stones and hazardous objects that were hurled at him by his own civilians. His keen senses and quick reflexes saved his face more than once as he knelt down to shade Nubbs from the hail of debris. Nutty reached behind him and felt for the door that he had just exited. Upon finding it, he yanked hard, and swung around to his front. This was just the shield he needed until he could figure out exactly what was happening and how to handle it.

Nutty extinguished the flames on his arm. He was surprised that he didn't feel any pain. Maybe he was lucky, and the fire didn't reach his skin. Coming through the doorway and shielding Nubbs took a few seconds. Yes, he was lucky, indeed. He cautiously peeked around the side of the door to see what he could, all the while, objects pounded the shield that he held for protection. Occasionally, a rock or a piece of iron pipe would bounce off the wall behind him and ricochet into his or Nubbs' back. It was more of a nuisance than anything else as these objects really didn't cause too much harm.

Nutty quickly surmised what was going on. There were several buildings on fire and vehicles were overturned in the streets. The debris that was coming down upon him was being thrown by his own town's orcs. This was a good, old-fashioned riot. He just needed to know why and how to stop it.

The door that was being held was leaned against a piece of pipe so that the two supported each other.

Nutty braced them to keep Nubbs protected while he readied himself to leave the comfort of the protection he was enjoying. He picked a target, a rather large male adult with an obvious leg wound. He recognized the orc as a parent he knew through an old schoolmate. Nutty sprang upon him without hesitation and wrapped his hands around the older male's throat. The male, a trained soldier, fought back.

Now, even as stupid as orcs were, they stopped pelting Nutty with rocks. They weren't so quick to harm the parent with whom they'd sided. Instead, a few of them froze, not sure what to do next. Sometimes, it took a little time for an orc to see something, think about what to do, and then have his or her body react. That was the case here. At any rate, a few precious seconds went by as Nutty and the parent squared off.

The parent fought to free his choked airway by pulling his arms up between Nutty's and loosening the grip around his throat. With one move, he did so and landed a pretty good right hand to Nutty's throat. Nutty, already a little short of breath from the smoke, found himself gasping more as the strike to his own airway left him in a bit of a predicament.

Still, Nutty found a way, as Nutty usually did these days, to make something out of nothing. The parent's drive forward to Nutty's throat caused him to reach forward. Nutty grabbed the parent's arm as it passed him, stepped forward himself, and swung him around. This gave Nutty his opponent's back. Nutty's other arm worked around the parent's neck, again choking him of the vital oxygen that he needed.

By this time, the other orcs had figured out what they were going to do. Some dropped their crude weapons and ran away, but some didn't. They advanced on Nutty in a hurry. Now preparing for close combat, a few took knives from holsters while others picked up sticks and pipes. In all, there were six armed veterans intending to make Nutty pay for the deaths of their children. They worked their way around him, without saying anything to each other.

Nutty stepped back against a wall with the parent struggling in his grip. He braced himself against the wall and released one of his hands. His other arm was still around his opponent's neck, bolstered by leverage from the wall. He unholstered his knife and brought it to the parent's throat. Nutty tried to talk, but his ability to communicate was hindered by smoke inhalation, heat, and the shot he just took to his throat.

Nubbs came up behind one of the orcs that had surrounded Nutty. He kicked behind the orc's knee, sending the unaware recipient to the ground. He pulled his gun and knocked another to the ground before the poor orc knew what hit him. The third orc that Nubbs engaged was looking down the barrel of a Big Town Army issue blasta before he had time to respond. Nubbs smiled as he pulled a flask from his pocket, opened the cap with one hand, and took a swig of alcohol. Without missing a beat, he teased, "Nutty, wanna kill dems?"

Nutty took time as he cleared his throat. He saw some of his troops rounding up other offenders down the street. His confidence grew. He didn't have to rush a weakened voice to give a response. Besides, waiting to talk gave the impression of mystery, and possibly, danger. He could be perceived as thinking about whether or not he would kill these guys, or he might have been pondering how he would do it. He gulped a hard swallow and found that his throat was feeling better. He cleared his throat again, ensuring that he had a strong sound before he spoke. When he finally did, he questioned the parent he was holding with a booming voice of authority, "Why you riot lika dis?"

The parent had a hard time getting sound out of his closed trachea. Nutty loosened his grip to allow the orc's response. The parent gulped like Nutty did, cleared his throat, and replied, "You killa my boy!"

Although Nutty was responsible, he didn't think that he killed anyone. He had put orcs in certain places at certain times to accomplish tasks. Random events, accidents, or gunfire from across the river were the real causes of death. "I kill no boys here. We fightin' da war."

"Yeah, a stupid war wit' Wivvaflow. Da real enemy is da Invadas. But our a kids dyin's cause a you makin's war wit' dems!"

Nutty understood the parent's frustration, albeit a little misplaced. Nutty actually thought he might feel and act the same way if the roles were reversed; maybe. He didn't think that he would set buildings on fire. He might go after the orc that he felt was responsible. He thought again. He would definitely go after the orc that was responsible. Nutty tried to coax the parent with kind words. "I knowed you kid. I lika him. Anda you good fighta. But dis is wrong. Wivvaflow was to attacks us. We found outs. We hit dem da day before dems attacks us."

"But, you not lose a you kid. You lose a mine."

Nutty empathized. "I know. I sorry. I lose brudder, friend, and my dad is missin'. Not a kid, I know. But, I lose my mum's kid. War a bad ting." Nutty released the parent.

Nubbs held out his flask as an offering of peace to the parent. "Have some. We still gots a war wit' Invadas comin' soon. It comin' if we want it or no."

Nutty added, "And you seed war is bad on Eastern Continent. We needs to fight togetha. I will pull you kids and wife from fight and da mines until Invadas come. Dat ok? Anda you stay wit' family until Invadas come here. You don't have to go back to Eastern Continent. Let it be knowed dat anyone who losed a kid or wife, don't have to work or fight until Invadas come. Spread da word."

The parent and the others were held until it was confirmed that there were no fatalities caused by the riot. The loss of some buildings and vehicles were irrelevant when it came to getting everyone on the same page. Nutty knew that he would miss the production of those he relieved from their duties, but he also knew that it was crucial to keep peace within his borders.

***

Later that evening, Nutty spoke to the tense crowd outside of the school. First, he addressed the town's losses. He paid tribute to the deceased, consoled those that lost loved ones, and thanked those that were wounded. He was sincere and charismatic. The crowd softened a bit.

Next, Nutty talked about the invasion from Wivvaflow that was going to happen. He explained why Big Town attacked her before she could bring her prepared troops a preemptive attack. He stressed the fact that war with a neighbor wasn't what he wanted, nor was it a war that he chose. He simply chose how he and his troops would fight to ensure the best chance of winning.

He let the crowd know about the loss of his brother, Gardawg, and the sacrifice he made. He did the same when it came to Kor. Gardawg, Kor, and others would be honored every year on the same date. It would be called "Heroes' Day". Their names would be written into history books that future generations would read.

Along the way, he emphasized Big Town's recent successes, accentuating his own wins against two top Wivvaflow officers. He boasted about the number of terrorists he beat with his bare hands while saving Uhra. Although it wasn't in his nature to boast, he whipped the crowd into a frenzy; their taste for victory was insatiable. He fed their appetite with as much as he could. The result was thunderous applause from Big Town citizens and his troops.

After several minutes of cheers and "Nutty" chants, he updated everyone about the stalemate on the Eastern Continent. He cursed the Invadas for their savagery and suggested that the stalemate was probably only temporary. He urged everyone to do their part to win against these evil, unwelcomed heathens. Furthermore, he swore that he would lead them to unconditional victory against the bastards and promised to free any orcs from their grip.

Then, he laid out his plan to form alliances with other orcs on the continent. In fact, he discussed meeting with King Basha the next day. He stressed the importance of freeing their troops from the Wivvaflow prison and adding them to his ranks. Not only had he hurt the enemy, but he showed good will to potential allies, and if nothing else, boosted his number of troops.

Finally, Nutty did something that was unprecedented in the history of orcs on his world; he referenced Grim, telling the crowd they were direct descendants of Da Rampage, one of the greatest orcs in the history of all orcs everywhere. He went on to indicate that they were special, and as such, were called upon to save their world from destruction. This inferred divine intervention, made victory not only seem possible, but sounded like a sure thing to the impressionable orcs that were awed by his words.

Nutty had outdone himself. The way in which he galvanized the population was even more impressive than his first speech. Hours of chanting and jubilation carried on deep into the night. The earlier day's events were a blip on the radar compared to the impending conflict that hung over his head. But at least one disaster was averted.

***

A slight mist burned off as the early sun, hot and determined, worked its way above the horizon. An orange sky to the east took over the dark blue blanket before it, distant stars fading amidst the gold speckled clouds that changed color and shape as the sun rose. The navy-blue sky to the west gave way to a lighter blue and green hue with white and gray clouds hanging like wool from the tail of a hyperdeer.

The humid air left morning due on the grass and on the leaves of plants. Light danced across the surfaces of the foliage as a slight breeze playfully nudged the greenery, sparkling as it did so in the same gold and orange, mirroring the beautiful sky.

Even at this early hour, Big Town bustled. Orcs came and went, eager to perform their required tasks. Trucks poured through the streets with machine parts, equipment, ores, and medical supplies. Things were loaded and offloaded with pats on the back and cheers for victory. Often, Big Town orcs recounted the speech from the night before and chose certain phrases as rallying cries. They urged each other on, joking as they passed each other on the dusty sidewalks.

Nutty was pleased with what he saw through the large double doors of the machine shop. He was working in the front room at dawn when the colorful sky illuminated the effects of his speech. As he saw orcs moving about, he smiled to himself. Thankfully, the fire hadn't affected anything here in the front room and this vantage point of the Crossroads was advantageous. However, the room wasn't his first choice for the meeting that was to occur.

After the fires were put out the evening before, troops immediately went to the task of rebuilding. The back room in which Nutty slept was no exception. However, it couldn't be finished in one night. This left Nutty upset because the room was damaged and not ready for King Basha's visit. *Oh well*, he thought. He would just have to make the best of it.

Nutty moved some tools and set up an oil lamp for better interior lighting. While he moved a workbench, he thought about how things changed over the last few months. It was this very room that he cowered in front of Guthrak. It was worse when he cowered to Gunza here, too. That was the time his pee was out. He urinated all over himself, Gunza, and everything nearby. He still cringed when he thought about it.

He thought about Uhra and how she licked his face, causing his phallus to reveal itself that time. He remembered the humiliation, but mostly, he remembered her eyes. He didn't understand her sexy, devilish look at the time, complete with curled lip. Although she was afraid of her father, she still took time to look at Nutty's surprise and smile at him. He thought about how intrigued she looked. Maybe she was amused. She was something else.

Then, Nutty wondered how he appeared when he saw her naked. There was nothing playful or sexy about that. He was abhorred by the brutality in which she was treated; abhorred and enraged. His poor little Uhra was alone, bound and naked for those bastards to abuse her. She was powerless to do anything as they tortured her. Not knowing if she was raped haunted his thoughts. He didn't want to bring it up; didn't even want to know.

Even if she was violated, she was still perfect to him. He just didn't want her to relive the shame of what happened. It didn't matter to him if her legs were in casts and she had burns on her stomach. He began to think about her smooth, soft green skin on her tightly muscled abdomen. Her small, oval belly button seemed to point downward to her pee. He had seen it! Well, sort of. The day he saved her was still a bit of a blur. He was curious if and when he might see it again.

As he thought about her physical features, he felt a little funny. *Oh boy*, he thought as he realized he was aroused. His large frame and heavy clothes couldn't hide the change that had just occurred. Nutty found it hard to walk as he strangled between his left leg and trousers. He tried to force Uhra out of his mind and he painfully made his way toward the workbench that he had relocated. He hoped to hide behind it until he regained his composure and hid his big problem.

No sooner did he turn away from the front doors than he heard Quicklip address him. "Nutty?"

Nutty reached down to rub his knee as he appeared to limp away to the workbench. He wanted to give the indication that his strange gait was due to an unrelated injury. There was no way in hell he would reveal something like this, especially to a big mouth like Quicklip. When he reached his destination, he carefully sat and turned in obvious discomfort. "What is it, Quick?"

If the limp belonged to Thunda, Quicklip would have been saying something about an object being stuck in his butt, or maybe that he was trying to hide an erection. Actually, a veritable plethora of insults came to mind. However, even Quicklip knew to keep his mouth shut at times. He simply said, "Umm, King Basha a here now."

Nutty continued to hide this situation from Quicklip. He needed some time to return to normal, so he could meet Basha with a standing handshake. "Imagine that," Nutty mumbled. He thought about the humiliation of being a little kid with his pee out in this same room. Now, the damned thing was acting the same way, only Nutty was meeting a king.

Quicklip puzzled, "Imagine what?"

Nutty nervously chuckled. "Oh, nuttin'. Please tella King Basha I be ready fo him in lika five minutes.

202

Dens come back and stand at da door. I gots papers to go ova first."

"Yessa," Quicklip replied. He turned and went to inform King Basha. He was back at the door thirty seconds later. He turned and stood at attention next to one of the guards that Nutty had posted there. He waited for Nutty to announce that he was ready to see Basha.

Nutty whistled as he made believe that he was writing things down. He shuffled some papers. He flipped through the pages of a book, then he flipped through the pages of another. For a full seventeen minutes and more, he distracted himself until he could stand without showing any visible signs that he exuded from thinking about Uhra. He called for King Basha and walked around toward the front doors.

Quicklip returned and announced the presence of King Basha. Basha came into view. He lumbered into the machine shop where Nutty greeted him.

"Welcome to Big Town, King Basha," Nutty joyfully exclaimed. He introduced himself and extended his right hand for a handshake.

"Tanks." Basha's eyes left Nutty's, followed his extended hand, and then came back to meet his eyes. Basha obliged with a hard handshake. His large hands matched the size of Nutty's. He squeezed with the might of an ox, and satisfied with Nutty's resilience to pain, smiled. He loosened his grip. "You a big kid, Nuttybomb. You lika you dad now."

Nutty, although aware of Basha's tight grip, was more attuned to his eyes and appearance. His eyes were bright and attentive. The way that they scanned Nutty and the room gave some indication of intelligence. The king wasn't just a bruiser. He was evaluating his surroundings. Nutty thought he remembered a story about Biggabomb and Basha. He didn't remember the whole story; just that they were friendly toward each other. Nutty responded, "Well, Dad say dat he lika and respect you. Dat's 'nuff fo' me. Anda if I anyting lika him, I be ok."

"Dat you will. Dat you will, Nuttybomb."

Nutty escorted Basha over to the workbench. He pulled up a chair for Basha and apologized for the conditions under which they were meeting. He explained what had happened in Wivvaflow and that he was using the machine shop because of its location. Basha understood. He also heard enough of what Nutty told him to confirm rumors about Nutty's victories. Basha was more than impressed.

"Nuttybomb, I talked wit' Mojo fro' Da Bend. He say he join me to fight. I say I fight if I fight fo' you. Nobody nevva beat Wivvaflow. Dems bastids puts our orcs in prison. We be nevva strong 'nuff to fight alone. Now, I tink you already kinda beat dems."

"King Basha, I no beat dems, yet. I justa stop dems and make war hard fo' dems to fight here. Dem still gots a army."

King Basha cut in, "No. No. Der army is fallin' part. Dem all leavin's now. Der leader, Fokra runned away anda hides when you killed Morbid anda Killa."

"You sure?" Nutty quizzed.

"Yeah. Dems can only comes through us or Da Bend or desert to west. I sure 'bout it. We see dems leave."

Nutty put his chin in his right hand as he thought for a moment. He did like the idea of having help to defeat Wivvaflow. Also, with Wivvaflow out of the way, Nutty could concentrate on the much bigger enemy. Wivvaflow was just a town, whereas the Invadas had whole planets to draw troops, weapons, and supplies from.

Nutty had some questions that he needed answered before he could commit. He first asked, "When can you fight?"

Basha bragged, "Anytime. We ready."

"Ok. When can we meet Mojo?"

"Oh. Couple days, maybe."

Nutty stated, "You talk wit' Mojo." Then, he asked, "Den, we all meet at you place in three days?"

Basha liked what he heard. He hated Wivvaflow. Their constant raids cost his city resources every time they attacked. There were the lives lost, too, not to mention the rumors of future attacks and other Clans looking down their noses at Gravestone. "Yes, three days."

"King Basha, now I ask you most important question. I ask you to be permanent part of army. We be one nation. Dat be four cities dat always fight together under my flag. You still control you army when we fight." Nutty had been thinking of the distinct possibility that Biggabomb might never return. Without unified forces and strong commitments, Hotta was doomed. Nutty was accepting that he might have to step up in a greater role much earlier than he ever would have imagined.

Basha laughed. "Really? I beed king fo' thirty years. You name been all over da continent fo' last two weeks. Maybe you should fight unda me."

"King Basha, I no wanna offend you. You great king, but you prisoners dat I freed already wanna fight fo' me. My army now as big as you and Da Bend put together."

"No wanna offend, kid? Dose are my orcs!" Basha exclaimed.

"Really? Dems wanna know why you nevva save dems. Dems can live wit' you, but dems fight fo' me when I call." Nutty wasn't sure if he was doing the right thing. Bullying a king probably wasn't the smartest thing he could be doing. He was trying so hard to appear arrogant and cocksure. He thought about this for weeks though. What he didn't know was how much Basha respected him. Basha had regarded Morbid and Killa as unbeatable. Nutty had beaten them both. Without being privy to Basha's thoughts, Nutty decided to be a bit more diplomatic to get Basha to commit. He continued, "We all be under da chief anyway, right? When Biggabomb come back, he be in charge. We be stronger together."

Basha wasn't completely buying into the plan. On the other hand, he wasn't discounting it, either. To call himself king was one thing; defending his city from the likes of Wivvaflow was something completely different. He decided to buy some time, so he could think. He engaged Nutty politely, "I take time to tink 'bout it, k?"

Nutty wasn't going to be less persuasive than he had been so far. He had a knack for knowing when to go for the throat. He sugarcoated his ultimatum with a meal as cover for his takeover. He humbly offered, "King Basha, please you stay fo' some food we gets you and you tink 'bout it. Der not time to wait anda decide. We too busy here in Big Town."

Nutty pointed out the large doorway where Basha could clearly see production moving at a staggering speed. The dizzying pace of it was something that Basha had never seen in his thirty years as king. Not many in any place at any time had for that matter. To Basha, the Crossroads looked like a large-scale ant farm with every inhabitant eagerly pitching in. But these were orcs. How was this possible? To Nutty, it looked like friends wrapped in determination, blanketed in joy, dipped in comradery, and consumed by pride with one unified goal. Nutty took Basha by the arm and led him to Quicklip where a proper meal was ordered. He thanked the baffled king and sent him on his way.

***

What appeared to be an opposing army was heading north on the road out of Wivvaflow. Nutty looked through a scope to count its numbers and troop types. He estimated it to be five hundred or so strong with, maybe, fifty vehicles.

Nutty's forces were heading south from Gravestone on the same road. They spread out into the fields on both sides of the road to maximize their potential fire power. Nutty, although in charge of the whole army, kept his eight hundred troops as the main force in the middle. He and his massive bike squadron were centered with infantry in trucks behind and to his sides.

To Nutty's far right was King Basha and his three hundred warriors. They were comprised of infantry units, used as support around a core of light propkoptas. Basha's orcs grunted in unison with each step they took toward Wivvaflow's demise. There was nothing as sweet as revenge and they were going to have theirs. Nutty soon found that the prisoners he had freed were also grunting along with their Gravestone brothers. They were unified in their cause.

Nutty saw Mojo's forces to his far left. They consisted of a mix of the ugliest vehicles that could be imagined. They brandished huge guns and patches of armor that were placed haphazardly wherever it would fit. Almost as impressive as the size of the guns was the disgraceful noise that belched out of the vehicles' exhaust systems and rattled within their frames. If Mojo's forces were grunting, chanting, or singing, they weren't audible above the sounds of his clanging, burping mechanical beasts. A small number of infantry walked among the sixty vehicles.

In all, Nutty had nearly fourteen hundred orcs and over two hundred vehicles at his disposal. This more than doubled the Wivvaflow forces that were coming toward him. He was thankful that King Basha finally accepted his proposal days before. He was also happy that Mojo came aboard as well.

Nutty raised his right hand and his army became silent; engines ceased to rev; all forward movement stopped. He waited for the Wivvaflow forces to close the distance, so he could unleash his full-frontal assault upon their narrow columns.

To Nutty's immediate rear, Booma's voice gave the order, "Den hup." A slow, methodical beat was formed by part of the infantry under his command. The bottoms of their weapons were struck against the ground. The volume increased as other troops joined in. Within thirty seconds, the whole army was stomping and grunting in time with the infantry. Still slow and rhythmic, the resonance was like the heartbeat of a sagecat lurking in the high brush, waiting for its victim.

The victim came within the distance that Nutty had decided to launch his attack at. But, as soon as it did, it raised a white flag. Then, it raised another. The vehicles that were approaching shut off their engines. Orcs from Wivvaflow began to lay their weapons on the ground and place their hands on their heads.

A lone Wivvaflow orc walked north on the road as he left his troops behind him. Nutty and his guards drove two hundred feet on their bikes. They dismounted and met the stranger.

The stranger said, "I be Devil froms Wivvaflow. We surrendas to you to be part a you army. We wanna follows Nuttybomb." Then, he took a step backward and bowed his head to Nutty.

Nutty walked up to Devil. He asked, "Are you in charge a Wivvaflow?"

"Yessa," Devil respectfully replied.

"What 'bout Fokra?"

Devil didn't want to give up anything he knew about his old leader. Fokra had never done him any harm. Still, the coward did leave his town to be conquered by Nutty. Devil reluctantly admitted, "Him leaves us and go to da Invadas. He a hope to joins dem to killa you. Anda dis ting too. Da biker dat had you gurl went wit' him. Dem are tellin' all secrets 'bout you and Big Town, so you gets destroyed."

Nutty wasn't sure what this meant. Was Devil telling the truth? Orcs didn't surrender, nor did they easily turn on their commanders unless there was something in it for them. Additionally, did Fokra and Jailbitch really think they would be spared from the brutality of the Invadas? What were the odds? After thinking for a minute and still being unsure as to why Devil was surrendering, Nutty questioned him. "Why you not fight us? Not normal to surrender. Many orc tink it is act of coward."

"No, not act of coward. We no really surrender. We join you, if you let us. We wanna fight fo' da great Nuttybomb."

Nutty turned his head slightly and raised one eyebrow. "Why you tink I'm great?"

"Cuz you killed Morbid anda Killa, anda all dose orcs. You blowed up town. Den, you broke prison. Anda you disappeared lika magic or sumptin'. You da greatest evva! Can we fight fo' you?"

Nutty's head was spinning. Did he just take Wivvaflow without firing a shot? Did he just add five hundred more troops to his army? Didn't this give him four cities and the largest army for hundreds of miles in each direction? He answered himself, "Yes, yes, and yes." Then, he answered Devil, "Yes."

***

Over the next few days, Nutty's troops took control of, and policed Wivvaflow. The town's army was absorbed into his and split up between his troops in an attempt to stave off an uprising. Many troops were actually used as manpower for production until they were needed to fight against the Invadas. Others rebuilt structures that were damaged or destroyed in the first attacks on Wivvaflow.

Nutty was amassing notes on everything that had transpired since he became Big Town Army Controla. He had hundreds of pages that he began to organize. Some pages were simple scribbling and crude drawings, others were detailed accounts of battle. Everything from inventory and production to ideas about reworking orc language were being outlined. He did this around his normal duties and reading, which he made sure to do daily. He was inspired by the books about Grim. He read as much as he could find time to do so. He was eager to catalog things as Grim had done. He might never achieve such greatness, but he wished to apply what he was quickly learning.

Twelve
The Future

Seconds seemed like minutes; minutes like hours. This cold, alien place was like the inside of a metal coffin, but it was bigger; much bigger. The room he was left in to rot wasn't, however. It was barely big enough to stand up in, not that he could do that easily. It wasn't difficult to stretch his arms out to touch each wall from the center of where he sat. Footsteps could be heard beyond the rusted steel walls that ran with scum, blood, and insects. They seemed to come from miles away and pass within a few meters, only to fade into an equally distant destination.

Biggabomb surmised that he was in a detention cell. But where? He felt a constant vibration that his body picked up through the floor. He thought that he may have been in a machine. Maybe he was inside the belly of a big boat. Or maybe the vibration was nothing more than a cooling unit next to his cell. No, it was a ship, alright. He deciphered the sound of feet on metal decking from the time they began until they ended. At least, his ears still worked.

Even his tough Orc body shuddered from the cold, trying to aid his weary mind to survive between the shivers from the fever that gripped him. A loss of his arm and burns to his skin, air passages, and lungs didn't help any; he was a wreck. He remembered the smoke that was probably a chemical of some sort. That may have been the source of his burns, maybe not. That's not why his stomach ached, though; he was hungry as hell. His survival instincts kicked in and he quickly began eating anything that moved within his reach.

His mind searched for answers. He reflected on the events that led to his capture. Surely, he could remember something that would help him to determine his location. He tried and tried, but in the end, he only thought of Muga, standing at his favorite chair. He saw her eyes, he tasted her boar cakes. By Gods, they were awful! Biggabomb smirked as he thought of a wisecrack to throw at her. She was so damned cute when she got angry. In that instant, he missed her and all her ways. He needed to protect her. He had to find a way to escape and get back to her.

He couldn't fathom what things back home were like; he didn't know how long he was away. Where was his army? Did his guards survive? Did he have any real chance of stopping the Invadas, even if he escaped? Was Nutty alive? Was Big Town still on the map? He ate as fast as he could, invigorated by his thoughts and new protein diet. But he was a mere shadow of himself. Getting out was going to take some doing.

He lied on the cold floor and thought of what to do. Lack of strength canceled out overpowering his foes. Careful planning and critical, split-second decisions would be necessary in his plan. He went right to work on his mission to escape, occasionally grabbing a critter or two as they wandered too close to avoid being devoured.

***

Nutty finished writing a message when a Runna showed up as expected. Nutty addressed his underling, "Hi, Friend. What is you name?"

213

The Runna looked stunned. He glanced behind himself, fully expecting an officer to be there, but there was no other orc to be found. His brow furrowed, and his eyes squinted as he looked around the room. He scratched his head and then put his chin between his thumb and fingers while he gazed aimlessly. It never occurred to him that Nutty was speaking to him.

Nutty smiled. "You gonna just look around or you gonna tell me you name?"

The Runna appeared befuddled; he looked around again. Why couldn't he see the orc Nuttybomb was talking to? This didn't make any sense. His malfunctioning brain was wired backward. This was perfectly normal for an orc. Sometimes, things had to be spelled out.

Then, something occurred to Nutty. Here was the epitome of the orc race standing before him, totally dumbfounded and unable to share his identity. The poor bastard didn't even know that he was being addressed. How was Nutty going to teach the masses an upgraded language when most of them weren't too far removed from this guy's thought process?

Nutty sighed a big puff of warm air from his bellowed cheeks, through his teeth, and passed the Runna. After watching retardation in full swing for a couple of minutes, Nutty decided to try a different approach. "Are you da Runna?"

The Runna perked up and stood at attention in full military form for his leader and no sooner blurted out, "Yessa."

Nutty found what he saw to be very interesting. He was somewhat entertained by the sudden change in the Runna's stance from a goofy mutt to an obedient soldier. Furthermore, Nutty's sense of amusement turned to admiration for a creature that had the ability to snap into rank after such a display of stupidity. For an instant, Nutty marveled at the accomplishments of his race. They had somehow become the dominant species, not just on his own world, but many throughout the galaxy. He swelled with pride.

"What is a you name, Runna?" Nutty asked.

"My name be Bump, Chief."

Nutty toyed with the Runna to bring out his full abilities. "BumpChief?"

Pause. Think. Pause. "No Chief, justa Bump."

"Ah, I see. Well, Bump, I have dese very important messages to givs to different leadas. You tink you can delivva dems?"

Bump replied, "Yessa."

Nutty asked, "You a sure? 'Cause only the bestest Runnas can works fo' me."

"Yessa, Chief. I is da bestest of all da orcs," boasted Bump.

"Awesome, Bump. Makes me proud."

Bump tipped his head up with pride. With his shoulders back and chest pushed out, he exclaimed, "Yessa!"

Nutty had just sent an idiot with plans to defeat the Invadas. He had already sent his most trusted Runna, Bigeye, with the first set of plans. But, there was nothing like redundancy, especially over the last few days. Invadas had begun to scout the area, searching for weaknesses to exploit. Orcs within a couple hundred miles had begun to go missing. These Runnas were traveling routes through these now vulnerable areas. Bump was simply insurance. Odds were that one of the Runnas would succeed.

Nutty walked outside and gazed at the beautiful building that was being erected. Opposite his location at the four corners was a fury of troop action. Only they weren't fighting, they were building. A library was going up, Da Grand Libury, to be exact. It would hold every book that Nutty could get his hands on. It would be a place to extract and share information.

The more impressive the building would be, the better the chance of other orcs learning, too. A monumental structure would give rise to curiosity. Orcs by nature were tinkerers. Nutty was betting that an ornate structure that housed books about vehicles, weapons, and war would establish the library as the impetus for learning; it had to. He wanted to eradicate the possibility of ever sending idiots to handle such important matters ever again.

Nutty's less idiotic friend walked over to him. Nutty smiled at Quicklip and asked, "How are tings?"

Quicklip rolled his eyes and smiled. He tugged at his trousers and began, "Well, first a all I hate dese new zippra tings. I keeps getting my pee stuck in 'em."

Nutty laughed and shook his head. Quicklip had a way. Nutty wasn't even sure if Quick was trying to be funny. He said such silly things at times.

Quicklip continued without missing a beat, "But goods. Food supplies more dan we can keep. Usin' extra buildin's to store dems. Da mines producing good, too. Anda since you not sendin' soldias back to East Continent, we got planes and weapons be builded again."

Nutty saw that Quicklip was still rubbing his trousers. "Ok, you can stops rubbin' you pee now."

"What, anda stop all da fun? Dis da most fun I have all day," Quicklip kidded.

"I bet," Nutty stated with a smile.

Nubbs strolled over to join in on the apparent fun. He took a flask from his pocket, and immediately, put it to his mouth.

Quicklip jeered, "You gonna share or what?"

Nubbs slowly lowered his drink and looked at Quicklip, who was still busy. "As long as you don't."

Quicklip taunted Nubbs with, "Try its. You might like its."

Nubbs wasn't amused. "You a hands clean? I know where dems been."

Quicklip ensured that they were with a firm nod of his head and a stout, "Yes!" Just as he gained possession of the flask and put it to his lips, he gleefully teased, "Clean 'nuff." With a mighty swig, he filled his mouth. Unfortunately, he made eye contact with Nubbs. He ended up spitting out half of his drink in the form of a geyser from the onset of overwhelming laughter.

Nubbs grabbed the flask from Quicklip. His face was soaked, and his temper was beginning to get the better of him. "You a nasty ass!"

Nutty changed the subject, "'Nuff, you two. Anda Eastern Continent? Quicklip, anyting on Biggabomb?"

Quicklip stopped rubbing and laughing. The seriousness of the question struck him. "No, Nutty. Nuttin' on you dad. But hims da best. He somewhere, I knows it."

***

Biggabomb tore his tattered shirt into strips. He used his mouth to hold one end while he pulled the fabric with his right hand. Then, he winced as he wrapped his shoulder with the pieces that he just made. He smelled his wound to check for infection. Thankfully, he didn't find the aroma to be like rotten milk. He knew all too well about the cheesy smell of infection that may have claimed as many lives on battlefields as the wounds themselves.

Most of his bleeding had stopped now. He had dark clots that had already scabbed over and began to fall off. He figured that he was probably injured a week or two ago, maybe more. He had eaten pretty well, all things considered, and was now bandaged up. After several minutes, he was satisfied with his medical work and lied on the floor. He readied himself for what was next. He didn't have to wait long.

The door to his cell opened and an orc peered inside. Confident that Biggabomb was sufficiently wounded, and still sleeping, he entered. As he reached for the feeding dish near Biggabomb's right foot, he was smashed across the cheek with Biggabomb's right fist. The orc didn't even know that he was struck at first. Before he could shake the cobwebs from his struggling brain, a second blow felled him.

Soon, Biggabomb found himself wearing the orc's clothes. If he couldn't fight his way out, he would have to use his smarts. *If only these Invadas were a little bigger*, crossed his mind. After popping a few buttons, he gave up and tucked his shirt into his trousers. He bound and gagged the orc and cautiously made his way out of the cell. Once again, orcs being orcs meant that the cell door was left open.

Something that didn't occur to Biggabomb, but was essential in his trying to integrate into the Invadas' personnel, was the fact that there was no language barrier. With hundreds, or maybe thousands, of years and millions of miles separating the two worlds, their languages were still very similar. Simple sentences and grunts were acceptable communication anyway. Biggabomb could nod if necessary.

The corridor was long and narrow. It was painted in an ugly pale green, similar to the color of orcs that died from the fever. Like the cell, it was made of steel. Conduit and plumbing lines ran its full length. It was lined on both sides by doors that matched the one on Biggabomb's cell. Girders and bulkheads could be seen for quite a distance. This ship was big, very big. He squinted as his eyes adjusting from his dimly-lit cell.

Biggabomb began his long trek down the corridor. He stopped at the first door and slowly opened it with the key he had taken from the guard. He steadied his weak legs and ordered the prisoner in the dark cell to turn around and walk backward to the doorway.

The prisoner asked, "Or what, Chief? You gonna shoot?"

Biggabomb instantly recognized the voice. "Gunza."

"It about time you get me out," Gunza half-joked.

Biggabomb entered Gunza's cell and leaned the door closed behind him. "Hey, we gettin' out. I bigga den you. Change clothes. I looka stupid. You be da guard. Sides, I weaka den a whore on a busy Friday night."

Gunza began to undress without hesitation. "Good, I getta use da gun, too."

"You see any mo' of us? I donta 'memba much," Biggabomb admitted.

"It bad, Chief. I hear da Invadas talkin' when we captured. Maybe half our army live. Da Wasp Legion held Invadas off fo' a while, but no. Hads to disband. East Continent a lost."

"Den, we a betta moves fast. Here, I put dis chain on my arm. You walk me lika I prisoner."

Gunza stated, "Already ahead a you, Chief."

The two friends entered the corridor and continued the task of searching and freeing their own. They confused two more guards and subdued them before freeing twenty more orcs. Two of those orcs were Guthrak and Nukklez. Along with the group, they covered more ground, freeing more Homeworlders and subduing more Invadas.

Just then, a gunfight ensued. Biggabomb and his orcs found themselves pinned down in the narrow corridor. They found themselves scrambling to take cover behind the rows of bulkheads that looked like ribs within the beast of this ship. Bullets were randomly hitting them as they ducked and dodged. Most of them were still feeling the effects of gas and wounds they had taken in battle; only a few had guns. It was time to fight or die trying.

***

Big Town was getting busier by the day. An influx of orcs from areas to the west, were showing up in droves. They told of the Invadas splitting them up and forcing them to fight or die. Reports of females being raped, while their males watched weren't uncommon. Children were taken and forced into labor. Those that

220

survived and made it this far were beleaguered for sure. They needed something to lift their spirits.

On this day, Nutty was greeted with more than eleven thousand refugees. Additionally, three thousand troops from the Eastern Continent found their way to Big Town, hoping to regroup. He quickly realized that the situation was critical. There were becoming too many mouths to feed. Plus, the newcomers were lost; they were down and out.

Locals were ordered to take in as many displaced orcs as possible. They dipped into their winter stashes and helped as best they could, assisted in aiding the wounded, providing lumber by cutting down trees and making bricks, and building simple shacks on the outskirts of town.

Skilled labor was sorted out from the twenty-six thousand orcs that had inundated the area over the last two weeks. They provided a boost to local production of weapons, vehicles, farming, and mining. Nine thousand were added to the army as well, giving Nutty the largest fighting force on the continent.

Late in the afternoon, after Nutty sorted out the best way to help and make use of everyone, he finally made his way down the street to the old builder school. The street was covered in bloody cloth and some odd body parts. Tending to the number of wounded and injured with so few docs left little time for cleanup.

Nutty wearily walked through the front doors and found wounded everywhere. Docs were performing amputations in front of other patients that were waiting for the same help. Some orcs growled as they anticipated experiencing the same pain forced upon their desperate comrades. Others placed bets as to how far the saw would cut into bone of the current, unlucky bastard before he screamed.

Females stitched gashes, wiped blood and dirt from the faces of the wounded or rushed back and forth with supplies. Screams echoed throughout the hallways. The sounds of saws and subsequent screams riddled the ward. A doc removed a limb in thirty seconds and removed somebody else's within another minute. Females followed docs everywhere.

The hurried sentiment in the room gave Nutty pause. He guessed how dire the situation was and wondered how long it would be before his orcs couldn't fight any longer. Would their numbers become so depleted that they wouldn't be able to attend to the wounded? At what point would they be defeated? Would it be a definitive moment, or would it be a gradual process? Attrition was more likely, he thought.

Nutty was interrupted by a soft voice that he knew very well. Only she could say his name like she did. Even as her voice sounded tired and sick from all she had seen, from all she had endured today, and from all that she tried to mask, it was a wonderful sound. "Younut."

"Uhra", he said with quiet enthusiasm. When he saw that her eyes were red and watery, his tone was a bit more apologetic. "You ok?"

Uhra put her body close to his and her lip began to quiver. "When dis all gonna end, Nutty?"

Nutty wanted to cry inside. No, he wanted to kill inside. He wanted to do whatever he had to do to ease Uhra's pain. All he could do was put his arms around her and escort her out of the bloody mess that was her world, so that's what he did.

"Wait", Uhra urged as she pulled away for a brief moment. "You eat yet?

Nutty looked in disgust. "Nope, not alla day."

"K, one sec." Uhra went into the back room and returned with a bowl. Then, the two started to walk to Nutty's house. Unlike days of old, they didn't joke; there was no kicking rocks down the road. By in large, they were quiet. Neither could, nor would, express the horrors they witnessed in war. Besides, they were orcs; they were tough and mean, at least on the outside.

Things didn't feel like they did just months before. They didn't feel playful. Each thought was about their jobs and what they needed to do to make things better. Hopefully, they could make things like they were. But somehow, they seemed different; jaded. The perceived reality was that things could never be the same.

Still, they moved forward, literally and figuratively. Uhra placed her hand within Nutty's. She was delighted to feel his fingers slide through hers, forming a bond that seemed stronger than the physical connection that it was. She was elated to see him smile, and he to see her in return.

After Nutty was interrupted several times to give orders to subordinates and receive updates, they arrived at his house. Uhra kicked her shoes off and grabbed some forks that hung on the back wall above the fireplace. Nutty started a fire below and the two sank into the dirt floor as comfortably as they could.

They made small talk about different things while the fire grew. As Uhra began to cook their meal in a grimy, old kettle, the conversation became more personal. They talked about loved ones. Uhra finally gave her condolences over Gardawg. She realized how fast time was going, even when the days dragged through the horrors of bloodshed.

Nutty quietly thanked her and fumbled through some odd sentences that didn't make much sense. He said, "Ok. Ya, tanks. Umm…sumptimes it happens. Lika da cabin where you wuz. You know? It a happens." Nutty looked confused as he searched Uhra's heart by seeing it through her eyes.

At first, she was busy pouring their food into bowls. Her distraction was only momentary, however, and she struggled to understand him. "What? Cabins happens?"

Nutty sighed. "No, not cabins. It do happens. Umm, at da cabin. You know?"

Uhra smiled a little as she puzzled over his words. "Younut! What a happens at da cabins?"

Nutty was visibly sweating now. His nervousness showed all over his stricken face. He fumbled for the words that eluded him. "No, Uhra. It. You know…It!!!

Uhra looked down and her eyes darted back and forth. Her face tensed as she tried to think of the thing that would cause Nutty to be so nervous that he sweated and made no sense. Then, it came to her. Her face flushed as she thought of "stuffin", a term used for the act of causing natural reproduction.

Uhra looked up and her eyes eventually met Nutty's. Now, she had a hard time with words. "What da hell?" she mumbled as she decided that one of them needed to get to the bottom of this. She nervously began, "Nutty? Umm…" Then, she paused before

224

forcing out the question, "Do you wants to do stuffin in da cabin wit' me?"

Nutty choked on his food. "What? No! Umm, yes. Wait, what?"

Uhra was getting the impression that somehow, she missed the mark here. She was humiliated. "I mean, no. I not a askin' to. Oh, I say it wrong." Her head violently shook in an undeniably "never!" motion. She tried again with, "I, I umm...I mean, are you askin' me?"

"No way!"

"No way?" Uhra was actually a little insulted. She thought she was probably more "stuffable" than most, as far as looks went, anyway. She had never stuffed before and she didn't know why boys might choose one girl over another to stuff. She hoped that she was pretty enough for Nutty to want to stuff her, not that she would admit it. It would be nice to know that he wasn't repulsed by her.

"Uhra, dis hard." Nutty was all mixed up. He was trying to ask if Uhra was violated the night that he saved her. Not only was it hard to ask before all the confusion, but now he had to address whether he wanted to stuff her or not.

"It hard?"

Nutty exclaimed, "Yes!" until he noticed her look down at his crotch. "I mean, no!"

Uhra was saying and doing one stupid thing after another. Her heart was pounding, and she felt short of breath. She wasn't helping things. She sighed and deflected, "You weird, Nutty." Although she felt better for a second, she realized that she may have insulted him. He was having a hard time getting his words out.

That's what he meant. She gathered herself and pried, "Nutty, it ok. What you really askin'?"

Nutty was rubbing his forehead in frustration. To ask or not to ask? To stuff or not to stuff? To clarify his original question or to justify his long-term intentions? He was all mixed up. Then, he looked into Uhra's eyes. She showed such compassion and understanding. He found the strength to ask the question that might humiliate her. He didn't want to, but he felt that he needed to know as if it was him that was violated. So, he asked, "Da night I get you from Wivvaflow...did dems do bad to you? I know dems did bad lika break you legs. But did dems do real bad tings? You know."

It finally made sense to Uhra now. "Oh, dat."

The door flung open and Nubbs busted in. "Chief, come quick!"

Nutty jumped up and followed Nubbs outside.

A hundred thousand orcs filled Big Town. There was so much commotion that Nutty couldn't get an answer from anyone as to what was happening. Several orcs just said, "We here to fight."

Nutty and Nubbs made their way down the street. They climbed into a truck and made their way west. The road was completely blocked by the mass of green beyond the Crossroads. They turned north and drove through a chanting crowd for the next forty-five minutes.

They finally disembarked just beyond the chaos and were met by several leaders. Just as Nutty was to sort things out, a shockwave was heard from above. They all turned to see a flash of light in the sky that was closing on them fast. It turned to the west and swung around. It appeared to be a ship, and a big one at that.

***

Biggabomb's orcs were in trouble. Not only were they being shot to pieces, but if they didn't move fast, other Invadas would come to aid their comrades. Biggabomb yelled to Gunza who was nearest to him, "Dis not good!"

They both turned to Nukklez when they saw him take a bullet. The shot ricocheted off his grenade and into his throat. The bullet lodged itself somewhere in the back of his neck, leaving a hole that spurted blood in time with his heartbeat. Worse was the fact that the grenade, which was securely strapped to his vest, was armed as soon as the bullet dislocated the pin.

Nukklez gasped, "Gods, dammit. Nukklez gotta do dis." He stood up, made eye contact with his friends one last, quick time, and ran down the corridor, screaming bloody murder, into the ranks that had shot him. His screams were cut short by a flash of light and discharge of smoke and debris. In an instant, bullets stopped flying and silence was heard.

The group got to their feet and began the process of reorganizing. Not much was said. It wasn't discussed that more should have been said before the explosion. Such was the way in war. An orc could be here one moment and then, gone the next. They all knew that their lives were lengthened because his was cut short. They carried on all the same.

Upon reaching the bridge, they were fifty-three in number. They easily took control of the ship and crew before them. Forty-five of Biggabomb's orcs backtracked to aid in securing the rest of the vessel.

The remaining troops took up positions throughout the bridge. Meanwhile, skirmishes continued within the bowels of the ship over the next fifteen minutes. In all, three hundred and eight orcs were freed.

Biggabomb was quick to assess the situation. The bridge was filled with controls and lights. He looked passed the few remaining crew members that his orcs held and saw an enormous window to the outside, encased by a display of beeping lights and monitors. Beyond that was traffic, not traffic like cars and beat up trucks. Nor was it traffic like battle vehicles he was accustomed to seeing on an almost daily basis. This was traffic on an almost unimaginable scale. There were thousands of ships dotting the star filled backdrop; ships of all sizes.

He started to count them all, but gave up as he walked closer to the window. He could see his home world of Hotta off to the right. A myriad of ships seemed to form imaginary lines as they moved to and from the planet. Figuring out each ship's purpose and function was impossible.

Biggabomb pointed to a crew member. "You, what is dat big ship ting in da middle?"

The crew member growled in defiance.

"No?"

One of Biggabomb's orcs brought the orc to Biggabomb and forced him to his knees.

Biggabomb seemed calm, but his tone was stern. "The ship in da middle?"

The crew member leaned forward and spat in Biggabomb's face.

Biggabomb was unphased. He looked into the crew member's eyes. "You a honor to you Chief and you world." With that, he pulled a gun that he had taken from a guard earlier and blew the crew member's brains out the back of his head.

Biggabomb turned to another crew member and asked pleasantly, "Do you know what da big ship is?"

He put his gun away and approached the crew member as he waited for a response. This orc growled much like the first. Biggabomb smiled and said, "You even bigga honor." After allowing what he felt was an adequate amount of time, he continued, "The ship?" But he was met with silence. Once again, he pulled his gun and planted the brains of the defiant crew member onto the face of the crew member behind him.

Guthrak giggled. "Chief, der ain't gonna be nobody to fly dis a ship." He scratched an itchy hand on the blade that protruded from his face. Then he smiled at the crew member that was wearing gray matter. He flicked the blade with his finger, making an audible ping and giggled some more.

The crew member looked around wild. He gulped. He soon began flinging ship classifications, weapons, armament, and anything else he could think of into the air to save his life. He even got clearance from "da big ship ting in da middle" to leave the fleet and head down to the planet. To top it off, he himself, piloted the prison barge all the way to the surface. His life and the lives of his comrades were spared. They were all sent to the detention cells until further notice.

Biggabomb found out that most Homeworlder prisoners were already being shipped off to the Invadas' planets. Most of them were women and children. He had watched the steady stream of traffic against the backdrop of stars. For a moment, he imagined all his fellow orcs being whisked away aboard the ships that faded into the distance. It was a sickening and helpless feeling.

Within ten minutes, the hijacked prison ship had pierced Hotta's atmosphere and landed without incident. Once the ship was safely on the ground, Biggabomb and his closest orcs found their way to the access hatch. Biggabomb was pretty sick. He knew that he was in no shape to lead his orcs into battle, at least not any time soon.

He turned to Gunza and Guthrak as the hatch opened and confided, "I makin' Nutty da Chief. I can't do it no more."

Gunza pointed to what came into view. Nuttybomb stood in front of over one hundred thousand chanting warriors.

Guthrak acknowledged, "Looka like him already da Chief."

Thirteen
Path to the Gods

"I don't know, Nutty," Muga told her son.

Nutty questioned, "What 'bout you, Doc?"

The Doc looked around as he searched for an appropriate answer; he simply didn't know what was happening. Still, he gave an answer that might explain what he saw. "Dems start havin' bad dreams anda stuff. Afta dat, dems sumptimes shake or can't move at all. Dunno."

Nutty dug for more. "Dreams? Shakes or not able to move? Hmm. Maybe from gas weapon?"

The Doc guessed, "Well, I thought a so. Maybe at first. But a no. Only cause dems all not be a gassed."

"Any dem patients here?"

"Yessa, Chief. Dis way." Doc led Nuttybomb and Muga down the builder school main hallway into a room off to the left. Nutty recognized the room as his old radio workshop where he was a student. Now, it was being used for the wounded. The wounded were restrained with straps that wrapped their arms and legs; two patients were gagged as well as being tied down.

Nutty expressed immediate concern. "Why dems gagged?"

The doc nervously answered when he saw Nutty's agitated facial expression. "We not want to. But dems crazy or sumptin'. Started a screamin' stuff. Make a no sense. All dems tied cuz dems try to hurt udders. But not all a dems screams."

Nutty walked over to a soldier nearest to his right; one that wasn't gagged. The soldier's eyes stared straight upward; they never blinked; they never moved. Nutty saw the soldier's arm jerking from side to side beneath the straps and his hand kept clenching. Nutty spoke quietly, "Hello, soldia." The soldier didn't respond.

Nutty addressed the doc with, "Him awake?"

"Yessa. Well, I tink so. Breathe ok anda blood pump normal."

Nutty tried to reach the soldier again. "Soldia?"

Just then, something happened. To be more precise, nothing happened. The soldia didn't move; he still hadn't blinked. Nutty's hair stood up on the back of his neck and he inadvertently snarled. His heart began to race, and goosebumps exploded all over his body; he became nauseous and stepped back from the soldier to protect himself.

Muga jumped and gulped. She followed Nutty's lead, unaware that she too was backing away. She saw Nutty's reaction and chills raked her from head-to-toe.

The Doc dropped his tools; he felt something, too. Like Muga, he reacted to Nutty. The sense of danger hung heavily in the room like the smell of death.

The soldier slowly turned his head and his eyes met Nutty's. Nothing more and nothing less. His eyes would remain fixated in that position for the next several weeks.

Nutty's eyes wouldn't remain there to look back at the soldier. They led Nutty out of the room in an immediate panic. He ran down the hallway, casting aside anything that was in his way; he crashed through the front doors and ran away. He stopped a couple miles away and went down an alleyway between two shops where he threw up and fell to his knees. He shook for a few minutes as he kept putting his hand on his chest to see if his heart was still inside his body. He continued to heave well after there was no more in his belly to be ejected from his mouth. Finally, he leaned back on his haunches, somewhat paralyzed by the experience.

Nutty was not himself. He couldn't completely shake the nausea and the feeling in his chest. He offered his apologies to the leaders that sought his attention. He delegated to his officers. He would be out of commission for the rest of the day.

***

It was two weeks since Biggabomb escaped with the Homeworld orcs. He was being fit for a new hand and partial arm; the new hand was a huge claw with hydraulics that he could use in combat as a destructive weapon against anything an enemy could throw at him. Additionally, his left lung needed to be removed. He was a candidate for a lung transplant as soon as a suitable one became available and found himself stuck in the builder school until then.

Muga visited her stinky ass husband, as she usually did. She always seemed to bring him something to eat, too. Biggabomb would joke about how much he loved hospital food over her cooking. A typical, "Choke on it, you fat bastid," was par for the course. She would check his vitals, kiss his forehead, and be on her way, but today she stuck around.

Biggabomb didn't mind her company; he liked picking on her and relished her comeback comments. However, today was different. He expected a wisecrack when he said, "I finally gots a hand big 'nuff to hold my pee." He held up the monstrous claw that was as big as his whole torso to emphasize how large it was. But Muga sort of smiled and said nothing. He tried again. "Now, it big 'nuff to grab you ass!" He laughed for a few seconds until he saw that Muga had no response; he thought that was comical. What the hell was wrong with her?

Muga stood up and walked over to the window. She was quiet as she looked out into the world, never seeing what was happening outside. Her mind was fixated on Nutty and what happened. She had checked on the soldier dozens of times over the last two weeks. She didn't know why Nutty did what he did. She felt Nutty's fear, or whatever unsettling emotion he felt, but why?

Muga left the room in search of Nutty, so she didn't hear the last couple of insults Biggabomb cast at her. She certainly wasn't going to trim his toenails by chewing them, or whatever the hell he said to her; she didn't have the time, anyway.

Muga headed out and began asking others if they had seen Nuttybomb. They all said yes. He was the Chief, and as such, highly recognizable. He easily attracted attention, but nobody seemed to know where he was now.

Muga found herself at the Crossroads. She saw an orc standing at the edge of the road. She noticed that he seemed fixated on the construction of the library which was coming along nicely. He was an older kid; by the looks of him, she guessed that he was around Booma's age. He looked familiar, too, but who could keep track of everyone with the sudden appearance of tens of thousands of newcomers?

Muga approached the teen and asked, "Hi, have you seen Nuttybomb?"

He turned and said, "Yes." Then, he turned back to look at the library.

Muga knew that orcs had short attention spans. She also knew that they could be rude while others just weren't that smart. She was sure not to assume anything. She thought to herself that her kids were all smart and good kids; she was lucky. She didn't care what this kid's deal was. She wanted to know where Nutty was, so she tried again. "You know where a he is?"

The teen turned and stated, "Yes," and went back to looking at the library.

Muga tipped her head to the side in a "Are you kidding me?" manner. She fought the frustration and purposely spoke softly. "Where is he?"

The teen turned, only this time, he didn't answer immediately. He looked at her for a few seconds, rolled his eyes slightly, and finally, said through his clenched teeth, "In da back room."

Muga was taken aback. First of all, she didn't know what back room he was referring to, and he seemed irritated that she was trying to get information from him. It was his inability to give complete answers that caused her to have to bother him repeatedly. This time she was direct and precise in her questioning. She didn't want any more half answers. "What back room is Nuttybomb in? In a house or a shop anda where? Here in da town? Who's house or shop?"

The teen turned and folded his arms. His eyes were angry; his nostrils flared. He said sarcastically, "Why you not ask so? Lady, him at a you house."

Muga reluctantly thanked the teen and headed home. The trip took nearly two hours. Congestion from all the new orcs, army movements, building, and the like were grinding traffic to a near halt. Along the way, Muga came across Pretty and Uhra. The three traveled together.

Muga was the first to enter her home, followed by Pretty and Uhra. It was dark; the early evening shed very little light through the small windows on the west side of the building. Muga raised her right hand into the air and felt for the pull string to the flimsy light that hung in the center of the main room. With a wave of her hand and a slight tug, the room became adequately lit for the three to see. The back room was still dark, though.

Muga slowly approached the back room as she called out easily, "Nutty? You here?"

Pretty made her way back to the front door where she was comfortable enough to run outside in a hurry if need be. The story of the day's strangest event, told by Muga, scared her. She remembered the night that Nutty attacked Gardawg. She had never seen violence like that. Even though Nutty was her brother, she figured she should be cautious.

As Muga reached the doorway to the back room, she turned quietly to see where the girls were. In doing so, Uhra, who was hot on her heels, stopped and wandered back a bit. Each movement made the faintest of sounds; skin rubbed against clothing and the weight of feet forced granules of sand and rock to crunch beneath them. In this eerie silence, everything seemed loud, everything made noise; well, almost everything. Before Muga turned back around, a heavy, warm breath ran over the back of her neck. She swung around to see her son.

She was startled. Her eyes were even with Nutty's chest. As she stepped back into the main room, Nutty advanced slowly. She hadn't seen him at first as she reached the doorway because of the darkness. Now, she saw him in a new light. He was big, very big; he was as big as any male she had ever seen. He was probably bigger than Biggabomb now. She never noticed how large he had become, not until this moment. The grains of sand had pushed the last few months by like a blur. She had seen him in is awkward posture and that had somehow masked his true size. But now she appreciated how dangerous he really was. His face had deep cuts through it that had scarred. His muscles were enormous, rippling bulges that hid his youth behind them. She couldn't speak.

Uhra's hair stood up on her arms and neck. She had seen Nutty in a frenzy the night he saved her. He decimated a room of hostile males single-handedly. He could easily kill the three girls in an instant, if he so chose. But, she knew that he loved her; he would never hurt her. She forced a fake, light-hearted giggle and called him, "Younut!"

Nutty stopped following Muga step for step. His eyes met Uhra's, just a few feet away now. He just stood there.

"You ok?" Uhra gasped.

Nutty looked around the room. He saw Pretty as his eyes drifted passed the door to the window. He walked in the window's direction as he rubbed his forehead with his right hand. His confused gaze was obvious.

Nobody could guess what he was thinking. The three girls could feel the tension between them and Nutty. They all felt something that they couldn't describe. A variety of goose bumps, hair standing at attention, and shaky knees clung to them. What was going on?

It took over an hour for the girls to get anything out of Nutty. Uhra embraced one of his arms with both of hers in a hug. She spoke softly and tried to reassure him that everything was okay, even though she had no idea what was wrong. Eventually, he turned from the window and began to speak.

He kept clenching his fists. He was still confused. He mixed his words. He made references to doing things at certain places during specific times that didn't happen. He was unsure of his surroundings and couldn't think of any of the girls' names. The only thing that made sense was that he was to lead his army against the Invadas in a few days. That didn't seem likely in his current condition.

The girls persuaded him to lie down for the night. He was told that all he needed was a good night's sleep. He did so, whether he believed it or not. Did he even understand it? As his broad, muscular back welcomed the blanket that was spread upon the floor, his eyes welcomed the ceiling. His mind welcomed the morning that couldn't come soon enough.

***

Morning light broke as darkness departed. Hues of orange and pink gave way to bright, light blue skies.

Beneath the warm blanket of early sun was an already active morning. Months of preparation for war had organized Big Town into a city much more capable than its population would have suggested. The newcomers were being organized and taught as soon as they arrived, and how they arrived.

The world outside was changing. More and more orcs from afar were convening upon Nutty's thriving metropolis; the population was growing so quickly, it was hard to tell where Big Town ended, and its neighboring cities began. Natural boundaries such as the river were the only way to determine one's exact location within which border. The surrounding cities were exploding, too, as orcs settled wherever food and water was plentiful enough for them to subsist.

A multitude brought their collective knowledge about battle, construction, mechanics, and farming. The prison ship that Biggabomb brought home was being taken apart and studied, piece by piece. Enemy weapons and armor were being looked over for strengths and weaknesses. The new orcs, with all their added skills, quickened the development of science and technology.

Yes, word had spread about his evolutionary changes. Books began to reach Nutty from every corner of the world to be used in this library of his. Other thinkers like him sought opportunities to learn and advance. This was the place to share knowledge and better their race. It was becoming a time of great change and direction on a global scale that had eluded the descendants of Da Rampage until this point.

A gifted Shaman, named Moonoak, brought with him a collection of books written by Grim and subsequent students. He and his followers of thought and religion would become elemental in shaping the changes that were evolving. The followers would spread the word of knowledge in accordance with Nuttybomb's visionary pursuit of advancements as his most trusted disciples. Moonoak would do much more than that.

First, he would seek out Nuttybomb. Curiosity about this kid in itself was enough to warrant an inquiry. Additionally, he wished to know what made this kid special. Was it circumstantial? Were there rumors that skewed the truth about a flawed individual? Were Nutty's accomplishments simply propaganda, even if at the smallest level? How much of the hype was based on fact? And, if this kid was for real, was there anything Moonoak could learn from him? As a thinker, he sought knowledge in a variety of ways, and as such, wasn't quick to dismiss the possibility of learning from this kid. Even if the kid was a fake, he would learn that, too.

Moonoak asked for a meeting with Nutty. Several times, Nutty's officers would pass along Moonoak's request with fifty others. The officers would inevitably respond, "Not at dis time." Sometimes, with an attached apology. They didn't know why Nutty wouldn't see anyone. They were unaware of his troubles. For all they knew, he was busy planning or working on war stuff. That's what Chiefs did, and they didn't question such things. It was common knowledge in Orcdom that questioning authority could mean death. The officers went about their officer business and continued to screen visitors.

Moonoak was getting an uneasy feeling about his new-found, sprawling surroundings. He began to hear rumblings about the ill that had fallen into coma-like trances over the last couple of weeks. This concerned him deeply; he had seen these symptoms before. Sometimes, orcs that were seriously injured went into comas before they died. He didn't rule out illness either. That didn't worry him. Sometimes, other forces were at work. The troublesome thing was that it sounded to him like the signs could mean something potentially worse.

As a patient orc, Moonoak settled down and waited for his turn to speak with Nuttybomb. Before he meditated, he read a section of a book that he knew well. It was an area that he occasionally reflected on and found important relevance in. He hoped to find answers as he opened the book and his mind reacquainted himself with the teachings.

He read:

The mind is a world of wonder. More complex than the secrets of the universe, its possibilities are unlimited. However, due to its complexity and our crude understanding of it, it is greatly misunderstood and widely misused. Therefore, we have barely begun to understand its true potential and power.

For some, it can be controlled to accomplish unimaginable feats. Those that learn to connect its pathways will understand essence in its truest form...to know what knowledge is...to fully understand understanding...to know all and nothing. No longer will we be bound by physical form, limited by bone, skin, and muscle; no longer will we feel pain, nor will we die; we will become beings that transcend space and time.

I have begun on a path to the gods. Through years of alchemy and ingestion of substances, I have learned to enter a state of limited understanding. Even in these relatively benign trances, I have seen events in the past, as well as images of the future. I have been visited by the dead and warned by the gods. I have learned to leave my body and take journeys to distant worlds. I have begun to communicate with others, from my mind to theirs. I am only able to accomplish this while the others are also in a state of sleep. I can see their dreams and enter their visions. I have found that I can alter their dreams by casting illusions and manipulating their thoughts. It is my goal to be able to converse telepathically while they are awake. I am confident that I will be able to control their minds. They shall be subject to my will, helpless to make their own decisions or perform actions by their own doing. One that can control multiple subjects could very well cause mass hysteria or brainwash subjects into total subjugation...a very powerful implement to have on a path to the gods.

As dangerous and sinister as mind control may seem, there are other forms of physical manipulation of objects that are possible. There are forces at work all around us that are more misunderstood than the brain itself. Energy and matter are connected in ways like thoughts controlling movement in the body. Energy, like thought processes or visions, is a somewhat intangible entity. However, it can control physical properties within the body. I have found the ability within myself and outside myself to move objects without the use of touch. No longer do I need to push an object with my hand; nor do I need to touch it to know what it feels like.

The Gods have warned me about this last topic. I am reluctant to incorporate this for fear that its inclusion may cause, rather than hinder, its use. However, I will, even with unrivaled trepidation and unmatched uncertainty, for it is directed and warranted by the gods.

Take heed! Goliath will return upon the sign and the heavens will fall! Thousands of years of suffering under his vehemence will mark his reign!

I am, as are all, forbidden to raise the dead! This goes against the fabric of the universe and is absolutely forbidden by the gods. Death may be unjust, but natural, whereas undeath isn't natural, but is demonic. The soul of one that plays with this evil will die a thousand times, times a thousand times in unmerciful anguish.

The Third Book of Grim/the Early Years

***

Nutty awoke later in the day. He looked around the room and figured that it was evening based on the lighting that shined through the window nearest to him. He rubbed his eyes and sat up.

Uhra was sitting at his side with an understanding smile. His eyes looked alive; he appeared to be Nutty again, normal to her. She said, "You sleeped a lot."

Nutty instantly took note of her devotion. He replied, "I tink I feel lil better. Weird, but better."

Uhra was so happy to hear that. She stayed awake all night and into the next day. For a moment, she thought that she was somehow willing him back to himself. She smiled an even bigger smile.

Nutty vaguely remembered that he wasn't alone with Uhra. "Momma and Pretty leave?"

"Yep. Dems go back to help da docs. But…" Uhra seemed troubled. Her brow dipped above her nose.

Nutty tried to persuade her to finish what she was saying. "But?"

"Well, I know you wuz sick or sumptin'. You had nightmares all da night long. You kept sayin's Darkster. What dat, Darkster?"

"Dunno. Hims just somewuns dat I fight in da dreams. Just dreams, Uhra."

Uhra, satisfied that her love was doing well asked, "You hungry?"

No sooner did she get the words out than did Nutty burst out with, "Yes!"

A meal never tasted so good.

Fourteen
Moonoak

It was the day before the army was to begin moving out and position itself to engage the Invadas. Nutty hadn't fully recovered, but felt well enough to see the leaders that had requested meetings with him. He had to make each one feel important and to show them their places within his ranks. He briefly looked at scouting reports that he had his officers create upon their first meeting with these leaders. From there, his insight helped him as far as how to best handle each new visitor. His thoughtfulness, quick thinking, and ability to call on his darker side allowed him to easily transition from nice guy to vicious killer as needed.

Nutty met each one, praised them, and assured them their place in history. Each would be given command of troops; some would be in control of whole legions, whereas others would lead smaller units. He took care to evaluate them based on their strengths, knowledge of battle plans, and background.

Upon completion of meeting the leaders and going over plans with his officers, Nutty sent for others who had requested meetings. Even with his officers screening many of them, he found a dozen or so to be a frivolous waste of time. However, one meeting would mark him for the rest of his life. He didn't know it at the time, but certainly realized the importance of it.

"Hello. Moonoak, is it?" Nutty extended a hand and led his visitor to a comfortable chair.

Moonoak engaged the boy with a welcomed smile. He sensed no threat of danger to himself, nor any reason to feel apprehension. He saw a youthful orc with warm eyes in a controlled setting. He understood the deliberate nature of the surroundings, the comfortable chair, and handshake to seem non-threatening. However, to be allowed to sit, and be offered to do so by a supreme ruler did strike him as odd. He wasn't sure if this was part of the illusion of comfort or if Nutty was truly humble. "I am Moonoak."

As Nutty was being evaluated, so too was Moonoak. Nutty saw an orc of average proportions that seemed larger than in the physical sense. Moonoak's long hair, graying at the temples gave him an appearance of someone with some importance, too. His floor-length, hand-woven cape flowed around his modest robe; his sandals appeared worn, but comfortable. Nutty laughed to himself, *Der is an orc who is comfortable in his own shoes.* As the two sat, Nutty also noticed how at ease Moonoak was. He wasn't clunky and clumsy; he carried himself well. He was much older than Nutty, although Nutty wasn't sure by how much.

Nutty began going through his mental checklist as he had done all day. He began with, "So, Moonoak, why you here today?"

"Der be several reasons, all because of dis I give gift to you." Moonoak handed Nutty a book.

Nutty's eyes widened when he saw what he was handed. He studied the ornate inlays and dark brown pages worn by the ages. He took just a second or two to flip through some pages and verify the book's authenticity. "Grim? How you get dis book?"

"I find Grim books in my travels. I have mo' of dems. Dis one fo' you or you new libury. You know how a read it?" Moonoak now sat back and waited to see how Nutty reacted.

"Tank you, Moonoak. Yes, I reads some already. Dis very special to me. I have udders as well. You are welcome to read dems, too."

Moonoak was curious. There was something about this kid. Nutty was polite and already had books by Grim.

Nutty placed the book on his desk and went back to business. "So, what dese udder reasons and how dems tied to dis book?"

Moonoak thought and spoke logically for an orc. "First, I set out to see who you are. Orcs say all kind of tings 'bout you. Second, I wanted to see how tings run here. It looka like even wit' all da new orcs, you have tings in control. But wit' all da new orcs come a trouble. Anda here how it ties to da book."

Moonoak cleared his throat and summed things up. "Years ago, my town started a havin dyin' orcs. Dems was havin' nightmares and den dems go into comas. Grim talks about orcs exploring mind controls. Dat's what it was. Da orc dat was entering into da dreams of my orcs was chased away. I hear no more 'bout comas afta dreams until Big Town ova da last two weeks. You gots a real problem here."

Nutty asked, "So you is sayin' dat da dream orc is among us?"

"No. He might be. Might be someone else. Maybe not at all. But you prolly gots enemies anyway. Can't be too careful."

Nutty was puzzled. "You come from Da Dunes Region?"

"Yes," Moonoak replied.

"Why you comes all dis way to tell me dis? Anda what can I do 'bout it? I don't know who do da dreams or how. Anda, why it mean anyting to you?"

Moonoak folded his hands with his fingers clasped inside each other. He leaned forward and implored with Nutty, "You must believe when I say dat dis could be worser dan da Invadas. At least wit' da Invadas, some of our species will live on. But if da dead rise, or if dems comas take us all, dens we are lost. All of us, lost."

Nutty said, "Ok. I don't have da time to read da whole book. Please, show me what to read and I will meet wit' you tomorrow."

Moonoak spent another twenty minutes with Nutty and pointed out pertinent sections of the gift he had just granted to him. The two discussed the dreams and how they might have been preludes to the eventual comas that would follow. Beyond that, there was too little time to share everything of importance. Additionally, there were dots that Nutty hadn't been able to connect. His lack of understanding inhibited his ability to ask crucial questions that Moonoak may have been able to answer.

Nutty didn't share his nightmares with Moonoak. He feared giving too much information too early in a relationship to his new friend. It wasn't that he didn't trust Moonoak. Time had a way of sorting out trust. He was simply unsure what the nightmares meant. Also, *he* was the orc in charge. He didn't feel comfortable talking about nightmares. Among orcs, they were considered scary dreams for babies. Even with Moonoak's explanation to the contrary, Nutty couldn't bring himself to embarrass himself.

The two shook hands and thanked each other before parting until the next evening. Nutty finished up a few more meetings and surveyed the city for any issues. Then, he checked on his army which was amassing thirty miles to the northwest. He and Booma flew above to see if any of its formations needed to be changed. They looked at each other in amazement and pride.

"Impressive, Nutty," Booma exclaimed.

Nutty was going to lead the largest Homeworld force in the history of his planet. He couldn't believe it. He couldn't help but question his own ability. He asked, "How many troops, Booma?"

"Wow. Dunno, Nutty. We try to keep track lika you say, but too many come every day. Maybe, I dunno how to count like dat, but two hundred thousand? Maybe three hundred? Anyway, dat what Gunza say. Oh, and three thousand tanks. Umm, two thousand fighta planes? Sumptin' like a dat."

"Oh my Gods, Booma", Nutty confided. "How I gonna lead dis many orcs?"

"Brudder, you already are. Plus, I keep reinforcements goin' to help you as more orcs come to Big Town. You gots dis."

Nutty sighed. "I sure hope so. I sure hope so."

The day continued with more inspections and orders given. Nutty set up to meet with his civilians the following morning at the Crossroads and then meet the troops after that. He went everywhere with a personal guard that consisted of Gunza, Quicklip,

Thunda, and Nubbs. He took Moonoak's advice and decided to protect himself; at least, while he was awake.

Booma became a temporary second to the more experienced Fighta Control officer that was leading things locally until he left for war. Not being much of a combatant, he would remain at Big Town and pick up his duties like he had done before the officer returned with Biggabomb on the prison ship.

Muga, Pretty, and Uhra would work with the docs and help with cooking when necessary. Runzda, younger than Nutty, would learn the updated language in the new school system. Then, she would be watched by one of Nutty's closest women. She would continue to sew as needed and learn healthcare, too. Kago would follow Biggabomb.

Biggabomb left the medical area to the dismay of his doctors. His lungs were still insufficient to supply adequate oxygen to his brain. This may have contributed to his unrealistic reasoning about his health. He told his docs, "If Muga's cookin' no kill me, nuttin' will." His inability to participate in combat basically relegated him to training Booma, Kago, and others here at home.

***

A hot and steamy night befell the Homeworlders. While exhaustion plagued those that continued to work through the night, it already laid claim to those who couldn't keep their eyes open any longer. About half of all adult orcs traded their tired muscles and achy feet for what they hoped would be blissful sleep. Some of those wouldn't sleep very well as the recent rains caused a population explosion in the insect population that exceeded that of Big Town's orc growth. Biting, blood-sucking mascrils fed on the hundreds of thousands of sleeping orcs in the area.

Along with pestilence, there were those that found themselves unable to sleep because of anxiety. The thought of war was exciting to warriors, but not so much to the ones that longed for peace. Then, there were the nightmares. Younglings dreamed of being chased by carnidawgs. Mothers dreamed of their children dying. Some dreamed of fighting enemy soldiers.

Booma dreamed of dismounting a tank during a heavy firefight. He ducked and dodged bullets, moving the troops forward that he led into combat. He rushed forward and met an enemy warrior face to face. They used their guns as close combat weapons until Booma landed a decisive blow, killing the enemy and leaving an opening for Booma to find another victim.

The next enemy came through the fogs of war. The figure was indistinct; devoid of features. It called Booma by name, "Booma. Booma. Booma." But Booma was undeterred. He smashed his weapon into the throat of the oncoming entity, dropping it to the ground. Again, he moved forward.

Then, Booma was dropping from the tank again. He killed an enemy face to face. Again, he faced an entity from the fog, and again, it called him by name. He killed it again. Back on the tank he went. He killed an enemy and found himself killing the same entity; that same shadowy figure.

The name Darkster played over and over in his head as his dream reset, time and time again. However, each time he faced the foggy entity, it became harder and harder to defeat. After dozens of encounters, Booma was fighting to survive. He was slow against the figure; he struggled to keep up with the much faster opponent. Booma's heart was racing. The voice called him, "Booma. Booma. Booma." Booma froze as the figure pulled a long saber and thrust into Booma. Booma screamed out, "Darkster!"

Booma awoke to Nutty shaking him and calling his name. He wasn't penetrated by the blade, but he was breathing heavily. He ran his hands across his heaving chest and stomach to make sure that he wasn't wounded. He was confused. Somehow, he was in his own quarters. But how? He was just on top of a tank. The battle was so real. It was as real as Nutty was, right here, right now. He looked to his younger brother in bewilderment.

Nutty was quick to console his brother. He had heard the name "Darkster" and knew how terrifying his own nightmares were. What he didn't know was how he and Booma were having similar dreams about the same character. Either way, his first task was to put Booma's mind at ease. He would deal with how and why later. He fought back the feeling of uneasiness that plagued him the same way that the soldier in the medical area did. Then, he talked with Booma. He asked open-ended questions to gather as much information about Darkster as possible.

Booma was slow to respond; he was having trouble conveying his thoughts. He was almost in a state of sleep, but not quite. In fact, Nutty had called him a bunch of times before his eyes opened from the dream with Darkster. It would be another hour before the older brother felt well enough to talk and make any sense.

Meanwhile, Nutty thought about Moonoak and what he had said in the earlier meeting. Was this Darkster the problem? If so, who was he? Why would he be haunting Nutty and his brother? For what purpose? What was this raising the dead stuff, anyway? Maybe it was all garbage. Who the hell knew? This was all new and very strange; none of it made sense, not to Nutty anyway. He would have to read the sections of the Grim book when he left Booma's side. Maybe he could figure things out with the writings in front of him. If not, he would see Moonoak sometime the next afternoon.

As Booma's mind became clearer, he told Nutty about his dream. He stated how surely he would have died if Nutty hadn't awakened him when he did. Also, one thing stuck out among the others. It was the fact that he believed Darkster wasn't the shadowy figure's name. He said, "It was, but it wasn't. Dunno, Nutty. It lika he use da name, but it not really him? Dunno."

Nutty tried to understand. "You mean he has da different name?"

"Yes! Well, no. Dat his name. But, maybe, it wasn't always his name."

Nutty understood. He opened up to Booma; he shared some things about his own dream. He, too, had confusion about the shadowy figure's name. He couldn't clearly identify Darkster as someone he knew, or even an orc, for that matter. They agreed, solely based on intuition, that Darkster may have had a different name in the past. Neither was sure, but they had hunches that they were probably right.

The last thing they discovered together was that both of their dreams became progressively more difficult to maneuver through. They seemed to be steered against their wills. The dreams repeated until they no longer controlled their respective situations. Nutty was able to wake himself before his impending death. Also, unlike Booma, he had faced death in the real world; a number of times, in fact. He didn't wake as wildly as Booma did. He thought that he might be better conditioned to combat, or maybe, he was wired differently.

Booma joined Nutty and the rest of the guards for the remainder of the night. Neither of them told anyone about their nightmares or the connections they were making with the coma patients. There was enough anxiety with the war against the Invadas. All the other orcs needed was some dim-witted story about being invaded in their dreams. Unsettling rumors and doubts about the sanity of their Chief wouldn't help any. No, this they would keep to themselves.

All those involved went over the plans again and again. Nothing could be left to chance. Some troops were moving out in the morning without the benefit of reorganizing, or even communicating with command. Nutty met these troops before dawn. He was counting on them and he told them so. He talked about pride, honor, and bravery; he went on about sacrifice; he let them know that he would be fighting alongside them. He would die if he had to. Mostly, he talked about the savage enemy and its plans to brutalize Homeworlders' families.

The troops moved out; half headed south-west to the coast; the other half went northwest to start supplying the battle area and to complete reconnaissance. Things were proceeding as planned.

Nutty was tired and his mind was numb. He found himself going through the motions of Chief as expected, but he was utterly drained. He retired to his home and asked for Moonoak to be brought to him within the hour. This gave him time to read portions of the newest Grim book that he had received from Moonoak.

It was decided that if he felt comfortable enough with Moonoak at this next meeting, he would tell him about Darkster and the dreams that he and Booma had experienced. He didn't want this hanging over his head too. Things were at a critical mass; the future of his race depended on him over the next few weeks. He had to be clear-headed and strong.

Against his better judgment, Nutty sat in his house alone. While his guards stood outside, Nutty read and read. His eyes were getting blurry as he pushed through each section. Lack of sleep and the trauma he had been through were just too much. Nearly half an hour into his reading, Nutty fell asleep.

Nutty awoke almost instantaneously to the sounds of gunfire. He jumped up and ran to the door. He was sleepy and weak. His movements were uncharacteristically sluggish, and he was somewhat disoriented. He fumbled with the latch to the door, but couldn't open it. He was half asleep and unable to act clearly. He hadn't fully awakened. Like a bad dream, he was stuck in slow motion. *Gods dammit*, he thought as he struggled with the imposing door. He went to his knees and tried to push through the door. His feet dug up dirt behind him as he planted his feet and pushed as hard as he could.

He heard the screams of his guards trying to defend themselves. Their struggles carried into the alley to his left. He saw Quicklip and Booma fall to their deaths through the window. He heard someone else yell, "Gunza is dead!" No, not Gunza; not his dad's best friend and Uhra's dad! He crawled over to the window to see outside. He rubbed away some dirt, so he could see more clearly. The bodies of his comrades lined the alleyway, limp with their blood spilling into the street. Gunza, Booma, Quicklip, and Thunda were all dead. Screams of chaos outside pierced the air. Mothers ran for cover. Children screamed in their beds. Fathers were being slaughtered.

Nutty scratched at the glass, trying to get out. He needed to help. He needed someone to wake him up. He was the Chief. He couldn't let them all die like this. The name Darkster played on his mind. He thought about his and Booma's dreams. It was probably this Darkster that was killing everyone.

Then, there was silence. The latch on his front door methodically unlatched, breaking the silence with a light metal against metal sound. Nutty turned to see his front door slowly open. The eerie creek of the rusty hinges was replaced by the vision of a shadowy figure that called out, "Nutty. Nutty. Nutty."

Nutty's heart was already beating fast. Was this death sent in a cloak? Was it his time to die? Nutty staggered to his feet and stood motionless. He couldn't find the words, nor the power to engage this dark entity. He wanted to fight, but he couldn't. He almost didn't want to. His mind was telling him that it would be easier to succumb to the wishes of the figure, rather than fight it in futility.

Nutty's internal struggle ended. He hoped to regain his strength to defeat this stalker of death. He wouldn't fade quietly into the night. No, he would find the strength to survive, like he had many times before. As the shadowy figure pulled a sword from his cloak and walked toward him, Nutty closed his eyes and screamed.

***

When he opened his eyes, he found Moonoak being subdued by Gunza and his guards at the doorway. Nutty was briefly unaware of his surroundings and what was happening when he heard Gunza questioning Moonoak. "What did you do, you bastid?"

Moonoak struggled to speak as he lied face down in the dirt. "Nuttin'. I help him."

Quicklip leaned over and smacked Moonoak in the back of the head with a sarcastic, "I help him. Yeah, right. You come here and dis happen. You did dis."

Moonoak pleaded his innocence, but it fell on deaf ears. Finally, he asked, "Nutty, who is Darkster?"

Nutty snapped into reality. Now, and only now, did he firmly grasp the situation. His eyes met Moonoak's as he said, "Gunza, let him up."

Gunza pulled Moonoak from the floor and to his feet with one hand. Moonoak wiped dirt from his face and looked at the guards. His eyes finally landed on Gunza as he said, "Tanka you?"

Nutty walked over to Moonoak and looked him directly in the eyes. "What you know 'bout dis Darkster?"

Moonoak replied, "Nuttin'."

"You know sumptin'. What you not tellin' me?"

Moonoak didn't panic. He was well-educated and mild-mannered. Also, he knew not to ignite an already flammable situation. "May we sit, Nuttybomb?"

Nutty reluctantly waved his guards out of the room. Currently, he had no reservations about Moonoak and his own safety. He was pretty sure that he could take down the passive orc before him if he had to.

Thunda made an offhanded remark about how he could have squashed the stranger in the cloak. That was followed by Quicklip's, "Yeah, what stopped you? He had no food fo' you to claim as a prize?" The guards laughed as Thunda pushed Quicklip through the doorway.

Nutty's eyes never left Moonoak's. "Darkster?"

Moonoak quietly and evenly began to talk. "I don't know a Darkster. Dat wasn't da name of da one who killed in my town. Dis name is different."

"Ok, what was his name?"

"Cracka. His name was Cracka."

Nutty mulled things over in his head. "Cracka, hmm? How dis Cracka different from a you?"

"I see your concern, Nutty. We both practice talk wit' da spirits. But, I don't mind control. Cracka did dat. I seek knowledge. Him seek power and glory. He used bad powers against me. I fight fo' my life and called to da Gods. I aska dems fo' peace, not to kill."

"How I know you tell da truth?" Nutty quizzed.

Moonoak admitted, "You don't."

"I would expected you to a defend youself."

"Why?" Moonoak asked. "I has no reason to."

"I could kill you. Dens what?"

Moonoak nodded his head. "Of dat I has no doubt. But Darkster may still haunt you."

Nutty chuckled. It was true. If he killed Moonoak, the dreams might continue. "Dis is great, Moonoak. I don't knows what to tink."

"All I can says is dat you know I wasn't in a you mind. I don't use dat power. It hard fo' me to do. But, as I get close to a you house, I could feel dat you wuz in a trouble. I brokes da door anda you woked up."

It was true as far as Nutty could prove. Maybe Moonoak was a master of deception, though. Nutty didn't know for sure, but he didn't think so. The timing of Moonoak coming to town and the dreams beginning around the same time were quite a coincidence, though.

Nutty began to drift a bit. It occurred to him that maybe Moonoak could read his mind. He tried to clear it for fear of being read. He didn't want any of his negative thoughts about this stranger or any information to get into the wrong hands. Once again, he thought about the burden of the world on his shoulders and how prepared he needed to be.

As if on cue, Moonoak stated, "I know you need to find dis Darkster. You has da war and all dat stuff. You a mind need to be right."

Fifteen
Today Begins da Rest of our Lives

This day marked the last day to get things done before the army left for battle. If Big Town seemed busier before this day, it paled in comparison to the overwhelming activity as orcs willed themselves to accomplish everything they could in such a short amount of time.

Muga pleaded with Nutty to set time aside for a final family dinner before he left in the morning. She was grateful to have Biggabomb, Pretty, Runzda, Kago, and Uhra in town, but Nutty's leaving was hitting her particularly hard. Biggabomb had just come back without an arm and lungs that would probably give out soon. Now, going up against a much stronger enemy was her boy. He was big and strong, but still just a boy. Biggabomb had years of battle under his belt before he became a Chief. Nutty had a couple months of experience.

Nutty agreed to the meal upon reworking his schedule in his head. He understood his mother's fear, and for good reason. If he could make time for hundreds of thousands and probably die, then surely, he could give his family an hour. He wanted to see Uhra, too, and it would be good to have her father there, so he could say goodbye to them and Biggabomb. Furthermore, Nutty would tell them about the dreams and Darkster. If he and his family were the targets of some kind of evil at work, then they should know what to look for. He shook his head in disgust when he realized that he was hoping they could wake each other up or something. *Dis damn Darkster*, he thought.

Nutty kissed Muga on the forehead and left for his flight. Like the day before, he checked progress from the air to get a better look at the overall picture from a better vantage point. This time however, he, Quicklip, Thunda, and Nubbs flew above Big Town and the surrounding residential areas.

Thunda looked through the window and moaned like a child. "Ooh. Ah."

Quicklip jabbed in a high-pitched voice, "Ooh, so pretty! Looka all da houses, Thunda."

"Dems prettier dan you, Bigmouff!"

"You a mouth not big 'nuff fo' what I stick in it," Quicklip teased.

Nutty cut them short. "Shutta up!" He surveyed the new roads and buildings. He saw the scale of his responsibility in that very moment. For miles in each direction were buildings and orcs. What used to be desert and grassland was now filled with small homes. What had been small homes in town, were now four and five story buildings. Irrigation canals stretched as far as the eye could see. It looked like every square inch of Hotta was used for living. Enormous tracts of desolate land had been converted to farmland on the outskirts. The view was spectacular! Nutty commanded the pilot, "Bring us south ova da mines."

Static broke with a voice that confirmed that it had received and was obeying the order. "Yes, Chief."

As the aircraft flew over the center of town, Nutty glimpsed what was easily the largest structure in Big Town; it was his library. It was tall and strong; it reached toward the sky; it's almost completed spires twisted upward unnaturally to the Gods. It cast shadows on the individuals that stood beneath it. They stared at its immense size and unmatched beauty.

Quicklip saw that guards had been placed on the steps and again at the base of the spires. He stated, "Nice touch wit' da stone carnidawgs, Chief." When Nutty said nothing in return, Quicklip turned his attention to Thunda. "Hey, see dat libury down der?"

"Duh, yeah."

"I finally seens sumptin' bigga dan you head." Quicklip laughed at his own stupid joke. It wasn't funny to anyone on board but him.

Thunda came right back with, "Den you ain't seen dis." He began to unbutton the front of his trousers.

This time, Nubbs had heard enough. "Shutta up you two! Thunda, evvyone a seen it. Half da time you fogets to wear pants."

Thunda chuckled. "Dat true." Still, he was a little irritated. He looked around and asked for an answer from anyone who could help. "What his problem?"

Nutty cut in a strict tone, "He drinked all night anda did stuffins. His head feel lika it esplodin'." Then, he looked squarely at Nubbs and dictated, "Not tonight. We leave in da morning."

Nubbs squinted beneath his pounding headache, "Yes, Chief."

Thunda was excited to hear more. Like an overgrown three-year-old, he had to know details. "Was dems da Wivvaflow whores?"

Nubbs smirked in agreement.

Thunda screamed, "I knowed it!"

A collective, "Shutta up!" rang out in the aircraft.

Thunda whispered as he fought back laughter, "How many dems?"

Nubbs held up four fingers.

Thunda screamed out in unbridled cheer, "Yeah, baby!"

Quicklip simply stated about Thunda, "Dat's it. I gonna kill him."

By this time, the aircraft had circled over the mountain area to the south of the library. Nutty spotted soft places in his defense there. "Ya, ya, ya. Afta you kill him get guns up on da peaks der anda der."

"I see it, Chief. Done," Quicklip submitted.

Thunda said, "No, you dumb."

Quicklip replied, "No, you dumb."

"No, you dumb."

"No, you dumb."

Nutty and Nubbs yelled, "Shutta up!"

***

Gunza and Guthrak were readying the troops and packing up supplies. The two old friends had a world of experience in getting prepared for battle. But neither had ever worked with the sheer numbers that they had to on this day. They weren't that concerned however. What really concerned them was the health of their closest friend and true leader, Biggabomb.

Guthrak, who knew that the relationship between Gunza and Biggabomb went back further than his and Bigga's, he asked, "You tink Biggabomb be ok?" He assumed that Gunza would know more than he did.

"Dunno, old friend. I be mo' worried 'bout his kid right now."

"How you mean?" Guthrak questioned.

263

Well, there it was. Gunza already put his foot in his mouth. He couldn't take back what he said. Besides, Guthrak was closer than a brother to him. He elaborated, "Nutty has a nightmares. Bad, too. Him got like demons or sumptin' in him from some Moon guy."

Guthrak commanded, "So, kills da moon guy. I would."

"I can't. Nutty don't a wants me to."

Guthrak scratched his head. "I knowed der was sumptin' strange 'bout dat kid. Nevva figure he lika demons, though."

Headhunta caught the tail end of the conversation. "Who lika demons?"

Gunza poked Headhunta in the ribs. "Look. Hims talks."

Headhunta didn't move. He just stared at Gunza and repeated himself, "Who lika demons?"

"Nobody lika demons."

"Guthrak say someone lika demons," Headhunta insisted.

Gunza tried to explain, but it came out backward. "No. Nobody lika demons. Well, someone lika demons, I guess. But no one I know. I tink."

Unsatisfied with Gunza's answer, Headhunta rotated his head slightly on axis and stared at Guthrak.

Guthrak shook his head and put his hands out as if to stop Headhunta from continuing the questioning. He said, "Quit starin' at me like dat, Creepo. If da kid lika demons, den he lika demons." He threw up his hands and walked away.

Headhunta asked as he followed, "What kid?"

Once again, Gunza thought, he was sticking his big foot in his big mouth. And once again, he would work while Headhunta went off and did whatever the hell he did. He ignored Headhunta and kept his head down, looking at maps. Headhunta eventually left.

As for Guthrak, he moved on as well. Gunza knew he was okay, even though he usually self-indulged in chemicals before battle; not that Gunza thought there was anything wrong with that. Guthrak had never let Gunza down when things got serious, but there were times when Gunza picked up the slack while Guthrak enjoyed some finer things in life.

Another officer approached Gunza and waited to be spoken to. Gunza put down the maps he was rolling and addressed the younger orc. "Yes?"

"You has been asked to be at Boss Nuttybomb house fo' dinna and drinks tonight wit' him anda Biggabomb at dark."

"K." Well, there you had it. While Headhunta disappeared and Guthrak did funky stuff with chemicals, he and Biggabomb drank before battle. Each had his own vices to get him through the toughest parts of war. Gunza thought about what they had seen, things they had done. It was a wonder they were still alive at all. A drink or a snort helped a bit, that's all.

Gunza went back to work. His mind continued to drift to the thoughts of war, his comrades, and Biggabomb. Was Biggabomb going to be alright?

***

Nuttybomb walked up the steps of the library to give his speech in front of a hundred thousand orcs. From the elevated height of the landing, he could be seen from this location at the Crossroads for a mile in each direction. Even though the library was far from finished, he wanted what it stood for to be a symbol of the future.

Hordes of orcs pushed tightly together, cramming to see their great leader. Many hadn't heard him speak. So many orcs were new to Big Town that so few recognized him as the Chief. This would be a first for many of them.

Speakers and connecting cables ran the length of the two roads that intersected at the library, giving all an opportunity to hear Nutty. Monitors were set up every two hundred feet to allow him to be seen at great distances. A huge, good-looking, battle-scarred teen is what they saw climbing the steps.

Nutty turned to the crowd, which was filled with applause. As he stepped forward to the microphone, they quieted. He reached into his pocket to get the speech that he had prepared, but it wasn't there. He calmly reached into the other pocket, but it, too, was empty. His face and neck felt a sudden flush of heat. This was the most important day so far in his life of speeches; he needed to rally his orcs to victory; to galvanize both home and abroad. He would give a speech to his troops a bit later to rally them, but the cause at home was nearly as important. He reckoned he would be embarrassed; no, he would be humiliated. He was so tired from the last few days, all he could do was try. He raised his hands to do three things. First of all, it quieted the rest of the crowd. Secondly, it built anticipation. Lastly, it bought him precious time to think and do some quick breathing exercises that Moonoak had taught him.

"Today begins da rest of our lives." That's how it started. He remembered that part with his newly reformed grammar from his notes. The rest was a blur. Although he fumbled to find what to say, the right words came through. He was clear and concise. He told the orcs of their place in history. He emphasized the importance of unity in unrelenting, non-negotiable defeat of their enemy. Not one Invada would be allowed to remain on Hotta soil. Not one Homeworlder would be allowed to remain a prisoner. They were the direct descendants of Da Rampage, and by Gods, Grim himself wrote of their coming from the heavens.

Nutty paused when the deafening roar of the green mass drowned out his voice on the sound system. The streets were never quiet again. He had to speak over a constant stream of excited chatter, whistles, and applause. He found himself raising his pitch and volume, accenting the most important things he had to say; his oratory proficiency was staggering. He talked about the library, its use for the children and the future generations. He vowed complete devotion to his following and offered to give his life in battle for their devotion in return.

There were other things said, fluff really. It was the type of stuff that further whipped the crowd into a frenzied, unyielding mass of production. He praised them. He told a couple jokes. Toward the end of his speech, he couldn't even be heard.

Muga was crying. She stood close to Biggabomb who was leaning on a building for support. He was silent. He had never given a speech like that; he didn't know how to. He hunched in stunned silence. The torch had been passed. There was no way that he wouldn't support his kid; *his* kid, the most powerful orc the world had ever known! Biggabomb gasped and had to sit. He had never been so proud. In this moment, just like the countless battles he had fought, he didn't think of himself. He would sit for hours until the crowds disbursed.

Uhra was jumping for joy and screaming, "Younut!" Her head was bobbing from side to side. Tears poured down her cheeks. Euphoria had gripped her for the first time in her life. That was *her* Nuttybomb, nobody else's. She didn't see the other thirty thousand screaming girls that wanted to have his babies. She didn't know how many would throw themselves upon his feet, offering all the pleasures they could to win his favor. She was in the moment, and what a moment it was!

Moonoak analyzed the things that unfolded before his eyes. Although Nutty had said special things for an orc, Moonoak didn't fully grasp how it was conveyed so effectively. He, himself, was taken by the boy. He could feel the excitement around him, the enthusiasm, and the willingness of the orcs to lay down their lives. He knew that Nutty wasn't near what he could be either. He knew about the dreams, the pressure, the uncertainty of his father's health, yet the boy did this. What was happening? What gifts did Nuttybomb possess? Where did he learn to do this?

After the speech, Nutty had a copy of what he said. He thought it wasn't bad, although he would have liked to say something different here or there, but overall, it was good. He didn't forget to get all his points across. He even remembered to thank everyone and pay tribute to those putting their lives on the line.

Quicklip escorted him through the library and out the back doors. He smiled and said, "Well, dat went well. Don't ya tink?"

Thunda agreed as he followed and walked alongside Nubbs. "Yeah, but four whores is good, too."

In unison, came the words, "Shutta up!"

Nutty reworked some things on his speech during his trip over to the troops. He tweaked some words that he thought might be more effective while in the back of a truck. He had several hours to do this as the crowd took forever to disband. He and his guards fought their way through, but made little progress. Sneaking out the back did little to expedite their travel.

When he finally arrived, this time it was to several hundred thousand screaming warriors. A buzz had already reached them about his effect on their loved ones. Luckily, his speech went off without a hitch, and much like the first speech, euphoria set in. They were ready for battle!

***

Later that evening, friends and family gathered at Biggabomb's and Muga's house. Excitement from earlier carried over into the house with each orc that entered. The atmosphere was one of celebration.

Nutty didn't understand it. Okay, he was able to comprehend that he got many of the orcs on board with his plan, but celebration was the furthest thing from his mind. The future was uncertain. Did he fool even those closest to him? Didn't they realize how many would die in the process of working toward victory?

He was also concerned with the whole Darkster thing; it weighed on him heavily. The truth was that he knew almost nothing about hocus pocus stuff. He couldn't protect himself against it. In fact, he was afraid to go to sleep. Plus, if he was away, which he was going to be soon, he couldn't protect any of them either. He decided to relinquish his troubled thoughts to those of sharing in good food and company.

Familiar faces came and went. Guthrak stopped by before heading back to finish preparing for war, as did Quicklip and Thunda. Their sarcastic comments toward each other were scarce as they engaged in simple pleasantries before making their departure. Several girl friends of Pretty and Uhra made brief appearances as well. Thankfully, Uhra hadn't noticed their batting of eyelashes and playing with hair to get Nutty's attention. They wouldn't be her friends much longer if she caught wind of their intentions. They left without incident.

Biggabomb became loud. He wanted food and was overly aggravated because of his lungs. He stared at the ceiling as he spoke at an overtly rude volume. "Where my food, Woman?" Muga had grown used to Biggabomb's incessant badgering over when and how to serve him. She had almost completely tuned him out at this point. He tried again, this time as loud as his battered lungs would allow. "Woman, where my food, dammit?"

"I gonna stick it in a you ass, Bigmouff!"

Biggabomb looked at Nutty and Gunza. He chuckled under his breath, "It prolly taste better."

"I heard dat you big bastid!"

"Can you hear dis?" Biggabomb lifted his leg. He cleared the main room of the house with a sound and smell that was incomprehensible.

"You asgusting!" came from the back room.

Biggabomb was laughing uncontrollably. "You sure you wanna stick it der?"

Pretty came in from the back room to open some windows. All she could muster was, "Yuck, Dad!"

Runzda and Kago were hysterical. But, being kids, and orcs at that, they soon went back to playing and totally forgot about the foul stench that hung low and warm in the room.

Uhra was laughing and gagging. She pushed passed Pretty to get outside as fast as possible. When she reached fresh air, she heard the beginnings of a quiet conversation that was hidden by the raucous inside.

Nutty was answering Gunza, "Dunno, Gunza. He need lungs. Wit'out dems, he will die."

"Dammit, Kid. I mean, Chief."

"It ok Gunza. Just call me Nutty."

"You dad beed my Boss fo' longa time. Dunno if docs can take my lung fo' him. You knows I give it if I can."

"Prolly not. Hims got strange blood. Me too. Not many orc have dat blood. So, lungs don't fit right or sumptin'."

"Hmm," Gunza frowned.

Biggabomb yelled from inside, "You can comes back in. Muga's food kill da smell in here."

Gunza smiled as he headed in, leaving Nutty and Uhra alone.

Uhra got on her tippy toes and leaned up against Nutty. She threw her arms around his neck and said, "I so proud a you. In case we gets no chance later, Younut...I wuvs you." Then, she embraced Nutty with

271

a long, warm, wet kiss. She felt his body respond against hers. She looked down and then, looked back up at his eyes. She bit her lip in a playful way and smiled. "Tink 'bout me, Younut." Then she turned and skipped into the house, her hair bouncing as her head bobbed back and forth in joy.

Nutty mumbled, "How can I not?" He didn't head right inside; he needed fifteen minutes to calm down before he could. He finally entered when it was time to eat. Uhra looked at him from top to bottom and smiled as she bit her lip again. She raised her eyebrows and winked at him.

Muga caught this interplay as she served Biggabomb. When she looked at Uhra, Uhra put her head down so no eye contact was made. She hid a smile beneath her long hair. Nutty wasn't much better. He forced a grin that looked like he was in pain. Muga asked, "What you two want?"

Like a child caught with her hand in a cookie jar, Uhra blurted out, "Nuttin'."

"Nuttin? You not hungry?"

Uhra scrambled to cover her rushed response. She always seemed to put her foot in her mouth when it came to talking with Muga while she was flustered over Nutty. She wasn't even sure why. In this case, she thought about the warm kiss, Nutty's large hands on her waist, and his physical reaction to her touch. She felt as if the whole room could sense what happened, even though she knew that it couldn't be the case. Still, her knee-jerk reaction to any questioning seemed critical to hiding her wanting Nuttybomb in every way a woman might. Uhra fought to compose herself. She said, "Well, yeah. I hungry. But I can wait till dems get der food first." She hoped that she covered her bases and her lie wasn't too obvious.

Muga picked up on Uhra's sudden change in tone. It seemed just a little too forced. She saw Uhra and Nutty make eye contact. Then, they would notice that she saw them, and they would look away. She decided to play along. "If dems eat first, der be none left a fo' you."

Biggabomb's mouth ran with the juices from the meal he was mutilating. He ran his tongue from his elbow to his wrist so as not to miss out on even the smallest drip possible. He paused just for a moment between slurps and snapped, "It true! I so hungry, I coulds eat da ass outta da stink rat!"

Muga shook her head in disgust. "Is der anyting you won't eat?"

Biggabomb hardily belted out a belch. Then added, "Not so far. I even eat all da stuff you cook, Muga."

Out of nowhere, a usually quiet individual had something to say. She had an issue that had been festering for quite a while, and although the timing wasn't great, it was necessary. Pretty was growing tired of the old man's insults. She had seen her mom get lambasted with indignities countless times. Maybe it wasn't her place to say anything, but it just came out, "Shutta up, Dad! Dat 'nuff. Nobody care fo' Momma cookin' jokes. Leave her alone."

Biggabomb dropped the bone that he was sucking on. He looked around the quiet room, but found no answer to the silent question he asked. He was a proud orc, a past Chief who had led his orcs to victory over insurmountable odds. He wore the scars of a battled veteran; his claw and ravaged lungs affirmed this. No big-mouthed bitch was going to talk to him that way, especially his daughter. His eyes finally fell upon Pretty's. He stated things as monotone fact. "First, you a lot lika you mom. If you anyone else anda talk to me lika dat, I kill you. Second, you got bigga rocks in you pants than most males. You needs dat to be strong as female in dis life, but be a careful. Anda last, you is right. Nobody care fo' Momma cooking, joke or not."

Slight chuckles faded in and then out.

Muga diffused things as quickly as she could. "Pretty, him put up with my cookin', and I put up wit' him stinky, crude, dirty, nose-pickin', fartin', and stupid ass jokes. I guess, I wuvs him."

Gunza added to the lightheartedness that was needed. "Muga, he such a catch, dat if you dump him, I mighta marry hims."

Everyone laughed. Muga thought it best to put things to rest, once and for all with, "Pretty, why don't you worka night shift fo' me. Anda I relieves you in da morning. Go 'head, gurl."

Pretty nervously finished up her food, forced down a last sip of water, and stood up. She walked around the clutter of crates, food, and bottles to get to Biggabomb. She leaned down and hugged him. "I sorry, Dad."

Biggabomb smiled and he put his good arm around her. "It ok. Someday you will undastand how moms and dads work. You turnin' into a woman now. Soon you be a mom, too."

Gunza found himself looking at his own daughter. Then, he thought of the compromised position he was in. He was pretty sure that Uhra had chosen Nutty as her mate for life. The signs were all there, regardless of how much Uhra tried to hide them. Nutty practically gave his life to save her. Now, the kid was his Chief. He thought to himself, *What a weaved web, or a tangled web, or whatever the hell it was that we weave.*

After Pretty excused herself and left for the medical area, Muga decided to load up some ammunition and fire some shots at Uhra and Nutty. "So, Nutty, I hears dat lil gurl, Sweeties, is back in da town."

"So?"

"So, didn't you used to kiss her?" Muga pried.

Uhra squinted in apparent pain. She immediately gritted her teeth, totally unaware of her facial expressions as she raised an eyebrow.

Nutty looked over at Uhra. At first, he was proud to have kissed anyone. He was bullied as far back as he could remember. He had actually forgotten about Sweeties. He forgot about her sister, too. He had kissed them both; actually, more than kissed. It was the kind of play that resulted from younglin's curiosity about the anatomy of the opposite sex. They had explored each other. Nutty was smiling until the grim reality of Uhra's face bled the color from his own. He gulped and answered, "Whatevva."

Muga pushed, "Just sayin'. She offerly pretty anda you is getting olda now. Times fo' you to start tinkin' 'bout pickin' a mate."

Uhra growled, "I hungry. I eats now."

Nutty had bigger things to worry about. In reality, he *had* picked his mate, but he had the war and Darkster on his mind. Also, for some reason, he didn't want to push fate by announcing his intentions toward

Uhra before he left for combat. He didn't want her to be hurt in the event he died in battle. It didn't occur to him that her feelings weren't limited by his declaration in return. On the contrary, she yearned for him, whether it was known or not to the world. Furthermore, this was his first real relationship with a woman. He didn't know what he should do, or when to do it. He knew the entanglements with Gunza. Nuttybomb literally had the weight of the world on his shoulders. He tried to persuade his mother by saying, "War here now. I can't tink 'bout udder stuff. Sweeties not fo' me, anyway."

"No?"

Nutty shook his head from side to side. "No."

"It Momma job to make sure her boy-"

"No, Momma!" Nutty exclaimed.

Biggabomb and Gunza watched as the two went back-and-forth. They turned their heads in unison, first to Muga, then to Nutty. Attention was drawn from one to the other, and as they spoke in turn, so too did Biggabomb's and Gunza's heads move from side to side. Biggabomb yelled at his wife, "Hey Fatass, you wanna move ova here so my neck don't hurt?"

Muga paid him no mind. She pressed on with Nutty. "What 'bout all da gurls dat you will be savin' in da war. Lots a dems would has you babies. You might be gone fo' longa time. Dems sneaks into your tent at night."...

"Ova my dead body," rang out. Uhra had heard enough. She was outraged to hear such things. She looked at Nutty and scowled, "Stuffins wit' dems and I kill dems first and den, I kills you! Gottit?"

Nutty gulped and shook his head up and down without thought.

Sixteen
Goodbye

In retrospect, orcs talked about the "Today begins da rest of our lives" speech with controversy. They have argued about what Nutty said and where he said it; they made bets over what he wore. But the details didn't really matter. What was important was the fact that they rallied behind him, and that Big Town was the rallying point. Production continued at a dizzying pace, and if possible, even picked up speed.

As Moonoak cited writings by Grim and others he had learned from, he explained to Nutty the intricacies of culture and how development occurred. As life-giving resources became abundant and the population flourished, so too did the availability of those who could work in specialized fields; they were no longer needed to provide necessities. There were more tinkerers, stone masons, and for the first time, artists of different types. Yes, even orcs became artisans. They built monolithic structures made of stone, painted in gaudy colors to highlight their accomplishments. A prominent creation of the time was the great number of statues, fashioned in Nuttybomb's likeness. Orcs competed to build the biggest and the best. Others came together to advance the development of vehicles and medicine.

Orcs emulated Nutty's actions and tried to repeat his words. A crude mixture of languages with simple barriers began to be overcome as dialects mixed and blended some; divisions that were created thousands of years earlier were slowly being eliminated.

Adversaries and rivals were now on the same side. Their common goals and language helped to spur further unity. Speaking in the same tongue brought easier trade and sharing of ideas. The cycle was self-fulfilling.

Moonoak sat on the stone floor with his arms crossed. His legs were spread apart at the knee with the bottoms of his feet touching each other. His head was lowered, and the hood of his brown robe was pulled back, revealing a perceptible wisdom through slight graying of the hair at his temples. For the moment, he was done teaching, at least in a physical sense. It was time to instruct Nuttybomb and the group to open their minds, to accept all, and to think of nothing.

The group consisted of Moonoak's half-dozen followers and several new students. Moonoak went through a series of basic breathing exercises and issued some benign drugs to help the process along. A wooden bowl was sent around the room. Each member took a healthy drink from it and passed it on to the left.

Nutty held the bowl with his left hand and picked at something in it with his right. His large pointer finger stirred the dark liquid that had gobs of muck mixed in. After a reassuring look from Moonoak, he lifted the bowl to his lips and drank. An occasional chewing of thick substances was needed to get the bitter cocktail down. But down it went, and with it, some of the anxieties he had been feeling.

Moonoak addressed him, "Nutty, you are a bit calmer, no?"

"Yes."

"Good. Put all tings out of you mind. No war. No problems. Don't even tink good tings. Breathe lika I been sayin' to. Tink only of breathin'. Nuttin' else. Breathe in, breathe out."

This was the most stupid thing Nutty had ever tried to do. How could he stop thinking? He was thinking about not thinking. By default, his irrational thoughts led him to the obvious, rationality. The harder he tried not to think, the more he thought about it. It was like asking someone who was drowning not to breathe.

"Nutty. Tink 'bout breathing. Hear you own breaths."

It took some time before Nutty could finally relax to a point where he could clear his mind. He had few moments of clarity though as his cluttered brain seemed to cast random thoughts. The relentless barrage of thinking was difficult to overcome, but he resolved to do his best in the future. One thing was certain. His apprehension was replaced by a current feeling of serenity. If he didn't become too complacent, he thought he could enjoy being at ease. It had been quite a while since he felt carefree.

Nutty asked if he could speak with Moonoak alone. Moonoak dismissed his followers and sent the newcomers on their way. He began cleaning up the bowl and various paraphernalia from the meeting. He sensed Nutty's welling uneasiness and addressed it. "What bodders you, Nutty?"

"Darkster."

"Of course. Dis sumptin' dat will take time to sort out, I tink."

That was an answer that Nutty wasn't willing to accept. "We don't has time."

"I undastand. But der many orcs here now. Too many. Dems clog my mind so dat I can't find him by tinkin' like we just a did. We will sort dis out. Maybe der is a way to set a trap."

Nutty nodded. He did understand what Moonoak was saying. Moonoak was a very wise orc; he was well-spoken, and the things he said, were accurate. He had certain attributes that were foreign to most orcs, too. There was a quiet air of confidence about him, not the sort of unsophisticated boasting that accompanied, or more accurately, defined most. Plus, he knew things that others didn't. Nutty began to realize that he would be a powerful ally.

Soon, Nuttybomb was with his officers, discussing reports that were coming back from behind enemy lines. Headhunta and a group of infiltrators had penetrated the enemy's perimeters without detection. They sent back information regarding size and movement of troops, weapons, and material. A long discussion ensued as Homeworlder positions and potential movements were reconfigured.

Afterward, Nutty walked around, inspecting his powerful army and giving last words of encouragement. The heat from the morning sun was blistering. Nutty felt it on his head, neck, and shoulders as he traveled. Even his tough, leathery skin burned from its unrelenting assault of scathing ferocity. The hot times were beginning, and with them, a long, punishing season of crippling weather. Hotta was so aptly named because of this unbearable spike in temperatures.

Nutty went to an area that was designated as his headquarters. It was nothing more than tarps that were hung along wooden poles. Mesh screening ran from the roof to the dirt floor to aid in insect prevention and was held in place with spikes that lined the outer walls. The enclosure was rounded out by use of sand bags. This whole rough and ready arrangement was easy to assemble and disassemble, perfect for a mobile operation that would come by day's end.

Nutty sat down in a folding chair with his back to the outside world. The shade of the tarp offered some shielding from the direct sunlight. He put his feet up on a desk and began going over supply lists. He decided to increase the water supply that would become progressively more necessary as the heat continued to rise in the weeks to follow. He reworked some other numbers, his attention broken at times due to the noise of his armies moving out.

Lastly, Nutty thought about contingencies. He even planned for the possibility of an Invada trap. Big Town wouldn't survive a full-scale barrage without proper defense. If his troops being pulled away to engage the enemy was a ruse, he needed ways to protect his civilians. Satisfied with the solutions he arrived at, he allowed his mind to drift.

***

The hot season was in full swing and the sun's rays were so strong. The warm water was only a temporary respite from the searing heat above. Nutty dunked himself over and over, enjoying this liquid playground. He was bathing in the river when he caught a glimpse of two girls approaching the bank ahead of him. He dunked himself one more time before wiping his eyes to see who was entering the water.

He recognized Sweetie, a girl from school. He guessed that the other girl was either her friend or her sister. He watched them undress, his eyes just above the waterline. They carelessly discarded all their garments, unaware that he was lying beneath the surface. Besides, they were a couple hundred feet away. They probably wouldn't have picked him out amongst the floating tree limbs and debris that washed into the river. He couldn't make out details at this distance either, but knew they were naked by the uninterrupted green skin that showed from their heads to their toes.

Then, something occurred to Nutty. He didn't have any clothes on either. His clothes were somewhere near theirs. He made his way in their general direction, but kept a safe distance so they wouldn't see him. As he attempted to swim around to the bank without them noticing him, he stepped on a crab which was not very happy. Its large claws dug into Nutty's foot as a defensive effort to fend off his intrusion, and an offensive attack to seek revenge on the stupid individual that dared to even test its dangerous grasp.

Nutty screamed out in pain. He bobbed up and down, trying to free himself from the crab. The more he fought however, the angrier it became. It attached to him in a death grip and clamped down harder than before. Nutty screamed even louder. He scrambled to get his footing, so he could make his way to the bank quicker. Unbeknownst to him, he caught the full attention of the girls. As he scampered ashore, their curious eyes followed him.

Nutty jumped around in circles for several minutes. He covered a hundred feet in each direction as he tried to dislodge the painful water beast from his sensitive foot. His only saving grace was a stick that he found. He pried the crab's claws open and flung it back into the water. The crab flew thirty feet over the girls' heads. They were now only ten-feet from him.

Reality rushed into Nutty's brain. He had been flailing around like a baby, kicking and screaming before the watchful eyes of two girls. Not only that, he was naked, every inch of him. He stood in front of them, dumbfounded. His mouth hung open as his eyes looked at them in disbelief. What was he to do next?

He laughed a nervous laugh and walked back into the water. He figured that the damage was already done; they had already seen everything. He would cover himself a bit by getting back into the river. Twofold, he would also benefit from the warm water that he would use to wash away the blood on his foot. As he entered the water, the girls said nothing. They did back away from him, though.

Nutty waited for them to say something, but nothing came from their mouths. He got in, up to his chest, and turned away from them. He didn't know if his embarrassment showed. Hell, everything else did. He closed his eyes and reopened them, hoping he was in a nightmare. Yep, it was a nightmare, alright, but not the kind that comes during sleep. He washed his foot, avoiding conversation with the girls that quietly watched him.

Finally, out of tension that enveloped him, he blurted out, "I hate da crabs!"

The two girls giggled. Sweetie admitted, "I hate dems, too."

Nutty got up the courage to turn around and face his onlookers. He didn't know what to say. He thought that casual conversation would at least mask his embarrassment, but words eluded him. He finally settled upon, "Yup." That was the best he could do. He was nine and had no experience with girls. Other than a few accidents where he was seen by his sisters, this was the first-time strangers had seen him fully exposed. What could he say?

The older girl didn't seem so embarrassed. She was quiet when she spoke, but seemed less shy than Nutty and Sweetie. She said, "Dat crab wuz big, too. Hims nasty. You ok?"

Nutty slowly replied, "Yes." He guessed that he was alright. He wasn't all that experienced in crab attacks either.

The girl insisted, "Lemme see." She approached Nutty through the somewhat murky water.

Nutty lifted his bleeding foot, but he was in the water deep enough that it wouldn't break the surface.

"Back up. Can't see you foot in da deep water."

Nutty reluctantly backed up, aided by her pushing forward. Before he knew it, water only came to the height of his thigh. It took time to sink in, though. As the girl took his foot and led him to shallow water, she exposed herself as well. Nutty's eyes were locked on her chest. Then, they found their way to the top of her legs.

The girl followed his eyes as she wiped his foot. She smiled. "Lemme wrap da foot."

"K." Nutty anxiously followed her ashore. She used hers and Sweetie's shirts as something to sit on and pushed Nutty into a sitting position atop them. Then, she used a headband to wrap his foot. He lay back clumsily while he watched her work.

Sweetie squatted beside him, making small talk as she took in the full view up close. "So, you builds dat motor ting at skool, huh?"

"What? Oh, yeah." Nutty turned to see Sweetie's torso just inches from his face. Before he answered, she leaned into him. She excused herself with, "Oops, I help with da foot, too."

Sweetie carefully leaned on Nutty's lower stomach with one hand while she massaged part of his exposed foot. She slipped slightly and rested her forearm in the crux of his pelvis. She deliberately brushed against him to get a reaction, and the reaction she sought, was given. He was nine. He just watched in disbelief. Sweetie looked back over her shoulder and smiled.

The other girl shook her head and pleaded, "Easy, Sweetie." Then, she leaned down to carefully move Sweetie's arm out of the way until Nutty was no longer hidden. She looked up into Nutty's eyes and smiled a big, devilish smile. "Well, good ting da crab gets you foot. Him coulda gotten you pee."

Nutty shrugged anxiously, "I guess so." His mouth was dry; he gulped from nervousness.

Playful gestures led to playful touching. Nutty's eyes widened. The older, not so shy, and fairly experienced girl led his hand to her body. She had him touch her stomach. Sweetie mimicked her sister and did the same with his other hand. Their necks and shoulders followed. Within minutes, there was little that he hadn't touched. Only the areas that were most precious to them were off limits. Adolescent kissing was tried, albeit awkwardly messy. If Nutty was any older, he would have been able to, and probably would have acted on his chance to have his way with these girls. As of yet, he was unaware of his body's ability to respond in these types of situations. In the meanwhile, he was more than happy to explore.

Sweetie, who was also new to seeing a male's body during arousal, was amazed by his body's reaction. Her inexperience caused her to inadvertently gasp and say in a startled way, "Look! It growed bigga."

The older girl smiled when she saw what Sweetie was pointing at. She wrapped her fingers around it and sighed, "Oh my."

Just then, Sweetie screamed, "What da? It shootin's lika gun!"

Nutty was shocked. He wasn't even sure why he was so rattled, but for some reason in that moment, he was terrified. In that instant, he felt totally naked and extremely vulnerable. His mind couldn't figure out what his body was doing. So, without any thought of how good the sensations were that pulsated through him, he jumped to his feet and scurried to get his clothes on. He hollered, "I gotta go now." Embarrassment kept his eyes from making any more contact with the girls. He left them by the water as he fled. He heard the girls giggling once he cleared the area.

Nutty's quest for knowledge was cut short that day by his panicked decision to leave so abruptly. It also marked the last time that he would have such an encounter with the opposite sex so far. He would go on to see Sweetie over the next several months before she moved away. He thought about her teasing eyes as she would taunt his curiosity with a tempestuous, "Hello, Nutty."

***

Nutty's daydream was broken by, "Younut. What you been tinkin'?"

Nutty looked up to find Uhra standing before him. His dreaming mind slowly came into focus. "What?"

"You ok? You seem funny."

Why was he cursed with such bad timing? "What? Oh. Nuttin'. Just tinkin'. Been busy. I was goin' ova war stuff before you a comes."

He didn't completely lie. The truth was that he had gone over such things earlier. He tricked himself into thinking that his rationalization justifiably covered his ass nicely. The sequential order of his thinking before her arrival was true, after all.

"Oh. Any bad dreams?"

"Umm, no." In fact, his dreams were quite nice; never better. He smiled. Uhra hesitantly dismissed his odd actions and strange reactions. "Well, I just sayin' goodbye. Ok, not goodbye. I see you soon?"

Nutty had completely forgotten about his daydream. His thoughts were only on Uhra now. He wanted to reassure her however he could. "I try to be backs as soon as I can."

Uhra thought that this was probably the best time to discuss something that had been on her mind for some time. "Nutty, ya 'memba when you asked if Dem orcs in da cabin did bad tings to me?"

"Yup."

"Not bad tings, like break my legs?" Uhra paused as she tried to say the right words. "Bad tings to my...umm...you know, my place below my belly?" She blushed and nervously kicked her toe into the ground. She put her head down because she couldn't keep eye contact out of embarrassment.

Nutty gulped. In that moment, he may have been just as nervous as Uhra. He simply scratched his head and replied, "Umm, yeah?"

Uhra's voice cracked a little and shook as she spoke this time. "Dem didn't touch me der. I justa has to tolds you. Umm, no orc has; none." She kept her head down.

Nutty smiled. He wasn't sure how to respond. He looked up to the sky and took a deep breath. Then, he exhaled through puckered lips.

Uhra looked up at him and then down again as he made eye contact with her. She did this several times before she had the nerve to look at him for more than a second at a time.

Nutty finally spoke. "Umm, I dunno what to say, but I really glad you not hurt der. I wuz really worried 'bout you."

He said enough. He obviously cared, and it showed. The two embraced one last time. Uhra wiped tears from her eyes as she ducked out of the headquarters and headed back to miserable work at the medical area. There was still plenty of prep work to do before wounded would arrive.

Nutty made it a point to say goodbye to his loved ones one last time. He didn't know if he would ever return. So, just in case, he did the best he could to convey his love to them. In turn, their wishes gave him strength to carry on with his responsibilities.

Soon, he was away. His first destination beneath the cruel sun was the local airfield. He was driven some fifteen miles or so through a harsh, sandy plain to the northeast. It was here, hidden among dead trees and stone, that aircraft were camouflaged to blend in with the tan surroundings.

He left his vehicle and was met by Booma. The thick air was sweltering and sweat ran from the two orcs as they briefly discussed their plans. Most importantly was Nutty's request for Moonoak to meet with him at the next destination. Booma guaranteed this to his younger brother with an affirmed pat on the back.

The two parted; Booma for his truck, and Nutty for the larger aircraft that was pulling in from the far side of the runway. Nutty looked back one last time. He looked back at his city on the horizon. He looked back at the comforts he was leaving behind. Finally, he looked back at his childhood. It was back there somewhere, too.

Things would never be the same. He longed for his childhood. He yearned for peace. All he could find were questions. How well did he leave Big Town defended? Would he ever return? Would he ever see Uhra again? And where the hell was Darkster?

In that moment, he longed for the oddest thing. He needed Moonoak. He needed to feel that peace that always seemed to elude him these days. He wanted to do breathing exercises across from his teacher, to forget his troubles, and to find clarity that had toyed with him. No, he couldn't wait to see Moonoak, but he had to.

Nutty was escorted aboard the aircraft by King Basha. "Chief? Dis way, please."

"A pleasure, my old a friend."

Basha walked Nutty down the center of the fuselage. He stopped at the row of seats where the two would sit. He asked his superior, "You wanna sit by da window or near da aisle?"

Nutty smiled. There were times when he seemed so unimposing. At other times, he was a monster, released with a millennium of penned up rage. At this time, he offered Basha the choice of seating.

Basha smiled, his gratitude obvious through the gaps in his teeth. "Da aisle fo' me, if dat ok. I fight harda dan any orc, but flyin' not my ting."

"Gotcha. I lika window seat, anyway." Nutty squeezed his large frame past Basha and sat by the window.

"Good. Tanks, Chief."

Nutty looked through the grimy glass. He watched the dusty runway change directions and drop beneath him as his stomach felt lighter. Air bound he was, again watching the formations below. What an oddity, he thought. The smaller things got, the better they came into view in the bigger picture.

For a moment, he thought about another irony. He was significant to his orcs, but just a dot compared to the expansive ground below. This insignificance was further dwarfed by the vastness of space. What difference could he really make? Was he able to make a difference at all? He hoped that Moonoak was able to teach him to step back, away from himself, so he could see himself in the bigger picture.

The aircraft flew at low altitudes so as not to be picked up by radar or satellite. However, it was high enough to show the long columns of vehicles from Nutty's army as far as the eye could see. These vehicles appeared desperately vulnerable, not unlike Nutty that day he was at the river with those girls. He chuckled to himself for a second, but too soon he realized how exposed his troops really were. Hopefully, his army's forward movements would buy enough time for his real weapons to get close enough and come in to play.

Once on the ground, more reports were brought to Nutty. He had barely gotten to his tent when Invada drop zone information was dumped in his lap. He looked over the reports and found some things to his liking. Apparently, the Invadas had a huge hole just south of their drop zone that he could breach. The problem was their technologically superior aircraft. Getting close was a problem to an area like this where incoming and outgoing aircraft could see for dozens of miles. Nutty went right to work on formulating a way to gain the upper hand.

To help him come to a decision, he called for his officers to go over all options. He valued their input; he figured that more eyes might see more problems that he may have missed. His humility and willingness to share responsibility were traits that were rare in Orcdom. Many too-eager leaders were willing to die, or worse, throw the lives of their troops into futility. Nutty was not such an irresponsible and callus wretch.

Concurrently, Moonoak was just arriving from Big Town in his usual unassuming garb. Although he didn't like to travel this close to the edges of battle, he thought of Nutty as a student and a friend. The usual handshake and smile preceded serious talks between him and Nutty. The two sat and briefly meditated at Moonoak's insistence when he found Nutty to be anxious.

Nutty was the first to speak as he came out of his trance-like state. "I no dreamed 'bout Darkster last night."

"Dat good. You not mention dat before."

"Guess I was relaxed and fogots."

"Meditation clears da mind of such tings."

Nutty agreed, but he had been thinking about things that seemed to make sense to him. Had he not dreamed about Darkster because of proximity? Maybe he didn't dream about him because Darkster knew that he was on to him. Nutty brought both possibilities to Moonoak's attention.

"Could be either, Nutty. I don't sense him, either."

"I wonder if he left town yestaday. Hey, stay at headquarters so we cans see if he come back near me."

Moonoak disliked war and violence altogether. He hardly liked the idea of being so close to battle. "I tink it be best if I go back to Big Town."

Nutty admitted a weakness to his new teacher. "I needs you here, Moonoak."

Seventeen
The Battle for Hotta

Nuttybomb, Biggabomb, all the leaders, and officers sought information from any and all thinkers to derive at the most accurate probability they could ascertain. Based on the planets' movements, by in large, they all agreed that the Invadas needed to conquer them within five weeks. If not, the Invada's possibility to resupply would be virtually impossible as the distances between the planets would widen to an expanse that would be too great to travel. They would have to wait five months or more for that.

So, did the Homeworlders have to defeat the Invadas before then? Probably. Would holding them off just long enough cause their eventual collapse without resupply? Probably not. The situation did not appear promising.

The Homeworlders were outnumbered twelve-to-one against a fierce and brutal enemy. They were technologically inferior and lacked the ability to square off outside Hotta's atmosphere. This was probably the greatest disadvantage they had. Their moves could be seen from high altitudes, giving away their positions. By all accounts, they had no chance against their opponent. But these descendants of Da Rampage would succeed or die trying.

The Invada's southern drop zone would be hit with a large enough collection of fighter planes, bombers, and junkers that it would appear to be the main thrust. Minimal damage inflicted on the enemy would be expected. Fighter planes would provide whatever fire support they could so the bombers could unload their devastating payloads upon the Invadas' heads. Junkers were bulky, unprotected pieces of metal and wood garbage that were laden with explosives. They were to follow the fighters and bombers on suicide runs, flying into key targets if possible. Orcs that flew these "cans of death", as they were referred to, had little training. They also had little time to eject before impact. Low level "shoots" were developed to help pilots get out at the last possible moment. Tests only showed around fifty-percent survivability of junker pilots to date.

Also heading toward the enemy positions to the south was a line of replica tanks and vehicles made of wood. They were being towed in columns by lead tanks like trains. The dummy vehicles had no propulsion of their own. They were simply decoys, without need for motors or guns. They would represent five hundred tanks and another eight hundred mixed vehicles. Fake troops would be dropped from the junkers just before their final approach. These shoots with thousands of phony troops would land somewhere near hundreds of other phony vehicles that appeared to be reserve troops. They were booby trapped to explode.

Nutty would lead the main attack to the north approximately two hours later. To further confuse the Invadas, he would send his troops from a number of different directions and converge on the enemy's flanks. Air power would take off from, and land at, different locations. To add insult to injury, things learned from the prison ship would be used to crack codes and cause more confusion. Nutty's own troops would be giving fake positions and troop movements on Invada channels.

Here was the real ploy. After Nutty got the Invadas to see their error, they would commit their troops to the north. By then, Nutty hoped to inflict as much damage as possible in the north, and sneak troops back in to the south. The drop zone might be left weak and vulnerable. Collecting some ships and other aircraft would be a nice prize. But coordination was essential.

The trap was set. Casualties were expected to be extremely high. Nutty's northern force hoped for a three-to-one disadvantage at best. Maybe the decoys, surprise, and hit-and-run tactics on the enemy's flanks would even the odds. Time would tell.

Minor skirmishes along the southern coast were already going on. The remnants of the Wasp Legion, with help from King Basha's Gravediggas, began reclaiming towns lost to the Invadas over the last month. These areas would become triage units for casualties and eventually, bases to launch air attacks from. Most of the Invadas had moved on to towns they hadn't taken yet, leaving small pockets of resistance that were easily cleaned up. More important, were the pieces found that might ultimately turn the tide of war in favor of the Homeworlders. Weapons, damaged vehicles, and ships were snatched up and rushed back to Big Town to be studied and reverse engineered. Maps that were found, as well as prisoners taken, were used to learn about, and confirm, Invada plans.

On the Eastern Continent, most of the Invadas had left and come to the Western Continent to finish off the pesky Homeworlders. Nutty sent thirty thousand troops and scouts to the old battlegrounds in hope of retrieving more information.

***

Evening had come. The lack of direct sunlight did little, if anything to comfort the troops from the oppressive heat. It did provide some cover of darkness by the time the Invadas began to counter attack.

The first hour went by. Nutty was kept abreast of enemy troop movements. He knew the numbers moving on both sides to the south. His decoy force was weak there; he knew that he was sending it on a possible suicide run. He waited impatiently for part of the Invada's northern troops to move south. Without their commitment, not only could his southern force be wiped out, but his northern force would still be vastly outnumbered. The troops to the south might be slaughtered for nothing.

Nutty began working on his contingency plans to save his southern troops. Before he executed orders to carry out those plans, the Invada's northern army blinked. Much of it raced south to meet Nutty's decoy army. The trap had been sprung and the bait had worked.

Over the second hour, Nutty confirmed what he suspected. His southern air force did the best it could to inflict damage and draw the Invadas into the trap, but they did fairly well. Nutty didn't believe that they would be so effective. Their being under the cover of darkness hid them from the better equipped Invada fighters that hunted them: nightfall was hiding them from the larger, more dangerous enemy air force.

On the ground, the Homeworlder's southern force left wooden tanks and fake troops, ready to blow up the enemy. The real troops found escape under the same darkness that saved their fighters and bombers. By in large, the main fighting force to the south was out of harm's way and fully functional. They would now wait for Nutty and the northern army to do their thing before heading to the drop zone.

Nutty wiped the sweat from his brow, screamed, "Letta us go," and raced ahead of his troops. Overhead, Homeworlder fighters screamed from behind him. They flew out ahead of him and drew enemy fire from the air and the ground. Bombers split the air with deafening roars as they advanced, low to the ground above the enemy positions.

Seconds later, the sky lit up. Homeworlder bombers were dropping their payloads onto unsuspecting Invadas. They softened key areas for Nutty and his orcs to take control of. A barrage from tanks and artillery decimated enemy troops that sought cover from the bombers' onslaught, clearing paths deep into the enemy's belly.

Nutty screamed out, "Letta us go, boys!"

Nutty was flanked by Gunza on one side and Guthrak on the other. Quicklip, Thunda, and Nubbs were close behind. They threw themselves into a melee before Nutty could register any fear. They cut through the stunned troops with ease. This was Nutty's land, his home. Every swing of his blade brought him closer to Uhra.

For nearly forty minutes, Nutty and his organized army pushed through enemy positions. What they didn't kill, they captured. Soon, they rested for a short period. It was during this time that Nutty assessed the situation. It seemed that his main force pushed right through the front line of the Invada's northern army. His intuition was correct.

While the Invada's main northern force moved south to meet Nutty's decoy, the Homeworlders had gained total surprise. So much so, that the Homeworlders that broke through the flanks, harassed part of the Invada's northern force that moved south. The Invadas were totally confused.

Intelligence confirmed the enemy movement south, and its eventual turn to the north. That was all Nutty needed to hear. He began withdrawing his army, but not before stripping the area of resources that he now controlled. Additionally, two hundred square miles were rigged with mines and explosives, waiting for the enemy's return.

While Nutty's main force fled and drew the enemy north, his southern force went to work. Nutty sent additional fighters and bombers to its aid from the north. The multitude of aircraft swung west, over the open water, dropped south, and wreaked havoc along the drop zone's west coast. His troops were parachuted into the drop zone.

Now, for all the Invada's technology and control of the atmosphere and beyond, it was useless in the hands of idiots. These were still orcs. Most didn't think quickly. They had a hard time determining what the enemy was doing, because they often confused it with their own troops. Such was the case here.

They were smart enough to make adjustments and pay closer attention to Homeworlder activity; it just took some time. Also, like the Homeworlders, they too had taken prisoners. They had plenty of information to seriously damage Nutty and his kind. Continued Homeworlder success wouldn't come so easily.

There was one orc in particular who would become a particular thorn in Nutty's side. He would provide key information about Nutty, his troops, and his hometown. This orc went by the name Pantha, but Nutty knew him as Jailbitch Bika Dude. Nutty learned of this by questioning a prisoner later that night. He also found Big Town and his loved ones to be at a higher risk than he thought. Pantha was going to lead the Invadas right to his home.

Nutty shuddered at the thought. Now, he had invisible enemies in Jailbitch and Darkster. Maybe the two were working hand-in-hand. Either way, the situation didn't seem great. Even if Nutty inflicted considerable damage on the ground army at hand, he was virtually defenseless where it really mattered. He wondered if he brought death and destruction to his loved ones back home.

Most of Nutty's northern army found protection in the Caves of Malice. There were enough locals in his ranks that could navigate through the thousands of miles that twisted beneath the towering mountains above. Darkness hid them outside, and then, inside the caverns as well. Behind them were the sounds of an advancing enemy being raked by explosions. Its leading troops were being shredded by a foe they couldn't find. Eventually, they would come to a halt to lick their wounds and regroup. By morning, the explosions would be a thing of the past and Nutty's army would be safe on the other side of the mountains.

King Basha brought his forces to bear against Invada forces on the outskirts of the drop zone. Here too, the Invadas had been hit hard, and as they gathered their strength to defeat Basha, they were hit from the air once again. The northern air force decimated their lines. Basha's troops captured ships and munitions before fleeing into the night. They were met by troops that dropped into the zone by air. In all, a dozen ships and thirty fighters were captured.

Throughout the night, Homeworlders continued to thwart Invada advances by using hit-and-run tactics. This gave their main forces the time they needed to escape beyond reach of ground attack. They hid in caves and several towns in the southwest portion of the continent. They would come out to attack and then, quietly slip away, undetected. This was a tactic that was unheard of to orcs from the other worlds. It was unheard of until now, anyway.

Nutty knew that his tactics worked to near perfection. In some ways, it worked better than anticipated. But, he knew the enemy would adjust. The Invadas wouldn't fall for the same decoy again. They would expect night attacks because it seemed to level the playing field. They would keep better track of Homeworlder movements, too. Nutty scrambled to keep one step ahead of them.

***

Daylight opened to a roar of blasting guns and incoming aircraft. Orcs were thrown about as concrete and block shattered around them. The hot, morning sun paled in comparison to the heat from explosions that came from the massive assault from above. Invada aircraft dove from the sky by the thousands. While some were shot down from the sky, many-upon-many

301

more unleashed devastation from their bombs that fell on Big Town.

Muga was covered in dust and debris. She staggered to her feet and wiped blood from her nose. She ran her tongue around in her mouth and found some teeth that were knocked out. To her right was a doc who was cut in half by a girder that crushed him below his ribcage. She saw wounded patients that were scattered around the room, no longer in their beds.

Sirens were blaring, and orcs were screaming all about. Uhra was yelling Pretty's name in an attempt to wake her from unconsciousness. She dragged her away from a fire that was spreading quickly along the north wall of the medical area. Muga came to her aid and the two dragged her outside.

The sight was horrific; bodies were lying about; explosion after explosion rocked the area. A bloody orc ducked and dodged as he ran up the street to Muga. He hollered as he passed, "Da Invadas landed near Wivvaflow! Dems comin'! Dems comin'!"

Muga was terrified. She asked Uhra to stay with Pretty until she returned. Then, she headed off to the mines to make sure Runzda and Kago were okay. She faded into the distance behind smoke that was billowing to the south.

As quickly as Muga disappeared, Biggabomb appeared. He was gasping for air. He jogged around large holes in the street that were created from falling bombs. He dropped to his knees in front of Pretty. He looked up at Uhra and pleaded, "She be ok?"

"Dunno. We should gets her to da mines. Bombs not get in der."

"Good tinkin', Uhra." Biggabomb paused to rub his chest and back. Then, he continued in obvious discomfort, "Where Muga?"

"She goin' to da mines already."

"K. Letta us go." He flung Pretty over his shoulder, coughed, and stumbled down the street along the edges of buildings while he followed Uhra to the mines.

Booma sent his small number of ragtag fighters into the air to defend Big Town, but they were easily brushed aside by the Invadas. His troops began to converge on Wivvaflow to engage the enemy. They moved in small numbers and moved from building to building to avoid being hit by incoming bombs.

On a hunch, Nutty had sent his fighters to defend Big Town. He pieced together code from transmissions that were sent between Invadas that suggested something big. His hunches were right. He chose to have his army hunker down for a day or two until he might have his fighters back as protection. Big Town needed protection more than he did. He just hoped he wasn't too late.

Homeworlder fighters screamed into battle behind the Invadas. They dived from directly in front of the sun; the blinded Invadas never saw them coming. In seconds, the fighters took out as many enemy fighters as possible. The Invada fighter, complacent because of their perceived dominance of the skies, were slow to respond. By the time they got into the fight, nearly a third of their numbers were lost, and many more bombers.

Now, the Homeworlder fighters fled as fast as they could. As soon as they lost the advantage of surprise, they began to take heavy losses. If it wasn't for Booma sending instructions to the Invada pilots in their own code, the entire Homeworlder air force would have been lost.

Booma redirected the Invada fighters north, where a large number ran out of fuel. He had others land at his airstrip, where they were captured by some of his troops. He obtained some bombers the same way. Then, he fueled them, put Homeworlder pilots in them, and sent them to Nutty. Not bad for the dummy in the family.

Nutty and his forces were running out of tricks. They were doing everything they could to gain every little advantage. Now, they were hiding during daylight, hoping not to be found. They were still grossly outnumbered, but they took a bite out of the Invada forces and put them back on their heels.

***

Bombs still fell on Big Town and her surrounding towns over the next few days. The ferocity and steadiness at which they fell, lessened though. Many bombers were redirected, shot down, or captured. But, there was still the large ground force that was closing in on the other side of the river. Big Town wasn't out of danger, yet; far from it.

Orcs fought to put out the blazes that raged in and around the town. They did this while bombs fell around them. The wounded were piling up in medical areas while the dead piled up outside. Big Town orcs struggled to keep order. Many sought cover underground in dug-out basements below their houses; others sought refuge in the mines, but there were thousands that worked, regardless of the danger to themselves. Some were simply unable to get to safety, either cutoff by debris or severely injured.

Biggabomb, Uhra, and Pretty were in the mines with Muga and her kids. Biggabomb's body was failing him; his lungs were filling with fluids and he was choking up blood; he was drowning in his own fluids. There were wounded and dying coming in to the medical areas that might be candidates for transplant, but the situation wasn't exactly perfect for such an operation to take place.

Uhra saw how Biggabomb had been deteriorating and brought up the subject. "Biggabomb, you not doin's too good. What I can do fo' you?"

"I could use da lung right 'bout now." Blood filled Biggabomb's mouth and ran down his chin as he spoke.

Uhra looked at him, then Muga, her kids, and Pretty who was still unconscious. She knew what she had to do. With no docs in the mine, she needed to get help. Obviously, the past Chief and son of the current Chief must have been important enough to warrant immediate attention. "I tries to be backs soon." Uhra jumped up and left for downtown.

The heat took one's breath away. It weakened legs and caused lightheadedness. The burning of oil, plastic, and every other contaminant in town didn't help. The sweet, sick smell of death wafted through the air and hung thick in the nostrils of Big Towners.

Uhra gagged as she stumbled in and out of doorways, trying to avoid the occasional explosion and gasp some much needed fresh air. She also hid from the Invada fighters that swarmed above, looking for targets that they forwarded to their bombers. They had complete control of the skies now and targeted at will.

The ground was hard and sharp. It jumped up and bit Uhra several times, playing with her by littering itself in debris hidden in the smoke. It cut and bruised as often as it could. It did its best work when it chipped her shin bone. It couldn't work alone; no, it used the heat, and stench; the pollutants that clouded the mind and weakened the legs. It was a formidable adversary.

Uhra covered several miles in almost an hour. Her hands and legs were bloody. Dirt, smoke, and soot darkened her torn clothing. Her hair was stiff and sticking up in every which direction. At one point, she found herself cursing the fact that she had brushed her long hair earlier in the day.

Collapsed buildings had fallen into the streets, making the road impassable. Uhra climbed over rubble as best she could. She chose a time to do so between aircraft flying overhead. She took a bad step or two, but eventually made it to the top and down the other side. Upon reaching the other side, she gasped and cupped her mouth. There, she saw outreached arms of a mother who was crushed by the building, only her arms were visible. Just out of the mother's outstretched hands was a dead baby. "Oh no!" Uhra cried.

Tears ran down her cheeks as she slowly made her way toward the Crossroads. She heard explosions and screams in the distance ahead of her. She thought she heard gunfire, too, but her senses were having a hard time differentiating between things. She was overwhelmed with sadness and grief for her town, Biggabomb, Pretty, and the baby she saw. What horrors she saw!

Uhra was getting closer to the Crossroads. Several orcs were crawling beneath rubble. She didn't know if they were hiding or trying to escape from these makeshift graves that were taking orcs by the dozens. Here, they might be entombed, only to die later. The thought gave her chills, but she continued on. The number of dead, dying, and trapped was more than she could bear. She couldn't help all of them; she couldn't really help any of them.

She came upon a doc who recognized her and lit up to see an orc alive and well in the area. "Uhra!" he exclaimed.

"Doc Cutstick, it bad 'round here."

"Yep. You ok?"

The two ducked as a hail of bullets came from somewhere to the northwest and ricocheted near them. Uhra shouted, "Yeah, sorta. Who shootin's?"

"Invadas come cross Wivvaflow bridge. Big fights wit' our orcs by Crossroads."

Uhra was stricken. "Doc, I tries to get lungs fo' Biggabomb. Him real bads now. How I get to da old skool? Umm, da medical area?"

"It gone, Uhra. Blowed up."

Uhra began to weep.

The doc didn't even look at her. He was busy picking up a medical kit that was thrown all over the street by the last explosion. "I got lungs fo' him. But dems on ice in Guthrak's old machine shop. But it danger der, Uhra."

"Gotcha. I gets dems. Doc, Biggabomb in da mines. I meet you der. Dis an orda from Nuttybomb." A little lie couldn't hurt at this point. Uhra needed the doc to help Biggabomb and Pretty, whatever the cost. Besides, Nutty would have approved.

The doc looked at her stunned. "But I gots no equipment to see if he do ok afta surgery."

"Doc, he die today wit' no lungs. It bad. Now, go."

Uhra headed north after the doc nodded and headed south. If she thought the trip so far was treacherous, she was sadly mistaken. Bullets ripped through walls with regularity. A few fragments of bullets found themselves in the top of her right leg. Concrete chips found their way into her face, neck, and upper left arm. During a nearby explosion, she found herself screaming, "Stop! Dis sucks!" Nobody heard her. Even if they did, they wouldn't stop.

To Uhra's left was the back of the library. It was damaged, but still stood tall. She guided her movements in and out of buildings and used it as the landmark to get to the Crossroads. Soon, she could see Guthrak's shop in the distance. She was getting so close.

Gunfire erupted in front of her. Orcs with guns were running and firing in different directions at the crossroads. Uhra recognized some as Big Town orcs, but others were foreign. She felt a pit down in her stomach. *They must be da Invadas*, she thought. She crouched inside a doorway to stay out of view and get a better look.

She counted eight Invadas coming toward her. They were only a hundred feet or so away. This was way too close for her liking. She only lurked for a second or two before ducking into the building. She hurried up the rickety stairs and found a bedroom. It had a window that she used to sneak a peek at what was going on just below.

Uhra pulled a blanket that hung above to one side of the window. While it hid her from sight, it revealed a horror. Now, she was sick with fear. The Invadas were going door to door. They were pulling Big Town orcs outside and killing them in the streets. Some were shot, others were stabbed; both genders and all ages.

Uhra remembered seeing a back door when she came into this house. She ran down the stairs with her shaky legs and flew out the back door. She closed it behind her and looked back in through a crack. Invadas came crashing through the front door. Two immediately headed upstairs. One looked around, flipping a table and sofa before walking to the back door.

Uhra turned and ran, but she didn't have anywhere to go. She was trapped in a little backyard that was formed by buildings on all sides. She turned back and saw a fence that had been knocked down. It led to the street, just beyond the entrance point to the house she just fled from. There was no choice. Within hundredths of a second, she was down the alleyway and lying near the street behind some rubble.

Although she heard the back door open and an orc climb over the broken fence that she had just traversed, she lay motionless. The sound of footsteps got closer. The Invada orc stepped behind her and said, "I got one." The other two orcs bolted down the stairs and out the front door. They ran over to Uhra.

The Invadas changed their codes to stop the Homeworlders from slowing their attacks like they had days before. Also, they were more accurately following Homeworlder movements as they adjusted to this new type of combat. Nutty struggled to keep Homeworlder casualties down, but things weren't going well. His first day's successes were replaced by brutal head-on engagements. Invada losses were higher, but there were so many enemies that it seemed to make little difference.

To make matters worse, reports were coming in of Big Town orcs being taken as prisoners by the Invadas. Parts of the town were in ruin and communication was spotty at best. Nutty's air force was all but gone, being wiped away daily, leaving his much slower ground troops at risk.

Something drastic needed to be done or Hotta was going to fall.

Eighteen
Darkster

Nutty was troubled. He had landed in a clearing near the crossroads. Big Town was in shambles; Dead bodies were everywhere; gray smoke and dark mist swept across the damaged landscape. He looked for anyone he knew. He couldn't find his mother or father. He didn't know where Booma or his other siblings were.

As he headed south toward the mine, he walked around the dead bodies that littered the street. He felt the need to go south, but he wasn't sure why. Somehow, he knew where Uhra was. Yes, she was in that direction. He picked up his pace, but stopped to check each body, hoping beyond hope that they weren't Big Town orcs, but everyone that he came across was.

Nutty marveled at how he knew where Uhra was. "I know where she is, I know where she is, I know where she is." He stopped in his tracks when he saw a woman lying face down near an alleyway to the right. He knew the shirt she wore; it was familiar, the pretty lace on the collar and the funny flower pattern; it was unique, handmade; it was Uhra's.

Nutty dropped to his knees in horror to see Uhra's body, limp and lifeless, haphazardly crumpled near a pile of debris. Her eyes were open, but there was no color in them. Her skin was a sickly, dead, pale yellowish-green. He cried out in pain, "No!" He hugged her body and brought her face up to his. It was stiff and cold, no different than the dusty concrete that she lay amongst.

Nutty cried and cried as he held his Uhra. He hated the Invadas, Gods how he hated them! Their senseless killing was for what? They even wrote something on her back. It was written in her own blood for gods' sake. It was hard to read at first, but as Nutty tried and tried through his wet eyes, he made it out. It read, "Darkster."

"Damn him! Darkster. Darkster. Darkster."

Nutty woke in a pool of sweat. Unlike other Darkster dreams, he found himself coherent after this one. His first thought was that Uhra wasn't dead; No, she was alive; he could feel it. Elation washed over him, but he knew other things that weren't good. She was in trouble; she was in real trouble!

Just then, a knock came at the door. It was followed by, "Nutty." There were two more hurried knocks, again followed by, "Nutty, open up."

Nutty slipped on some pants, rubbed his eyes, and opened the door for Moonoak.

"What is it, Nutty? What happened?"

The words couldn't come out fast enough, but Nutty pulled Moonoak inside and closed the door, away from wandering ears. "It wuz Darkster. He here anda he know where Uhra at. I dunno how, but he do."

"We musta finds him."

"Der more. In da dream, he beed wit' da Invadas."

Moonoak looked befuddled. He asked, "So, he a Invada? You sure?"

"No, not sure. Wuz in my dream, though." Nutty paused as he tried to piece his thoughts together and make sense of his dream. He continued, "No, he one of

312

us, but he want me deads so he can rule. If he can't gets me, den he goes to anywhere he can rule."

"How you know dis?"

"Dunno, but I do."

"You should meditate and clear you mind."

"No. No times fo' dat. My mind as clear as evva. I know wutz to do anda you comin' wit' me." Nutty saw Moonoak roll his eyes. "Yeah, ok. You hate war. I get it. Good, you can help stops it. From now on, you stay by me."

***

Uhra lay as still as she could. She heard one of the Invadas above her ask, "Dis one?" He nudged her with his foot.

The orc who had said, "I got one," exclaimed, "No!" He pulled a gun, cocked it, and fired.

In that split second, Uhra fully expected to feel searing pain in her head or back, or maybe, she expected to feel nothing at all. She had heard all kinds of crazy stories about orcs that had died, been revived, and talked about a bright light, or a friendly orc that accepted them in death. *Whatever*, she thought. She didn't know what to feel. What she did realize was that a bullet had found its way from the gun to an orc on the second floor across the street. She saw him fall through his window and land on the street below. That was the "one" that he got.

The Invadas laughed. One said, "Good shots!" Then, they moved on, southward. They checked a number of buildings over the next hour or so and were finally far enough away to pose no threat. During this time, Uhra witnessed more murders, more troops, more fighters overhead, and more explosions. When she thought she was safe to move, she methodically dragged her hurting body off the ground and made her way to the machine shop.

Uhra slid between a building and the library and entered through the back door, carefully hiding low along the perimeter walls. The crackle of grit and debris echoed in the vaulted construction. Every step brought a slight moan that she tried to conceal from the amplified room she negotiated. She moved as fluidly as possible.

The front double doors were tall and wide. They were made of solid wood with large, ornate iron hinges and details. Uhra peeked through one of the stained-glass arches to see what was going on outside. To her surprise and delight, she saw Homeworlder troops taking up positions at the Crossroads. She decided to move.

Within seconds, she was yelling orders to the troops. One followed her and laid down covering fire, so she could make it to the machine shop. She ran with her head down, covered by her arms across the street. She made it to the other side and threw her body into the large doors. Her little body, helped by the power of her legs thrusting her forward, pushed the doors open. She landed face down, unharmed. She had made it!

Uhra looked around and jumped to her feet. She saw the soldier stumble in behind her with a gunshot wound in his shoulder. Two more Homeworlder troops were running passed the shop. One was yelling, "Retreat, retreat!"

The soldier with the gunshot wound yelled, "Get dat stuff quick, lady! We gotta goes."

Uhra worked her way around the room and searched in boxes and bags. She made her way around a desk and found a metal container under it. Before she crouched to open it, she was startled by a torrent of noise.

A grapple was going on in the street. Orcs from both sides of the conflict were fighting hand to hand. The Homeworlders were outnumbered. They were generally bigger than their opponents, but that didn't always equate to victory. The soldier in the doorway rattled off several shots from his hand gun before pulling a knife and rushing into the street. He was met by a tide of Invada orcs. He screamed, "You bastids!" He swung his blade and cut several enemies, then ducked and swung again. The last thing he yelled was, "Save da gurl anda get dose lungs to da mines!" He fell back under a wave of orcs that were dressed in leather and red trim. He would never yell again.

Uhra checked the container and found the lungs in it. She jumped over the desk and headed for the door. As she got close to the door, an Invada orc entered. He smiled as he walked toward her. He smiled and said, "I'ma not gonna hurts you." He held his knife out in front of him, showing anything but what he told her. He licked his lips and panted from excitement.

Uhra looked from side to side as he approached. She sought any weapon she could find to defend herself, but she saw no guns and no knives. She barely took her eyes off the menacing figure before her when he raised his knife above his head. Uhra jumped to her right and pulled a rope that she had seen. It was attached to a huge, steel pulley that hung from the rafters. The rope slipped from a hook and released the pulley, sending it swinging into the orc's head. He still had a smile on his face after the pulley embedded itself in his forehead. Within a few seconds he said, "Uh oh," and dropped the knife. He fell to his knees and fumbled with his hands about his head. He knew the pulley didn't belong there; he wasn't sure how it got there, either. He looked at Uhra with a blank stare as she carefully walked around him.

Uhra slowly stepped backward toward the door. She faced him the whole time, so he couldn't get her from behind. At the doorway, she stopped. She dropped the container and became confused. She looked down to find something long and shiny. It was about as long as her arm, but it looked sharp and extended from her belly out toward the orc with the pulley in his head. It dripped a red liquid that ran into a small puddle that was accumulating on the floor below her. She couldn't breathe; she gasped as it disappeared into her belly and exited via her back.

Uhra fell to the floor. The room appeared sideways; from her vantage point, everything was skewed at ninety degrees. She saw a younger adult male standing in the doorway, straddling her. He held a long saber that glistened in the sun. She couldn't believe that the whole three feet of blade that he held had entered her back and pierced her, straight through her stomach.

She wanted to pick up the lungs that had spilled onto the floor, but she couldn't. She wanted to fight back, but she couldn't. She wanted her Nuttybomb to save her, but she knew he couldn't. She laid there helpless and watched the orc lick the blood from his blade. Then he used it to slice her shirt open in the front. He smiled and said, "My, you a cute one." He got down to his knees and began to play with her navel. He pulled his dark cloak to one side, so he could squat without ripping his own clothing. Then, like the other orc, he began to pant from excitement; he began to drool. He dribbled piles of spit that splashed all over Uhra's face. She closed her eyes, so she couldn't see anymore.

***

Headhunta hid in the closet. He had been here for two days and remained undetected. As hungry as he was, his patience and duty dismissed the want for food. His thirst for blood quenched his thoughts of weakness. He patiently waited until the time to act; it was time.

Jailbitch Biker Dude flipped the light switch on and entered his quarters. The quarters were much better than the dirt and wood crap hole that he had back on the planet. These Invadas knew how to treat Homeworlders that gave up their brethren. He gave away their positions and handed critical information to the Invadas on a silver platter. He smiled as he wiped his face and hands from the blood that he had taken from the "stupid orcs on Hotta".

He laughed when he said, "I tink I will have Nuttybomb blood next." He laughed as his belly spilled onto the ground. He was sliced and diced in an instant. His throat was cut. He gurgled as he fell to the floor. A shadow of a body exited his room and went down the hallway beyond.

Headhunta slipped beneath this and hid behind that. Sometimes, he hid in plain view, covered by a shadow or the stupidity of the orcs he stalked. He walked among them, just off to their sides. Many times, they thought they saw something or thought they were being watched. Those that weren't hunted dismissed those eerie feelings as just one of those weird things that we all have. Those with cut throats and spilled guts never second guessed themselves again.

From ship to ship he traveled; a stowaway in a cargo hold, or a passenger that was ill and didn't want to leave his room. Anything that got him where he needed to go was what he did. He managed to find his way through the Invada ranks, even to those that were considered untouchable. His list was nearly complete. He scanned it from top to bottom and his eyes settled on the last name. It was the final name, just after Pantha. He whispered it to himself as an overwhelming excitement gripped him, "Orcilla."

***

The doc worked feverishly. He had no way of knowing if he would be successful with any of the Bomb family members, let alone all of them. Pretty was finally conscious so the doc did little for her. He gave her some fluids and a shot of something. She had a broken wrist and, "A hell of da headache fo' a few days," according to doc.

Biggabomb was heavily medicated. His new lungs were in place, his back and chest marked by stitches that closed the long cuts from neck to belly. Breathing tubes ran from his mouth and nose while drainage tubes ran from several places from his back. The drainage tubes emptied into milk jugs that sat on the floor by his cot.

Doc Cutstick told Muga, "Da worst ain't ova. Surgery bads, but most don't live afta. He in real danger now. Lungs might die or infections he get, maybe. Dunno. Might bleeds to death. Sorry, Muga. I still tries all I can. At least, he gots lungs now. Da udder ones didn't work."

Nutty cut in, "What bout Uhra?"

The doc didn't want to respond, but he knew that he had to. "She bads, Boss. I fix her stomach. It all messed up, but I tink it will be ok. But I can gets no pictures. I tink her back beed cut in half. She got no use da legs or arms. She might die. I sorry."

"So put it backs together."

"I can't. Dunno how. No doc does."

Nutty was filled with emotions. He felt anger, sorrow, loss, and denial. Mostly, he felt guilty. This was his fault; he should have protected her. He raised his palms upward as he shrugged, "So dat's it?"

Regrettably, the doc admitted, "'Fraid so, Chief. Just gots to wait anda see."

Nutty sent orders to his officers to be carried out. He knew how desperate things were. Big Town was being overrun by Invadas and his army was beginning to fail in the west. The enemy was just too strong. Furthermore, half of his loved ones were hurting, some maybe even dying.

He recounted the steps that brought him to this point. He remembered Gardawg, the cabin, Captain Morbid, the speeches, all his stupid plans. They all meant nothing if Uhra wasn't okay; she had to be okay.

There was still the matter of finding Darkster. But Nutty knew that his most hated enemy would have to wait for death to come. And death would come to him, Nutty swore it.

In the meantime, Nutty organized his local troops and set out to hit the Invadas here in town. He may have been too late to save Uhra, but he wouldn't wait any longer to do what he must. He was going to drive these bastard enemies home.

Nutty had no guards this night. What he had were a few thousand well-trained warriors who were exhausted and/or wounded. They would follow him in the final battle of Big Town. Their heroism would be legendary; their stories, the stuff of myth.

Once again, he and his troops were saved by darkness. They cleared building after building. They followed their fighters, bombers, and tanks that were summoned. Civilians joined the fight. Nothing was left to chance. A well-coordinated attack, backed by the souls of revenge, decimated the enemy without recourse. There was no pity; there was no pause.

The Invadas, reluctant to pull their main force from the northern drop zone area, allowed Big Town to be liberated. They refused to blink this time, assuming that Big Town was a decoy. But it wasn't. Nutty had used the entire remnants of his air force and armor divisions, betting on the Invada's overcompensating for earlier losses. It worked!

A long night of intense fighting led to the capture of over sixty thousand Invadas, along with fighters, bombers, tanks, vehicles, munitions, and a few capital ships. The world was told of this event. It was a total rout of the enemy. All of this was accomplished with Nutty's main army of two hundred thousand troops still a thousand miles away. He still had his main fighting force. Not bad; no, not bad at all.

Fires were being fought and debris removed from the streets. The gruesome task of gathering the wounded and dead was finally at hand. On the way back to the mines, Nutty came across old acquaintances of his, one of which was also wounded.

Sweetie was being attended to by her sister, Hottie. Her disfigured leg was wrapped in bloody cloths. The bone protruded the temporary wrap that bound her calf and shin together. Sweetie looked up to find Nutty walking toward her. She cried out, "Nuttybomb?"

Nutty shook his head. "Yep."

Hottie smiled as she questioned, "Nuttybomb from da wivva?"

Nutty wasn't embarrassed this time. For whatever reason, he was self-assured. It had nothing to do with his experience with females. He had virtually none of that, but life had caused him to mature faster than most. These girls were nothing to him. The day at the river was the stuff that kids did, plain and simple. He checked out Sweetie's leg. When he twisted it, she screamed. Impassive, he said, "You be fine."

Hottie didn't see the kid from a few years before. She saw a powerful, handsome, self-assured male. He was candy to her. Then, something occurred to her. "You is Nuttybomb?"

Nutty looked at her annoyed, "Yes!"

"Warchief Nuttybomb?"

He had no reason, nor need to repeat himself. He picked up Sweetie and held her against his muscular chest. Her eyes looked up at him, her heart beat wildly in her chest and neck. Nutty exclaimed, "Letta us go."

Hottie called out, "I be damned."

Vehicles still couldn't pass the collapsed buildings that covered the roads. Nutty carried Sweetie all the way to the mines. She stared up at him the whole time. She studied his warm eyes and nicely carved features. She imagined running her fingers across his lips. She memorized his strong chin and jaw. She watched the veins pulse blood through his muscular neck. She wanted to rub his scars and his damaged ear. *Dat poor baby*, she thought, as she surveyed every inch of his face, neck, and shoulders.

That was it! She wanted him! No other female could have him. They had fooled around in the past; well, sort of. She knew that he liked her; he certainly liked her that day at the river. Yup, she would have him. She absolutely loved him at this moment. She imagined a life of loving him, and him loving her.

However, the many miles it took to walk to the mines were more than enough for Nutty. He had been in hard fought combat all night. This was just after he carried Uhra down this same road just hours before. His arms were dead, his legs were weak. He still had a bullet or two in one of his shoulders. He was cut and bruised everywhere. On top of all of that, *Dis bitch gots heavy*, he thought. She wasn't the little girl from a few years before.

They got to the mines and found the doc still attending to Biggabomb. He was waking up at this point and wasn't happy. "Who da hells cut me whole chest?"

The doc quickly explained, "I gived you new lungs, Chief."

"New lungs?"

"Yep. Try a sleep now."

Biggabomb drifted back into forced unconsciousness. Even though orcs endured all levels of pain better than most, the procedure that cut him from end to end and replaced organs was fresh. Plus, he had a very small amount of pain killers in his system. His best chance of comfort was sleep from the anesthesia. He accepted it.

Nutty approached the doc who had turned to treat Uhra. He was more concerned about Uhra than the girl in his arms. "Doc, Uhra?"

"She awake, Chief. Her toes mova some. Dat real good sign."

Nutty looked over the doc's shoulder and saw Uhra's eyes. She was in pain and cried out, "Nutty!"

Nutty pushed the doc aside and stood at Uhra's side. He leaned down and kissed her forehead, clumsily bouncing Sweetie's head against the wall as he lifted her out of his way.

Sweetie hollered, "Ouch! Dammit!"

Uhra looked around. First, at Nutty. Then, at Sweetie. And then, back at Nutty. "Who dis?"

"Oh, dis is Sweetie."

"Oh, really?"

Nutty grasped the gravity of the situation. He begged, "Lemme esplain." He would try to "esplain" for over an hour. Eventually, he gave up. He told her about the river some years before. He told her that was the only time and there was nobody else. Sure, Sweetie being in his arms this night didn't look good, but it was nothing more than him finding her injured. It was just coincidence.

Uhra had a hard time swallowing it. Nutty apologized for anything and everything, kissed her again, and sought Moonoak.

The two discussed what they should do next. Moonoak talked about meditation again, and this time, Nutty agreed to try it. The condition was that it was a short meditation; there was too much to do and he was so damn tired.

A half hour passed...Nutty was calm. But once again, things were chaotic. The doc urged him to have the bullets removed from his shoulder. It couldn't wait because the doc needed to leave the mines to attend to other wounded orcs. Nutty grudgingly agreed.

There were no antibiotics, no anesthesia. Nutty sat and cringed as the doc dug into his tough, leathery skin, and strong, dense muscle. Thankfully, he was distracted by Hottie. She kept making eye contact with him and smiling. After a different doc set Sweetie's leg, she did the same.

Uhra was not happy. She was in a lot of pain, not just physically, but emotionally. She was told that she may never walk again. She might still bleed out and die. It didn't occur to her that Sweetie was stuck in the same room as her because of her broken leg. Even if she was wounded, it was a stupid broken leg. She thought, *Go heal outside you lil wench. Anda taka you big-boobed, smiling, eyelash-batting hussy sista wit' you!"*

Nutty looked over at Uhra and smiled when he saw her. It didn't matter if she was upset with him. Eventually, she would understand. He knew she was hurting. He loved her.

Uhra growled at him and spit, "You shoulda hurt, Nutty? Dat too bad." Then, she half-smiled with her tongue half sticking out between her teeth.

Sweetie was getting a feel for the relationship between Nutty and Uhra. Jealousy got the best of her. "I so prouds a you, Nuttybomb. You becomes da Chief afta we played in da wivva."

Hottie exclaimed, "Anda how!"

***

Orcilla strode confidently from his office to his quarters. His handful of elite guards walked along with him. There were two in the front, one on each side, and two behind the Invada leader. He snapped some commands as he walked the long passageway of his flagship.

As he approached his room, his lead guard approached the two guards that were posted to each side of the door. He addressed them and pushed a button that opened the door. The two guards entered and came out a minute or two later with an "all clear" signal.

Orcilla and his guards entered the room in much the same order that they had traveled down the hallway. While four guards stood around Orcilla, the others checked the room for anything out of the ordinary. They lifted ceiling panels and checked up above and checked the ventilation ducts. They proceeded to look in the closets and bathroom. The desk, under tables and beds, and every other inch of the quarters were checked. The door guards went back to their posts and the door was closed and sealed.

Orcilla had a guard pour drinks for all of them and they began to talk about Big Town being allowed to fall as part of the "master plan". Orcilla finished his drink and excused himself to use the bathroom. He put his glass down and walked a few feet to his destination, closed the door behind him, and undid his pants.

He began to empty his bladder, but needed to make some room for full flow to occur. His body emptied some air with a loud whoosh sound from his rear. The flow was strong and continued for thirty seconds. He chuckled when he heard his guards laugh because of his flatulence. The high-tech auto flush whooshed even louder. Orcilla opened the door when he was done. He was buttoning his pants as he stepped back into the main room of his quarters. He looked up and found his guards sprawled on the floor with their throats cut and their stomachs emptied on the floor. By the time reality checked in, Da Great Orcilla of Da Crimson Guard was another casualty. He fell to the floor, gasping for air that couldn't find its way through the deep cut that virtually severed his head from his neck.

"I seldom do dis, Orcilla. But you should know dat it me who taka you life. I Headhunta, Rula of da Dead. Anda now I rule you."

Orcilla tried to protect himself from the slicing that was occurring in his abdomen. His extended arms didn't keep Headhunta's determined blade from carving him up though. He lost some fingers, and eventually his hands, in the process.

Headhunta laughed. "Oh, one more ting. I just da deliverer. Der is one who I fear. You lucky dis kill come from me."

Nutty and Moonoak were talking as quietly as they could. They didn't mention the nightmares. They

326

still felt the need to hide details from others. The name Darkster did come up. They didn't think that the name could be associated with any nightmares. Who, other than them and Booma, would know anything? The name seemed benign by itself.

Biggabomb asked in a weakened state, "Is Headhunta ok?"

Nutty turned to see his father trying to sit up. "Lay down, Dad."

"Nutty, Headhunta ok?"

"Yeah. Well, I tink so. He on a mission, but he really good, right?"

"Him real good. But he ok?"

Nutty looked at Moonoak. The two exchanged an inquisitive glance. Nutty questioned, "Why?"

"Oh, you said Darkster."

"So, who is Darkster?"

"Dat Headhunta's kid."

Nineteen
Life Hangs in the Balance

Gunza led two hundred thousand Homeworlders against a million Invadas. His night attacks chipped away at the enormous force that opposed his. He continued to implement Nutty's hit-and-run tactics at night and made use of decoys and ambushes when possible. As his losses mounted and he was forced to retreat, he stripped the land of every resource he could. However, there always seemed to be more enemies on the horizon.

Over the last week, powerful thunderstorms rattled the troops on both sides. Lightning accounted for a few dozen additional lives lost. This was inconsequential to the survivors who basked in the cool torrents of rain that accompanied most of the storms. Nighttime temperatures stayed well above one hundred degrees, but that was still more comfortable than the oven-like conditions during the day. A bit of soothing rain was welcome.

To the Invadas, unaccustomed to such violent weather and heat, this hellish planet was more than unbearable. A great number were becoming ill. They were used to cooler, less severe conditions. Water supplies were stretched to near breaking points as Invadas seemed to drink around the clock. Ten thousand or more were reported to have had delusions. Hundreds died because they drank fuel and other toxic liquids. By comparison, the Homeworlders collected every bit of rainfall that they could and were fairly well adjusted to their own planet's conditions.

Gunza had formulated his own plan that wasn't half bad. He dropped troops behind the enemy at night. They destroyed or poisoned whatever water supplies they could, further inflicting damage on the enemy. Gunza figured he could eliminate part of the enemy without engaging them. He was right.

After his infiltrators completed their missions, Gunza's army moved. Part of his troops lured the Invadas into the caves where they had been hiding. They had an advantage here. Bottlenecking the larger enemy meant an even number of troops fighting on each side at any given time. The disadvantage in numbers was nullified. Furthermore, as the Invadas were unable to advance past their own dead, they were besieged by fires that were ignited around them. Over sixty thousand enemies lost their live in the caves on the first day.

Gunza's main force engaged the Invadas head on. Early in the week, his losses were heavy due to Invada air superiority. His solution? He saved his few fighters, bombers, tanks, and artillery for night combat. He rushed his troops into the enemy and fought among them. The Invada aircraft couldn't differentiate between his troops and theirs. They were essentially out of the fight. Although still outnumbered five-to-one, he and the Homeworlder army fought valiantly. Within hours, they were taking substantially lower casualties than they were inflicting on the Invadas. The heat worked to his orcs' advantage.

Basha swung around from the south and took control of the drop zone, attempting to halt any further reinforcements from landing with supplies. This time, he didn't flee at night. He and his Gravediggas welcomed a fight with the Invadas. His troops didn't fare as well as Gunza's, though. He lost nearly forty-percent of his troops. But he was successful in holding the drop zone for several days and pulled part of the main Invada force away from Gunza.

After several days, the Homeworlders' persistence began to pay off. Invada orcs began to succumb to dehydration. Those that didn't die were sluggish, and their minds were cloudy. Their fighting abilities were diminished by lack of the simplest requirement- water. Without it, they couldn't function. Tens of thousands began to surrender to Gunza's army. Things were looking up for the Homeworlders.

***

On the other side of the continent, things were much different. Prisoners had escaped. Booma's woefully sparse forces could no longer keep tens of thousands of prisoners under control. While most were contained, a few hundred from Camp Twelve eluded capture and made their way aboard the prison barge that Biggabomb had stolen. They quickly lifted off and left the atmosphere. Soon, they would dock with their massive prison station in space.

Booma said to Nutty, "It only one ship, I guess."

Nutty acknowledged his brother with, "I know, but we don't has many."

"At least dems will lead us to da udder Homeworlder prisoners."

Nutty had learned about Invada protocols. The ship was destined to be checked by communication before being routed to its normal destination, in this case, one of the docking bays at the prison station. This is where dozens of other ships like it held

Homeworlders that were captured. "I gladly exchange three hundred of der prisoners for nine hundred, sixty thousand a ours. Problem is, I already hearin' dat mosta da nine hundred, sixty thousand a our orcs already bein' shipped to da Invadas' planets."

"Woulda be nice." Booma changed the subject, "How Uhra doin', Nutty?"

Nutty cringed. "Nots so goods. She has a hard time wit' arms anda legs. Finawy gots pictures to show dat her back was cut almost all da way thru. Bad pains and stuff. But maybe some a it canna be fixed."

"I hopes so, brudder. She a good gurl. Anda she goods fo' you." Booma smiled.

"I not goods fo' her. Darkster got her thru me. I dreamed it. He used me to finds her."

"Hmm. I not dream 'bout Darkster since you anda me talked 'bout it lasta time."

"Docs said no mo' patients in comas at Big Town anymo', too. Maybe Darkster left."

Booma made the connection. "So, him has to be near ya to get inna dream?"

Nutty shook his head. "Dunno. Maybe. If yes, den how he be in my dream a thousand miles away and dan get Uhra here so quick?"

"Good question."

***

"Dis ain't a you ass, Woman! You supposed to wipes it to keep it clean. Doc said wounds a get infected if no wipes it right."

"Biggabomb, shutta up. You ain't crippled. Do it youself," Muga spewed out of frustration. Then, she looked over at Uhra and realized what she had said.

Uhra struggled to feed herself. Her chest was full of mudbread that never made it to her mouth. Her hands seemed to be permanently tucked downward under her wrists, her neck braced, unable to support the weight of her head. Every simple motion was a monumental task to her. The effects of atrophy were unknown to orcs. The longer her condition went unchanged, the worse she would continue to get.

Muga growled at Biggabomb, "Useless poop!" Then, she attended to Uhra. "I sorry, Uhra. Lemme helps with you food. Soons you canna do it youself. I just helps till den."

Uhra smiled. "Tanks, Momma."

Muga smiled. At first, she was mildly pleased to have Uhra's acceptance as a potential mother. Actually, her first thought was that Uhra was confused, but she knew that her brain wasn't hurt. She guessed that this was Uhra's way of telling her that she had chosen her son to be a life partner. Within seconds, Muga was elated. Uhra was never any trouble. Muga never heard about any derogatory words or stories spoken of her. Plus, her son loved Uhra with his whole heart; that was evident from his actions.

Muga fed Uhra, one small piece of food at a time. She gave her drink through a straw and stew from a spoon. She massaged severe leg cramps that came on every so often due to the spinal injury. The partially severed nerve was an electric shock that found its way throughout Uhra's body. Until her wound could heal some, she couldn't have surgery to repair the nerve. Muga continued to nurture her new daughter over the next few hours.

Pretty was up and about. Her headache had subsided. She had returned from work at the hospital to check in on her loved ones. She was visibly tired as her head hung and her eyes were little more than slits to see through.

Muga asked, "It getting busy ova at da medical area now?"

"It terrible, Momma. So many soldias comin' back wounded. We can't keep up. Anda we still helpin's Big Towners too. It too much."

Muga nodded her head in understanding. "Nutty said dat he maybe end war in a week or two if evvyting go ok."

Biggabomb burst in with, "Dat boy is sumptin' else. If any orc cans do it, he can. Him lika his old man." Biggabomb smiled as pride enveloped him.

Muga added, "Well, him smart and good fighta, too. Plus, him not vulgar."

They all nodded in agreement and laughed.

Finally, Biggabomb caught on. "You too funny, Muga."

***

"What da hell am I supposed to a do, Moonoak?" Nutty was not sure how to end the war. Uhra was to the point that she was pretty stable, but she would need a very dangerous surgery soon and he didn't want to leave her. But, he had to give one hundred percent to ending this dreadful war. If the war was lost, it wouldn't matter what her condition was. She would be a slave; she would be used for sex and hard labor. When used up beyond her perceived value, she would be killed. He had to decide what to do.

Moonoak didn't have many answers. Things were obviously complicated, but he hoped to work toward some resolution by asking some additional questions and putting things in perspective. "You now know who Darkster is?"

"Yes, da kid of a top officer in our army."

"Where dis officer now?"

Nutty rubbed his forehead. "Comin' back fro' killin's da leader of da Invadas."

"So, dat is good. No leader, no war? Maybe dat all we needed to break da hearts of da Invadas."

"Hasn't worked, yet, my friend."

"Has you summoned fo' Darkster, yet?"

"No. Timin' is bad. Anda I don't know how to do it wit' his dad comin' back. Very tricky, ya know?"

"I do."

"Moonoak, der more, too. Da more I find out 'bout Darkster, da more he worry me. He got very powerful mind. I can't beat hims."

"Yes, but you gots da whole army."

"But, if he jumps to da Invada side, we gots bigga problems."

"I see. You must be da one to kills him, Nutty. It has to happen quick and sneaky."

"Don't know if dat will work either. He got Uhra thru me. Can he read my mind all da time? He will know I'm comin'. Do he already know?"

"If yes, dens he very powerful. Anda what if he get away and show these powers to some of da Invada army? Dems would be unstoppable."

"My Gods, Moonoak. Can you use you powers to stop hims?"

"No, I not dat strong."

"Can you helps me? Anyting you canna do might helps."

"I will try, Nutty. I will try."

***

Nutty had said goodbye to Uhra. She still wasn't scheduled for surgery. The blade that cut through her spinal cord had also nicked her heart and part of her esophagus. She was estimated to be ready in a week's time. Nutty kissed her, shared his love, and readied for what was to come.

Now, with his goodbyes behind him, he stood where he planned to put Darkster behind him. He surveyed his surroundings and made mental notes of the exits, distances from area to area, and the contours of the floor. It was easy for him to see that the room was cavernous. An underground cave had been dug to hide the new ships that the Homeworlders had taken from the Invadas. The digging was complete, but the room had no ships in it so far. Steel supports lined the walls and held up beams that carried the weight of the massive stone ceiling. Nutty noticed small stone chips and dust beneath areas that had cracked in the walls and the ceiling above. The small pieces of debris had showered down from weaknesses in the structure around him. Mild concern left him as the real threat was addressed.

Gunza and Guthrak stood in amazed disbelief. Surely Headhunta wasn't an enemy. What they were being told didn't make sense. Even their fairly well-developed orc brains struggled with the fact that they might have to confront and kill one of their closest brothers in battle.

335

"I don't want to kills him," Nutty exclaimed. "But if we confronts his kid, whatcha tink he will do?"

Gunza laughed, "Cut you belly open anda cut you throat."

Guthrak admitted, "Gots to admit, he a lil scary. Don't a looks at me lika dat. I not scareds. I just say he scary; umm…creepy. He kills by sneakin' around and stuff. Hims real good fighta, but he don't fight head-to-head."

Nutty asked a question that he wasn't sure that the two knew how to answer. Would they answer honestly? Pride sometimes skewed one's perception. Pride sometimes hid the truth. "Can two a you beat hims?"

Gunza and Guthrak looked at each other. Gunza said, "Yeah, right?"

Guthrak shrugged his shoulders. "Well, hims fast, real fast. Anda hims sneaky, likes I said. Really strange, too. I tink I can takes him, tho. I stronger."

Nutty had more to say. He found the best way to do so and began, "You may has to a kill hims. Don't hesitate. I tink he will kill you to protect his kid."

Gunza needed to know exactly why they were confronting Headhunta. He asked several times in different ways to get an answer.

Nutty confessed to the dreams and Darkster finding Uhra. Guthrak finally understood what the nightmares were that he and Gunza had talked about. Then, he admitted that Headhunta had followed him around and asked questions.

Nutty appeared stricken. "You talked to Headhunta 'bout da dreams?"

Guthrak was on the defensive. "N, n, no! Gunza said you was havin' nightmares anda Headhunta overherd its. I told him to get away from me. He was a creepy. But he knowed you has da nightmares. Oh, anda sumptin' 'bout demons, but I don't 'memba."

"Demons?"

Gunza spoke up. "Yeah, Chief. Dat one kind of on me. Well, sorta." He pointed at Guthrak and continued, "Dummy ova here misundastood dat you wasn't killin's a Darkster ting, even tho it was you nightmares. He said sumptin' like no way you lika demons or some crap. Dat when Headhunta heard and asked stuff."

"Really, you two? I worry 'bout troops hearin' dis stuff anda you talks 'bout it to da possible enemy."

Guthrak apologized. "We didn't know, Chief."

Gunza took full responsibility. "It my fault, Chief. I talked 'bout it to Guthrak. I hoped you ok to fight even with da nightmares. Headhunta came at bad time. But still, it my fault. I da one who said it stupids to Cracka."

Moonoak's ears pointed forward and his usually calm demeanor appeared shaken. "Cracka?"

"Yea. Dat his old nickaname."

Moonoak unwittingly revealed, "Oh, my Gods."

"What? I know I said wrong stuff to him."

Moonoak explained Headhunta's hidden powers and that he was Cracka in reality. Headhunta was the nickname he used to hide his true identity.

Nutty disliked the facts, but liked the accountability from Gunza. He looked into Gunza's eyes and saw all that he needed to. Gunza was sincere. It didn't help things, though. Nutty looked down for a minute and thought. He said, "He might know. Dis not good. His kid gonna be here, too. His kid wants me a dead. He is da enemy."

Moonoak strode easily alongside Thunda, Quicklip, and Nubbs. Nutty, Gunza, and Guthrak turned to hear the usual bickering between Thunda and Quicklip.

Quicklip had muttered something to the effect of, "Yea? You a mudder liked it."

Nutty screamed, "Shutta up, you stupids!"

"Dems gonna do dis durin' fight time, too?" Guthrak scowled.

Nutty exclaimed, "Not wit' my foot up der asses."

As the group laughed, Nubbs offered a drink. The group discussed the situation at hand as they shared in the offering. Within minutes, they were all well informed and the flask of drink was empty.

Nutty checked the time. "It almost time, guys." He decided to finish up with the last couple bits of information. He began, "Ok, settle down. It almost a time. Gunza, I has to tell you dat we gots to survive dis anda win da war. I choosed you a daughter, Uhra, as my partner. Now, fo' you anda everyone else…"

Gunza stopped Nutty in mid-sentence. "Whoa, whoa, whoa. Ok, kid. In battle, you is my Warchief. I follow you anda die if I must. Outside battle, you still justa kid. But you is a good kid. If dis you choice, you betta takes care a her. Got it?"

Nutty walked closer to Gunza. "Yeah, I got it. I be goods to her anda protects her."

Gunza pressured, "You betta."

Nutty looked to the rest of his officers. "Anda fo' da rest a you, I gots one mo' ting to say." He took a deep breath and rubbed his chin. He delayed until he decided to finally tell the truth of truths. "Darkster is raising a army from da deads. Him's very strong! We musta kills him. Headhunta is his father and more powerful than we all thought."

Moonoak concurred, "It true. I face Headhunta once. Him a fearsome warrior and an enemy of da Gods. You musta fight you hardest to win against him and his son!"

Half of the group's mouths dropped. Orcs, although considered fearless when it came to battle, admittedly cringed when it came to certain superstitions. The thought was, how could they kill what was already dead? Was it wrong to attack a dead body? Even barbarian races like orcs paid tribute to their dead. What Nutty said bordered on some strange, unknown quantity that none were familiar with.

Quicklip was the first to ask a question. "So, we gots to maybe kill dead orcs?"

Nutty replied, "Dunno. But yes, maybe."

Next, Guthrak asked, "What happen if we a die? He raise us from da dead?

Nutty responded, "Again, dunno."

Around the room, questions flew. "Is he bringin' a dead army? Does Headhunta has powers, too? Will dems find our family thru our dreams?"

The answers were consistently the same: "Dunno."

Nutty summed things up nicely. "Kills dems anda you don't has to worry 'bout all da udder stuffs."

Thinking about his battle brother, Guthrak questioned, "We gots to kill 'em?"

Nutty firmly asserted, "Yes. If dems live, der powers too strong and dems can even kill you in you dreams. Once dems find out, it us or dems. Headhunta comin' first. I do da talkin', got it?"

Guthrak answered, "Yes."

The others followed the direction of Nutty.

***

Two more ships were taken by Invada prisoners that had escaped. Booma informed Nutty about the details and elaborated on what steps he was taking. The two discussed what further actions were necessary to secure the prisoners, Big Town, and a final victory over the Invadas. Odds of everything working to perfection were slim at best.

Booma quickly sent two ships in pursuit of the escaped prisoners. Within minutes, they had pierced the atmosphere and entered space just outside Hotta. They were spotted by Invada capital ships and chased back toward the planet. They avoided destruction by ducking into massive storms that had developed over the open ocean to the east of Big Town, leaving the Invada ships no option, but to withdraw.

What the Invadas didn't know was that the ships sent by the Homeworlders were part of a trick. They were intended to appear that they were pursuing the Invada prisoners. In truth, the illusion of pursuit hid their true nature. The escaped ships were laden with explosives that were set to explode upon a series of timed events. It was hoped that they would detonate near other Invada ships. Once again, tricky timing and elaborate planning would wait for time to show its workings.

Booma sent a report to Nutty, who was pleased. Coordination between the two would continue over the next half hour. Defenses were bolstered, offenses were readied. The next step was to tell the Homeworlders of Headhunta's success, if he had indeed assassinated the Invada leader. That would have to wait until Headhunta showed up for his scheduled meeting with Nutty.

Nutty and his officers didn't have to wait long. They turned to see the door open and Headhunta glide into the room. He approached the group and stopped in front of Nutty.

"Headhunta, good. You on time." Nutty played coy.

"I am reporting to you."

"Anda?"

Headhunta smiled. "It is done."

Nutty tipped his head slightly as he guessed what was done. "Which part is done?"

"All of it."

"The whole list?"

"Yes."

"Are you sure?"

"Yes. I don't allow any of dems to live. I sure."

Nutty looked around to his officers. He saw their concerned faces. He wondered if they were weary of what they might have to do shortly, or if they were aware that Headhunta killed everyone on the list he had been given. He didn't exactly kill little girls; he killed an empire's leader and his elite guard. He sought out and killed everyone at different locations in the hazardous void of space, and he did it among enemies. This was virtually impossible!

Headhunta also saw their conflicted facial expressions. "What wrong wit' all a you?"

Nutty answered for them as quickly as he could.

"Headhunta, it not lika everyday dat someone can kills so many, so easy. You very skilled."

"Yes, I am."

Nutty held his pointer finger up and said, "No talkin'. One minute." He pulled a crank phone from one of his pants pockets and gave some commands to hail Booma. He spoke into the crackly box, "Booma?"

Booma heard him from a thousand miles away. "Yeah, Nutty?"

"It done. Spread da word. Orcilla is dead."

"You got it, Nutty."

Nutty pushed one of the buttons on the phone to end the transmission and put it back in his pocket. All the while, he wondered if he should ask Headhunta about Darkster. He didn't want to tip Headhunta off. To this point, it appeared that Headhunta hadn't picked up on the group's knowledge of his son. This gave them the advantage of surprise. Any conversation might take that benefit away. Nutty said nothing.

Headhunta looked at Guthrak and said, "Looka like you seen a ghost."

Nutty's hair stood up on the back of his neck. His muscles tensed; he felt the anxiety in his officers. Nutty had the feeling that he was being watched. He turned toward the door and saw Darkster.

Darkster calmly stated, "He did."

Twenty
Creeps

Nuttybomb dashed toward Darkster and stopped, his eyes just inches from Darkster's. "Tell me why I shouldn't kill you right now."

Darkster thought for a second and began, "Well, shouldn't prolly not the right word. I undastand dat you want a kills me. Fo' good reason, too. But can't prolly a betta word." Darkster grinned.

All those in the room began the dance of taking up positions to defend themselves and others on their side. Gunza and Guthrak carefully put themselves between Nutty and Headhunta. The others hung close to Nutty.

Headhunta rang out at Nutty with, "Careful, boy. You talkin' to my kid."

Gunza snapped back at Headhunta, "You be careful! You kid tried a kills my daughter."

Guthrak added, "Anda has some respect. He not a boy. He is you a Warchief now."

Headhunta corrected, "No, Biggabomb wuz my Warchief. Dis justa his kid."

Nutty yelled out, "Evvyone, shutta up!" He turned his attention to Darkster and continued, "Can't kill you? I can anda I will."

Darkster sneered. "But you can't use you a right arm."

He was right. For some reason, Nutty's arm hung useless at his side. As hard as he tried to move it, he simply couldn't. He tried to hide this fact, but his eyes gave him away.

Darkster was full of himself. He showed no fear and he would do whatever he needed to as long as he and his father made it out of the cave alive. But that wasn't enough. He wanted to play with Nutty and his guards. He wanted to show them just how powerful he was. He looked away from Nutty and pointed to Thunda's arm. He said, "Anda you. You no goods wit' you arm on fire."

Thunda looked at Darkster, down at his arms, and around the room at the others. He wondered if he heard Darkster correctly. "What?" He chuckled in defiance. "Fire?"

Darkster pointed to Thunda's left arm. "See? It definitely on fire." Just like something in writing, like the air that is breathed, like the world itself, Darkster's words were firm and factual; the certainty was unquestionable. Thunda looked down at his vulnerable appendage in horror, as if his arm was actually aflame. And then, Thunda's left arm ignited, as if by will.

Stunned observance cost Thunda the quick response that he so desperately needed to avoid severe burns. After several officers jumped away from him, Moonoak and Quicklip rushed to help him. They tried to extinguish his bare skin before the fire spread, but the heat lit his vest as his engulfed arm threw small cinders of flesh and material around him in a flash. Quicklip wrestled him to the ground where he and Moonoak worked to stop the blaze that caused Thunda's agony and distracted others.

Nutty stepped back in disbelief. What had just happened? Nubbs dropped his flask. He was shocked by what he just saw, too. In fact, none of Nutty's guards were immune to the spectacle they witnessed.

It happened all too quick! Guthrak was too slow to stop the blade that Headhunta swung from severing his jugular vein. He too had been jolted by the fire that was consuming Thunda. His clumsy response was simply a knee-jerk reaction to movement that he caught from his periphery. He barely got his own blade lifted to deflect the lethal strike that crossed below the souvenir blade that he wore in his jaw. He was only fast enough to lose a couple fingers and cause Headhunta's knife to swing in somewhat of a horizontal strike. The original upward swing of the blade would have cut the vein along its full length. However, the minimal deflection caused a clean cut across his brain's vital blood supply. As a result, it could have been worse. If Guthrak could get attention from a doc, maybe he would survive.

Gunza engaged Headhunta in a heartbeat. His enraged strikes, heavy and powerful, were countered by Headhunta's fluidity. While Gunza had all the anger of his wounded daughter flowing throughout his body, Headhunta had a clear head and a determined spirit on his side.

Before long, the two were using multiple weapons. Gunza used a twenty-inch knife in his right hand and a lean battleax in his left. Headhunta had somehow replaced his knife with two long swords. Two dissimilar styles with practically unparalleled skills were set upon each other. Virtual brothers were now matched as enemies, and each knew how deadly the other was.

Guthrak entered the fight in spurts. However, the best that he could do was to engage Headhunta at the same time Gunza attacked. He staggered forward, swung, and retreated. He was forced to rely on his weaker, left hand to swing a weapon since losing some fingers and part of his right hand and thumb. Being predominantly right-handed, and not ambidextrous like Gunza and Headhunta, he struggled to keep pace with them. Each time he stepped back, he held his torn throat with the damaged hand that somehow prolonged his life.

Meanwhile, Nutty didn't miss a beat. He had countered Darkster's first thrust, even without the use of his right arm. He was, however, in a defensive position as Darkster had a marked advantage.

Darkster gritted his teeth as he swung two long swords like his father. He wasn't nearly as skilled, but was just good enough to push his right blade through Nutty's left shoulder. Nutty's arm felt the force of a lightning bolt from his neck to his fingers. He pulled himself from Darkster's blade as he dropped his own. One of the nerves in his shoulder was completely severed. Nutty fell backward and landed on his back. Both of his arms lay beside him, limp and useless.

Darkster jumped over Nutty and pushed his right sword down into Nutty's chest. The blade pierced the thick leather that Nutty wore and found its way into flesh and muscle. Nutty wanted to fight back, but it was not to be. He couldn't move his arms. He was fixated on their inability to defend him.

Moonoak saw this and yelled to Nutty, "Fogets you arms Nutty. Use you legs!"

Nutty blinked and kicked upward into Darkster's groin. It worked. Darkster stumbled to the left and away from Nutty. Nutty had the time to get to his feet, and he did. He wearily trudged toward Moonoak with the sword hanging from his chest. He was unaware that Nubbs had been in a trance and unable to fight until Moonoak had worked him back into consciousness.

Darkster stood up from a crouch and began mumbling. His head swung as he looked upward. His eyes rolled back. His arms reached upward to some invisible target. He muttered pleas to something beyond.

Within seconds, Nubbs was near him. He readied himself for battle against this strange foe. He braced himself for fire, or a trance, or whatever ungodly things might be cast upon him, but he was not prepared for what came next.

Quicklip was now standing after putting out the fire that ravaged his friend's body. In horror, his eyes were fixated on the figures that were entering the cave. He blurted out, "What da hell?"

Everybody stopped in their tracks. Even the intense clash between Gunza, Guthrak, and Headhunta halted. All eyes were drawn to the ghastly beings that were beginning to fill the entrance of the cave.

Reality was something strange now.

***

"I so prouds a you, Uhra."

Uhra had taken several steps on her own. They weren't with the usual grace that epitomized her before the injury. They weren't even steady, but they were footsteps, unassisted and clumsy. Still, they were footsteps all the same. Uhra smiled and responded back to Muga with, "Tanks, Momma."

Muga somehow straddled Uhra to keep her from falling if she stumbled. The "Momma" looked somewhat like a defensive lineman on a killball team. She didn't care. What she did care about was the well-being of her son's love interest. She had just been called "Momma" by her and it felt good. Muga thought that she couldn't have enough children. Too many had been lost to disease, and now, this Gods forsaken war!

Just as Muga needed children, so too did Uhra need a mother. Uhra's mother had succumbed to the "fever" as did many orcs. Her mother was beautiful and vibrant before contracting the disease that took her. Yet, even though she died before she could make lasting impressions on Uhra, her traits seemed to carry on in her daughter.

Uhra was too young to remember life lessons that her mom may have taught her. In fact, she barely remembered what she looked like. Vague images of her mom holding her hand or seeing her cook something in the other room was all that Uhra had to go on. Now, almost a teenager, she sought guidance. A time that her hormones raged, and this injury left her disabled, was a time that she could have used the knowledge and comfort of her mother. Muga was all too happy to oblige.

Muga was also aware that Nutty would be fighting for his and the worlds' lives over the next few days. She had spent twenty-plus years dealing with Biggabomb going off and fighting. She dealt with his problems. She thought of the loneliness when he was gone. She thought of the fear of not knowing if he would come home; the fear of not knowing that each time she said goodbye, it may have been the last. Now,

Biggabomb had left again, this time to check on Nutty. She had said goodbye to both of them.

As if on cue, Uhra mentioned Biggabomb. Maybe she saw that Muga was upset, maybe it was coincidence. Either way, she knew how Muga felt. Her Nuttybomb had said his goodbyes, too. She hoped to be walking when he returned…if he returned. Maybe talking about Biggabomb deflected her feelings about Nuttybomb and distracted her tortured mind.

Muga showed a brief smile. "Dat big bastid will be fines. He always is. His lungs doin' good. Anda him already tolds me what he wanna do to me wit' dat big claw he gots now. Oh my Gods!"

The two laughed for a while as they told funny stories about each other's partners. The levity of everything being at risk was lost in the moment's denial of such. Things that weren't the least bit humorous left them in tears. Such were the results of stress, fear, and nervousness.

***

Biggabomb left the truck that brought him from the airfield to the foothills where he hoped to find Nutty. He waved to the grunt that drove him and began to walk along the dusty trail that led over a hill a short distance beyond.

The grunt, seeing Biggabomb walking alone, questioned his former Warchief. "You sure, Chief? Be ok alones?"

Biggabomb laughed. He raised his enormous bionic apparatus. "See dis claw?"

The grunt nodded hesitantly. He wasn't sure if he said the wrong thing and that the claw would mean his demise. Biggabomb was still a big SOB. He could easily handle the grunt that questioned his male prowess. The grunt hung his head.

"I can smash a tank now. I goods." Biggabomb headed to locate Nutty.

The grunt, relieved that he hadn't killed himself out of stupidity, which he also knew was something that happened all too often to orcs, kept his mouth shut and drove off. His run-on thoughts kept him busy for a few more minutes. Then, the truck died. The grunt was too stupid to remember that it ran on fuel. Now, he was alone and left without a running vehicle several miles from Biggabomb.

He dismounted and headed back to where he dropped off his former Chief. He decided that there was no way he would risk walking thirty miles to a base...not with all the enemies that traveled these parts.

Meanwhile, Biggabomb climbed the hill that had been ahead of him just minutes before. His breathing was a bit labored for a task that was so easy to him just a few weeks earlier. Now, he had to come to grips with his limitations. He thought it better to not think about his limitations and just push on. He felt that he might be forced to reckon with his inadequacies soon enough.

The view was amazing from his new vantage point. The sky had hues of light blue, mixed with yellows, oranges, and reds. The mountains all around him were tall and majestic. They gave way to a valley that opened to a plateau around ten miles to the west.

Smoke rose from a battle that was raging out there. It mixed with the low, ominous clouds that were forming. The lights from gunfire and explosions flickered in the distance. Biggabomb couldn't make out the dots that moved around in the conflict, but he guessed that the small ones were orcs and the larger ones were probably vehicles. He wasn't so feeble that he couldn't figure that much out, even with all the smoke and dust that was kicked up in the battle. He smiled a bit.

While he took in the view, he realized that he must be feeble after all. His new lease on life caused him to look at the beautiful sky and the wonder that amazed him from afar. He saw these things in a new light, but now wasn't the time. The wonder on the plateau was death unfolding in countless numbers. The swirling clouds and colored atmosphere were signs of an impending storm, and from the looks of it, a bad one at that.

Biggabomb made his way down the other side of the hill. He tried to get rid of the sick feeling in his gut. He was wrong to pause and look at the backdrop. How stupid could he be? His orcs were dying while he watched like an idiot. Furthermore, his son might be in serious trouble. His stomach churned.

He walked around a corner where he had fought a month or two before. He was unsure of time since he was wounded. It didn't really matter when it was, but that it was. It was an intense fight where both sides took heavy casualties. He remembered the dead being buried along the cliff wall. He called this place "Da Valley of Heroes". The valley ran along the side of the cliff where he assumed Nutty would be. Recent construction equipment confirmed his assumptions.

His stomach was really plaguing him now. He bent over and held it with his good arm. As nausea gripped him, his breakfast was deposited on the ground in Da Valley of Heroes. His head ached. He stumbled as his unsteady legs shook beneath him. But they didn't shake because he was ill; the ground was convulsing under his feet. He, like his breakfast, ended up on the ground.

Thunder rang in Biggabomb's ears. He watched the walls of the valley crack. First, the tops of the walls ripped and carried down to the floor below. Each crack found its way to a raised section in the floor of the valley. Each section was about four feet wide and seven feet long and each section was marked with a headstone.

One by one, the sections began to cave in. Dirt, rock, and sand filtered downward, leaving lumps that were becoming visible. The shaking had become more localized now. Although the ground rumbled, it gave way to a rhythmic shaking that seemed to focus on the lumps.

Years of battle told Biggabomb's brain how many sections had drained of Hotta's materials and sifted down beneath the lumps that began to writhe. There were fifteen in all. He knew without thinking. He might have taken pride in this, had all his attention not been drawn to the open graves that came to life around him.

"Good Gods," was all that he muttered. Biggabomb stumbled to his feet, his head a mix of skepticism. Surely, his eyes weren't seeing what he thought. They just couldn't be. All those years of battle, in countless engagements, in all kinds of weather, against many kinds of enemies, this was a first.

Orcs that weren't truly dead and not truly alive gathered in the small corridor where they had been buried. They had the weapons from their graves in their hands and they were quick to use them. They began coming at Biggabomb in groups.

Biggabomb hesitated to strike the "creeps" that started to attack him. He didn't know what he should do to his fallen battle brothers. He had shed blood with them. Now, he would have to shed blood against them. They were tainted by some ungodly curse; it was the vilest and most grotesque thing he had ever encountered. The smell of rotten flesh gave testament to his senses.

He found himself swinging a short sword in his hand and crushing things with his claw. The instinct to survive acted for him. He couldn't think about how creeps got their name. Was it because they were creepy? Did the name point out their slow movements? These thoughts had occurred to him briefly, but were pushed aside by the innate sense to defend himself.

The creeps moved like they were in pain. They walked slowly, but attacked with a fury. They defied logic on every scale. Some were just skeletons with tattered clothes hanging from them. Others had muscle and flesh that was still being consumed by insects and bacteria. None had sufficient muscle, tendons, and ligaments to provide them the motion that they obviously showed. They didn't have working brains and nervous systems. None had working hearts or lungs, yet they functioned...and functioned well.

The creeps functioned so well, in fact, that Biggabomb wasn't keeping up with their thrust. He was facing too many. He had dropped a few, but they got back up and attacked again. The harder he seemed to fight, the more they came back for punishment. And...they were dangerous.

Several creeps slashed cuts across Biggabomb's chest and arms. Some cut each other as they wildly sought to ravage their foe. They moaned as they walked and growled as they bared gnarly teeth that drove for Biggabomb's face. A few rattled off shots from their guns. For a second, this fact bothered Biggabomb. The fact that they shot at him didn't quite annoy him as much as the fact that they had been buried with ammunition in their guns.

What the hell was he thinking? "Fight! Fight! Fight! Drive forward you old feeble bastid! Slay these unfathomable horrors. Maybe you can put them to rest and save your life in the process." Well, that's what his brain was trying to tell him. "Ugh," and "Fukka," was what actually left his lips.

The grunt, hearing foul language by the truck load, barreled around the corner and started shooting the creeps as he closed in on them. He wasn't alone. No, he was with Biggabomb at last! It did occur to him that he might have been better off walking thirty miles to base, especially when he realized what he was shooting. He stood in shock.

"Fight dems you stupid a bastid!" Finally, Biggabomb had commanded himself and his lips stated it. The grunt mistook the command as an order to him though. This benefited them both. Five minutes of grueling, desperate, unimaginable horror was over when Biggabomb and the grunt were the last standing. Mangled body parts still moved on the ground, but weren't much of a threat without accompanying bodies.

Biggabomb joked with the grunt. "I thought I said I be ok and fo' a you to go."

The grunt chuckled. "Well, Chief, sorry I no listen too good."

Biggabomb laughed. "Hey, I knows you. You is Guthrak's sista's kid, right?"

The grunt was elated that Biggabomb recognized him. "Yup. Me is Grotta."

"Good fightin', Grotta. Tanks."

"Tanks, Boss Biggabomb. Hey, was dems creeps?"

For thirty-four seconds, Biggabomb and Grotta talked about the unlikelihood of ever coming across a creep. They also talked about a much-deserved promotion for Grotta. He was acknowledged for saving Bigga's hide.

On the thirty-fifth second Biggabomb cautiously pushed open the door to the cavern. He saw the backs of Gunza, Guthrak, and Headhunta. Further away in the dimly lit room were the others, also facing the other way. Biggabomb blurted out, "Did you guys sees all dem creeps?"

The startled group in the room stirred to find him standing at the entrance. Their movements gave way to another couple dozen creeps encroaching upon them from the other side of the room. The wounds from those in the group were also becoming apparent.

Nubbs said in sarcasm, "Yeah, we saw 'em."

Darkster aimed his sarcasm at Biggabomb too with, "Dems impressive, right? I made dems myself."

Biggabomb didn't answer. He watched the evil kid, never taking his eyes away from him, as he walked over to Nuttybomb. He put his hand on Nutty's shoulder. "Dis him son?"

Nutty was comforted by his father being there. But he was also conflicted with knowing how vulnerable his father was to the deception and potential acts from Darkster. Nutty said as much as he could as quickly as he could. "Yeah. He maka creeps and he can set you on fire wit' his mind if you let him."

Moonoak cut in. "Don't believe what he say, Biggabomb. He say you on fire, but you not. If you tink you on fire, then you be on fire, ok?"

Biggabomb scratched his head and turned it several times as his thick neck cracked. Still, his eyes were fixated on Darkster. "Neat trick, kid."

Headhunta commanded Biggabomb to, "Stop! Don't do it, Chief."

Biggabomb stopped in his tracks. He growled under his breath and whispered, "You are next, old friend."

Darkster had held his creep troops at bay with his hand in the air. He lowered slowly as he spoke. "I gots one ting to say Biggabomb."

Biggabomb waited for the kid to threaten him or tell him he was on fire. But that didn't happen. Instead, something else did.

Darkster brought his hand to his face where he spoke into a crank phone. He said, "Dems all in da cave now."

How things unfolded next is anyone's guess. Battles are chaotic. Why orcs can't shoot worth a boar cake is more bewildering. A few well-placed bullets may have decisively ended the conflict in a matter of seconds. Instead, they tangled in an epic clash of hand-to-hand combat.

Biggabomb fought his way toward Darkster, but was mauled by creeps. Quicklip came to his aid as fast as he could, but he, too, was halted by the same. This left Nubbs against Darkster and Gunza against Headhunta. While Moonoak patched up Thunda, he verbally worked Nutty back to reality. Grotta, who had some medical experience, worked on his uncle Guthrak.

Darkster kept taunting Nubbs with, "You are burning," but it didn't work. He went to, "Wow, da ground is soft. It slowin's us both down." At first this didn't work either, but it began to work as Nubbs thought about it; he fell into the trap. It was the wording that tricked him.

Darkster knew the ground wasn't soft, no matter how much he said it. But to a simple-minded orc it had to be. Nubbs believed that they both were slowed by the ground. Why would Darkster talk about slowing himself? It was believable.

Footwork was important in combat. It was very important when balance was needed to attack and defend in close quarters. To lean a little more forward or backward or to one side over the other could have spelled disaster. Warriors have been trained throughout the millennia to adjust without thought; to practice through repetitive sparring. Training has been used to make movements second nature. Therefore, a warrior who didn't have to think about what he did, and actually did it, was far more dangerous than one who was deliberate.

Darkster had Nubbs thinking. But it wasn't quite enough yet. Nubbs doubting the rigidity of the ground meant that his mind was beginning to open. The sinister, egotistical manipulator sought to find even the smallest hole in his enemy's psyche, so he could widen the crack into a permanent channel for his plot.

Nubbs was hanging in there with his volatile enemy. His legs were slow, but functional. Darkster swung his weapon, ducked a counter and stepped to the side A swing here, another duck, and some play with balance had the two grappling. Darkster seized the moment. "When you die, who gonna cry?"

"I not gonna die. You are."

"No, I don't a tink so. You gonna die and leave a momma or a maybe sista behind I tink. Maybe."

As they wrestled for advantage, Nubbs couldn't help but to think about the small family he would leave behind if he did indeed die. He didn't think that Darkster could kill him by thinking it or saying it. He wasn't going to fall for that anyway. He made sure that he knew he wouldn't die because Darkster said it. Besides, he did have a mother and a sister to protect back home.

Oh no! It was a horrifying moment. Nubbs eyes opened wide. They saw the smile on Darkster's lips. Darkster knew that he had a mother and a sister. How did this happen? Nubbs was sure to not think about dying. He was so careful not to be concerned about that part, that he missed the real threat. He was forced to think about his loved ones.

Darkster felt the grip from Nubbs' right hand loosen slightly. He felt Nubbs shift his balance ever so slightly. Darkster pleaded, "Don't do it, Nubbs."

Nubbs wasn't going to do anything that Darkster told him to. In fact, he decided that doing the opposite was the best thing. Furthermore, he wanted to end this fight quickly before Darkster got into his head any more than he already had so far. He released Darkster and swung...

Moonoak screamed, "Nubbs, no!"

Darkster sidestepped and buried his sword deep under Nubbs' armpit.

Nubbs had no free, useable arms to defend himself and his legs were so heavy that they couldn't kick or even attempt to trip Darkster. Instinctively, he headbutted Darkster and fell backward as a stunned Darkster released his competent arm. Nubbs staggered as he held off attacks from creeps. He was getting cut up and was in severe pain from the sword that leaned skyward in his shoulder. He backtracked in the direction of Nutty and Moonoak.

By this time, Grotta had sewed up Guthrak and pulled a sword from his holster. He turned and ran into battle to help whoever he could. The timing and his circumstances were unfortunate. He ran to Gunza and Headhunta, fully expecting to fight creeps. Instead, he was confused for a second as he saw the two champion warriors battling each other. He was totally unaware of Headhunta's intentions until it was too late. He never saw the slashes that severed his head from his neck and spilled his entrails all over the floor.

Guthrak jumped in to help him, but it was too late. He watched his nephew's hands fumble for an empty stomach and a head that wasn't attached. The confused body dropped to the floor.

Guthrak roared as he flew across the room at Headhunta. He took a deep cut to his right hip and leg as he broke Headhunta's ribs due to such a violent collision. He smashed Headhunta's face over and over with his forearm. A dazed Headhunta reequipped himself with a knife and used it. As Guthrak's arm came down to crush Headhunta's face for the eleventh time, it was torn by the razor-sharp blade.

Gunza never did capitalize on Guthrak's attack. He was stabbed in the back by Darkster who had just been freed up by Nubbs. He threw a quick backhand that sent Darkster flying twenty feet. Gunza picked up where Guthrak left off and engaged Headhunter yet again.

Moonoak was desperately monitoring Darkster while taking up arms against creeps. He wasn't much of a warrior, but the situation called for his suddenly unexpected trial by fire. He and Thunda, who was all but dead at this point, drove each other forward into battle. As Moonoak struggled mightily against the creeps, he continued yelling things to Nutty.

Quicklip was wounded, too. He had been cut a few times that he remembered and another few that he didn't care to. He didn't want to die, but he knew his duty to guard Nutty was his priority. He continued fighting with his back to Biggabomb. This gave him and his Warchief's father's protection on their weakest sides. It also allowed him to see Nutty the whole time. He could see his mutilated friend doing everything that he could to serve his Warchief, too.

Quicklip was moved; so much so that he almost cried. He couldn't imagine being cooked alive like his friend, Thunda. He saw Thunda's flesh slide up and down the bone in his forearm when he moved it, like a cooked piece of chicklen thigh. Only these most important words came to his mind. He may have never said anything so pertinent or poignant in his life, and perhaps, never would again. He said, "Thunda, you fat, stupid bastid. You fights like a lil gurl. Fight harda dan dat!"

Thunda responded wearily, "I fightin' nots to tink about you momma from last night!"

Quicklip wiped his watery eyes between attacks and smiled.

Nutty was starting to come around. He talked himself into believing that his arms would work, even the one that had been wounded. It wasn't long before he was back on his feet and looking for weapons to use. He wasn't at one hundred percent, but then again, who was?

Nutty walked sluggishly behind Moonoak and waited for a moment to get his hands on a sword. He fought instinctively with his bare hands against the creeps that Moonoak and Thunda were facing. He freed some weapons from the falling creeps and gathered himself. He swore that he wasn't going to let Darkster's trickery work on him again.

The addition of Thunda, Moonoak, and now, Nutty swung the odds against the creeps. As creep after creep was separated from their limbs and heads, Moonoak stepped into the more adequate roll of shaman. He, like Darkster earlier, muttered words to a God from beyond. Only, his words were used to give final rest and comfort to the beleaguered souls that were forced into their bodies against all compassion.

Nutty fought furiously to get to his father. He thought that he, along with his father, could finally destroy Darkster and Headhunta. That plan was laid to rest when Nutty heard Biggabomb squealing as he breathed. He saw the pain in his father's eyes.

Biggabomb whispered, "Nutty, my lungs collapsed."

"You done fightin', Dad?"

"Dunno how to quit, son. But can no fight none neither. I gots eleven a dems creeps outside and ten mo' in here." Biggabomb went to one knee. His coloring wasn't good.

"It ok, Dad. You did 'nuff."

Nutty called Nubbs and Moonoak over. Thunda stumbled along as well. Quicklip fought the remaining few creeps on his own as he, too, made his way back to the group.

Nutty said to Moonoak, "Come wit' me. Try a keep der mind stuff off me and I try to keep der swords offa you."

"Ok, Nutty."

Nubbs got Nutty's attention. "What 'bout dems?"

Nutty's eyes followed Nubbs' finger as it pointed to ten Invadas that came into the cavern. He shrugged his shoulders and sighed, "Do da besta you cans."

Gunfire rang out. Bullets tore into the group of Homeworlders. Quicklip and Nubbs rushed the Invadas and forced them to fight in close combat. Against whatever physical laws when it came to the limitations of wounded animals, Biggabomb and the others forced their way to confront the enemies that had just entered.

Nutty rushed into combat alongside Gunza against Darkster and Headhunta. Gunza was so badly wounded that he struggled to defend himself by now. He had finally collapsed from blood loss. All the others were fighting Invadas. Nutty had to face Darkster and Headhunta alone. Gunza couldn't even stand up from all the wounds he had received. Nutty commanded him to fall back and protect Moonoak.

Nutty attacked Darkster with his left hand while defending against Headhunta with his right. He soon found that this was too perilous as his wounded arm was no match for the lightning fast Headhunta. It was a mistake that nearly cost Nutty his life. He adjusted quickly to fend off the rapid-fire assault of Headhunta and dodged a variety of slashes that came from different angles.

Darkster began his own assault. "Too much fo' you Nutty?"

Nutty replied, "Yup." He smiled and worked his feet around to the right.

Darkster didn't expect admission that Nutty was outmatched. "So, you know dat you will die?"

"Yup. We all gonna die."

Moonoak chimed in. "Darkster, you know how dis ends. Nutty kills a you."

Darkster thought clearly as he struggled to keep up with the pace of his father and Nutty. "No. Nutty gonna die."

Moonoak continued, "Yeah, but not by you or you a dad. He kills a you. I have seened it."

"No! I not die from him. I kill him, and he know it, too!"

Nutty had worked his way consistently around to the right so Darkster couldn't make effective strikes. By doing so, he forced Darkster to get close to Gunza, who was still a wild card and a potentially deadly threat. Darkster would have none of it. He stayed behind his father and struck when he could find an opening, but these attempts were futile.

Darkster stepped back and began calling to his God again. The ground shook as he muttered gibberish. His eyes rolled back as his hands reached upward.

Many more figures were on their way and none of the Homeworlders in the cavern were able to fight any more after facing the Invadas. The Invadas were cut down, but so were Quicklip and Nubbs.

Bodies were strewn everywhere. The stench of decay was impalpable. The amount of carnage that these enemies set upon each other in the cavern was unfathomable. There were so many dead, so many dying, and so many in between. What souls would find rest?

Creeps began to come into the cavern. Moonoak wouldn't be able to face them all, even if Nutty could handle Headhunta and Darkster. Gunza was done. He floated in and out of consciousness, each time verging on death.

Nutty stepped out of the fray for a moment to semi-protect Moonoak. He saw a fairly fresh Darkster and his deadly father with a couple broken ribs and a mangled face. He counted seven more creeps at the entrance.

Headhunta cautiously followed Nutty. He spit hatred from his bowels through his teeth, "Hello, Moonoak. Remember me?" This was not good.

Twenty-One
Da Libury

Booma was trying to reach Nutty. He was trying to inform Nutty about the prison ships that made it to their destinations. They exploded as planned and took out a large number of Invada ships. Others were captured by Homeworlder infiltrators. Also, the Invadas were leaving Hotta. They had a new leader and they swore they would return, but they were pulling out. The combination of their losses and the time constraints to resupply in the vastness of space did them in.

Lastly, Booma wanted to say that the Homeworlder population was chanting Nutty's name in the streets of every city. He wanted to share this personally with his little brother. However, the information would have to wait until Nutty was able to respond. That was in question, though. Booma didn't know what was transpiring in the cavern.

***

Moonoak did his best to calm Nutty. Of course, he didn't think that he and Nutty were going to survive the onslaught that was imminent, but he didn't show it. Instead, he advised Nutty to breathe and focus. He told him to basically stay in the moment, not to listen to Darkster, and not to worry about the outcome.

Nutty knew the odds. However, he told Moonoak to fight any creeps to his furthest right. Nutty had to take on more than what he thought he was capable of handling. It was his duty, his responsibility, and his need to succeed after leading everyone to this point.

So, he would fight Headhunta, Darkster, and most of the creeps on the left. He was keenly aware of the odds.

As Headhunta made his move, Nutty pushed Moonoak into the group of creeps and to the right. Nutty deflected a barrage of attacks from Headhunta and positioned himself within the group of creeps, too. He fought off attacks from them as well and did the best he could to keep a few of them between Headhunta and himself.

The fight was awkward and sloppy. A chaotic mix of weapons being swung, punches being thrown, and pushing creeps into Headhunta and Darkster was the theme. It wasn't spectacular like the fight between Gunza and Headhunta. The mastery of that art wasn't to be seen against creeps. No, it was simply the will to live during a desperate fight against insurmountable odds that gave an "anything goes" kind of street brawl look to this free for all.

Moonoak had succeeded against one creep. Nutty took out another three. The odds were slightly better than impossible now. Nutty didn't want to completely eliminate the creeps, though; he needed them for his next move. He and Moonoak would just have to survive the onslaught a little longer.

Nutty decided to try and communicate with Moonoak through telepathy. He figured it probably wouldn't work, but if Darkster could do stuff with his mind, maybe anyone could. Nutty kept imagining that he was telling Moonoak to bait Darkster. He said it over and over in his head. He gave instructions and waited for a response.

Moonoak stopped for a second and looked at Nutty. He furrowed his brow with a look of confusion. Then, he nodded that he had understood Nutty. He winked and began to taunt Darkster.

"Darkster. It shame dat you die today."

Darkster was indignant. "No, I already said I no die. Nutty does, you stupid shaman."

"But, you can't a kill him anda we no listen to you stupid tricks. Dems works no more."

Darkster sneered and exclaimed, "But, looks. Nutty can't breathe. See? The creeps make da air dead all around dems."

Nutty calmly stated, "Well, dat would be scary if it true. But it not. You tricks don't works, Darkster."

Darkster kept it up. "So, why can't you breathe?"

Nutty retorted, "I breathes ok, just a lil winded from all da fightin'. Sorry to disappoint you, Darkster."

"No. Da air is thick anda heavy. Death fillin's you lungs right now, Nutty."

Moonoak took a bad cut down his left arm. He screamed out as he went to his knees. He fought from this compromised position as he worked to calm himself and shield the pain from his brain. Then, he spoke. "Darkster, da air is fine. But you not looks too good."

Nutty added, "You can't even fights, Darkster. You is too tired."

The impetuous Darkster was irritated at this point. His willful thoughts and words weren't working on Nutty. Also, he wasn't particularly fond of them telling him how he looked and felt. He said, "I fine. I not tired."

Moonoak asked him, "Why you drop a you sword den?"

Darkster defiantly said, "I didn't." He held his hand out to show the sword and checked to make sure. As he questioned himself, Moonoak managed to turn Darkster's own tactics against him. The sword dropped from Darkster's hand.

Nutty anticipated this, grabbed a creep by the arm, and flung him at Headhunta. Before Headhunta or Darkster knew what happened, Nutty drove his sword through Darkster's gut and turned to slice Headhunta's right arm.

It was a bold and miraculous turn of events. Darkster fell to the ground in a pool of blood. Headhunter dropped the long sword from his damaged arm and staggered backward. He was overwhelmed at the sight of his son falling from a severe wound and the amazing speed in which Nutty worked.

Nutty never stopped attacking. He didn't give Headhunta time to gather himself. He swung his blades in rapid succession until Headhunta, who struggled to defend himself with one good arm, also fell. Nutty cut his throat and slashed his stomach open. Nutty exclaimed, "Dat how all a you victims feel."

However, as Nutty felled his dangerous opponents, he left one unchecked. He assumed that Moonoak would have slain the last creep. But, Moonoak was still on his knees and unable to do it. Instead, the last creep drove its blade through Nutty's back. Before Nutty finally fell, he turned and cut the creep's head off. Then, he managed to cut its arms off, too.

Nutty slumped on the floor and watched helplessly as Darkster struggled to crawl to his father. He saw Darkster stumble to his feet and slowly drag Headhunta out of the cavern.

Moonoak, exhausted and bleeding, dropped on his back.

It would be several minutes before he could attend to Nutty. They kept talking to each other to ensure that neither lost consciousness. Moonoak made sure that he didn't forget to tell Nutty something. "Nutty?"

"Yeah?"

"So, we can use our minds like Darkster, too."

"Yeah. But sumptin' tells me he can do more. Anda he won't let us do its again."

Moonoak added, "You mean, if he lives?"

Nutty was confident about his next words. "No. He will live. I knows it."

"How you know?"

"I just do. Anda I kill Headhunta, but..." Nutty had a hard time concentrating and articulating his thoughts as his blood continued to drain from his body.

"But, what, Nutty?"

"Headhunta died. I know it. But he not dead. He not dead."

At that moment, a Homeworlder patrol showed up at the cavern. They were looking for Grotta, who never got back to base. They radioed for help and began helping the wounded. The healing process could begin.

***

The war was in a lull, both sides licking their wounds and preparing for the next conflict. The

Homeworlders tore apart Invada ships and weapons to learn about their technologies. They rebuilt them and began to experiment with building their own ships. Also, they organized and implemented better defenses. They prepared for another invasion.

But the orcs on Hotta still had nearly a million of their own that were taken away to the Invada's planets. Nutty had sworn that no prisoners would be allowed to be removed. Bolstering their defenses wouldn't get their orcs back. No, the only way to get them back was to go after them. Nutty implemented a shipbuilding and arms program. He decided that the next fight would be brought to the Invadas.

On the home front, rebuilding was in full swing. The library was finished and stocked with thousands of books. Nutty sat with Moonoak and went over some of the titles and content. The two laughed as they discussed the writings.

"I da Bestest Trukk Driva Evva."

Moonoak laughed. "How 'bout dis one? I Katched da Biggest Frog."

Nutty smiled. "Dat one a kid book?"

"Nope."

They laughed some more.

Nutty had another book in front of him that he wanted to share. "I lika dis one...Nuttybomb, da Greatest Warchief."

"Yeah, you would likes dat one."

Moonoak became more serious. "Hey, Nutty, look."

Nutty read the title and then thumbed through the pages. It read, "Advanse Farm Tekneek fo any Orc."

Nutty nodded and exclaimed, "Now, dat what I talkin' 'bout. Dat is real stuff to help orcs get betta."

Nutty became hysterical. He laughed so loud that he could be heard outside the massive stone walls. My momma wrote one, Moonoak."

"Yeah? What is title?"

Nutty's high-pitched voice was something Moonoak had never heard before. Actually, it was a little embarrassing. But Nutty couldn't control himself. He finally burst out between belly laughs, "Biggabomb, Gets Away Fro Me Wit Dat Claw!!!"

Moonoak laughed, too, but not like Nutty who was wiping his eyes and screeching. He settled down quicker than Nutty and changed the conversation. "Nutty, all da books is good for us. I put da farm one in our science area. You know, ders a whole wall 'bout you? You saved da planet."

A different voice chimed in, "We helped, too." Nubbs was sure to get his deserved props in as well.

Thunda sat down and shook his head in disgust. "We beed here on time if Quicklip could drive."

Quicklip stared at his scarred friend. "I drived you momma last night."

Nutty intervened. "Alright, you two. Dat 'nuff."

Quicklip questioned Nutty with, "It really happen tomorrow?"

Nutty perked up. "Yup. Right here on da steps of da libury."

They were all starting to show up now. Biggabomb threw the doors open and announced his arrival. Gunza and Guthrak followed. Three dozen more former kings and military leaders joined them as well. It was customary on such an event for all the bigwigs to share in this momentous occasion.

Nubbs rudely shut everyone up. Orcs weren't a very forgiving race. Given the circumstances, however, even the meanest, toughest orcs allowed this new warrior to put them in their place. Well, he had to with the importance of what he asked. He yelled, "Where is the Shlogger?"

Cheers erupted from all. Barrel after barrel was wheeled in to keep the war stories going all night. Food was abundant and supplied in massive quantities. Tales of unimaginable content were heard as each orc boasted, trying to outdo each other. One described killing a hundred orcs with his pinky. One irritated everyone by talking about getting caught in his zippra all night long. Another claimed to be a great frog catcher. Nutty and Moonoak laughed when they heard that.

Toward the end of the festivities, toasts were made; not that they needed to be. They were probably done so more drinks could be pounded down. It was tradition as well, so they happened.

Biggabomb took his turn and stood up. The room fell silent. He looked around and slurred, "I know I a lil sloshed right now…"

The room erupted in laughter and fist pumping. Then, it quieted again.

Biggabomb held up his mug. "To my son, Nuttybomb…He lead us to win against da Invadas. He a real Warchief…Da meanest, toughest, bestest leadingest bastid on da planet!"

The roar in the room was deafening. Biggabomb sat down and gave way to Nutty.

Nutty looked around the room. He stood for several minutes as he waited for the cheers and comments to stop. He looked down at his father. "You taught me, Dad."

A loud chorus of "Awe!" was followed by laughter. Things like, "Dat so cute," and, "Kiss him," were heard above the raucous hilarity.

Nutty chuckled and began pointing to each orc in the room. "But we win cuz a you anda you anda you." After each orc was recognized, more claps and cheers added to the noise. Then, Nutty asked who da bravest orc was. The orcs looked around at each other.

When Nutty got no response, he said, "All a you. Anda you females, too. Anda da kids."

After some more drunken cheers Nutty wrapped up with, "Ya knows why we win dis war? Cuz we all are da meanest, toughest, bestest, leadingest bastids on da planet!"

To Nutty's dismay, he was carried around Big Town on different orcs' shoulders for the remainder of the night. He didn't relish the attention, but he allowed the public display because he thought the war-torn orcs from his world needed it. He was right.

He directed them to carry him home. He washed up, changed his clothes, and out he went again. Cheers followed him all the way back to the library. He looked at the opulent structure as he arrived. The columns were decorated in ivy and white flowers. A red carpet had been rolled out upon his arrival.

Above was a beautiful, light blue sky. The sun had just risen, and the heat was already starting to be felt. The streets were filled with citizens and troops who made sure they were here to see this event. The younger ones were told by their mothers that they would want to tell their offspring about it someday. Music played in the background.

Nutty stood at the top of the stairs and waited. While he waited, he watched Pretty trying to stop Kago from kicking Runzda. Ole Man Boppa was there behind them, along with King Basha, and Bigeye. Booma was there with Muga and Biggabomb, as were three-million of the planet's inhabitants. Everyone was there.

Sweetie yelled above the crowd, "I wuvs ya, Nuttybomb!"

Then...the music changed.

Through the back doors of the library stepped Uhra. She tried to ignore the bothersome screams from Sweetie, and for the most part, she succeeded. But Sweetie would always be in the back of her mind, haunting her, and keeping her vigilant when it came to her soon-to-be husband.

She walked slowly down the full length of the red carpet until she stood alongside Nutty on the steps out in front. She wore her hair up in curls that accentuated her face.

Nutty had watched her the whole time she walked. He couldn't take his eyes off her.

To Uhra's credit, she didn't stumble, nor did she limp. She was still injured, but on the mend. She wanted this day to be perfect. She wasn't going to be Nutty's partner in front of the world as anything less than perfect. She cried most of the night before as she tried again and again to walk. It didn't show now, though. No, on this day she did it without incident.

Uhra couldn't keep from smiling. She was bursting inside. Her Nutty was standing next to her all handsome and strong. Mostly, she loved him. She wished they would grow old together and have a family.

Nutty quietly felt the same; he wanted a family, too. He put himself in situations to give his life for her countless times. He wondered if she knew it. It really didn't matter; he didn't need for her to know. He simply needed her.

The music stopped.

Moonoak said, "Nuttybomb, Son of Biggabomb anda Muga...Warchief of Hotta...You choose Uhra as you a partner?"

Nutty smiled wider than he had been. "Yup."

Moonoak continued, "Anda you, Uhra, Daughta of Gunza anda Hinda...You choose Warchief Nuttybomb as you a partner?"

Uhra was shaking with excitement. "Yup."

"Ok. Now, you be partners."

Uhra bit her lip in the way that drove Nutty crazy for her. Then, they kissed before the millions of onlookers. She looked into his eyes and whispered, "Younut."

Nutty had to go back to work as Warchief. He was done heaving and panting in rhythm with Uhra. He wiped the blood and slime from his hands and shirt. He left Uhra to recover while Muga watched over her son's and daughter-in-law's new prizes. They were twins!

As Nuttybomb proudly left his front door and thought about what had just happened in the back room of his house, he said, "Dis gonna be a great day!"

The End

If you enjoyed this work, please leave a positive review where you purchased it, if possible. Thank you for your involvement in the Hyadeswars universe.